D1449699

BETRAYAL

Also by R. L. STINE

Temptation

BETRAYAL

THE BETRAYAL • THE SECRET
THE BURNING

By R. L. Stine

SIMON PULSE
NEW YORK LONDON TORONTO SYDNEY NEW DELHI

This book is a work of fiction. Any references to historical events, real people, or real places are used fictitiously. Other names, characters, places, and events are products of the author's imagination, and any resemblance to actual events or places or persons, living or dead, is entirely coincidental.

SIMON PULSE
An imprint of Simon & Schuster Children's Publishing Division
1230 Avenue of the Americas, New York, New York 10020
This Simon Pulse paperback edition December 2015

For information about special discounts for bulk purchases, please contact Simon & Schuster Special Sales at 1-866-506-1949 or business@simonandschuster.com.
The Simon & Schuster Speakers Bureau can bring authors to your live event. For more information or to book an event contact the Simon & Schuster Speakers Bureau at 1-866-248-3049 or visit our website at www.simonspeakers.com.
Cover designed by Regina Flath
Interior designed by Mike Rosamilia
The text of this book was set in Meridien LT Std.
Manufactured in the United States of America
2 4 6 8 10 9 7 5 3 1
Library of Congress Control Number 2015950978
ISBN 978-1-4814-5041-6 (pbk)
ISBN 978-1-4391-2034-7 (*The Betrayal* eBook)
ISBN 978-1-4424-0741-1 (*The Secret* eBook)
ISBN 978-1-4391-2035-4 (*The Burning* eBook)
These titles were previously published individually by Simon Pulse.

TABLE OF CONTENTS

The Betrayal

THE FIER FAMILY TREE

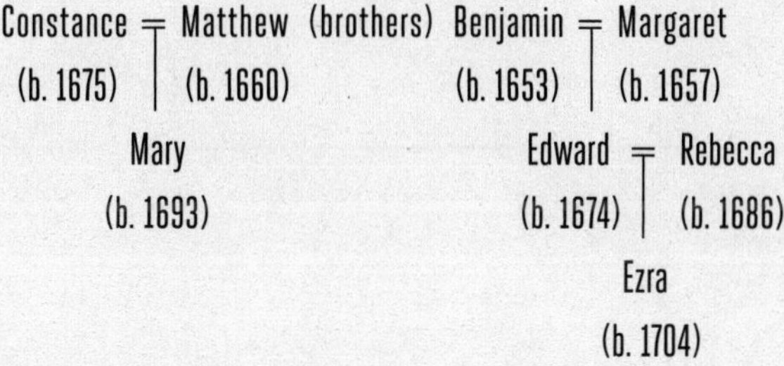

Village of Shadyside

1900

The fire roared like thunder. Above the choking clouds of black smoke, the night sky brightened with a wash of angry scarlet.

The flames tossed and crashed like ocean waves, rolling over the blackened mansion, pouring out every window, sweeping up the walls and over the roof until the house was nothing more than the dark core of a raging fireball.

Staring down at the fire from the low hill that overlooked the wide lawn, Nora Goode pressed her hands over her ears. But even with the fire's roar muffled she could hear the screams.

The screams of those trapped inside the blazing Fear mansion.

The screams of everyone she knew, of everyone she loved.

"Daniel! Come out!" Nora cried, her small voice buried under the avalanche of terrified shrieks, anguished moans, and the unending roar of the spreading flames.

"Daniel, I'm here! I am alive! I ran out! I escaped the fire!" Nora shouted. "Where are you? Are you coming out too?"

The flames roared louder, as if to answer her.

Nora's entire body trembled in dread.

She lowered one hand to the amulet on a chain around her neck.

The fire had already blazed for more than an hour. Daniel wasn't coming out. No one was coming out.

Only minutes after the fire had begun, the Shadyside volunteer firefighters had pulled their horse-drawn water truck onto the lawn of the mansion. But the flames had already swallowed up the entire house.

Their faces revealing horror and awe, the firefighters stood by helplessly and watched with the other townspeople who had gathered on the low hill, huddling in small groups, their faces red in the light of the flickering blaze.

"You're not coming out, are you, Daniel?" Nora said. "I'll never see you again."

She shut her eyes. But even with her eyes closed she could still see the angry red and orange flames tossing across the inside of her eyelids.

Squeezing the small round pendant tightly, Nora sighed. This silver amulet with its sparkling blue jewels held in place by a silver three-toed claw, like those on a tiny bird's foot, had been given to her by Daniel Fear as a token of his love.

"It is all I have left of you, Daniel!" Nora wailed.

Voices rose around her, close by, louder than the thunder of the flames. Nora opened her eyes and turned her gaze on the horrified faces of the people from the village. They clung together, as if frightened for their own lives.

"The fire will burn forever!" a bearded man cried, his face scarlet, the flames reflected in his eyes.

"Look at the house," a frail woman a few feet from Nora cried, pointing. "It is covered with flames, but it does not burn!"

"It looks as if the *sky* is on fire!" screamed a little girl, hiding her face in her mother's dark skirt.

"I always knew this place was evil," the bearded man declared, shielding his eyes with one hand. "I always knew the Fears would come to no good."

"They burned up inside their house," someone said.

"May their evil perish with them," another person added.

"The firemen did not even try to put it out."

"They could not put out *this* fire. It is not an ordinary fire. It is not a fire from this world."

"The evil of this house feeds the fire."

"The house is cursed! The ground is cursed!"

"No! Please . . . stop it! *Stop it!*" Nora shrieked.

Unable to shut out their voices, she began running toward the house. Her cloak flapped behind her as she stumbled down the hill and over the lawn.

Slipping on the dew-wet grass, she could feel the heat of the fire on her face. Strange shadows flickered over the lawn, black against the reflected scarlet light.

"Daniel, why is your family so cursed?" Nora cried as she ran. "What kind of evil brought you and your family to this fiery end?"

Nora's long dark hair floated wildly above the flapping cloak. As she ran, she held her arms out as if ready to embrace the flames.

"Who *is* that?"

"Where is she going?"

"Somebody stop her!"

Alarmed voices rang out from the crowd.

Panting loudly, Nora raised an arm to shield her eyes as she ran. She could feel the precious silver amulet bobbing against her throat.

"Daniel, are you in there? Daniel?"

"Somebody stop her!"

"Has she gone mad?"

"Who *is* she? Is she a Fear?"

The voices finally faded, drowned out by the crackle and roar of the blinding red-orange blaze.

It's so hot, so hot! Nora thought. She loosened the cloak and let it fall.

I feel as if I am running into the sun! Now I feel as if I am on fire too.

She stopped, choking on the hot smoke.

Where am I?

She gazed into the flames and suddenly realized she was standing in front of a window. The window of the grand ballroom.

The tossing flames made the window glow.

"Ohhh!" Nora moaned in horror as the faces inside came into view. Faces among the flames.

Nora's breath caught in her throat as she stared through the window at the wriggling dark bodies.

Are they dancing in there? Dancing with the flames?

No.

Their faces were twisted in agony. Their dark bodies writhing in pain.

She saw screaming women, flames rolling up from their hair.

She saw the tortured faces of young men, dark holes where their eyes should have been, their clothing wrapped in fire.

Who *are* these people? Nora wondered, unable to turn her eyes from the ghastly nightmare inside the house. Why are they in the ballroom? Why aren't they consumed by the flames?

Why don't they *die*?

And then Nora's eyes focused on a figure in the center of the writhing, screaming crowd. A young girl. Wearing a long maroon dress and an old-fashioned cap.

Nora gasped as the girl raised her head and their eyes met.

The girl's eyes were eggshell white. Glowing white.

As Nora gaped in horror, she saw the girl's mouth open wide into a tortured scream, a scream of rage, of unbearable pain.

Then Nora noticed that the girl's hands were tied behind her. Tied to a tall wooden pole.

The girl was tied to a stake.

And now her dress was billowing with fire. And the flames were rising up to her face, up to her long blond hair. The cap burst into flame then.

Struggling against the stake, the girl shrieked as she burned.

Then, with a low explosion, the flames hid them all behind a rippling yellow curtain.

The window burst, glass shattering and flying out. The fire's roar rumbled over her.

And still Nora stood motionless, staring where the screaming girl had been, staring into the wall of flame, staring, staring into the bright, dancing horror. . . .

PART ONE

Wickham Village, Massachusetts Colony

1692

CHAPTER 1

The fire crackled softly. A loud pop sent up a shower of glowing red embers.

Susannah Goode uttered a cry of surprise and jumped back from the hearth. The embers died at her feet.

After straightening the starched white apron she wore over her heavy, dark maroon skirt, Susannah bent over the bake kettle to lift the heavy lid and peer inside.

Behind her in the small borning room, the baby started to cry. Susannah heard the floorboards creak as her mother made her way to the cradle to see what the problem was.

"Susannah!" Martha Goode's tone was scolding. "You have wrapped George too tightly again. The poor baby can barely breathe!"

"The blanket is too small. I had trouble covering him," Susannah complained, still bent over the kettle, a few long golden curls falling out of her bun and over her face.

"The blanket will have to do," her mother replied. "It is the best we can afford." She lifted the squalling baby and held him up to her face. "Poor George. Poor George. What did your sister do to you?"

Susannah sighed. "These biscuits are taking so long to bake."

Martha Goode stepped up behind her. George's cries had softened to quiet whimpers as he lay his head against his mother's stiff white collar.

"The fire is too low," her mother said, shaking her head disapprovingly. "You cannot bake in those dying embers. Put more wood on, Susannah."

Frowning, Susannah straightened up and tossed the locks of escaped hair behind the white collar that covered the shoulders of her dress. "We need firewood."

Susannah was tall and thin. She had sparkling blue eyes, creamy pale skin, and dimples in both cheeks when she smiled.

Whenever Martha Goode found Susannah gazing into the looking glass or toying with her golden hair, she scolded her with the same words: "True beauty comes from deeds, not appearance, Daughter."

As a Puritan, Susannah had been endlessly taught the virtue of modesty. She had been taught that all righteous people are beautiful and the same in the eyes of the Maker.

She felt embarrassed whenever her mother caught her admiring herself, as if her mother had peered inside her soul and found it flawed and unworthy.

But at sixteen, Susannah felt stirrings that excited her as much as they troubled her. She found herself thinking of a certain boy, daydreaming about him as she worked. And she couldn't help but wonder if she was pretty enough to win him over all the other girls in the village of Wickham.

Martha Goode held the baby and rocked him gently as she stared disapprovingly at the fire. "Where is your father? He will want his biscuits on time, but he will not have them if he is not here."

"I believe he is at the commons, tending the cows," Susannah told her.

"Cows," her mother scoffed. "Bags of bone, you mean." She lowered her gaze sadly to the baby she held. "It is a wonder we survive, George."

Susannah started toward the door. "I will get the firewood and fetch Father. I was going out for a walk anyway," Susannah insisted.

"Susannah. Please," her mother said, fear clouding her eyes. "You must stop taking solitary walks. You must not do anything—anything at all—to attract attention to yourself."

She gazed intently at her pretty daughter. Then she added in a low whisper, "You know the dangers. You know what is going on here."

"Yes, Mother," Susannah replied impatiently. "But I think I can go out for a walk without—"

"They took Abigail Hopping from her house last night and dragged her to the prison," her mother said softly. "The poor woman's screams woke me."

Susannah uttered a shocked gasp. "Abigail Hopping a *witch*?"

"That's what Benjamin Fier says," Martha Goode replied, swallowing hard. "Benjamin accused Abigail of singing songs of the Evil One as she prepared the evening meal."

"I cannot believe that Abigail Hopping is a witch," Susannah said, shaking her head. "Has she confessed?"

"Her trial is at the meetinghouse tonight," Martha Goode said darkly.

"Oh, Mother! Will she burn like the others?" Susannah cried, choking out the words.

Her mother rocked the baby and didn't reply. "There is so much evil about, Daughter," she said finally. "Three witches uncovered in our village by Benjamin Fier since summer began. I beg you to be careful, Susannah. Stay in the shadows. Give no one reason to suspect you—or even to notice you."

Susannah nodded. "Yes, Mother. I am only going to

the commons for firewood. I shall be back quickly." She pushed open the door, causing a flood of bright sunlight to wash over the dark room.

"No! Stop!" her mother cried.

Halfway out the door Susannah turned, her blue eyes flashing, an impatient frown on her face.

"Are you going out with your head uncovered?" Martha Goode demanded. "Where are your thoughts, dear?"

"I am sorry." Susannah returned to the room, took her white cap from its peg, and pulled it down over her hair. "I will hurry back," she said.

She closed the door behind her and, shielding her eyes with one hand from the bright afternoon sunlight, made her way past the chickens pecking the dirt in front of the house.

Susannah turned onto the path that led into the village. Walking quickly, her long skirt trailing over the dirt, she passed the Halseys' house. The glass for their windows hadn't yet arrived from England, Susannah saw. The windows were boarded up. Mr. Halsey was bent over his vegetable garden and didn't look up.

At the meetinghouse she saw someone up on the shingle roof working to attach a brass weather vane above the chimney.

The village magistrate, Benjamin Fier, a troubled expression on his face, was just entering the building. Susannah stopped short and waited until he had disappeared inside. A cold shudder ran down her back as she thought of Abigail Hopping.

I know Benjamin Fier is a good and righteous man, Susannah thought. But I am afraid of him, just as everyone else in Wickham is.

As village magistrate, Benjamin Fier was the most powerful man in Wickham. He was also the wealthiest.

His home, the biggest in the village, stood across from the meetinghouse. The aroma of roasting beef wafted out from the summer kitchen as Susannah strode past.

The Fiers are so prosperous, Susannah thought, unable to suppress a feeling of envy. They won't be having biscuits and gravy for their dinner. The Fiers can have roasted meat every night.

Susannah knew that the Fier brothers, Benjamin and Matthew, were the most prosperous men in Wickham because they were the most worthy. Since she had been a little girl, she'd been taught that good fortune goes to those who are the most righteous.

Thus, Benjamin Fier became magistrate because he was the wisest, most pious man in the village. It was he who conducted the witchcraft trials. And he who insisted the guilty ones be burned—rather than hanged as they were elsewhere in Massachusetts. Benjamin's younger brother Matthew had a farm that prospered when others failed because Matthew Fier was more righteous and faithful than the other farmers.

That was plain and simple knowledge.

As she passed the meetinghouse and glanced toward the commons, Susannah found herself thinking about Benjamin's son, Edward Fier.

Edward, where are you?

Are you thinking about me?

"Oh!" she cried as she stumbled over an enormous pink pig spotted with black, and went sprawling onto the hard ground.

The pig grunted a loud protest and scrambled off the path.

Susannah picked herself up and brushed the dust off the front of her white apron. That will teach me not to have improper thoughts, she scolded herself, straightening her cap over her hair.

But how can thoughts about Edward be improper?

She saw her father at the far end of the commons, the large, rectangular pasture in the center of the village. He was busily raking a section of ground and didn't see Susannah wave to him.

Mr. Franklin, the blacksmith, was at his anvil in front of his shop, pounding noisily on a sheet of tin as Susannah hurried past. She smiled at Franklin's apprentice, a boy named Arthur Kent, who was tending the bellows, which were nearly twice as big as he was.

Behind the blacksmith's shop were the shimmering green woods. Tall poplars and beech trees leaned in toward the village. Behind these the woods grew dark with pines, oaks, and maples.

A village woodpile stood at the edge of the woods, logs neatly chopped and stacked. But Susannah's eyes were focused on the woods.

Sunlight filtered down through the shimmering leaves, sending rays of light darting over the ground. Black and gold monarch butterflies fluttered in and out of the shafts of white light.

I shall take a short walk into the woods, Susannah decided.

It felt good to be out of the dark house, away from the heat of the cooking hearth, away from the crying baby.

Away from her chores and the watchful eyes of her mother.

Away from the heavy fear that hovered over the entire village these days.

Susannah stepped into the woods, dry twigs cracking beneath her heavy black shoes. As soon as she was hidden by the trees, she pulled off her cap and shook her hair free.

She walked slowly, raising her face to the shafts of bright sunlight. Her dress caught on a low bramble. She tugged it free and kept walking.

A scrabbling sound nearby made her spin around, just in time to see a brown and white chipmunk scurry under a pile of dead leaves.

Susannah tossed her long hair back and took a deep breath. The air smelled piney and sweet.

I'm not supposed to enjoy the woods, she thought, her smile slowly fading. Susannah had been taught that the woods were a place of evil.

As if mirroring her thoughts, the trees grew thicker, shutting out the sunlight. It became evening-dark.

Away from civilization, deep in the woods, was where the Evil One and his followers dwelt, Susannah had been taught.

The witches of the village came here to dance their evil dances by moonlight with the Evil One and his servants. The Evil One and his servants lived deep in holes in the ground, hidden by scrub and thick shrubs. Susannah believed that if she wandered alone into the darkness of their domain, they might reach up and grab her and pull her down, down into their netherworld of eternal torture and darkness.

The air grew cooler. From a low branch just above Susannah's head a dove uttered a deep-throated moan, cold and sorrowful.

Susannah shuddered.

"It is so dark, suddenly so cold," she said.

Time to go back.

As she turned, she felt strong hands grab her from behind.

"The Evil One!" she cried.

CHAPTER 2

"Let go of me!" Susannah screamed.

To her surprise, the hands obediently released her.

She spun around, her blue eyes wide with fright, and stared into the laughing face of Edward Fier. "Do I look like the Evil One to you?" he asked.

Susannah felt her face redden. She glared angrily at him. "Yes, you must be the Evil One," she said. "Why else would you be out in these woods?"

"I followed you," he replied, his expression solemn.

Edward was tall and good-looking. He wore a wide-brimmed black hat over his straight dark brown hair, which fell below his ears. His gray doublet was made of the finest linen. The cuffs at the end of his sleeves were white and stiffly starched.

His navy blue breeches ended just below the knee. Gray wool stockings covered his legs. On his feet were Dutch-style clogs fashioned of dark leather.

No other young man in the village dressed as well as Edward. He seemed to take his clothing as seriously as he did everything else in life. In private some villagers criticized his fancy dress, accusing him of the sin of pride.

But no one dared criticize him in public. For Edward was a Fier, Benjamin Fier's son. And no one would dare say a word against Magistrate Fier or his son.

As the trees shuddered around them in a sudden cold breeze, Edward's dark brown eyes locked on Susannah's. "We should not joke about the Evil One," he said, lowering his voice. "My father says the Evil One's slaves have overrun our village."

"I—I am so afraid these days," Susannah confessed, lowering her gaze to the dark ground. "I keep dreaming about Faith Warburton. She—she was my friend," Susannah stammered.

"I know," Edward muttered softly.

"They seized her as a witch . . . because she wore a red ribbon in her hair. Th-they *burned* her—!" Susannah's words were cut short by a sob.

Edward placed a hand on Susannah's trembling shoulder. "I know that my father must have had proof of your friend's evil practices. He appears stern, but he is a fair and just man, Susannah."

"We should not be here together. We have to stop our secret meetings. They put me in great danger," Susannah said softly.

"You are in no danger," Edward replied. "I . . . wanted to talk to you, Susannah. I wanted to—"

Before Susannah could back away, Edward had his arms around her waist. He lowered his face to hers and kissed her.

The hat tumbled off his head, and he pressed his lips against hers, urgently, hungrily.

Susannah was breathless when she finally pulled free. "You—you are suffocating me!" she exclaimed, grinning at him. She raised a hand to his shoulder. "What if the Evil One is watching us?" she teased.

To her surprise, he pulled away from her touch. His dark eyes flared with anger. "I *told* you," he warned, "do not joke about the Evil One."

"But, Edward—" she began. His intensity always startled her.

"You know I cannot bear blasphemy," he interrupted in a low, steady voice.

They had been meeting secretly for weeks, stealing moments behind the grain barn or behind the trees at the riverbank. Susannah had been surprised by Edward's seriousness, by his solemn attitude about most things.

She liked to tease but quickly learned he didn't share her sense of humor.

Why did she care so much about him? Why did she think about him night and day? Why did she dream about being with him forever?

Because he needed her. Because he seemed to feel as she did.

She gazed up at him coyly. "Being here alone together in the woods, that is a crime against village custom," she said. "What do you think your father would say?"

He picked up his hat from the ground, gripping it tightly in one hand. "Being here with you, Susannah, is no crime."

"Why is that?" she teased.

He hesitated, gazing at her as if trying to see inside her head, to read her thoughts. "Because we love each other," he said finally.

And before she knew it, they were wrapped in each other's arms again.

I want to stay here, Susannah thought happily. Stay here with Edward in the dark woods. Live in the wild together, just the two of us, away from the village, away from everyone.

She pressed her cheek against his, surprised that his face was as hot as hers.

A sudden noise made her cry out and pull away.

Voices!

"Edward—someone else is here!" she cried, raising her hands to her cheeks in horror. "We're caught!"

CHAPTER 3

Edward's dark eyes grew wide with fear. He grasped Susannah's hand tightly.

They listened, frozen together in the dark woods as if they'd been turned to stone.

The voices rose, carried by the wind.

Chanting voices.

"Burn the witch! Burn the witch! Burn the witch!"

"Ohhh!" Susannah gasped.

The chanting voices weren't coming from nearby. The wind was carrying the sound from the commons.

"There is no one here," Edward said, smiling with relief.

"Poor Abigail Hopping," Susannah whispered.

"If she is a witch, she must face the fire," Edward replied, still holding Susannah's hand.

Susannah rested her head against his shoulder. "We should get back. I went out for firewood. I should have been home. My mother will think the Evil One has taken me."

"You go first," he told her. "I will wait here a while before I return."

"Are you going to tell your father . . . about us?" Susannah asked eagerly.

"Yes," Edward told her. "When the time is right."

She leaned forward and kissed him again. She didn't want to leave. She didn't want to go back to her tiny, dark house. She didn't want to return to all the anger and fear of the village.

Edward gave her a gentle push, his hands on her shoulders. "Go."

She forced a smile, then turned and ran off, pulling on the cap and covering her hair.

We're going to be married, she thought, her heart pounding.

Edward and I are going to be married.

I am going to be the wife of Edward Fier.

She felt as if she were floating through the trees.

Susannah ran right past the woodpile and through the commons, and was nearly home before she remembered she had come out for firewood, and had to go back.

* * *

"The carrots are small but sweet," William Goode said. He sat stiffly at the head of the table, rubbing gravy off the wooden plate with a biscuit.

Susannah watched her father eat his dinner. He looked tired to her, tired and old. He was not yet forty, yet his face was lined, and his once-blond hair had turned prematurely white.

"Susannah baked the biscuits," Martha Goode said.

"Would you like more gravy, Father?" Susannah asked, gesturing to the gravy pot still simmering on the hearth. "There are more boiled carrots, too."

"I am going to mash some carrots and give them to George when he wakes up," Susannah's mother said.

"I do not know why our carrots are so small," Mr. Goode grumbled. "Matthew Fier's carrots are as long as candles."

"Why do you not ask him his secret?" Susannah's mother suggested.

William Goode scowled. He narrowed his gray-green eyes at his wife. "Matthew Fier has no farming skills that I do not have. He has no secrets that I—"

"The Fiers have plenty of secrets," his wife interrupted. "Who *are* they, these Fier brothers? Where do they come from? They did not come to the New World from England, as we did."

"I do not know," Mr. Goode replied thoughtfully. "They come from a small farm village. That is all I know.

They were poor when they arrived, both Fier brothers and their wives. But they have prospered here. And that proves they are pious folk, favored by the Maker."

His wife sighed. "These carrots are sweet enough, William. I did not intend to hurt your feelings."

William Goode frowned. "Sweet enough," he muttered.

"Help me clear the dinner table, Susannah," Martha Goode ordered. "Why are you sitting there with that dazed, faraway expression on your face?"

"Sorry, Mother." Susannah started to get up, but her father placed a hand on her arm to restrain her.

"Susannah will clear the table in a little while," he told his wife. "I wish to speak with her first." He stood up, pulled a clay pipe down from his pipe rack, filled it with tobacco from his cloth pouch, and went over to the fire to light it.

Susannah turned in her chair, her eyes trained on her father, trying to read his expression. "What did you wish to speak to me about, Father?"

"About Edward Fier," he replied, frowning as he puffed hard to start the tobacco burning.

Susannah gasped. She had never discussed Edward with either of her parents. She and Edward were merely acquaintances, as far as her parents knew.

Holding the long white pipe by the bowl, Mr. Goode made his way back to the dinner table. He pulled back the stool next to Susannah's and sat down stiffly.

"Wh-what about him?" Susannah stammered, clasping her hands tightly in her lap.

Her father leaned close to her. Pipe smoke rose up in front of him, encircling them both in a fragrant cloud. "You and Edward Fier have been seen walking together," he accused. "Walking together without a chaperone present."

Susannah's mouth dropped open. She took a deep breath, then started to speak, but no sound came out.

"Do you deny it, Daughter?" Her father's white eyebrows arched over his gray-green eyes, which burned accusations into hers. "Do you deny it?"

"No, Father," Susannah replied softly.

"You were seen in the woods together," her father continued sternly. He held the pipe close to his face but didn't smoke it.

"Yes, Father," Susannah muttered, her heart thudding in her chest. Then the words just burst out of her. She had been longing to tell her parents. Now she could hold back the news no longer.

"Edward and I are in love!" she cried. "He wants to marry me! Is that not wonderful?"

Her mother turned from the hearth, her eyes wide with surprise.

William Goode's face reddened. He lowered his pipe to the table. "Daughter, have you lost your senses? Are you living in a world of dreams?"

Susannah gaped at him. "Didn't you *hear* me, Father? Edward wants to marry me!"

Her father shut his eyes. He cleared his throat loudly. The pipe trembled in his hand. "You cannot marry Edward Fier," he said quietly.

"What are you saying?" Susannah whispered. "Why can't I?"

"Because Edward Fier is already betrothed," Mr. Goode replied flatly.

Susannah gasped. "What?"

"Edward Fier is engaged to be married," her father said. "Edward is to marry a young woman of Portsmouth. His father told me this morning."

CHAPTER 4

The hearth fire flickered low. Long shadows slipped across the floor. In her sleeping alcove, huddled under an old feather quilt, Susannah turned her face to the wall.

How could Edward be so cruel? she asked herself for the thousandth time.

How could he lead me to believe that he cared for me, that he *loved* me?

Susannah pressed her face into the pillow to muffle her sobs.

She had gone to bed early, hoping her parents wouldn't see how upset she was. Hours had passed now. A pale half moon was high in the late night sky, and Susannah was still wide awake, still tossing in her narrow bed, crying softly and thinking about Edward with anger and disbelief.

I trusted Edward, she thought. I believed everything he said. I risked my reputation for him.

And all the while he was engaged to another girl.

Breathing hard, Susannah rolled over and stared at the glowing embers in the fireplace across the room. Her secret meetings with Edward Fier rolled through her mind. She remembered his words, his touch, his kisses.

Edward always seemed trustworthy, she thought miserably. So honest and upright.

So good.

Susannah kicked off the quilt and pushed at the pillow, punching it with both hands.

I will never trust anyone again, she told herself bitterly. *Never!*

Across the commons, firelight blazed in the windows of Benjamin Fier's two-story house. In the dining room Benjamin was standing at one end of the oak table, gripping the back of a hand-carved chair.

Benjamin's son Edward glared at him defiantly from the other end of the table.

Benjamin was big and broad-shouldered, an imposing man who looked as if he could wrestle a bull and win. He had straight black hair that fell below his ears and bushy black eyebrows over small dark eyes that seemed to be able to pierce through anything.

Benjamin's face was red and almost always set in a hard frown. He was so powerful in appearance, his expression so angry, that most people in Wickham were afraid of him, which didn't displease him in the least.

Standing with his back to the fire, Benjamin unfastened the long row of brass buttons down the front of his black doublet, his dark eyes studying Edward.

"I will not obey you, Father," Edward insisted, his voice trembling. He had never defied his father. He knew it was wrong.

Benjamin stared across the table, his features set. He didn't reply.

"I cannot obey you, Father," Edward said when his father did not reply. "I will not marry Anne Ward." Edward gripped the back of the chair. He hoped his father could not see his trembling knees.

"You will marry the girl in the autumn," Benjamin said in his deep baritone. "I have arranged the marriage with her father."

He turned away from Edward to indicate that the discussion had ended. Picking up a poker, he jabbed at the logs in the fireplace, sending a shower of sparks flying up the brick chimney.

Edward swallowed hard.

Can I do this? he asked himself. Can I stand up to my father? Am I strong enough?

Another question nagged at Edward as he struggled to

find words: Is it *right* to argue with my father? Is it not my duty to obey his wishes?

No! Edward answered his own question. I love Susannah Goode. I will marry Susannah and no one else. I *cannot* obey my father's wishes this time. I will not!

Edward took a deep breath. "Sir," he called, causing Benjamin to turn away from the fire. "I cannot marry Anne Ward. I do not know her. She is a stranger."

"You will become acquainted with her after the wedding," Benjamin said sternly. "It is a very fortunate arrangement for us."

"It is not fortunate for *me*!" Edward declared heatedly.

"Do not raise your voice to me, Edward," Benjamin warned, his face a dark crimson. He raised the fireplace poker and pointed it at his son. "Anne Ward is an excellent match for you."

"But I do not know her, Father! I do not love her!" Edward cried shrilly.

"Love?" Benjamin tossed back his head and laughed. "Edward, we did not come to these colonies for love. My brother, Matthew, and I did not leave our village for love. We came here to succeed! We came here to escape the poverty of our lives, to escape it *forever*!"

"I know, Father," Edward said, sighing. "But—"

"Do you know how poor our family was in the Old Country?" Benjamin demanded, setting down the heavy iron poker and returning to the table. His eyes burned into Edward's, hotter than the fireplace flames.

"Do you know how poor Matthew and I were? We ate *rats* to survive, Edward!"

"I know, sir—" Edward tried to interrupt. He had heard this speech before.

"Many was the night we huddled together to keep warm," Benjamin continued. "We had no fire, no blankets . . ."

Edward lowered his gaze to the floor. He held his breath, waiting for his chance to speak.

"We came to the New World to succeed, Edward. Not just to succeed but to prosper."

"You have done well, sir," Edward broke in. "You are the respected magistrate of Wickham. And Uncle Matthew's farm is the most—"

"We can do better!" Benjamin exploded, slamming his fist on the tabletop. "Your marriage to Anne Ward will help us do better, Edward."

"Why, Father? I don't see—"

"August Ward is the tea importer for Portsmouth," Benjamin explained, lowering his voice. "It has made him a very wealthy man. As his son-in-law, you will become a tea importer too. You will share his wealth."

"No, Father." Edward shook his head. "I cannot. I will not."

"You will," his father insisted sternly. "You must. You must marry August Ward's daughter."

"I cannot, Father! I am in love with someone else!" The words burst out of Edward's mouth before he could stop them. He gasped, realizing what he had revealed.

For a brief moment Benjamin's eyes widened with surprise. Then his expression quickly darkened. "In love?" he asked, his voice rising sarcastically. "With whom?" He made his way down the long table to confront his son. "With whom?" he demanded again, bringing his face a few inches from Edward's.

"Susannah Goode," Edward replied weakly. He cleared his throat and tried to avoid his father's harsh stare.

Benjamin hesitated, stunned. Then he closed his eyes and began to laugh—scornful laughter.

"D-do not laugh, sir," Edward stammered. "I am in love with Susannah Goode, and I wish to marry her."

Benjamin Fier shook his head, his smile lingering. "William Goode owns two scrawny chickens and two cows. His daughter is not a match for you, my son."

Edward took a deep breath, trying to calm his pounding heart. In his seventeen years he had never argued with his father, never dared to disagree with him.

Please, he prayed silently, *give me the strength to stand up to my father now. I know I am right. I know I cannot betray Susannah. Please give me the strength.*

"Sir," Edward began, "Susannah is a pious girl. She is the girl I will marry. I cannot marry a girl for her wealth. I must marry for love."

Benjamin closed his eyes. A log cracked loudly in the fireplace. The floorboards creaked as Benjamin shifted his weight. He sighed wearily. "Your engagement to Anne Ward is arranged. We will travel to Portsmouth in the autumn for your wedding. I wish your mother, Margaret, bless her soul, were alive to see you wed so profitably."

"No!" Edward cried. "No, Father!" He could feel his anger rise, feel the heat of it in his chest, feel himself losing control—for the first time in his life. "I have always obeyed you, sir. I know you are a wise and honorable man. But it is *my* life!" Edward screamed, his hands balled into tight fists at his waist. "It is my life, and I will marry Susannah Goode! I will marry her even if we have to run away to do it!"

Edward turned from his father and ran from the room.

I did it, he thought, relief mixing with his anger as he made his way to his bedroom. I said what I had to say. I stood up to my father.

Back in the narrow dining room Benjamin Fier slumped heavily into a chair. He fingered the shiny buttons of his doublet as he stared thoughtfully into the fire.

Before long, a dark smile spread over the man's ruddy face. "I am sorry, Edward, my poor, confused son," he said, grinning into the leaping flames. "You will never marry Susannah Goode."

CHAPTER 5

"I dislike peeling potatoes!" Susannah groaned.

Her mother, seated in front of the hearth with the baby on her lap, raised her eyes to Susannah, her features tight with concern. "Are you feeling well, Daughter? It isn't your nature to complain."

"I am feeling well," Susannah replied, sighing.

I shall never feel well again, she thought miserably. Never, never, never.

She wanted to tell her mother everything, tell her about Edward and how he had lied to her, how he had betrayed her.

But Susannah knew she had to keep her broken heart a secret. Her meetings with Edward were against all rules of conduct.

Susannah had sinned, and now she was paying for her sins. Paying with an empty feeling that gnawed at her without relief, paying with a heavy sadness she knew she'd never shake.

Martha Goode rose from her chair, cradling the sleeping baby in one arm, and stepped up behind Susannah at the table. She put her free hand to Susannah's forehead. "Hmmm. You feel a little warm, Daughter. Do you feel feverish?"

Susannah lowered her knife and gazed up at her mother. "I am not ill," she said impatiently. "I just detest peeling potatoes. They are so wet and slippery."

Martha Goode took a step back, startled by Susannah's vehemence. "We should all be thankful that we have been given potatoes for our meal," she said softly. "Your father works so hard, Susannah. It is a sin to complain if there is food on the table."

"Yes, Mother," Susannah relented, lowering her eyes.

Edward's face flashed into her mind. His thick brown hair. His dark eyes.

Where are you now, Edward? Susannah wondered, picking up another potato to peel. What are you doing?

I know you are not thinking about me.

Are you thinking about your bride? Are you packing your bags? Preparing for your journey to Portsmouth?

She uttered a long sigh and stabbed the knife blade into the potato.

"Susannah, are you sure you are not ill?" her mother demanded.

"No. Not ill," Susannah muttered, unable to shake Edward from her mind.

"The potatoes can wait," her mother said, returning to the hearthside chair and carefully lowering the baby onto her lap. "It is a beautiful afternoon. Put on your cap and step outside. Breathe some fresh air. It will refresh you, Daughter."

"I do not feel like breathing fresh air," Susannah snapped.

I might see Edward, she thought, her heart skipping a beat at the idea.

And what would I do if I saw him again? What would I say?

She could feel her face redden in shame.

I was such a fool.

Struggling to hold back the tears, Susannah picked up another potato.

The door burst open without warning.

Susannah and her mother both cried out in surprise as two village men stepped into the room, grim expressions on their faces.

"What—?" Martha Goode started, but her voice caught in her throat.

The baby opened his eyes and gazed up at her, startled.

The two men stepped to the center of the room,

revealing Benjamin Fier in the open doorway.

"My husband is not home," Martha Goode told the two officers. "I believe he is at the commons."

The two men stood stiffly, their expressions set, as Benjamin Fier strode into the room. His black boots clonked heavily on the floorboards, his face red beneath his tall black hat. "We are not here for your husband, Martha Goode," he said coldly in his booming baritone.

"I do not understand—" she replied, alarm creeping into her voice.

The baby uttered a squawk, preparing to cry. Martha Goode pulled him close to her chest. "What business have you with me, Magistrate Fier?" she asked, climbing reluctantly to her feet.

Benjamin Fier ignored her question. "Keep watch on them," he instructed the two men. "I will search for the proof."

"Proof? Proof of what?" Susannah cried, tossing down her knife and jumping to her feet. "Why are you here? Why can you not wait for my father to return?"

Benjamin ignored Susannah, too. He strode quickly to the hearth, his black cloak sweeping behind him. "Aha!" He bent down, as if picking up something from behind a kettle.

When he turned around to face them, Benjamin held a purple cloth bag in one hand. His lips spread into an unpleasant smile. "I believe we have the proof we need."

"Proof of *what*?" Susannah demanded shrilly.

Benjamin walked quickly to the table and overturned the bag, spilling its contents onto the tabletop.

To her astonishment, Susannah saw a chicken's foot, some feathers, dried roots of some kind, a small bone, and a glass vial containing a blood-colored liquid.

"What *is* that?" Susannah cried.

"That does not belong to us!" her mother cried, her face pale, her troubled eyes darting from the items on the table to Benjamin Fier.

"We have the proof we need," Benjamin told his men, holding up the empty bag. He gestured to Susannah and her mother. "Take them to the prison. Tie them securely to await their trial."

"Trial?" Martha Goode shrieked, holding her baby tightly against her chest. "Trial for what crime?"

"For the crime of witchcraft!" Benjamin Fier declared, eyeing Susannah coldly.

The two officers moved quickly, grabbing Susannah and her mother firmly by the shoulders. Benjamin strode quickly to the door, still gripping the empty purple bag.

"Benjamin Fier—you *know* us!" Martha Goode cried desperately. "You know we are a God-fearing, humble, and pious family!"

"You cannot do this!" Susannah shrieked, fear choking her throat. "You cannot do this to us!"

The officers dragged Susannah and her mother to the

door. The baby whimpered in confused fear, one tiny pink hand breaking free of his mother's grasp and thrashing the air wildly.

As Susannah and her mother were pulled out the door, Benjamin Fier stepped back to watch. His eyes gazed hard at Martha Goode, then lingered for a long while on Susannah.

He didn't smile. His face was set in rigid coldness.

But Susannah thought she caught a gleam of merriment in his dark eyes.

Just then their neighbor, Mary Halsey, attracted by the commotion, appeared at their door.

"Please take the child," Martha pleaded, and handed the baby to Mary. "Keep him safe."

The baby's whimpers turned to frightened cries.

As the two men dragged Susannah and her mother away, Benjamin Fier followed close behind, his eyes on Susannah all the while.

This is not happening, Susannah thought, her heart pounding, the blood pulsing at her temples. *This cannot be happening to us.*

She heard surprised murmurs as they passed through the commons. Whispered questions. Muffled cries of surprise.

The prison loomed ahead, a low clapboard building behind the meetinghouse.

"Why are you doing this to us?" Susannah cried, the

words bursting from her throat. "Why are you dragging us from our home?"

Benjamin Fier stopped on the path. His voice was low and steady. His eyes locked onto Susannah's.

"You two witches will burn before the week is out," he said.

CHAPTER 6

Torches were hung on the meetinghouse walls. Their flames flickered and threatened to go out every time the door was pulled open, allowing a gust of wind into the hot room.

In the prisoners' box at the front of the court, Susannah gripped her mother's hand and stared at the flames. Her mother's hand felt so small, like that of a cold, frightened animal.

Without realizing it, Susannah had nervously started chewing her lower lip. Now she felt the bitter taste of blood in her mouth.

They burn witches, she thought, staring at the torchlight. *They've burned three already.*

Her entire body convulsed in a shudder of fear. She

squeezed her mother's hand tighter. Even though witches in other parts of Massachusetts Colony were hanged, Benjamin Fier believed that burning was the only way to punish a witch.

But I am not a witch!

Surely if there is justice in Wickham, I will not be found guilty.

The long, low-ceilinged room was filled with shadows. Solemn faces flickered in the orange torchlight. Eyes, dozens of eyes, peered at Susannah and her mother.

The rows of wooden benches stretched to the back of the long room. People crowded quietly into them, the frightened citizens of the town, whispering their fears, staring at Susannah and her mother with curiosity and surprise and pity.

The whispers and hushed voices grew louder, until Susannah wanted to cover her ears. "Mother, why do they stare at us like that?" she uttered in a frightened voice, leaning so close she could feel her mother's trembling. "They know us. They know who we are."

"Some believe they are staring into the faces of evil," Martha Goode replied, squeezing her daughter's hand.

"But they *know* us!" Susannah repeated shrilly, her heart thudding in her chest.

"Our innocence will soon free us," her mother replied softly. Her words were brave, but her entire body shook with fear.

Edward, where are you? Susannah wondered.

Have you spoken to your father? Have you told him about us?

"Edward will not let us burn," Susannah said out loud without realizing it.

Her mother stared at her in surprise. "What did you say?"

Susannah started to reply, but someone in a front bench cried out loudly.

Susannah heard a flapping sound and felt a cold ripple of wind close to her ear.

Startled voices called out.

Susannah heard the flapping again, like the beating of wings. A shadowy form darted overhead.

"A bat!" a man shouted from the back of the room.

The creature swooped low toward the flickering light of a torch, then flew over the prisoners' box again, its wings beating like a frightened heart.

Matthew Fier appeared at the front of the room. "Open the doors! Let it out!" he ordered.

The bat swung low over the spectators, and Susannah saw several heads duck. She felt a cool ripple of air as the bat flew past her face.

"Hold open the doors. It will fly out," Matthew Fier said in his high-pitched voice.

The doors were obediently pulled open. The torches flickered and bent in the invading breeze. A moment later the bat swooped out, disappearing into the starless sky. The doors were closed.

Matthew Fier shouted over the buzz of voices, calling for silence. He served as trial warden, keeping order during his brother's trial proceedings.

He did not have Benjamin's booming deep voice. He was not as large or imposing as his brother, but he had the same fire of ambition in his dark eyes.

The room grew silent. The shuffling of feet made the floorboards creak. Someone near the doors coughed loudly.

Matthew turned to the prisoners, adjusting the white stock he wore over his robe. "You may summon as many evil creatures as you wish," he told Susannah and her mother, his eyes glowing like dark coals. "You may summon bats or snakes—or the Evil One himself. But it will only serve to prove your guilt."

"We did not summon that bat!" Susannah cried.

"Silence!" Matthew ordered. "Silence! A dark creature like that would not enter our court unless summoned!"

Loud murmurs burst forth from the rows of benches. Accusing eyes, reflecting the torchlight, glared at Susannah and her mother.

"Silence! Silence!" Matthew shouted, gesturing with both hands.

As the room grew quiet, Susannah saw a man at the end of a row rise to his feet. "Release my wife and daughter!" he demanded.

"It is Father!" Susannah cried to her mother, leaning forward to see him better.

"Release them, Matthew Fier! You know they are not witches!" Mr. Goode cried passionately.

A tall man in dark robes strode to the front of the room and stood beside Matthew Fier. "Be seated, William Goode," Benjamin Fier ordered. "We do not place innocent women on trial here."

"But *they* are innocent!" William declared. "I swear it by all that is holy!"

"Be seated!" Benjamin commanded in his booming voice. "Be seated, William, or I will remove you from this court."

Susannah saw her father open his mouth to protest. But he uttered only a helpless groan before slumping onto his seat.

Benjamin Fier turned to face the accused. His straight black hair and dark eyes glowed almost red in the torchlight.

"Martha Goode, do you wish to confess your guilt?" he asked, leaning close to the prisoners' box.

Susannah's mother cleared her throat. Her voice came out in a choked whisper: "I have no guilt to confess."

Sneering, Benjamin turned his harsh gaze on Susannah. "Susannah Goode, do you wish to confess your guilt?"

Susannah clasped her trembling hands tightly in her lap and lowered her head, a couple of blond ringlets falling loose from her cap, over her face. "I am not a witch," she managed to mutter.

Edward, where are you?

Edward, aren't you going to save us?

Isn't anyone going to save us?

"Confess now," Benjamin demanded. "There are witnesses. Witnesses in this hall tonight. Witnesses who saw you both dancing with the Evil One in the moonlit woods."

"That is not true!" Susannah shrieked, on her feet now.

"Susannah—!" She could hear her mother's warning, feel her mother's touch on her sleeve.

"That is not true!" Susannah repeated. "We have never—"

"Be silent, witch!" Matthew Fier commanded, stepping up beside his brother, a fierce scowl on his slender face. "You have already tried to bedevil us by summoning that creature of the night into our meeting hall. Do not disrupt the trial again!"

"Confess now," Benjamin urged. "Your hollow protests only serve to demonstrate your guilt."

"But we are *innocent*!" Susannah shrieked.

"Release them! Release them now!" Susannah heard her father cry.

Low murmurs spread through the long rows of benches, growing to a roar.

"Release my innocent wife and child!" William Goode

cried desperately. “My son needs his mother!”

Matthew turned to point to Susannah’s father, who stood with his hat gripped tightly in one hand. “Remove him from the hall!” he shouted angrily.

Suddenly John Halsey, Mary Halsey’s husband, stood in the back of the meeting house.

“Let him speak, Matthew. You’ve known the Goode family for years,” he cried.

“Release my family!” William insisted. “This trial is a mistake! A mockery!”

“Remove him!” Matthew ordered, silencing John Halsey.

From out of the shadows two militia officers moved quickly, pushing their way into William’s row, grabbing him by the shoulders.

Staring over the startled, silent faces of the onlookers, Susannah saw her father struggle. She heard angry shouts. Scuffling. A hard blow, followed by her father’s cry of pain.

A few moments later she could see her father’s limp body being dragged up the aisle. The doors at the back were flung open.

The sudden breeze threatened to extinguish the torches against the walls. The flames dipped low. The darkness deepened. Then the flames rose up again.

The room returned to heavy silence.

Her father had been taken out.

You cannot save us, Father, Susannah thought, cold dread tightening her throat.

You cannot save us. So who will?

Will it be you, Edward?

Are you here? Will you speak to your father? Will you rescue us from the fire?

Or will you betray me again?

"We have all witnessed their dark powers," Benjamin Fier announced to the rows of onlookers. "We have seen them try to darken this hall just now. The torches nearly went out. But our goodness prevailed over their evil power!"

He turned to Susannah and her mother. "Your evil could not douse our torches. Your evil could not put out the light of truth in this room!"

"It was the wind that nearly doused the torches!" Susannah cried.

"Silence, witch!" Benjamin screamed, his booming voice ringing off the dark wood walls.

He raised one hand high above his head. Susannah saw that his hand was gripping the purple bag, bulging with its odd assortment of items.

"I found the proof of your blasphemy!" Benjamin declared. "I myself found the tools of your witchcraft. I found this near your hearth, a hearth made cold by the presence of the Evil One!"

"It does not belong to us!" Susannah screamed,

feeling her mother's restraining hand on her sleeve once again.

"Silence!" Benjamin warned, his dark eyes narrowing at Susannah.

"We have the proof of your evil practices," Benjamin continued. "We have witnesses who have seen your moonlight dance with the Evil One and his servants. And we have seen your attempts to frighten us tonight by bringing a bat into our meeting hall and trying to douse our light."

"No!" Susannah shrieked, tugging at the sides of her hair with both hands. "No! No!"

"Good shall always triumph," Benjamin continued, ignoring Susannah's shrill cries of protest. "Good shall always triumph over the Evil One. Those of us with pure hearts shall always triumph over your kind, Martha and Susannah Goode."

Susannah's mother lowered her head, but Susannah could see her shoulders trembling and knew her mother was crying.

Susannah wanted to scream out her protest, to declare her innocence until Benjamin Fier would listen to her. But she could see that her shouts were of no use.

Her heart pounding, her head spinning, Susannah slumped over and leaned her head against her mother's trembling shoulder.

"A dark evil has descended on Wickham," Benjamin

Fier was saying. "As magistrate, it is my duty to battle it wherever it may appear."

He faced the onlookers and lowered his voice as he spoke to them. "It is not my desire to put on trial the wives and daughters of our village. But it is my *sacred duty* to protect all who are innocent from those possessed by the Evil One, such as these." He pointed to Susannah and her mother.

"There is nothing left but for you to confess!" he demanded, stepping up before the prisoners' box. "Do you confess, Mistress Goode? Do you confess to your evil practices?"

Susannah's mother was crying too hard to reply, her shoulders heaving, her face turned away into the shadows.

"Do you confess to practicing the dark arts, Susannah Goode?" Benjamin demanded.

"I am innocent," Susannah uttered in a choked whisper.

"Your refusal to confess," Benjamin shouted, "your unwillingness to confess to the truth *proves* your guilt!"

He stood over Susannah and her mother, leaning close, so close that Susannah could smell his sour breath. "We have found you, Martha Goode, and you, Susannah Goode, guilty of witchcraft. It is my duty as magistrate to sentence you both."

"No—please!" Susannah shrieked, reaching out to him.

He backed away, eyeing her coldly, his face half

hidden in shadow. "You both shall burn tomorrow night," Benjamin announced without any emotion at all.

A pale half moon, poking through wisps of dark cloud, cast a faint rectangle of light through the tiny window of the prison cell. Susannah leaned against the cold wall and stared down at the patch of light on the dirt floor. Her hands were tied behind her, so she could do no witchery, the warden at the jail had told her.

Martha Goode lay in darkness against the opposite wall. Breathing hard, uttering low moans, calling out for her baby, she slept fitfully.

Too frightened and upset to sleep, Susannah suddenly saw a shadow making its way up the front of her skirt. A spider.

She bent toward it, struggling to free her hands. But they were fastened tightly. She could not brush the spider away. She could only stare at it helplessly as it made its way up her dress.

Outside, the white moonlight fell on two large mounds of straw, golden under the pale wash of light.

Is this the straw we will burn in? Susannah thought with a shudder.

Are these mounds of straw waiting to be our final bed?

The spider was up to her waist, its legs moving quickly over the coarse fabric of the dress.

As she stared at the mounds of straw and pictured them afire, a strangled sob burst from her throat.

She turned her eyes from the window.

I am not a witch, she thought with fierce bitterness. *My mother is not a witch.*

What of the three who have already burned? Were they innocent, too?

Are the innocent burning in Wickham? Can that be true?

Suddenly the moonlight appeared to be snuffed out.

The tiny cell was cast in deep darkness.

Startled, Susannah turned to see a silhouette on the other side of the window, blocking the light.

"Wh-who's there?" she stammered.

"Susannah," came a hoarse whisper.

"Edward!" she cried, feeling a burst of joy lighten her chest. "Edward—have you come to save us?"

CHAPTER 7

Edward Fier stared at her, his face half hidden in darkness.

"Have you come to save us?" Susannah repeated in an eager whisper.

Edward hesitated. Susannah could see his dark eyes staring in at her, studying her coldly. "Save you? Why would I save you?" he demanded finally, his voice as cold as his eyes.

"Edward, I thought—"

"How could you betray me like this?" Edward asked, spitting the words angrily.

Susannah gasped. "Betray *you*? Edward, I did nothing to betray you. *You* betrayed *me*. You toyed with my heart. You were engaged to be married, and yet you continued to—"

"I was never engaged!" Edward insisted vehemently in a low whisper. He pulled back from the window and glanced quickly from side to side. When he was certain there was no one around, he pressed his face close to the opening again.

"I was never engaged. I told my father that I was in love with *you*!" Edward told her bitterly.

Susannah swallowed hard. "You did?"

"But you betrayed me, Susannah."

"No. I never—" Susannah started.

"You betrayed me with the Evil One!" Edward accused, his dark eyes glowing with anger.

"No! I am innocent, Edward!" Susannah whispered fiercely. "You must believe me! You *must*!"

"You cannot be innocent," Edward whispered. "You are a witch, Susannah. You tried to lead me astray. But your evil was exposed in time."

"No! I am innocent!" Susannah declared. "Edward, you *know* me. We have been so close. We have meant so much to each other. How—" Her voice caught in her throat. She took a deep breath and tried again. "How can you be so certain of my guilt?"

He stared at her, his features set, his eyes as cold as his words. "I told you, Susannah. I revealed my feelings about you to my father. I told my father of my love for you. Do you think that knowing this, my father would put you on trial if you were innocent?"

"But, Edward—"

"Do you think my father would put me through this pain? Do you think my father would *hurt* me like this? Deliberately hurt me by trying an innocent girl?" Edward shook his head, his eyes still burning accusations into Susannah's.

"No, Susannah," he said sadly. "My father may be stern and hard, but he always does what is right. He is a good man. My father cares about me, about my feelings. He would never do this to me. He would never put you on trial unless he was certain of your guilt!"

"I swear to you, Edward—" Susannah started.

But he wouldn't let her finish. "To think that I defied my father on your behalf," Edward cried. "To think that I went against my father's wishes in order to stand up for you. To think that I risked my father's goodwill, my father, who is a good and pious man, who only wants the best for me. To think that I was ready to defy him, for *you*—a witch!"

"Edward, your father is *wrong*!" Susannah shouted desperately.

His eyes narrowed. He lowered his voice to an icy whisper. "Do not speak of my father, witch. Your spell over me is ended."

"Edward, no! Edward, please!" Susannah wailed.

The face in the window was gone. The pale moonlight returned.

Susannah sobbed quietly. Across the room her mother stirred but didn't awaken.

Susannah felt the spider inching along her neck now. Her skin tingled as it made a path up to her chin.

Go ahead, spider. Bite, she thought with a bitter sigh of defeat.

Go ahead and bite.

Across the village in the Goodes' small house, William Goode sat hunched in a tall-backed chair. The fire had burned low, purple embers sizzling quietly. The room grew cold. William, staring blankly at the darkening hearth, didn't notice.

Deep in despair, he had been sitting motionless for more than an hour. Unable to focus his eyes, unable to focus his mind. The sounds of the trial, the shadowy faces, and the accusing eyes all washed across his distressed mind.

All is lost, he thought, picturing his wife and daughter, picturing them at home by the fire, picturing them in the peace and tranquillity that would never return. Even his baby was lost to him—a neighbor had George for the time being.

All is lost.

When a knock came at the door, William didn't move.

Sinking deeper and deeper into his despair, he didn't hear it.

The knock repeated. And then again even more loudly, a third time.

William stirred, raised his head, listened.

Yes. A knock on the door.

Who could it be at this hour? Who would have the nerve to come to his door, knowing how he must be suffering at this moment?

Knowing how he would suffer the rest of his life. How this night would be played out again and again in his mind until the day he died.

The loud knocking was repeated.

Someone was being very insistent.

With a groan William pulled himself unsteadily to his feet.

The purple embers came into focus.

The fire is dying, he thought.

Everything in my life is dying.

More loud knocking.

"Go away," William muttered.

But he made his way to the door and pulled it open.

The bright light of a torch caused William to shield his eyes. Slowly the face of the torch bearer came into view.

"Matthew Fier! What do you want of me?" William demanded weakly. "Have you come to take me away too?"

CHAPTER 8

The torchlight fell over Matthew Fier's face, casting it into deep shadow. His dark eyes stared out at William, black circles ringed by black as black as the grave.

"I have come to help you, not accuse you, William," Matthew said softly. He raised the torch high, and once again his face disappeared under the shadow of his hat.

"Help me?" William asked weakly, his body sagging in the narrow doorway.

"May I come in?"

William nodded and took a step back. Matthew Fier set the torch down in the dirt and edged into the house, pulling his cloak around him. He removed his hat, revealing tousled brown hair. He hung the hat on a hook on the wall.

The two men stood awkwardly in front of the door, staring at each other.

William was the first to break the silence. "My wife and daughter have been unjustly accused. Your brother has made a dreadful mistake. Martha and Susannah know nothing of the dark arts."

Matthew started to move past William, his eyes on the dying fire. But William grabbed the front of his cloak. "Your brother is wrong!" he cried. "He is wrong! Wrong!"

"My brother is human," Matthew said softly. He pulled away from William's grasp and, straightening the front of his cloak, stepped to the fire.

William stared after him, bewildered by his remark.

Matthew picked up a log from beside the fireplace and dropped it onto the dying embers. "You let your fire die, William," he said, staring into the hearth.

"I do not care about fires now," William replied, his trembling voice revealing his emotion. "I care only about my wife and daughter. I implore you, Matthew—"

Matthew turned to face William, clasping his hands in front of his gray doublet. He had rough hands, William saw. Farmer's hands.

"I believe I can help you, William," Matthew said slowly, softly.

"You mean—?"

"I believe I can save your wife and daughter."

William uttered a loud sigh. He gestured to the straight-backed chair near the fire.

Matthew shook his head. He began to pace back and forth in front of the hearth, his boots clicking against the floorboards. "My brother is human, as I said."

William scratched his white hair. "I do not understand. Do you mean to say . . ." His voice trailed off.

"I have influence with Benjamin," Matthew said, raising his dark eyes to William's.

"You can talk to him?" William asked eagerly. "You can reason with him? You can explain to him that he has made a tragic error?"

A strange smile formed on Matthew's face. He stopped pacing and nodded. "I believe I can persuade my brother to change the verdict. Your wife and daughter need not burn tomorrow evening."

"Oh, thank you! Thank you, Matthew!" William cried joyfully. He dropped to his knees and bowed his head in a silent prayer.

When he raised his eyes, he saw that Matthew still had a strange smile on his lips. A wave of doubt swept over William as he climbed heavily to his feet. "You really can sway your brother?" he asked hopefully. "Your brother will listen to you?"

Matthew nodded. Sweeping his cloak around him, he

lowered himself into the tall-backed wooden chair. "I can persuade Benjamin," he repeated. He narrowed his dark eyes. "But it will be costly."

"What?" William wasn't certain he had heard correctly. Was Matthew Fier asking for payment? For a bribe?

"It will be costly, William," Matthew repeated, his smile fading. "My services in this matter must be well rewarded."

William Goode swallowed hard. "I have little money," he choked out. "But I will spend every shilling I have to save Martha and Susannah."

"The price is one hundred pounds," Matthew announced flatly, staring hard at William.

"One hundred pounds?" William cried, unable to conceal his surprise. "But, Matthew, I beg you!"

"One hundred pounds is a small price to pay," Matthew said, rising and walking over to the hearth. The fresh log had just caught flame. Matthew held out his hands to warm them.

William gaped at him in disbelief.

He is willing to spare Martha and Susannah in exchange for a bribe, William thought. I knew the Fier brothers were ambitious. I knew their characters were weakened by the sin of greed. But I never dreamed they were *so* corrupt. I never dreamed they would try to increase their wealth by threatening the lives of an innocent woman and girl.

"Matthew, I have only eighty pounds," William

protested. "Eighty pounds is all that I brought from England, all that I possess in the world. If you take it, I will have nothing."

Matthew's dark eyes lit up, reflecting the leaping flames in the hearth. "You will have your wife and daughter," he said flatly.

William lowered his head, knowing he would pay the huge sum to Matthew Fier. Knowing he would pay *anything* to rescue Martha and Susannah from the flames.

When he looked up, Matthew was examining a long-handled pan hanging on the wall beside the hearth. "Very nice warming pan," he said, taking it down and turning it over in his hands, admiring it. "Is it brass?"

"It is of the finest brass," William replied. "It was crafted by my father."

"I will take it as part of the payment," Matthew announced, still examining it. "Since you do not have the full one hundred pounds to pay me."

"Take it," William replied with a wave of his hand. "Take everything I own, Matthew. Just return my family to me safely."

Matthew lowered the warming pan and gazed around the small room. "Speaking of your family, where is little George?" he asked.

"Mary Halsey next door has taken the baby," William replied unhappily. "He needed a nurse. And I could not bear to look upon him, to see his innocent face and know that he would grow up without ever knowing his mother or sister."

A loud sob escaped William's throat. He wiped tears from his eyes. "I will get you your payment, Matthew," he said in a voice trembling with emotion. "Then will you speak to Benjamin tonight?"

Matthew nodded solemnly. "Your family will be released tomorrow at sunset. Your troubled heart may rest easy, William."

His head still spinning, William eagerly made his way to the back of the house, where his life savings were hidden. As he pulled the heavy cloth bag up from under a loose floorboard, he felt as if his heart were about to burst.

Martha will be home tomorrow night!

Susannah will be home too!

We will all be so happy again. What rejoicing we will do!

He hoisted the bag to the front room and sat down at the table to count it out. Matthew Fier, carrying the brass warming pan in one hand, made his way to the table and peered over William's shoulder at the large coins.

"Eighty pounds," William said finally, shoving the pile of coins toward Matthew. "I am left with two copper shillings. But I am a rich man!"

"Yes, you are," Matthew agreed, his face completely expressionless. As he leaned forward to collect the coins, the pendant he wore around his neck fell in front of William's eyes.

It was so unusual that William couldn't help but comment on it. "What an interesting amulet you wear, Matthew," he remarked.

Matthew stood up and fingered the amulet, as if seeing it for the first time.

The silver disk sparkled with blue jewels. The jewels were grasped by a silver three-toed claw. Matthew twirled the disk in his fingers. On the back three Latin words were inscribed.

William struggled to read the words: *"Dominatio per malum.*

"Quite unusual," William said. "What do the words mean?"

Matthew tucked the amulet back inside his doublet. "Just an old saying," he replied with a shrug. "The amulet was given to me by my grandmother before I left our village. I wear it only as a reminder of that wonderful old woman and of my previous life, a life of poverty and struggle."

William raised his eyes to Matthew's, studying his face in the dim firelight. "I have heard such a claw referred to as a demon's claw," he told his visitor. "It is said to have powers."

For a brief moment Matthew's mouth remained open in surprise. When he regained his composure, he said, "I know nothing about powers or demon's claws. Nor should you, William Goode."

"No, of course not," William said quickly, lowering his eyes.

Matthew Fier collected the remaining coins. Then, carrying the brass warming pan, he made his way to the door, his cloak sweeping behind him. He lowered his hat onto his head and turned to gaze back at William.

William hadn't risen from the table. His entire body was trembling. Trembling with joy. With eagerness. With relief. "My family—" he managed to say.

"I will make sure of everything," Matthew Fier promised. Then, pulling his heavy cloak closer about him, he opened the door and disappeared into the night.

CHAPTER 9

The next evening William Goode hurried across the commons toward the prison. A small flock of sheep interrupted their grazing to raise their heads and mutter their surprise in his direction.

The sun spread rose-colored waves across the evening sky as it lowered itself behind the trees. A pale half moon was already visible, just poking over the shingled roof of Benjamin Fier's two-story house.

The day had gone by in a haze for William. Mary Halsey had brought him his midday meal, but it had gone untouched. He had intended to mend the fence around his wife's small kitchen garden but hadn't the strength.

Time had stood still, and William Goode frozen with it.

Only when the sun had begun to sink and evening

approached had William sprung to life. Now he moved quickly past squawking chickens and a lowing herd of scrawny cows, eager to be reunited with his beloved family.

Eager to hug them, to touch them. Eager to share the warm tears that would flow, the happy tears that would wash away the terror, erase all of the nightmares. Eager to bring Martha and Susannah home.

As the low, gray prison building came into view, William's heart began to pound. So much joy! So much relief! Panting loudly with excitement, he slowed his pace. Then he stopped to catch his breath.

A yapping hound ran across his path. William looked up to see a crowd in front of the prison entrance.

They've come to share my joy, he realized.

Their faces were hidden from him, hidden by dark hats and hoods. But he knew they were his neighbors, his friends, grateful for the reversal of the unjust verdict, grateful for the Goodes' change of fortune.

As he approached them his knees felt weak, his legs trembly. He forced himself to take a deep breath and hold it. He could hear their murmuring voices as they huddled near the prison doorway.

This is the happiest day of my life, he thought.

And then the door swung open. An officer appeared.

Another officer stepped out in front of the murmuring crowd.

Susannah came next, her head lowered as she walked through the doorway. Martha Goode followed close behind, her shadow blue against the hard gray ground.

"Susannah! Martha!" William called, pushing eagerly through the crowd of well-wishers.

They both raised their eyes and searched for him.

"Here I am! Martha! Over here! Susannah!" William called happily. He stepped to the front of the group of onlookers, breathing hard, his face red, his vision already blurred by happy tears.

"Martha! Susannah!"

He watched for them to be released.

But to his surprise, their hands were tied behind their backs.

William gasped as one of the officers turned and shoved Martha from behind, pushing her hard, causing her to stumble forward.

"Martha!" William cried.

She saw him finally and called out to him, a mournful expression on her face.

"Do not worry!" he called. "They are releasing you now!"

"Father!" Susannah cried shrilly, her face also twisted in anguish. "Help us, Father!"

"Do not worry—" William started. But his voice caught in his throat as he saw the officers force his wife and daughter toward the low mounds of straw.

"Father—!" Susannah pleaded.

"William! William! Help us!" Martha cried.

"Wait!" William shouted.

Someone tried to restrain him. "It is all in the hands of the Maker," he heard someone mutter. "Let us pray for their souls."

"No!" William screamed. He pulled away, jerked himself free, and began running toward them. "Stop! Stop!"

To William's horror, Susannah and Martha had already been marched to the straw piles and were being tied to tall wooden stakes.

"Nooooo!" William's scream of protest raged in the evening air like the howl of a desperate animal.

His vision blurred by angry tears, he burst forward, howling his rage, a frantic wail of protest. He stopped short when he saw Benjamin Fier at the edge of the crowd, overseeing the proceedings, hands on the sides of his long black cloak, his face hidden in the shadow of his wide-brimmed hat.

"Benjamin—!" William screamed, grabbing the magistrate from behind by the shoulders. "Benjamin—you must stop this now! Free them! Your brother promised me—!"

With a desperate sigh William spun him around by the shoulders . . . and gazed into an unexpected face.

"Giles!" William croaked, his voice a shocked whisper. "Giles Roberts!"

"William, please let go of me," the deputy magistrate said softly.

"Giles? But . . . but . . ." William stammered breathlessly, too astonished to think clearly.

Susannah and Martha were now tightly secured to the stakes. The two officers were moving forward with lighted torches.

"Stop them, Giles!" William demanded. "Stop them at once. Where is Benjamin? Where is Benjamin Fier? I must speak to him before . . . before . . ."

Giles Roberts took a step back, freeing himself from William's grip.

"William, have you not heard?" he asked, staring into William's tear-filled eyes. "Benjamin and his brother, Matthew, fled the village before dawn this morning."

CHAPTER 10

"Fled the village?" William cried frantically, staring over Giles Roberts's shoulder to the straw piles where his wife and daughter were twisting in terror against the wooden stakes that held them.

"Before dawn," Giles repeated solemnly.

"But I paid Matthew—!" William cried. "I paid him to—"

"The Fiers robbed us," Giles told him. "They emptied the storehouse. They left us no food for winter. They took everything. Everything."

"I—I don't understand!" William cried, feeling the ground tilt and whirl beneath him. He shut his eyes, tried to steady himself.

"They loaded all their belongings onto wagons," Giles told him. "And they disappeared with all of our supplies."

"But didn't they speak to you before they left?" William demanded, desperately clutching at Giles. "Didn't Benjamin tell you? Didn't Matthew tell you?"

"They didn't speak to me, William," Giles replied softly. And then he added firmly, "Please let go of me."

"But the sentence against my wife and daughter was to be reversed! They are to be freed, Giles! Benjamin should have told you. He should have—"

"He told me nothing," Giles said. The deputy magistrate's features grew hard. "The sentence must be carried out."

There was no use struggling, Susannah realized.

Her hands were tightly bound. She could not free herself from the stake. It poked uncomfortably into her back. Her wrists throbbed against the tight cords. Her shoulders ached.

She raised her eyes to the sky. The sun had lowered itself behind the trees, the trees she had loved to walk among. The piney sweet-smelling trees that had brought her so much joy. The trees where she and Edward had hidden during their brief secret meetings, during her brief happiness.

Lowering her eyes, she thought she saw Edward.

He stood at the edge of the crowd, staring back at her.

At first Susannah saw hurt in his eyes. Pain.

But as she gazed at him, his face appeared to harden before her eyes, until it became a mask of cold hatred.

She cried out—and realized it wasn't him.

It wasn't Edward.

The boy didn't look at all like Edward.

Two circles of yellow light approached from out of the grayness.

Two torches.

"Mother—" Susannah cried. "Mother, will it hurt?"

Tears streamed down Martha Goode's swollen cheeks. She turned her face from her daughter, struggling to stifle her sobs.

"Will it hurt, Mother? Tell me, Mother—will it hurt?"

CHAPTER 11

William Goode pressed his hands against the sides of his face. But the anguished screams of his wife and daughter invaded his ears.

I'll hear their screams forever.

Eyes closed, he could still picture their bodies twisting on the flaming stakes, still see their melting faces, their fiery hair.

He had tried to run to them.

But the two officers had held him back, pushing him to the ground, holding him on his knees as the choking black smoke fogged the sky and the howls of agony rose higher than the flames.

Martha. Susannah.

My family . . .

William was still on his knees when the fire had been doused and the silent crowd had departed. He hadn't noticed that he was alone now.

Alone with his grief.

Alone with the stench of the smoke in his nostrils.

Alone with the screams of his wife and daughter ringing in his ears.

They burned so brightly, he thought, sobbing.

They burned as bright as stars.

The ground beneath him was puddled with his tears.

He raised his eyes to the night sky, the color of coal, pierced with pale white stars.

I know you're both up there, William thought, climbing unsteadily to his feet.

I know you are both up there, bright as stars.

He uttered one last, wrenching sob. Then his grief quickly gave way to his fury.

He strode home through the silent, deserted commons, his eyes held straight ahead. The fire faded in his mind, faded to dark, shifting images, pictures of Benjamin and Matthew Fier.

His fury grew with every step.

Betrayed.

They betrayed me and stole my life.

"William?" A voice startled him at his front door. It took him a while to erase the hated images of the Fier brothers and focus on the dark figure in his doorway.

"Mary Halsey!" he whispered.

She held the baby up to him, wrapped tightly in a wool blanket. "Take the baby, William. Take George."

"No." William raised his hands as if to fend the baby off.

"He is your only family now," Mary Halsey insisted, thrusting the baby forward. "Take him. Hold him, William. He will help you get over your grief."

"No," William repeated. "Not now, Mary Halsey. There is something I must do first."

He startled her by pushing past her and entering his house, closing the door hard behind him.

The house was dark, nearly as dark as William's thoughts. The fire had long since burned out.

William moved quickly through the darkness to the back of the house. He pulled open the door that led to his special room, the tiny, secret room behind the wall, where even Susannah and Martha had never gone.

The room where the black candles were always lighted.

He stepped into the flickering orange light and pulled the door closed behind him.

Whispering the ancient words of the purification ritual, William removed the scarlet hooded robe from its hiding place beneath a stack of wooden boxes and pulled it around him.

William could feel the power of the robe even before he lowered the hood over his head.

Bowing his head three times, William gazed around

the circle of candlelight. Then he dropped to his knees on the dirt floor and began to chant the ancient words he knew so well.

My wife and daughter were innocent, William thought bitterly as he chanted.

They were innocent.

But I am not.

They had no knowledge of these dark arts.

But I have practiced them well.

Whispering the ancient dark curses, he began to scratch signs of evil in the dirt floor. He was breathing hard now, his heart pounding in his chest.

Under the satiny scarlet hood he glared, unblinking, at the ancient symbols he was scratching in the dirt. A grim smile formed on his trembling lips.

Innocence died today, William Goode thought as he summoned the spirits of evil he had summoned so many times before.

Innocence died today. But my hatred will live for generations.

The Fiers shall not escape me.

Wherever they flee, I will be there.

My family's screams shall become the Fiers' tortured screams.

The fire that burned today will not be quenched—until revenge is mine, and the Fiers burn forever in the fire of my curse!

Village of Shadyside

1900

"That's how it began. That's how it all began more than two hundred years ago," Nora Goode said.

Staring into the yellow candle glow, she set down her pen. Her slender hand ached from writing.

How long have I been here? she wondered, allowing her eyes to trail down the melting wax on the side of the candle.

How long have I been seated at this narrow table, writing the story of my ancestors?

The candle flickered, reminding her of the fire. Once again she saw the burning mansion. Once again she heard the anguished screams of her loved ones trapped inside the blaze.

How did I escape? Nora wondered, staring intently into the flame.

I don't remember.

How did I get here?

Someone brought me here. Someone found me. Someone found me on the lawn, staring into the fire, watching the mansion burn.

Someone helped me away from there and brought me to this room.

And now I must write it all down. I must tell the whole story. I must explain about the two families and the curse that has followed us through the decades.

Nora picked up the pen. With a trembling hand she straightened up the stack of papers on the small table.

She leaned toward the smooth yellow candle flame.

I must finish the story before the night is ended, she thought.

So little time.

Susannah and Martha Goode burned in 1692. Now my story picks up eighteen years later.

Benjamin and Matthew Fier are once again successful farmers. Matthew's wife, Constance, has given him a daughter, Mary.

Benjamin's son, Edward, is a grown man. He never married Anne Ward, but he has married Rebecca, a woman from a nearby village. They have a son named Ezra.

So much to tell. So much to tell . . .

Taking a deep breath, Nora bent over the table. A few seconds later her pen scratched against the paper as she resumed her dark tale.

PART TWO

Western Pennsylvania Frontier

1710

CHAPTER 12

"Sometimes I think this family is cursed," Benjamin Fier muttered, pulling his chair closer to the long dining table. He shook his head unhappily, his disheveled white hair glowing in the fading evening light that filtered through the window.

"You are starting to sound like a crotchety old man, Father," Edward said, laughing.

"I *am* a crotchety old man!" Benjamin declared with pride.

"How can you say we are cursed?" Benjamin's brother, Matthew, demanded, sniffing the aroma of roast chicken as he entered the room. "Look how our farm has prospered, Benjamin. Look how our family has grown."

"I can see that *you* have certainly grown," Benjamin teased.

Matthew had become quite stout. As he took his place at the table, everyone could see that his linen shirt was stretched tight around his bulging middle.

"Uncle Benjamin, are you teasing my father again?" Mary Fier scolded. Matthew's daughter Mary set a serving platter of potatoes and string beans in front of Matthew.

"Well, don't you look like Queen Anne herself!" Benjamin roared at Mary.

Mary blushed. "I put my hair up. That is all."

Mary was seventeen. She had long copper-colored hair, as did her mother, Constance Fier. She also had her mother's creamy, pale complexion and shy smile. She had her father Matthew's dark, penetrating eyes.

"Why do you scold Mary?" Constance demanded of Benjamin, sweeping into the room, holding the platter of roast chicken in front of her long white apron. "Mary worked all afternoon, peeling potatoes and snapping the beans for your dinner."

"I also picked the beans," Mary added grumpily.

"He was only teasing, Cousin Mary," Edward said. "Weren't you, Father?"

Benjamin didn't reply. He had a faraway look clouding his dark eyes. He stared at the narrow window.

"Father?" Edward repeated.

Benjamin lowered his eyes to his son with a frown.

"Were you addressing me?" he barked. "Speak up! I am an old man, Edward. I cannot abide mutterers."

"Where is Rebecca?" Matthew demanded, his eyes searching the long, narrow dining room.

Rebecca, Edward's beautiful young wife, always seemed to be the last to the table.

"I believe she is tending Ezra," Edward told his uncle.

"Your son has been trouble since the day he was born," Benjamin grumbled. His booming voice had become raspy and harsh.

"Ezra is a difficult child," Edward admitted to his father, accepting the platter of chicken. "But I believe you go too far."

"I'm his grandfather. I can go as far as I please," Benjamin bellowed unpleasantly. "If you don't like my remarks, Edward, go eat your dinner at your own house." He pointed out the window toward Edward's house across the pasture.

"Hush, Brother," Matthew instructed, raising a hand for peace. "Let us enjoy our dinner without your usual sour complaints."

Rebecca entered, pulling Ezra behind her. It was evident from Ezra's wet eyes that he'd been crying. Ezra was six but acted as if he were much younger. Rebecca, sighing wearily, lifted him into a chair and told him not to squirm.

Rebecca had straight black hair pulled back from a

high forehead, olive-green eyes, and dramatic dark lips. She had been a high-spirited, giggly girl when she married Edward, but six years of mothering Ezra and helping out on the farm had brought lines to her forehead and a weariness to her voice.

"Will you eat some chicken now, Ezra?" she asked.

"No!" the boy shouted, crossing his arms defiantly in front of his chest.

"He has a strong will. He is a true Fier," Benjamin growled approvingly.

"I am not!" Ezra cried peevishly. "I am Ezra. That is all."

Everyone laughed.

Rebecca dropped a chicken leg onto the boy's plate. "Eat your dinner," she instructed softly.

"What a fine family we are," Matthew said happily, patting his large belly. "Look around this table, Benjamin. Look at our children and grandchildren. And think of our prosperous farm and trading store. How can you say this family is cursed?"

Benjamin chewed his food slowly before replying. "Cursed," he muttered after swallowing. "The new roof shingles. Edward finished putting them up just last week. And last night that thunderstorm washed away half of them. Is that not a curse?"

Edward chuckled. "Only a few shingles were blown off, Father," he said, reaching for his pewter water cup. "There will still be light after dinner. I will go up on the roof and examine it closely. I am certain it is but a minor repair."

"Cousin Edward, it will be too dark," Mary warned. "Can it not wait until tomorrow?"

Mary and Edward were more like brother and sister than cousins. Mary was also close to Edward's wife Rebecca. There were few young people in the village for Mary to befriend. She had only her family to turn to for companionship.

"There will be enough light to examine the shingles," Edward assured her, helping himself to more string beans. He smiled at Mary. "Do not fret. Wipe your uncle's words from your mind. There is no curse on the Fier family. The only curse around here is my crotchety old father!"

The family's laughter rose up from the long dining table. It floated out the window, out of the two-story stone house to reach the ears of a white-bearded man in ragged clothes who was hidden behind the fat trunk of an old oak tree just beyond Mary's small flower garden.

Careful to keep out of view, the man leaned toward the sound of laughter, the sleeve of his worn coat pressed against the rough bark. His tired eyes explored the steep shingled roof of the sturdy farmhouse. Then he lowered his gaze to the window where the tangy aroma of roast chicken floated out.

The man's stomach growled. It had been a while since he had eaten.

But he was too excited to think about food now.

Too excited to think about his long journey. A journey of years.

He could feel his heart pound beneath his thin shirt. His breath escaped in noisy wheezes—such rapid breathing his sides began to ache. He gripped the tree trunk so tightly his hands hurt.

"At last!" he whispered to the tree. "At last!" A whispered cry of joy, of triumph.

The white-haired man was William Goode.

For almost twenty years I have sought this moment, he thought, staring intently at the flickering light through the window, listening to the chime of voices inside.

For twenty years I have searched the colonies for the Fiers, my enemies.

At last I have found them.

At last I can carry out my curse. At last I can avenge my wife and daughter.

I have found the Fiers. And now they will suffer as I have suffered. All of them. One by one.

He heard the clatter of dishes, the scrape of chairs.

Then, to his surprise, the door opened and a young man came out of the house, followed by several others.

With a gasp William pulled his head back out of view and pressed himself even tighter against the tree's ragged bark. The sun was low behind the trees. The sky was a wash of pink and purple, quickly darkening.

From his hiding place, William Goode squinted hard, struggling to recognize the faces of those he had hunted for so many years.

He had somehow expected them to look the same. Now he stared in surprise to see the changed faces and bodies.

Can that be Edward Fier? he asked himself, watching the young man prop a wooden ladder against the side of the house. Edward was but a boy when last I saw him. Now he has become a sturdy young man.

And that white-haired man, stooped over his walking stick? William squinted hard. Can *that* be Benjamin Fier?

He has aged badly, William decided. Back in Wickham he was tall and broad-shouldered, a man as powerful as his booming voice. And now his shoulders are hunched, and he leans heavily on his stick with a trembling grip.

All the better to help you topple into your grave, Benjamin Fier, William Goode thought with a grim smile.

I still have my powers, William thought with satisfaction. And I plan to use them now.

Recognizing Benjamin's brother, Matthew, William nearly laughed out loud. Why, he has become as fat as one of his cows! William declared to himself. Look how he struts with his belly hanging out.

You will strut to your grave, Matthew, William decided, feeling a wave of bitterness sweep over him. It will be a painful journey for you, Matthew. You will beg for death.

But I will make your death agonizing and slow. For you are my betrayer. You are the one who robbed me of my money—and my family!

William couldn't have known the little boy who was scampering through the flower garden, unheedful of the blossoming flowers. Nor did he recognize the copper-haired young woman who held the side of the ladder.

What fine linen shirts the men all wear, thought William bitterly. And the girl's dress is of the most expensive fabric.

What are the young people's names? Are they the children or the grandchildren of the Fier brothers?

It doesn't matter, he thought, closing his eyes, a broad smile hidden behind his scraggly mustache and beard. It doesn't matter what your names are. You are Fiers.

And all Fiers shall start to suffer now.

All.

CHAPTER 13

"The sun is nearly down," Mary told her cousin, gripping the sides of the ladder.

"There is enough light," Edward insisted. "Move away. I am only going up for a moment."

"But the shingles are still wet from the rain," Mary insisted. "Wait until morning, Edward."

"Please. I shall be down in a moment," Edward said stubbornly. "Why do you always treat me as if I'm Ezra's age, Mary?"

"Why do you always insist on being so reckless?" Mary replied. "It's as if you have to show off to Uncle Benjamin and my father. You have nothing to prove to them, Edward."

"Maybe I have things to prove to myself," Edward

muttered. "Now, please, Cousin—allow me to make my inspection of the shingles before the moon is up."

Mary obediently took a step back. "May I hold the ladder in place for you?" she asked as Edward began to climb.

"You know you should be in the kitchen helping Rebecca and your mother clean the dinner dishes."

Mary groaned and rolled her eyes. "I am seventeen, Cousin Edward," she said sharply. "I am not a girl. I am a woman."

"Your place is still in the kitchen," Edward called down. He had reached the roof and was edging his way off the ladder. "It appears much steeper up here than it did down on the ground," he said.

Mary backed up a few paces to see him better. The sun had disappeared. Edward was a dark figure against an even darker sky.

"Please be careful!" Mary called. "You're up so high, and it's so dark, and—"

Her voice caught in her throat as Edward's arms shot up. She saw his legs buckle and his body tilt.

And then she opened her mouth wide and began to scream as she realized Edward was falling, falling headfirst to the ground.

CHAPTER 14

Edward hit the ground with a sickening crack.

The horrifying sound split the air, louder than Mary's screams.

A second later another scream burst from the house.

Matthew came hurrying from the toolhouse at the end of the garden, followed by Benjamin, hobbling as fast as he could with his walking stick.

Rebecca was the first from the house, with Constance right behind her.

Mary, her hands pressed against her face, hurried to Edward, diving beside him on the dark ground. "Edward—?"

He gazed up at her lifelessly, a startled expression frozen on his face.

"Edward—?"

He blinked. Swallowed hard. Took a noisy, deep breath.

"My arm—" he whispered.

Mary lowered her gaze to his left arm buried beneath his body at an unnatural angle. She gasped.

"I—I can't move it," Edward whispered.

"You broke it," Mary told him, gently placing a hand on his chest.

"What happened?" Benjamin cried breathlessly, still struggling to get to the house.

"Is Edward injured?" Matthew demanded.

"Edward, can you get up?" Constance asked softly.

Mary turned and raised her eyes to her mother and Rebecca. "Oh, Mother!" she cried in horror, her mouth dropping open in disbelief.

The front of Constance's dress was splattered with blood.

"I—I—" Constance lowered her gaze. She held up her hand. Blood poured down her arm.

"I was cleaning the carving knife when I heard you scream, Mary," she explained. "The sound startled me. The knife slipped, and—" She hesitated. "I shall be fine. I just—"

"Let us get you into the house!" Mary cried, jumping to her feet. "We have to stop the bleeding."

As Mary led her mother back to the kitchen, Matthew

and Rebecca lifted Edward to his feet. With his good arm around Rebecca's shoulders, Edward took a few unsteady steps.

"I think I can walk," Edward said, his jaw clenched against the pain. "But my arm . . . it is badly broken, I fear."

Leaning heavily on his walking stick, Benjamin Fier watched them walk off, shaking his head. "Cursed," he growled to himself. "The whole family is cursed."

The harsh crowing of roosters woke Mary at dawn. Gray light filtered through her tiny bedroom window. The air in the room felt hot and heavy.

She pulled herself up slowly, not at all rested. The back of her shift stuck to her skin.

What a horrid night, she thought, stretching, her shoulders aching. *I don't think I slept an entire hour. I just kept picturing Edward lying on the ground in a heap. I kept hearing the crack as his arm broke. And I kept seeing the blood pouring down Mother's arm.*

I tied Mother's wrist as tightly as I could. But it seemed to take forever to stop the flow of blood.

Meanwhile, Edward howled in pain as Matthew struggled to set the broken arm. Ezra was screaming and crying in the corner. Poor Rebecca didn't know which of her family to comfort—Edward or Ezra?

Finally a sling was fashioned for Edward from a bolt of

heavy linen. Rebecca led her family back to their house, Ezra's frightened wails ringing through the air.

What an unfortunate night.

Mary lowered her feet to the floor, then made her way to the dresser, squinting against the gray light.

Why do I have this feeling? she wondered. Why do I have this dark feeling that our bad luck isn't over?

Mary returned from the henhouse after breakfast, a large basket of white and brown eggs pressed against the front of her long white apron.

The sun was just climbing above the trees, but the air was already hot and sticky. Puffy clouds hovered overhead. A rooster crowed. Somewhere in the direction of the barn a dog barked in reply.

Mary walked with her head lowered, her copper hair flowing down her back nearly to the waist of her linen dress.

She nearly dropped the egg basket when a strange voice behind her called out, "Good morning, miss!"

Uttering a short cry of surprise, Mary spun around and stared into the sky blue eyes of a smiling young man. He grinned at her, his eyes lighting up as if enjoying her surprise.

"Oh. H-hello," Mary stammered. "I didn't see you."

She realized she was staring at him. He was a good-looking boy, about her age, maybe a year or two older. Above his sparkling blue eyes he had heavy blond eyebrows on a broad, tanned forehead. The skin beside his eyes crinkled when he smiled. He had wavy blond hair the color of butter, which fell heavily down to his collar.

He wore a loose-fitting white shirt, the front open nearly to his waist, over Indian-style deerskin breeches. His boots were worn and covered with dust.

"I am sorry to trouble you," he said, still grinning, his eyes locked on hers. "I am looking for the owner of this farm."

"That would be my father," Mary replied, turning her gaze to the house. "Matthew Fier."

"Is your father around?" the young man asked, the morning sunlight making his blond hair glow golden.

"I believe so. Follow me," Mary replied shyly.

He reached out and took the egg basket from her. "I'll carry it for you," he said, smiling pleasantly at her. "It looks heavy."

"I carry it every morning," Mary protested, but she allowed him to take the basket. "We have a lot of chickens."

"It's a very big farm," the boy said, gesturing to the far pasture with his free hand. His boots crunched loudly over the hard ground. "My father and I settled here recently. We live in a small cabin outside the village. I don't think I've ever seen a farm this big."

Mary smiled awkwardly. "My father and uncle came here before I was born. The farm has been growing ever since."

"What is your name, miss?" the boy asked boldly, his blue eyes flashing.

Before Mary could answer, Matthew appeared, lumbering out the back door. His flannel shirt hung loose over his big belly. His knee breeches had a stain on one knee.

Matthew yawned loudly and stretched his hands over his head. Then he noticed the young man holding the egg basket beside Mary.

"Oh," Matthew said, furrowing his brow and clearing his throat. "And who might you be?"

Matthew's brusqueness didn't seem to bother the young man. "Good morning," he said with a confident smile. "My name is Jeremy Thorne, sir."

"And what might your business be, Jeremy Thorne?" Matthew asked. "Has Mary hired you to be her egg carrier?"

Jeremy laughed even though Matthew's remark wasn't terribly funny. "No, sir," he replied cheerfully. "But I have come to your farm in search of work."

Matthew Fier stared rather unpleasantly at Jeremy. "I regret to say I'm not looking for farm help right now," he told Jeremy. "If you would kindly—"

Matthew was interrupted by Edward, perspiring from his walk across the pasture from his house. "Wait a moment, Uncle Matthew!" Edward cried. He raised his free hand to halt the conversation.

Startled, Matthew turned to his nephew. "Good morning, Nephew. Does the arm give much pain this morning?"

"Enough," Edward replied dryly, glancing at his arm, suspended in the sling. "I overheard your conversation with this young man, Uncle Matthew. I believe we do need an extra hand."

He gestured to his heavy sling. "You have lost my services for a while," Edward continued. "I believe this boy's timing is perfect. He can take some of my tasks—until my arm is healed."

Matthew rubbed his chins thoughtfully, his eyes trained on Jeremy. "Maybe . . ." he muttered reluctantly. "Where do you come from, boy?"

"From the village," Jeremy replied, eyeing Edward's sling. "My father and I settled here recently. My father is ill, sir. I am our sole support."

"No sad stories, please," Matthew cut him off, still rubbing his many chins. Matthew studied him. "You look strong enough."

Jeremy raised himself to his full height, throwing back his broad, muscular shoulders. "Yes, sir," he said quietly.

Mary stood stiffly, watching them all. She wanted to urge her father to hire Jeremy, but she knew better than to utter a word. It was not her place.

Matthew nodded. "All right, Jeremy Thorne. You may begin by cleaning out that toolhouse." He pointed to the low wooden structure behind the garden. "Pull all of the equipment out. We plan to build a bigger one."

"Thank you, sir!" Jeremy exclaimed happily. "I am very grateful. And my pay?"

"Ten shillings a week," Matthew replied quickly. "But let us see what kind of worker you are before we begin to think of you as more than temporary help."

"Very good, sir," Jeremy said. He glanced quickly at Mary.

She felt a shiver at the back of her neck.

He's so good-looking, she thought, lowering her eyes to the ground.

All kinds of thoughts raced through her mind, surprising thoughts, exciting thoughts.

But of course Father would never approve of anything between a mere farmhand and me, she realized, stopping the flow of wild thoughts in midstream.

Jeremy Thorne.

Jeremy. Jeremy. Jeremy.

She couldn't stop his name from repeating in her mind.

Her heart pounding, Mary took the egg basket from Jeremy and hurried to the house.

The talk at lunch was of the dreadful mishaps of the night before. Poor Edward. Poor Constance.

They all lowered their heads in prayer before starting their soup.

Mary couldn't stop thinking about Jeremy.

All morning long as she'd done her many kitchen chores, she had sneaked peeks at him from the door. She saw that he was proving to be as hard a worker as he had claimed.

At the back of the garden she could see the pile of tools and heavy equipment he had dragged out of the toolhouse. She watched him working alone back there, lowering his head to enter the structure, then appearing again with another handful of items.

"Mary—what are you daydreaming about?" her mother demanded, breaking into Mary's thoughts after lunch as they began washing the dishes.

"Nothing at all, really," Mary lied, blushing.

"You barely said a word at lunch. I watched you," Constance said. "You hardly touched your soup."

"I wasn't hungry, I guess, Mother," Mary replied dreamily.

"Please stop gazing out into the garden and help me with the dishes," Constance ordered. "You see I have only one hand."

"Go rest, Mother," Mary insisted. "I will clean the dishes by myself."

After the dishes were washed and put away, Mary picked up a basket and headed out to the garden to pick vegetables for the evening meal.

The sun blazed down. Mary could see waves of heat rising off the near pasture.

As she bent to pull up some turnips, a movement at the back of the garden caught her eye. Jeremy was emerging, drenched with sweat, pulling out several heavy iron hoes and rakes.

On an impulse Mary dropped her vegetable basket to the dirt and hurried to the well at the side of the house.

A few seconds later she was standing in front of Jeremy, a tall pewter mug of cold well water in her hands. "Here," she said, thrusting the mug at him. "I thought you might be thirsty."

He smiled at her, breathing hard. His blond hair was matted flat to his forehead. He had removed his shirt, and his smooth, muscular chest glistened with sweat.

"You're very kind, Miss Fier," he said. He raised the mug to his lips and, keeping his blue eyes on her, thirstily gulped several mouthfuls. Then he tilted the mug over his head and dumped the rest on his hair. It poured over his hair and face and onto his tanned shoulders.

They both laughed.

"You may call me Mary," she told him shyly, feeling her cheeks redden. "You're a very hard worker," she added quickly.

Her remark seemed to please him. "I believe in doing a job well," he replied seriously. "My father and I, we have always been poor. My father's health has never been good, so I have known hard work since I was barely out of swaddling clothes."

Mary gazed over his shoulder toward the rolling green pasture. "I work hard, too," she said wistfully. "There is so much to do on a farm this size."

"It is an admirable place," Jeremy said, turning to follow her gaze.

"It is very lonely here," Mary said suddenly. She hadn't planned on saying it. The words escaped before she could stop them. Her cheeks suddenly felt as if they were on fire. She lowered her eyes to the dirt.

"Do you have friends on other farms?" Jeremy asked softly. "Friends in town? Church friends?"

"No. I have my family. That is all," Mary said sadly. She cleared her throat. "But I have so many chores that I am usually too busy to think about friends and—"

"You're very pretty," Jeremy interrupted.

Startled by the compliment, Mary looked up to find his blue eyes staring intently at her.

"I like your hair," he said softly. "It is the color of sunset."

"Thank you, Jeremy," Mary replied awkwardly.

He took a step toward her, his eyes locked on hers.

What is he doing? Mary asked herself, feeling her heart start to pound.

Why is he staring at me like that? Is he trying to frighten me?

No. He's going to kiss me, Mary realized.

She started to take a step back, to move away. But she stopped.

He's going to kiss me. And I *want* him to.

"Mary!"

A voice behind her made her cry out.

She turned to see Rebecca running through the garden, waving to her wildly with both arms, her white apron flapping at the front of her dress as she ran.

Jeremy thrust the mug back at Mary, then turned and headed quickly toward the toolhouse.

"Rebecca, what is the matter?" Mary demanded, gripping the empty pewter mug in both hands.

"Have you seen Matthew? Edward? Where *are* they?" Rebecca cried, her features twisted in fear.

"Rebecca, what is the matter?" Mary repeated.

"Come quickly, Mary," Rebecca insisted, grabbing Mary's arm. "Please. Come. Something *horrible* has happened!"

CHAPTER 15

With Rebecca's shrill, frightened cry still ringing in her ears, Mary raced after her through the garden to the house.

"This way!" Rebecca shouted breathlessly, running through the kitchen and into the sitting room.

It took Mary's eyes a while to adjust to the sudden darkness. She gasped out loud when she saw Benjamin sprawled stiffly on his back on the floor.

"Look—that is how I found him!" Rebecca cried, pointing with a trembling finger. Her black hair had come undone and fell in disarray over her shoulders. Her dark lips formed an O of horror as she stared at the fallen man.

Mary dropped to her knees beside Benjamin. "Is he . . . is he . . . ?" she stammered. "Is he dead, Rebecca?"

She peered into Benjamin's face. His eyes were frozen in a glazed, wide-eyed stare. His mouth hung open loosely, revealing two rows of perfect teeth.

"I—I think so," Rebecca replied in a whisper. Then she ran back to the doorway, shouting, "Matthew! Matthew! Edward! Come quickly!"

Mary reached for Benjamin's hand and squeezed it. It was as cold as ice.

She swallowed hard, gaping down into the blank dark eyes that stared lifelessly up at her.

I've never seen a dead person, she thought.

"What's happening, Rebecca?" Edward had appeared in the doorway. "I heard you calling, and—" He lowered his eyes to the floor. "Father?"

"He—he must have been sitting there," Rebecca stammered, pointing to the high-backed chair against the wall. "He must have fallen. I think—"

"Father!" Edward cried again and dropped beside Mary. "Is he breathing?"

"I don't think so," Mary said softly. "I think—"

She and Edward both cried out at once as Benjamin blinked.

"Father!"

"Uncle Benjamin!"

He blinked again. His lips quivered. His mouth slowly closed.

"He's alive!" Mary told Rebecca happily. Rebecca let

out a long sigh and closed her eyes. Slumping against a wall, she began whispering a prayer.

Benjamin raised his head groggily.

"Lie still, Father. Take your time," Edward urged, a hand on Benjamin's shoulder.

"I am able to rise," Benjamin insisted gruffly. "Let me up."

Edward moved his hands behind Benjamin's shoulders and helped him to sit up.

"Uncle Benjamin, what happened? How do you feel?" Mary asked.

"I must have been dozing," Benjamin growled, shaking his head, blinking several times to clear his eyes. "Fell from the chair, I guess."

Matthew burst into the room breathing hard, his round face bright red from the exertion of hurrying. "Was someone calling me?" he asked breathlessly. He cried out when he saw his brother on the floor.

"I am fine," Benjamin told him. "Do not get hysterical."

He started to climb to his feet, then hesitated. His expression turned to surprise.

"Uncle Benjamin, what is it?" Mary asked, still on her knees beside him. The others drew near.

"My left leg," Benjamin muttered. "I can't move it." He moved his right leg, drawing it up, then making the foot roll from side to side.

"I have no feeling," Benjamin said, sounding more startled than worried. "No feeling at all in the left leg."

Glancing up, Mary watched as her father grasped the odd three-toed medallion he wore around his neck. "How strange!" Matthew declared.

"Edward, help me to my feet," Benjamin ordered.

Edward obediently wrapped an arm around his father's shoulders and with great difficulty hoisted him to his feet.

Benjamin's eyes narrowed as he tried to put weight on his left leg. He would have fallen if Edward and Mary hadn't caught him.

"No feeling in the leg at all," Benjamin said thoughtfully. "It does not hurt. There is no pain. It does not feel like anything. It is as if the leg has been taken away from me."

Wisps of clouds floated low in a bright sky. The white trunks of the beech trees at the end of the pasture gleamed in the late afternoon sunlight.

Mary stepped along at the edge of the woods, lifting her skirt over low shrubs and rocks. Above her the leaves trembled in a soft breeze.

She turned where the trees ended and felt the blood pulse at her temples as Jeremy came into view. He was working shirtless as usual, his back to her, tugging with gloved hands at a tangle of brambles at his feet.

She crept closer. The tree leaves appeared to tremble harder.

Or is it my imagination? Mary wondered. Is it just my excitement?

For three days Jeremy had been working to clear the brambles from this new section of land. Each afternoon Mary had met him there. She brought him water from the well. Jeremy would take a break from his solitary efforts. They would sit together on a fallen tree trunk and talk.

Jeremy was so sweet, so understanding, so kind, Mary came to believe. She could feel herself growing close to him. She could feel herself beginning to fall in love with him. The feelings swept over her gently, almost like pulling on a favorite wool cloak.

Comfortable. Reassuring. Warm.

"I feel as if I've known you all my life," she told him after he had finished the mug of cold water. Her eyes trailed a gold and black butterfly as it fluttered near the trees.

Sitting beside her on the smooth tree trunk, he kicked the soft dirt with the heel of one boot. "Every afternoon I worry that you won't come," he said softly.

"Here I am," she replied, smiling.

"But if your father found out—" Jeremy started, staring into her eyes as if challenging her, a wave of blond hair tumbling over his forehead.

Mary's smile faded. "My father would not approve," she admitted. "After all, you are only a poor farmhand, without a shilling. And I—"

"You? You are royalty!" Jeremy joked. But there was

bitterness behind the joke. "Queen Anne!" He rose to his feet and dipped his head in a courtly bow.

Mary giggled. "Please stop. I am sure that after time—"

"Time," Jeremy muttered. His eyes went to the thick brambles that rolled over the rocky ground. "Time for me to get back to work," he said. "Your father has instructed me to clear this field before the week is out."

"My father is not the true snob of the family," Mary said, lost in her own thoughts. "My uncle Benjamin would be much more alarmed than my father if he knew—"

"How does your uncle Benjamin feel?" Jeremy interrupted, his features tensing in concern.

"Not well," Mary replied, frowning. "His left arm has given out along with the leg."

"You mean—?"

"He cannot move the left arm now. He has no feeling in it. It is completely numb, he says. His entire left side is paralyzed."

"And how are his spirits?" Jeremy asked.

"Hard to tell," Mary replied thoughtfully. "He is as difficult and cantankerous as ever. He is not a man to give in to illness or affliction." She sighed. "Despite his strong spirit, he is as helpless as a baby."

"He is lucky to have you as a nurse," Jeremy replied, his eyes lighting up.

And before Mary could cry out or protest, he leaned over and pressed his mouth against hers.

Closing her eyes, Mary returned the kiss eagerly.

This is not proper. This isn't right.

But I do not care, she thought.

"Edward, please wait for me," Mary pleaded. "Don't walk so fast." Twigs snapped beneath her shoes as she hurried to catch up to him.

"Sorry," Edward said, turning to her. He pulled up a long, straight reed with his good hand and stuck one end in his mouth. "I was thinking about something."

Mary stepped up beside him breathlessly. "About your father?"

Edward nodded.

A bird cawed loudly above their heads. Mary gazed up into a red sunset sky to see two large blackbirds standing side by side on a low limb.

"Are blackbirds good luck or bad?" she asked her cousin lightly.

"Bad luck, I believe," he replied thoughtfully. "Black is the color of death, is it not?"

"You do not have to be so gloomy," Mary complained. "I asked you to come out for a walk to cheer you up."

"Sorry." He frowned. "I am gloomy. I cannot help it, Mary."

"Because of your arm, Edward? It will heal."

"No," he replied, glancing down at the heavy sling. "I am worried about my father. And Rebecca. And—"

"Rebecca?" Mary interrupted, stepping over a tree stump. "Is Rebecca ill?"

Edward shook his head. "No. But she seems so weary all the time, so exhausted. So dispirited. She seems so different to me."

"I think she *is* tired," Mary told him. "Ezra is not an easy child."

Edward didn't reply. They continued their walk through the woods in silence. The last rays of sunlight slid between the slender trees, casting rippling blue shadows at their feet.

"It is nearly dinnertime," Edward said finally, chewing on the end of the reed. "Rebecca will worry."

"Let us head back," Mary agreed, running her fingers along the trunk of a tall oak as she turned around.

"I tried to speak to my father this afternoon," Edward told her, letting her take the lead. "I needed to speak to him about the receipts for the store. But he would only talk about his paralyzed arm and leg."

"Oh!"

They had walked into a swarm of buzzing gnats. Mary raised her hands to shield her eyes. She quickened her pace, nearly stumbling over a jagged white rock in her path.

"It is so strange about Father," Edward continued, still scratching his neck, even though the gnats had been left behind. "He feels perfectly fine. He seems to be in good health. He has no pain. And yet—"

"Perhaps his strength will return," Mary said hopefully. She stopped and turned to him. "You seem so troubled, Cousin. You can talk of nothing but our family's gloomy problems and mishaps."

"Everything was going so well for us," Edward replied with emotion. "We were all so happy. And now, all of a sudden—"

He stopped walking.

Mary saw his eyes grow wide and his mouth drop open. The reed fell to his feet.

"Edward—what is it?"

She turned as he pointed.

At first she thought the yellow glow was the sun poking between the trees.

But she quickly remembered that the sun was nearly down. This yellow glow was too bright, too fiery.

"Fire!" Edward screamed, the flames reflected in his frightened eyes. "The woods are on fire!"

"No!" Mary cried, grabbing his good arm. "Edward—look!"

Inside the glowing fireball a figure writhed.

"Someone is trapped in the flames!" Mary shrieked.

CHAPTER 16

"It cannot be!" Edward cried in a hoarse whisper. "It cannot be!"

But they both saw the dark figure of a girl clearly. The head rolled from side to side. Her arms were tied around a dark post behind her back that also burned with yellow fire.

Inside the flames.

Inside.

Being burned alive!

Gasping in horror, Mary began running toward the fire. Edward, struggling because his sling threw him off balance, followed behind.

"It is a girl!" Mary cried, raising both hands to her face. She stopped. She could feel the heat of the flames on her face.

Breathing hard, Edward stopped behind her.

Mary's breath caught in her throat. The fire seemed to grow hotter. Brighter.

She could see the girl clearly now inside the flames. Her mouth was open in a scream of agony. Flames climbed over her long curly hair. Flames shot up from her dark, old-fashioned-looking dress.

As the girl twisted in the flames, struggling against the stake behind her, she stared past Mary to Edward. Stared with wide, accusing eyes. Her entire body tossed with the fire. And through the flames her eyes burned into Edward's.

It took Mary a long time to realize that the terrified howl she heard behind her came from Edward.

She turned to see his entire body convulsed in a shudder of terror. Edward's dark eyes bulged in disbelief. The hot yellow firelight cast an eerie glow over his trembling body.

"Susannah!" Edward cried, recognizing at last the girl in the fire. "Susannah Goode!"

As he cried out her name, the vision darkened and disappeared. The burning girl vanished.

The woods were dark and silent—except for Edward's horrified howl.

"I have had nightmares about the fire for the past two nights," Mary told Jeremy. "When I close my eyes, I see that poor girl, her hands tied behind her, her hair in flames, her entire body in flames. It was two days ago, Jeremy, but I still . . . I . . . I . . ."

Mary's voice broke. She leaned her head against Jeremy's solid shoulder.

They were seated close together on a low mound of straw in the corner of the new field. Ahead of them, at the tree line, she could see the brambles and tree branches Jeremy had cleared from the field that morning.

The late afternoon sky was gray and overcast. Occasional drops of cold rain indicated a storm was approaching.

"Sometimes the light plays tricks in the trees," Jeremy suggested, speaking softly, soothingly, his arm gently around Mary's trembling shoulders. "Sometimes you see a bright glowing reflection, and it's only the sun against a mulberry bush."

"This was not a bush," Mary replied edgily. "It could not have been a bush."

"Sometimes the trees cast strange shadows," Jeremy insisted.

"Jeremy!" Mary rose angrily to her feet. "Edward recognized the girl! It could not have been a shadow! He *recognized* her!"

Jeremy patted the straw, urging her to sit down. "I am sorry," he said softly. "How does your cousin feel? Has he recovered?"

"Edward has become very quiet," Mary told him,

dropping back onto the straw but keeping her distance from Jeremy. "He will not talk about what we saw. He will not talk about much at all. He seems very far away. I—I think he has nightmares, too."

Jeremy gazed at her but didn't reply.

"I am sorry to burden you with my troubles," Mary said, frowning. She gripped the basket she had carried with her from the house. "I had better be going and let you get back to work."

She could see the hurt in his eyes. "I want you to share your troubles with me," he said. "You do not burden me, Mary." He lowered his eyes to the basket. "What is in there?"

"Sweet rolls," she replied. "I baked them this morning for Rebecca. I'm going to take them to her now. Rebecca has been in such low spirits lately. I thought to cheer her."

He gazed at her with pleading eyes. A smile slowly formed on his lips as he pressed his hands together in a prayerful position.

"Do not beg," Mary scolded, chuckling. "You may have one." She reached into the basket and pulled out a large sweet roll.

"I would rather have this," Jeremy said, grinning, and he sprang forward and began kissing her.

The sweet roll fell out of her hand into the straw. Mary made no move to retrieve it. Instead, she placed her hand behind Jeremy's neck and held him close.

When the kiss ended, she jumped to her feet, brushing the straw off the long white apron she wore over her dress. She adjusted the comb that held her hair and gazed up at the sky.

Dark storm clouds rolled over the gray sky.

"I had better go on to Edward's house," she said.

"Have you told your father?" Jeremy demanded, picking up the sweet roll from the straw and examining it. "Have you told him about us? About how we feel?"

Mary frowned. "No. It is not the right time, Jeremy. Father is so terribly troubled."

"You told your father about the fire? About the girl burning in the flames?"

"Yes." Mary nodded solemnly, her skin very pale in the approaching darkness. "I told him about what Edward and I saw. He had the strangest reaction."

"Strange?"

"He wears a silver disk around his neck. He always wears it. It was given to him in the Old Country by his grandmother. It is jeweled and has tiny silver claws. Well, when I told Father about the girl in the fire, he cried out as if he had been stabbed—and grabbed the disk tightly in one hand."

"And what did he say to you, Mary?" Jeremy asked quietly, carefully picking straw off the sticky roll.

Mary's face darkened as the storm clouds lowered. "That is the strangest part," she whispered. "He didn't say anything. Not a word. He just stood there gripping the silver disk, staring out the window. He didn't say a word."

"That is very strange," Jeremy replied, lowering the sweet roll, a thoughtful expression on his face.

"I must leave now," Mary told him sadly. "Before the storm." She lifted the basket and straightened the linen cover over the sweet rolls.

She took a few steps toward the pasture, then suddenly stopped and turned back to Jeremy. Still seated in the mound of straw, he gazed up at her, chewing a mouthful of the roll.

"What of *your* father?" Mary demanded. "Have you spoken to him about me?"

The question appeared to startle Jeremy. He choked for a moment on the roll, then swallowed hard.

"I would like to meet your father," Mary told him playfully. "I would very much like to see your house and meet your father."

Jeremy climbed to his feet, his forehead knitted in concern. "I am afraid that is not a good idea," he told her, avoiding her eyes. "My father is . . . quite ill. He is not strong enough to welcome company."

Mary could not conceal her disappointment. "I guess we are doomed to meet in the woods for the rest of our lives," she said with a sigh.

* * *

Edward's house was a small one-story structure, built of the stones that had been cleared from the crop fields and pasture. It had a sloping slate roof and two small windows in the front.

The house sat at the edge of the woods. From the front, one could gaze across the pasture to Benjamin and Matthew's house on the other side.

As Mary made her way from the back field where Jeremy worked, she felt the first large drops of rain start to fall. She thought about her father as she hurried on.

I wish I could tell him about Jeremy, she thought sadly. But he is in no mood for more troubling news.

Her thoughts turned to her ailing uncle Benjamin. The poor man had awakened them all, screaming at the top of his lungs in the middle of the night.

Mary had reached his room first, followed by her frantic father and mother. At first they thought Benjamin was suffering a nightmare. But his screams were not because of a dream.

During the night, he had lost the use of his right leg.

Mary's uncle could now move only his head and right arm.

Matthew was becoming more and more distant and aloof, lost in his own thoughts. Her cousin, Edward, had become glum and silent. And Rebecca—Rebecca appeared wearier and older, as if she were aging a year every day.

Mary gripped the basket of sweet rolls tightly in one

hand and approached Edward's house. "Rebecca?" she called.

No reply.

"Rebecca? It is I, Mary."

Still no reply.

The storm clouds gathered overhead. Raindrops pattered against the hard ground.

Mary knocked on the front door.

It is so strangely quiet, she thought, shifting the weight of the basket. I can always hear Ezra's shouts and cries when I approach this house. Why do I not hear him now?

She knocked again.

Receiving no response, she pushed open the door and entered.

"Rebecca? Ezra?"

The front room was surprisingly bright. The candles on the wall were lighted, as were candles on a small oak table beside the hearth. A low fire crackled under a pot in the hearth.

"Rebecca?"

Where can she be? Mary wondered.

"Rebecca? Are you home?"

As she set the basket down on the floor, Mary heard a soft creaking sound. She listened for a few seconds, trying to figure out what was making the sound.

Then she suddenly noticed the black shadow swinging back and forth across the floor.

Confused, she stared down at the slowly moving shadow for a long while, following it with her eyes narrowed.

Creak. Creak.

The odd sound repeated in rhythm with the shadow.

Then she raised her eyes and saw what was casting the shadow—and started to scream.

The rain couldn't drown out the *creak-creak* of the body as it swung gently back and forth.

"Edward! Father! Mother! Help me!"

Mary ran through the rain, her arms outstretched as if reaching for help. Ran screaming without hearing her own cries.

Rebecca, you cannot be dead.

Please do not be dead!

Do not be dead, Rebecca.

Mary was halfway across the pasture now, slipping over the puddled grass. Rainwater matted her hair against her head, ran down her forehead, and blurred her vision.

The house loomed ahead of her, gray against the low black sky.

"Edward! Where are you? Edward? Father? Father?"

Her feet slid out from under her, and she fell, sprawling facedown in the soft cold mud. She landed hard on her elbows and knees.

"Oh!"

Maybe I will not get up. Maybe I shall stay here forever.

Maybe I shall just lie here in the mud and let the rain carry me away, float me away from—everything.

With a desperate cry she pulled herself to her feet, her clothes covered with mud, her hair hanging heavily in her face.

She took a few steps, then stopped with a shocked gasp.

Who is that?

A stranger standing in the middle of the pasture.

Dressed in black, standing as still as death.

Am I seeing things?

She pushed her hair out of her eyes with both hands and wiped the rainwater from her face.

No.

He was still there.

Who can it be?

Why is he standing so still in the pouring rain and staring at me?

She called out to him.

The dark figure stared at her without moving.

CHAPTER 18

Mary called again.

Beyond the pasture the trees shivered and were bent low in a howling gust of wind.

The man didn't move.

Trembling from the cold, from the horror, Mary took a reluctant step toward him. Then another.

The wind picked up and swirled around her. The rain swept over her like cold ocean waves.

Her shoes sank into the mud as she made her way closer.

He was standing so still, Mary saw, squinting through the heavy curtain of rain.

As still as a statue.

A statue?

It is a scarecrow, she realized.

Of course. That is why it doesn't move.

A scarecrow.

As she ventured closer, she saw rainwater rolling off the brim of its black hat, saw the dark sleeves of its long coat flutter in the sweeping winds.

Who put a scarecrow here? Mary wondered.

Then her next thought made her stop short: Why would anyone stand a scarecrow in the middle of a grassy pasture?

She shielded her eyes with one hand and squinted hard.

And took another step closer. Then another.

Finally through the heavy downpour she recognized the face under the wide-brimmed black hat.

"Uncle Benjamin!"

Once again Mary stared into the blank-eyed face of death.

Benjamin Fier was the scarecrow.

His body was propped up nearly as straight as if he were standing. His arms hung lifelessly at his sides.

His face was bright purple. His hair spilled out from the hat and lay matted against his head.

He gaped at Mary with blank eyes, deathly white eyes, the pupils rolled up into his head.

"Uncle Benjamin!"

The wind gusted hard, shaking the body, making the limp arms swing back and forth.

The body turned again. Benjamin's mouth dropped open, as if he wanted to speak. But the only sound Mary could hear was the heavy groan of the wind.

Mary's body convulsed in a cold shudder of horror. She spun away from the ghastly sight, the dark grass tilting and swirling wildly around her. Her stomach heaved, but there was nothing left to vomit.

Rebecca. Benjamin. Both dead.

Dead. Dead. Dead.

The word repeated in her mind, pounded into her thoughts, pounded against her brain like the cold rain.

The cold, cold rain that poured off her uncle's hat. Cold as death.

Is everyone dead?

Has my whole family been killed?

Mary stared toward the house. It seemed so distant now. So dark and distant. Far away, on the other side of the storm.

Has everyone been killed? Mary wondered.

Everyone?

And then: *Will I be next?*

CHAPTER 19

The funeral for Rebecca and Benjamin was held two days later. The rain had stopped the day before, but the sky remained gray and overcast.

The graves had been dug in a corner of the field Jeremy had been working to clear. White rocks had been placed at their heads since there were no gravestone carvers in the village.

Standing at the side of the open graves as the minister delivered his funeral speech, Mary gazed at the dark-suited mourners.

Several people had come from the village and neighboring farms to attend. Their blank faces and hushed whispers revealed more curiosity than sadness.

Mary glanced at them quickly, then turned her

attention to the members of her family. As she studied them one by one, the minister's droning voice faded into the background.

The past two days had been a waking nightmare in the stone farmhouse that had so recently rung with laughter. Now the faces of her family, Mary saw, were pale and drawn, eyes red-rimmed and brimming with tears, mouths drawn tight, in straight lines of sadness—and fear.

On the far side of the graves Edward Fier stood with his shoulders hunched, his head bowed. His hands were clasped tightly in front of him.

At first Edward had reacted to the deaths of his wife and father with stunned disbelief. In a frenzy he had shaken Mary violently by the shoulders, demanding that she stop telling such wild tales, refusing to believe her gruesome descriptions.

But her racking sobs forced Edward to see that Mary hadn't been dreaming. With a wild cry he had burst from the house, out into the driving rain, running awkwardly with his sling bobbing in front of him, running to see the horrors for himself.

Afterward, Edward had become silent, barely speaking a word. He spent a day in silent prayer. When he emerged, his eyes were dull and blank.

Edward wandered silently around the house like a living corpse. Constance, crying without stop, was forced to tend to Ezra. Matthew made the funeral arrangements and supervised the digging of the graves since Edward was unable to speak to anyone.

Ezra sensed immediately that something terrible had happened. He had to be told that his mother was never coming back.

It had fallen to Constance to tell the boy. Mary watched from a corner of the room, huddled next to the hearth.

Constance had drawn Ezra onto her lap and, tears running down her cheeks, told him that his mother had gone to heaven.

"Can I go, too?" Ezra had asked innocently.

Constance tried to hold herself in, but the boy's words caused her to sob more, and Mary had to carry him away.

Afterward, Ezra had acted troubled. He stayed underfoot while the funerals were being planned and cried loudly if anyone spoke a harsh word in the house.

Poor Ezra, Mary thought, gazing at the boy, so tiny and solemn in his black coat and breeches. Ezra's black hat was several sizes too big for him and fell down over his ears.

The minister droned on. Mary turned her gaze to her father. Matthew stood beside her, his large stomach heaving with each breath he took, his eyes narrowed, staring straight ahead.

He had reacted more strangely than anyone when he heard the news of the two murders. Mary had expected him to crumple with grief, especially at the news of the loss of his brother.

But Matthew had only reacted in fear. His eyes had narrowed. He had glanced nervously around the sitting room as if expecting to see someone who didn't belong there.

Then, gripping the three-toed amulet at his throat, he had disappeared from the room.

Late that night, while the house was cloaked in silent sadness, Mary had spied Matthew in his room, seated at his worktable, his face deep in shadow. Holding the strange medallion in front of him with both hands, Matthew was repeating its words aloud, again and again like a chant: *"Dominatio per malum."*

Mary wondered what the words meant.

Was it some kind of prayer?

She didn't know any Latin.

The next day Matthew had still seemed more frightened than sad. His eyes kept searching the farm, as if he expected an unwanted visitor.

Mary was desperate to talk to him about what had happened. But he avoided her each time she approached. She was forced to spend most of her time trying to comfort her mother.

The minister continued his prayers. One after the other the two pine coffins were lowered into the graves.

Mary suddenly saw Jeremy standing at the edge of the crowd of villagers. He was dressed in black breeches and a loose-fitting black shirt. He was wearing a battered old hat with a broken brim.

Despite her grief, a faint smile crossed her face. She had never seen Jeremy in a hat before.

Mary hadn't seen Jeremy in two days. Nearly all work had stopped on the farm, and Jeremy had been sent home.

She was surprised to see him now. Their eyes met. She stared at him, wondering what he was thinking.

He lowered his eyes, his expression troubled.

After the graves were covered over, the minister and villagers departed quickly. Constance and Matthew led Ezra back to the house. Edward remained standing stiffly, staring down at the graves.

Mary saw Jeremy walking slowly in the direction of the toolhouse behind the garden. Taking a deep breath, she decided to follow him.

"Jeremy—wait!"

She caught up with him at the side of the toolhouse and threw herself into his arms. "Jeremy. Oh, Jeremy. I—I have missed you. I need you. I really do!"

Grabbing both of his hands, she tugged him behind the toolhouse, out of view of the house, and breathlessly kissed him, pulling his head to hers.

To Mary's surprise, Jeremy resisted. He gently pushed her away.

"Jeremy—it has been so horrible!" Mary cried. "The past two days. A nightmare. I—"

She stopped when she saw the troubled expression

on his face. She reached for him again, but he took a step back.

"Jeremy—what is wrong?" Mary demanded, suddenly frightened. "What has happened? Why are you looking at me like that?"

He locked his eyes on hers. "Mary, I have to tell you something," he said in a low, trembling voice.

Mary started to answer, but her voice caught in her throat. She searched his eyes, trying to find a clue in their blue depths.

"Jeremy . . . I . . ."

"Please. Let me talk," he said sharply. "This is hard. This is very hard."

"What?" she managed to whisper.

"I—I know who killed Rebecca and Benjamin," Jeremy told her.

A cold chill ran down Mary's back, a chill of fear. And heavy dread.

"Who?" she asked.

CHAPTER 20

Jeremy lowered himself to a sitting position on the ground and pulled Mary down beside him. They sat with their backs against the wall. Jeremy gripped her hand tightly.

"I prayed this would not happen," he told her. He tore off his ill-fitting hat and tossed it away.

"What, Jeremy?" Mary demanded. "Who killed Rebecca and Benjamin?"

Jeremy's eyes were tense as he raised them to hers. "My father," he told her. "My father killed them both."

Mary gasped and pulled her hand away. "I—I do not understand." She started to get to her feet, but Jeremy pulled her back down.

"I will explain," he said. "Please. Let me explain."

"You told me your father was ill!" Mary cried angrily. "You told me he was too weak to have visitors. And now you say—"

"My father is an evil man," Jeremy admitted, burrowing his hands into the dirt beside him. "But there is a reason. He had much evil done to him."

"I—I do not understand a word you're saying!" Mary declared.

"I will explain it all, Mary," he replied quietly. "You shall hear it all. The whole unhappy story. Just as my father told it to me. For I was born after it all happened."

Mary sighed and pressed her back against the toolhouse wall. She clasped her hands tightly in her lap and listened with growing horror to Jeremy's story.

"My father's name is William Goode," he began. "I told you my name was Thorne because I needed work, and my father instructed me that your father would never hire a Goode."

"So you lied to me?" Mary asked sharply. "You gave a false name on the day we met?"

"It was the only lie I ever told you," Jeremy replied softly. "It was a lie I regret. Please believe me. My name is Jeremy Goode. I was born after my father left a village known as Wickham in Massachusetts Bay Colony."

"My family also comes from Wickham!" Mary cried with surprise.

"I know," Jeremy said darkly. He tossed a handful of

dirt past his shoes. "I have a brother. George. Two years ago he chose to return to Wickham. He could no longer tolerate my father's insane obsession."

"Obsession?" Mary asked, bewildered.

"Let me go back farther in time, Mary. You will soon understand. Although you will wish you did not."

Jeremy took a deep breath and continued. "When my father lived in Wickham, he had a wife named Martha and a daughter named Susannah," he told her, staring straight ahead. "He had a life, a happy life. But your father and your uncle robbed him of that life. They robbed him and the entire town."

Mary swallowed hard, then gazed at Jeremy in bewilderment. "How can that be?"

"Your uncle Benjamin was magistrate. His brother Matthew was his assistant. Benjamin accused Martha and Susannah of practicing the dark arts. He put them on trial. He burned them at the stake as witches."

"Susannah Goode!" Mary cried, raising her hands to her face. "That is the name Edward cried when we saw the girl burning in the woods!"

"Benjamin burned Susannah as a witch to keep her from marrying your cousin, Edward!"

"No!" Mary exclaimed, shaking her head as if trying to shake away Jeremy's words. "No! Stop!"

"I cannot stop until my story is finished," Jeremy said heatedly.

"But Edward is the most pious man I know!" Mary declared. "Edward would never allow his father to burn an innocent girl!"

"Edward did allow it," Jeremy replied in a low whisper. "He did nothing to save Susannah or her mother. Edward trusted his father. He did not know the villainy that Benjamin Fier was capable of."

"But—" Mary's voice caught in her throat.

"Your father, Matthew Fier, was also a villain. He promised to save Martha and Susannah. He took money from my father in exchange for saving their lives. He robbed my father. Then Benjamin and Matthew robbed the village and fled. And Martha and Susannah, an innocent woman and girl, burned at the stake."

"No!" Mary uttered in a hoarse whisper. "I cannot believe this, Jeremy."

"This is the story my father has told me all my life," Jeremy said, grabbing her hand. "All my life he has sought revenge against your family, against the Fiers. And now . . . now my father has begun to take his revenge. He has murdered two Fiers. He will murder you all—unless we do something."

Mary stared into the gray sky as if in a daze. She didn't move or speak.

Jeremy's words hung in her mind, lingered, repeated, creating ugly pictures, pictures of fire and suffering and treachery.

"Why should I believe you?" she demanded finally, her voice small and frightened. "Why should I believe these horrible accusations you make about my father and uncle?"

Jeremy's reply stunned her. "Because I love you," he said.

She gasped.

"I love you, too, Jeremy," she replied breathlessly.

He wrapped his arms around her and pulled her close. They held the embrace for a long time, her face pressed against his, their arms around each other, not moving, barely breathing.

When he finally pulled away, Jeremy stared at her intently. "We can stop the hatred now, Mary," he said softly. "You and I. We can stop the hatred between our families so that no one else will die."

"How, Jeremy?" she asked, holding on to him. "How can we?"

"We love each other," Jeremy said with emotion. "We will marry. When we marry, our families will be one. The old hatred will be forgotten. And the Goodes and the Fiers will live in peace."

"Yes!" Mary cried.

As they kissed, they didn't see the dark-coated person move silently away from the side of the toolhouse.

Wrapped in each other's arms, they didn't realize that this figure had been so near the entire time, had heard their conversation, had listened in shock and dismay to Jeremy's story.

Edward Fier took a deep breath, then another, trying to calm his pounding heart.

After the funeral he had followed Mary, planning to ask her to look after Ezra. To his surprise, he had spied her with Jeremy. Leaning against the side of the toolhouse, Edward had eavesdropped, clinging to every word with growing horror.

Now Edward's horror mixed with anger as he strode quickly to his uncle Matthew's house.

"Lies!" he declared to himself. "The boy speaks lies. And he has filled poor Mary's head with these unthinkable false tales!"

My father did not accuse Susannah Goode unjustly, Edward told himself. My father was a righteous man. Susannah burned because she was truly a follower of the Evil One.

Halfway to the house Edward stopped short.

The fire he and Mary had seen in the woods flashed into his mind as brightly as if he were seeing it again. And inside the fire was Susannah Goode, twisting in agony, screaming in pain.

"No!" Edward cried. He closed his eyes to erase the image. "Susannah burned because she deserved to burn! My father and uncle are righteous men!"

His heart racing, he burst into the house. Ezra and

Constance were in the front room. "Edward," Constance started, "come sit down and—"

"Not now," Edward said brusquely.

Her mouth dropped open in surprise.

"Hello, Papa!" Ezra called.

His mind blazing, Edward ignored the child. He rushed past them both, heading for Matthew's room.

A fire crackled in Matthew's fireplace despite the heat of the afternoon. Edward pushed open the door without knocking. "Uncle Matthew?" he called breathlessly.

Matthew was seated at his worktable, papers strewn messily across the top. Still in his mourning coat, he appeared to be gazing into the fire.

He turned in surprise as Edward burst into the room. "Edward—the funeral. It went well, I suppose. I—"

"Uncle Matthew, I must ask you something!" Edward cried, his dark eyes burning into his uncle's. "I heard a horrifying story just now, about you and my father. About the days when we lived in Wickham."

Matthew's lips twitched. His eyes widened in surprise. "What kind of story, Nephew?"

"About Susannah Goode," Edward blurted out. "That she was falsely accused. That she was condemned to burn by my father even though he knew of her innocence. That you and my father robbed the town and fled."

Leaning over his table, Matthew Fier closed his eyes and rubbed the lids with his thumbs.

"These stories cannot be true!" Edward declared breathlessly. "Tell me that they are lies, Uncle. Tell me!"

Matthew slowly opened his eyes and trained them on Edward. "Calm yourself, Edward," he urged softly. "Rest easy, my boy. Of course those stories are lies. There isn't a word of truth in them."

CHAPTER 21

"All lies," Matthew repeated, staring hard into the fire. He rose from his chair and turned to Edward. "I must know who is spreading these false stories."

Edward hesitated.

To his surprise, he saw that Matthew's entire body was trembling.

The door burst open and Mary entered, her face flushed, her expression troubled. "Father, I must speak to you. I—"

Seeing his daughter, Matthew fell back into his chair. Uttering a low, mournful sigh, he covered his face with his hands. "Mary, poor Mary," he muttered to himself. "Will he kill you, too, before this is over?"

"Father, what are you saying?" Mary demanded, still in the doorway.

Matthew remained with his face hidden behind his hands. When he finally looked up, he had tears in his eyes.

"Edward," he said in a whisper, "the stories are true."

Edward cried out in shock. "No, Uncle Matthew! Please—do not tell me this!"

"I must!" Matthew choked out. "I must. I cannot carry on with my lies. Seeing Mary made me realize it is time to finally tell the truth. We are all in too much danger."

Mary took a few steps into the room. "What are you saying?" she demanded of her father. She turned to Edward. "Cousin, what are you talking about?"

Edward stared at her in stunned silence. "An innocent girl—a girl I loved—died because of my father." He gave a pained sob. "And I condemned her as much as my father did!"

Slumped at the table, Matthew suddenly looked very old. His jowls sagged. All the life seemed to drain from his eyes. "Your father wanted the best for you, Edward."

"The best?" Edward cried bitterly. "You never told me why we left Wickham. My father never gave me a choice!"

"Yes," Matthew insisted, avoiding Edward's accusing stare. "He and I both wanted to make sure you never experienced the poverty we experienced. But we went too far."

"You overheard my talk with Jeremy," Mary accused Edward.

Edward nodded. "Yes. And I came directly here. To confront your father. To learn—"

"The stories are all true?" Mary cried shrilly, raising her hands to her cheeks.

"I am afraid they are," her father confessed sadly.

"Poor Susannah Goode. How I wronged her," Edward said, swallowing hard.

"You and Uncle Benjamin burned an innocent woman and girl?" Mary demanded, her eyes burning into her father's.

Matthew turned away. "It was a long time ago. Before you were born," he told Mary weakly.

"And now William Goode has had his revenge," Edward said in a trembling, low voice. "He has murdered my wife and my father."

Matthew rose to his feet, his face bright red, his hands shaking. "We will make him pay!" he shouted angrily.

"No!" Edward and Mary shouted in unison.

"We are even now!" Edward cried passionately. "We will make peace with the Goodes."

"Peace?" Matthew protested heatedly. "Peace? Edward, have you lost your senses? He *murdered* Rebecca and Benjamin!"

"We will make peace," Edward insisted, narrowing his eyes at his uncle, his features set in firm determination.

"Jeremy Goode and I are in love," Mary blurted out.

"The farmhand?" Matthew cried. "The farmhand is a Goode?"

"Jeremy is William's son," Mary told him. "And we wish to marry."

"No! Never!" Matthew declared, pounding his fist on the table, sending papers flying to the floor.

"Yes!" Edward insisted. "Yes, they *will* marry. The wound between our families will be healed. And you, Uncle, will offer your apology to William Goode and his son."

Matthew glared at them both. Then his gaze softened. He sighed wearily and shrugged under the heavy black mourning coat. "I will never apologize to a murderer," he muttered.

"You and Benjamin are also murderers!" Mary cried.

Her words stung Matthew. He closed his eyes. He was silent for a long while.

"Well, Father?" Mary demanded.

"We will heal the wounds," Matthew replied finally. "I will apologize as you wish. You may marry William Goode's son if you so desire."

"I do so desire," Mary replied quickly.

"This murderous feud will be ended," Edward said solemnly. "The two families will no longer be enemies."

"Yes," Matthew agreed. "When a week of mourning has passed, invite them both—William and Jeremy—to dinner. At that time I will do what is necessary, I promise you both, to end this bitter feud forever."

"Thank you, Father!" Mary cried happily.

"Thank you, Uncle," Edward declared.

"It will be done," Matthew said softly.

The week of mourning passed slowly for Mary. Sadness hovered low over the house and farm.

Mary did her household chores and helped Constance care for Ezra. Ezra kept asking when his mother would return. He didn't seem able or willing to understand that she was never coming back.

Edward remained at his house, buried in thoughts of the past, awash in regret, reliving the painful memories as if they had happened the day before instead of eighteen years earlier.

Matthew made an effort to do his work. But he seldom spoke to anyone in the house. His eyes remained empty, cold, focused far away.

Dinners were eaten in uncomfortable silence. Mary found herself thinking of Jeremy.

This sadness that covers the house like a dark curtain will lift when Jeremy and I are together, when Matthew makes his apology to William, and the two families are as one, she thought.

And finally the evening arrived, a cool, clear evening with a hint of autumn in the air. Inside the house the tangy aroma of a roasting goose floated through the rooms. Candles in a silver candelabra glowed in the center of the dining room table, which Mary and Constance had carefully laid out with the family's best dishes and serving utensils.

Mary sat, tensed, waiting for Jeremy and his father to arrive. Ezra tried to climb on Edward, but Edward impatiently pushed him off.

Hands clasped behind his back, Matthew paced the floor, frowning. Constance remained in the kitchen, tending to the goose.

Everyone in the family is so nervous and silent, Mary thought. And I am the most nervous of all.

How difficult it will be for Father to see William Goode after all these years. How difficult for them both.

But how fortunate that Jeremy and I will be able to bring them together, to end the years of hatred.

What a tragedy that Rebecca and Benjamin had to die before this horrid feud could end, Mary thought sadly.

A loud knock on the door jarred Mary from her thoughts.

She jumped to her feet and hurried across the room.

"Hello, Jeremy!" she cried, pulling open the door. She gazed over his shoulder. "Where is your father?"

Wearing a loose-fitting white wool shirt that was tied at the waist over black breeches, Jeremy stepped into the room, a fixed smile on his face. "Good evening, Mary," he returned her greeting quietly but did not answer her question.

This is so wonderful, Mary thought, gazing at him.

This is a dream come true.

Jeremy is here—in my house! I'm so happy!

Mary couldn't know that in two seconds' time—two ticks of the clock—her happiness would turn into unspeakable horror.

CHAPTER 22

As Jeremy crossed the room to greet him, Matthew Fier raised the silver disk over his head and pointed it at Jeremy.

Jeremy hesitated. His smile faded.

Matthew called out the words on the back of the disk: *"Dominatio per malum!"*

Jeremy's head exploded with a low *pop!*

At first no one was certain where the sound had come from.

Mary was the first to realize that something horrible had happened.

Jeremy's skull cracked open, and the skin on his face blistered and peeled away. Pink brains bubbled up from his open skull. His face appeared to melt away, and another face pushed up from under the shattered skull.

Another head appeared on Jeremy's body.

The head of a white-haired man, his cheeks scarlet, his eyes brimming with hatred.

"William Goode!" Matthew declared, still holding the strange medallion above his head.

"Yes, it is I," William replied weakly. "I almost stole your daughter from you, Matthew. But your powers are stronger than mine."

"Jeremy!" Mary shrieked, finally finding her voice. "Jeremy! Jeremy! Where is my Jeremy?"

"There *is* no Jeremy!" her father told her. "There *never was* a Jeremy, Daughter! It was William Goode all along! He used his powers to make himself appear young!"

William Goode glared across the candlelit room at Matthew, his hatred too strong for words. He raised a trembling hand to point an accusing finger at Matthew.

"Jeremy!" Mary cried, her eyes darting frantically from face to face. "Jeremy! Where are you? Where is my Jeremy? Where have you hid him?"

"Constance—help comfort Mary!" Matthew ordered.

But Constance remained rigid with terror against the wall.

With an animal cry of rage Matthew again pointed the amulet at the figure of William Goode. *"Dominatio per malum!"* he screamed. *"Power through evil!"*

William's entire body trembled. His eyes rolled up in his head. The skin on his face began to crumble.

He sank to his knees. His clothing appeared to fold over him as he crumbled, crumbled in seconds to powdery gray dust.

"Jeremy!" Mary shrieked, racing back and forth across the room, her eyes wide and fearful. "Jeremy—where is my Jeremy?"

As Matthew stared down at the pile of dust under the crumpled clothing, a triumphant smile crossed his face. He tossed back his head, opened his mouth wide, and began to laugh.

A loud, gleeful laugh.

"Jeremy? Where is Jeremy?" Mary demanded.

"Where did the man go?" Ezra asked Edward.

His eyes wide with horror, Edward grabbed Ezra up into his arms and held him pressed tight against his chest.

Matthew laughed harder, joyful tears pouring down his face.

"Stop laughing, Matthew!" Constance screamed, running over to him. "Stop it!"

Matthew laughed even harder.

"Where is Jeremy? Where is he hiding?" Mary cried.

Holding Ezra over his shoulder, Edward grabbed Mary's hand. "Come on," he urged her firmly.

"What? I cannot go without Jeremy," Mary replied, gazing at Edward with dazed, unseeing eyes.

"Come on, Mary." Edward tugged her hand. "We have to leave. We have to get *out* of here!"

Holding his bulging sides, Matthew roared with laughter.

"Stop laughing—please, Matthew!" his wife pleaded.

Matthew laughed harder.

Constance began pounding her fists on his chest. "Stop laughing! Stop laughing! Matthew—can you not stop?"

"Mary—come on!" Edward pulled Mary to the door.

Ezra, clinging to his father's shoulder, began to cry.

Edward pulled Mary out the door into the cool night.

"Jeremy? Is Jeremy coming with us?" Mary demanded.

"No," Edward told her. "Come with me. We have to leave this farm. Tonight." He pulled her into the darkness.

In the house Constance continued to plead with her husband. "Matthew—stop laughing! Stop! Can you stop? Can you stop now?"

Despite his wife's desperate pleas, Matthew continued to laugh.

His round face bright scarlet, his enormous stomach heaving, his mouth gaping open, he laughed and laughed.

Loud, helpless laughter.

Maddened by his triumph, Matthew would laugh without stop for the rest of his life.

PART THREE

Western Pennsylvania Wilderness

1725

CHAPTER 23

Ezra Fier dug his bootheels into the horse's sides and urged the old mare on. Low branches and shrubs brushed against his worn leather breeches. Ezra kept his eyes straight ahead.

Twenty-one now, a slender young man, Ezra had his mother's straight black hair and broad forehead and his father's thoughtful eyes.

As he rode through the thick brush, Ezra thought of his father and his aunt Mary, and his bitterness grew.

My poor father, he tried so hard to keep us alive in this lonely wilderness. He worked so hard to keep a roof over our heads and food in our mouths.

But he was never the same after that strange night, my last night at Great-Uncle Matthew's farm.

Ezra remembered that night as one might view a faded photograph. He could picture the young man Jeremy Goode. Something bad had happened to Jeremy Goode. Aunt Mary had started to scream. Great-Uncle Matthew had started to laugh crazily.

And then Edward—Ezra's father—had pulled Ezra away, pulled him into the night, away from the farm, along with Aunt Mary.

Ezra had been only six. But the frightening memories of that night haunted him still.

As he rode through the thick woods to his Great-Uncle Matthew's farm, the bitterness of the past fifteen years washed over him, blanketing him in darkness despite the dappled gold of the bright sun filtering through the trees.

Edward had died of exhaustion, still a young man. Ezra's Aunt Mary had never recovered her senses. She would go for weeks without speaking, then suddenly declare, "I am a witch! I am a witch!"

Often Mary would stare out into the trees for hours on end. "Is Jeremy coming?" she would ask in a pitiful small voice. "Is Jeremy coming soon?"

Ezra took care of his aunt after his father's death. Then, one horrible afternoon, he had found Mary floating facedown in the pond behind the small cabin they had moved to. She had drowned herself.

Now I am alone, Ezra thought, after burying Mary beneath her favorite beech tree.

Thanks to William Goode, I am alone in the world.

The Goodes cursed my family.

The Goodes ruined our lives.

And now it is up to me to pay them back.

But where to begin? Where can I find out if any Goodes remain in the Colonies?

Ezra needed information to start his angry quest for revenge. Strapping his few possessions on his back and abandoning the small cabin in the woods, he returned now to Matthew's farm.

As the farmhouse came into view, Ezra urged the exhausted horse on, kicking its sides, whipping its neck with the worn leather reins.

I remember it, he thought, gazing at the two-story house in wonder and surprise. I remember that toolhouse at the edge of the garden. And that little house on the far side of the pasture—that was *my* house!

His heart pounded with excitement.

Are Matthew and Constance still here? he wondered.

As he rode closer, his excitement faded to disappointment. The pasture was high with overgrown weeds. There were no cows or sheep in sight. No crops. No bales of wheat or straw. The garden was barren and weed choked. Brambles and weeds stretched across the unplowed field.

The farm hadn't been worked in years, Ezra could see.

Did Matthew and Constance die? Did they abandon the farm after Father, Aunt Mary, and I left?

Eager to solve the mystery, eager to gain the information he needed to begin his quest for revenge against the Goodes, Ezra jumped down from the horse.

His legs ached from the long ride as he made his way to the front door. He took a deep breath. And knocked.

Silence.

The whisper of the wind through the shimmering trees was the only reply.

He knocked again. "Is anyone home?" His deep voice echoed strangely in the empty yard.

Ezra pushed open the door. Stepping inside, he found the front room dark and cold, despite the warmth of the afternoon. A layer of dust had settled over the furniture, making everything appear ghostly and unreal.

"Anyone home?" Ezra called loudly.

The floorboards creaked under his boots.

This room hasn't been used in years, he realized, rubbing his hand over a table, making a long smear in the covering of dust.

He had come so far, driven the horse so hard. He had been so eager to find his great-uncle, to speak to him, to hear the story of the Goodes, to learn where he could seek his revenge.

He had come so far to find only dust and silence.

"No!" Ezra cried. "I will find what I need in this dark old house!"

He began a rapid, determined search of all the rooms.

The dining room was as gloomy and dust covered as the sitting room. In the common room two field mice gazed at him from the barren hearth, as if he were intruding in their domain.

Retracing his steps, Ezra moved quickly back toward Matthew's study, his features set in a disappointed frown.

Perhaps Matthew left some papers, Ezra thought hopefully. A journal or diary. Something that will tell me what I need to know.

The wooden door had become warped.

Ezra struggled to pull it open. It wouldn't budge.

"I cannot give up!" he cried. "I must see what lies behind this door!"

He sucked in a deep breath, grabbed the edge of the door, and pulled. With a burst of strength he finally managed to slide it open partway.

Breathing hard, he peered inside—and gasped.

CHAPTER 24

Ezra stared in amazement. At first he didn't believe his eyes.

The opening was covered by a wall of stone!

Ezra pulled the study door open a little farther.

"What on earth!" he exclaimed, scratching his dark hair. The room had been completely walled in.

Gaping in astonishment in the dim light, Ezra saw that the stones had been piled one on top of another but not cemented together.

"What I am looking for must certainly be on the other side of this strange wall," he said. The sound of his voice reassured him.

He reached for a stone and attempted to pull it away.

It was then that he heard the scratching sound.

He lowered his hands.

The scratching continued, low and steady.

Scratch, scratch, scratch.

More field mice? Ezra wondered, listening hard.

No. The sound is too regular, too steady.

Scratch, scratch, scratch.

What is making that sound?

With renewed energy Ezra began pulling the heavy stones out of the wall and tossing them down on the floor behind him.

Dust flew as he worked, choking him, burning his eyes.

The scratching sound grew louder.

Did my great-uncle wall in his own study? Ezra wondered as he worked, pulling the stones away, heaving them behind him.

Did he hide something in here that he didn't want anyone to find?

He could see only darkness through the small opening he had made. With a quiet groan he pulled away more stones.

He worked feverishly for several minutes, thinking about what he might find on the other side, pulling away stone after stone.

"So much dust," he muttered. "So many stones. . . ."

Blinking, he resumed his back-breaking work—and gasped.

A grinning decayed brown skull leaned toward him from the darkness on the other side of the wall.

Ezra tried to cry out—but he was too late.

The skull slid toward him.

The skeleton's brittle arm slid out through the hole in the wall, and its bony fingers closed around Ezra's throat!

CHAPTER 25

Ezra shrieked and fell backward, stumbling over the stones strewn at his feet.

He landed hard on his back. Stunned, he lay there for a moment, panting and staring up at the hole in the wall.

The skeleton arm was draped over the wall, not moving.

Still breathing hard, his back aching from his fall, Ezra climbed to his feet.

He peered into the opening he had made. The skeleton had merely fallen forward, he realized. It hadn't really grabbed him. But what was that scratching sound? Had the skeleton been trying to break free?

Ezra pushed the skeleton out of his way, raised himself up on his hands, and peered into the room. Too dark in there to see anything.

Grumbling, he turned back into the room, his eyes searching the grayness until he found a candle on a low table. Carrying the candle into the kitchen, he located a tinderbox near the hearth.

It took several minutes of concentrated work, rubbing the kindling together in a hard, fast rhythm, to get a small fire started. Then Ezra was able to light the candle. It flared, then flickered out, then flared again.

Eagerly he returned to the dark walled-in room.

A second skeleton greeted him on his return. This skeleton was seated at a low worktable.

Ezra held the candle close to the grinning skull. From all the decay he couldn't even tell which skeleton was his great-uncle Matthew and which was his great-aunt Constance.

In the yellow candle glow Ezra's eyes came to rest on a document on the table under the skeleton's bony hand. Pushing away the hand, Ezra carefully lifted the brittle papers.

Raising the candle close, he struggled to read the scrawled words on the page. "It's a journal!" he cried. "Written by Matthew Fier."

Eagerly Ezra read the words on the last page of the journal:

> I still laugh the hideous laugh without cease, the laughter an unending torture for me and for Constance. But the wall is in place, and at last we are safe from the Goodes and their treachery.
>
> Constance attempted to escape. The poor woman did not realize that the wall is for our safety. I had to hit her over the head and render her senseless so that I could put in place the final stones and secure our safety.
>
> We are now as safe as we were in the old days in Wickham, and will remain safe from the Goodes for the rest of our lives.

The manuscript ended there.

Ezra set it down gently.

The Goodes, he thought.

The Goodes have destroyed my family. I will not rest until I find them. The Goodes must pay for their evil.

His heart pounding, Ezra took a step back.

The skeleton seated at the table suddenly creaked and toppled backward. In the dim light Ezra spied a strange object at its neck.

Holding the candle in front of him, Ezra leaned over the skeleton and lifted a round silver amulet from around the neck bone. He stared at the tiny three-toed claw in the center of the disk. Words were inscribed on the back of the medallion, but Ezra could not make them out in the dim light.

With a wistful sigh Ezra slipped the cord around his neck and adjusted the amulet over his chest. "My only inheritance," he said bitterly.

A few moments later he was out of the cold, dark house, walking into the sunshine, thinking about the village of Wickham, thinking about the Goodes, driven by his bitterness toward the sweetness of revenge.

The Secret

THE FIER FAMILY TREE

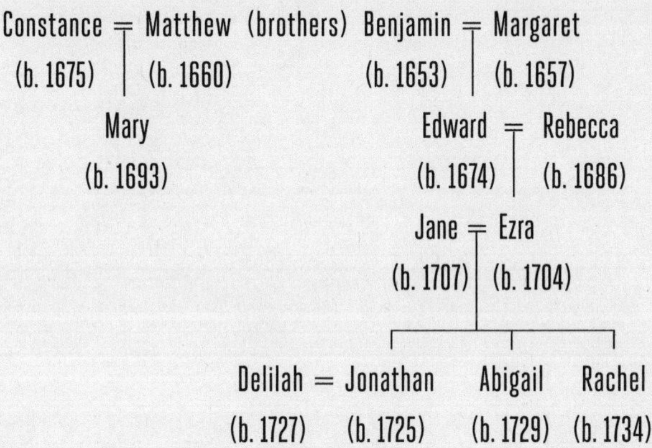

(100-Year Break)

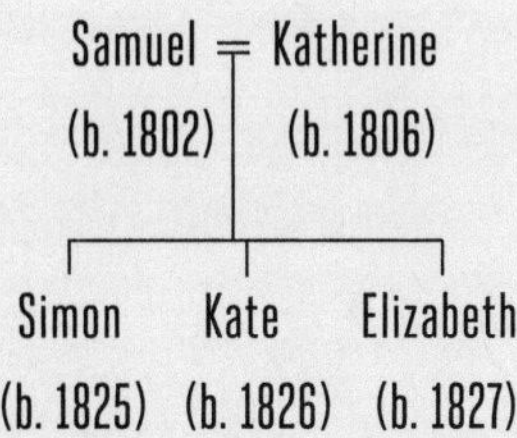

Village of Shadyside

1900

Nora's pen scratched against the paper. Dry again. Wearily she thought of dipping the point into the inkwell, changed her mind and, yawning, set the pen down on the small writing table.

Just for a minute. Just for one minute's rest . . .

Her back ached and her fingers were cramped. She had been scribbling furiously all night by the light of a single candle.

Nora knew she had to tell her story. And she had to tell it tonight.

She touched the silver pendant that hung from a chain around her neck. Her fingers picked out the silver claws, the blue stones. Then fire appeared before her closed eyes, burning in her memory. Fire that burned the innocent

Susannah Goode in 1692. Two hundred years of hatred and revenge followed Susannah's death. And then, at last, the terrible fire that consumed the Fear mansion . . .

Nora's eyes filled with tears. *Daniel . . . my Daniel . . .*

After so many fires, all was in ashes now.

Sighing sadly, Nora dipped her pen into the inkwell. No time to rest. The story must be told.

She heard a noise and stopped writing. She listened.

Footsteps. Someone was coming!

Her hands trembling, Nora frantically shoved the paper and ink into the desk drawer. No one must see this, she thought. No one can see it until it is finished. And it is far from finished. There are so many horrors left untold.

So many horrors . . .

She held her breath, listening. The footsteps moved closer, closer . . .

PART ONE

Wickham Village, Massachusetts Colony

1737

CHAPTER 1

Village of Wickham.

Jonathan Fier sighed with relief as the wagon rolled past the wooden sign. Their long journey was over at last.

He glanced at his father sitting beside him on the box of the wagon. Ezra Fier's face was haggard and drawn, but his black eyes sparked with excitement. He snapped the reins with renewed energy, and the chestnut horse trotted faster down the rutted, tree-lined road.

"We are here, Jonathan," Ezra said to his son. "After all those weeks in this wagon, we are finally in Wickham. George Goode is going to wish he had never been born." Ezra's voice dipped lower, almost to a whisper. "Revenge at last. It will be so sweet!"

Jonathan felt a cold chill. *Revenge*. Revenge for what?

I still do not understand, Jonathan thought. Who is George Goode? I have never even met anyone named Goode. Goodes have never done me any harm. So why did we have to leave the farm in Pennsylvania? Why have we spent the last six months driving east in this cramped and dirty old wagon?

Jonathan stole a glance at his father's gaunt face. We've come here to seek revenge against the Goodes, Papa says. Everything he does is for revenge.

Sometimes I think Papa is crazy.

Jonathan immediately wished he could take back that thought. How could I think such a thing? he scolded himself. He is my father. He cannot be crazy. There must be a reason for all the misery we have suffered. There *must* be.

"I have searched for the Goodes through five colonies," Ezra muttered. "And found no one. But now—" He paused to lift his hat and run a bony hand through his straight black hair. "Now I feel sure. I *know* they are here. I know I have found them at last."

"Ezra!" Jonathan's mother called from the back of the wagon. "Please slow down. The girls are being tossed all around!"

Ezra scowled and pulled on the reins. Jonathan turned on the box and looked back into the covered wagon.

His mother, Jane, and his two sisters, Abigail and Rachel, were huddled back there, along with all the family's possessions: pots and pans, dishes, utensils, clothes, blankets, the Fier family Bible, and the little food they had left.

"We have arrived, Mama," Jonathan said quietly. He wondered whether she would be glad or sorry.

"Hurrah!" cried three-year-old Rachel, clapping her hands. She was a chubby angel in a homespun muslin shift with a mop of blond curls peeking out from under her cap.

Jane Fier only nodded. She was fair, with worry lines beside her clear blue eyes. She wore a printed linen dress and a loose white cap.

"I will be so happy to leave this wagon," said Abigail, a red-haired eight-year-old with mischievous blue eyes. She wore a blue- and white-striped linen dress and a white cap with blue ribbons. She looked up to her brother, Jonathan, who at almost twelve was nearly grown up. "Mama, will we be able to stop for good this time? Will we be able to sleep in a bed tonight?"

"I hope so, Abigail," Jane said.

"I will ask Papa," Abigail said.

She started for the front of the wagon, but her mother pulled her back.

"Do not bother Papa about that now," Jane whispered. "He has other matters on his mind."

He always has other matters on his mind, Jonathan thought with some bitterness. Or rather, *one* other matter.

Jonathan faced front again and lowered his black hat

over his eyes. He wore his long brown hair tied back. His white linen shirt was dirty from weeks of traveling, and he was growing out of his brown homespun waistcoat and knee breeches.

As soon as we settle down, he thought, Mama will have to make me some new clothes.

No one passed them as they rolled down the leafy lane toward the village—not on horseback or on foot. It seems strangely quiet here, Jonathan thought. It is not the Sabbath. Where is everyone?

At last he saw a carriage up ahead. It was headed toward them on its way out of town.

Jonathan kept his eyes on the carriage as they approached it. It was shiny and black, a fancy carriage for rich people.

But, wait, he thought. The carriage is not moving. And where are the horses?

Something is wrong, he realized.

Something is terribly wrong.

The Fiers' wagon drew closer. Jonathan could now see two horses, but they were lying on the ground. Are they hurt? he wondered, leaning so far forward he nearly fell. Are they *dead*?

Closer.

A foul smell invaded Jonathan's nostrils. He nearly gagged.

He could see the horses clearly now. Long dead. Their

flesh was rotting, their bones shoving up through the decaying skin.

"Ohhh!"

Jonathan heard his mother utter a cry of shock. He glanced back into the wagon. She had pulled his two sisters close and was covering their eyes.

Ezra slowed the wagon but did not stop.

Why was it left here on the road? Jonathan wondered. Why would people abandon such a fine carriage?

The wagon wheels creaked as they pulled close enough for Jonathan to see inside the carriage.

To his astonishment, the carriage was not empty.

Three women were inside, dressed in gowns of fine silk and white lace caps.

Jonathan stared hard at the women. Their faces.

The faces were purple, nothing but bone and chunks of decaying flesh, poking out from beneath their fancy caps.

They're dead, Jonathan realized, covering his nose with his hand. And they've been dead a long, long time.

Rotting corpses, going nowhere in a fancy carriage.

CHAPTER 2

Jonathan stifled a cry and covered his face with both hands.

Why have these decaying bodies been left here? he wondered. Why have the villagers not taken them away to be buried?

Was the carriage and its rotting cargo left here as a warning?

Stay away!

Still holding his breath from the stench, Jonathan turned to gaze at his father.

Ezra was staring intently into the carriage window. Was he shocked by the figures inside? Jonathan could not tell. His father's face revealed no emotion.

"Ezra—" Jane pleaded, her voice tight and shrill. "Turn

back. We cannot stay here. That carriage. Those women. I have such a bad feeling."

Ezra turned and silently glared at her in answer. She kept her eyes leveled on him defiantly. Then, without a word, he snapped the reins and urged the horse forward. They headed into town.

Ezra guided the wagon into the village common and stopped.

Jonathan glanced around.

No sign of life. Not another person in sight.

Jonathan could hold the questions back no longer. "Papa, why are we here? Why are we searching for the Goodes? What did they do to you?"

"Jonathan, hush!" his mother cried. Her eyes were wide with fright and warning.

For a moment no one spoke. Jonathan turned from his mother back to his father. What have I done? he wondered. What will Papa do to me?

Then Ezra spoke. "He is old enough now, Jane. He is right to ask these questions. He must know the truth."

With a groan Ezra climbed down from the wagon and beckoned to his son. "Come with me, boy."

"I will come too!" said Abigail.

Her mother pulled her back inside. "No, Abigail. You will stay here with me."

Jonathan followed Ezra across the common. He stopped short when he saw a man locked in the stocks, his head and hands thrust through the three holes in the wooden frame. His eyes were open and staring but empty. *Dead.*

Jonathan's stomach lurched. "Papa—" he managed to choke out.

But Ezra strode quickly past the wide-eyed corpse. "Our family once lived here, in Wickham," Ezra told Jonathan. "My grandfather was the magistrate. Everyone knew him and his brother to be good and righteous men. But that very righteousness ruined their lives."

How could that be? Jonathan wondered. But he said nothing.

"Witches were discovered in Wickham. My grandfather had them burned at the stake. Two of them were Susannah and Martha Goode. They were put on trial by my grandfather, found guilty, and burned."

Now Jonathan swallowed hard. "Your grandfather—he—he burned people at the stake?"

"Not people—*witches!*" Ezra boomed. "Vile and evil creatures of the devil!" Ezra paused, breathing hard. "My grandfather and his brother did their duty."

Jonathan shuddered at the thought of women being burned alive. But he said nothing.

"Our family moved from Wickham to Pennsylvania," Ezra continued, calmer now. "But William Goode, the father of Susannah, the husband of Martha, followed them. He believed his wife and daughter to be innocent.

Driven by revenge, William used dark powers against my grandfather and his family.

"William disguised himself as a young man. He took advantage of my aunt Mary's innocence and—" Ezra paused again, searching for words.

"And what, Papa?"

"William Goode destroyed our family. He killed my grandfather and my mother. The rest he drove insane. I found my great-uncle and his wife buried behind a brick wall—nothing left of them but bones."

Jonathan gasped. *This* was his family history! And it was the reason behind his father's obsession. It explained why his father hated the Goodes with such passion.

Still, something did not make sense to Jonathan. In his almost twelve years, Jonathan had never seen a sign of this William Goode or his black magic.

No member of the Goode family had ever appeared during Jonathan's life to seek revenge against the Fiers. So why was Ezra keeping the evil feud alive? Why was Ezra determined to spend his life searching for Goodes?

"Papa," Jonathan asked hesitantly, "is William Goode still alive?"

"I do not know," Ezra replied bitterly. "He would be very old. I do know he had a son, George. George lived in Wickham once. I am hoping—"

He did not finish the sentence, but Jonathan knew what he was hoping. He hoped to find this George Goode, or other Goodes, and bring them misery.

And that is why we have come to Wickham, Jonathan realized.

But so far we have not seen a living soul. Only corpses.

This town *must* be cursed.

"Come," Ezra said. "We will go to the tavern and ask after the Goodes." Ezra led Jonathan up the tavern steps.

The innkeeper will tell us what has happened, Jonathan thought. Innkeepers always know the news.

Ezra opened the tavern door. They stepped inside.

The room was empty. The fireplace stood cold and dark, the tables covered with dust and cobwebs. Plates of food had rotted on one of the tables. It may have been a meal of roast lamb and a pudding. Rats scurried around the table, gnawing at the mold-covered meal.

Ezra grunted unhappily, his features set in disappointment. Jonathan saw a pile of dust-covered letters on the bar, probably left there for the villagers to pick up. The letters had been delivered a long time ago.

The floorboards creaked under Ezra's boots as he walked over to the bar to sort through the letters. About halfway through the pile, he stopped. He rubbed the dust from the front of the envelope and carefully studied the address.

"Papa?" said Jonathan.

Ezra looked up at his son. "Go find the village magistrate's house," he ordered. "Ask if the magistrate will see me. I will be along in a minute."

"Yes, sir," Jonathan replied meekly and walked quickly from the tavern. Outside he hesitated.

Where could he find the magistrate? The street was empty. There was no one to ask.

Then he spotted a large house on the other side of the common. It was the grandest house in the village, sided with clapboards weathered brown, and enclosed by an unpainted picket fence. It stood two stories tall, with glass windows and two chimneys.

This *must* be the magistrate's house, Jonathan told himself, making his way across the common, half walking, half running. It felt good to run after his long journey.

Jonathan lifted the heavy brass door knocker and let it drop. No answer. How strange that such a fine house should have a broken parlor window, he thought.

He cupped his hand around his eyes and peered through the window beside the door. The parlor was dark.

He turned the doorknob and uttered a soft cry of surprise when the door opened easily at his touch.

"Hello?" he called. His voice echoed through the house.

Jonathan quietly stepped inside. "Hello?" he repeated in a trembling voice. "I am here to see the magistrate."

The house remained silent. Jonathan made his way into the parlor. The heavy thud of his boots on the floorboards was the only sound. "Hello?"

No one was in the parlor, which led to a smaller room.

Some kind of office, perhaps? "Hello? Is the magistrate at home?" Jonathan stepped into this second doorway.

Squinting into the dim light, Jonathan saw an old man at a desk with his back to the door. Jonathan could make out long gray hair falling onto the collar of a brown coat.

Jonathan knocked lightly on the frame of the open door and said, "Sir? May I come in? Sir?"

The old man did not move.

Jonathan took a deep breath and stepped into the room. He made his way up to the high-backed chair and gently tapped on the man's shoulder. "Sir? Sir?"

The man moved—and Jonathan started to scream.

CHAPTER 3

Jonathan's scream echoed off the walls of the tiny room.

The man toppled and slid to the floor.

Panting loudly, struggling to keep from screaming again, Jonathan gazed wide-eyed at the hideous face.

The man's long gray hair rested on nothing but bone. The grinning skull stared up at Jonathan, its teeth yellow and rotting. As Jonathan gaped down, frozen in horror, a spider crawled out from the deep, empty eye socket.

Jonathan shrieked out his horror. He wanted to run, but his feet seemed to be nailed to the floor. He couldn't take his eyes from the white-haired, grinning skeleton.

He screamed again.

"Jonathan! Jonathan! What is wrong?" Ezra shouted, bursting into the room. Ezra stopped and stared down at the corpse. "Come. We must go," he said softly. Placing his hands on Jonathan's shoulders, he guided the boy from the room.

Outside, Ezra ordered, "Go back to the wagon and sit with your mother and sisters. I will be there soon. Just stay put and wait for me."

"Yes, Papa," said Jonathan, grateful to be out in the fresh air. He walked slowly back to the wagon, breathing deeply, trying to slow his racing heart.

He didn't want to scare his mother. But he knew she would ask him what he had seen. And there was no way to describe it without frightening her. No way to say it that wouldn't be horrible to hear.

No one lived in the town of Wickham, Jonathan realized as a wave of terror swept over him.

Every single human had died.

Wickham was dead, a town of rotting corpses.

"What have you found?" his mother asked eagerly as Jonathan stepped up to the wagon. "Where is your father?"

"Papa will be back soon," said Jonathan. "He is exploring the village."

"Did you talk to the innkeeper?" Jane demanded.

"Why was that carriage left on the road? Did he say anything?"

"No, Mama," said Jonathan softly. "There was no innkeeper. There is . . . no one."

Jane leaned forward, her eyes burning into his. She chewed her lower lip. "Jonathan, what do you mean?"

"Everyone is dead," said Jonathan. "Everyone. There is no one left alive in the whole town."

Jane gasped. She started to say something, but Ezra returned. He climbed up beside Jonathan on the box and, without saying a word, cracked the reins. The wagon lurched forward with a jolt.

"Ezra?" cried Jane. "What is it? Where is everyone? What did you find out?"

"Plague," Ezra answered flatly, narrowing his eyes and staring straight ahead. "No survivors."

"And the Goodes?"

"We shall soon see," Ezra said.

Ezra drove the wagon out of town, the wooden wheels bouncing over the rutted dirt road. He said nothing. His expression remained set, hard and thoughtful.

He didn't slow the horses until they came to a farmhouse. It was a wooden saltbox house, smaller than the magistrate's, but still two stories tall with a small attic. A brick chimney ran through the middle of the house. A shed connected the kitchen to a big barn.

Ezra pulled the wagon up to the door of the house and stopped the horse.

Is this the Goodes' house? Jonathan wondered. Will they be dead, too? Will they be alive?

Ezra lowered himself to the ground and made his way to the door. He knocked. Three solid knocks.

And waited.

No answer.

Jonathan watched his father open the door and step inside. "Jonathan," Jane whispered, giving him a shove. "Go with him."

Jonathan climbed down from the wagon. Abigail slipped out, too, before her mother could stop her. They followed Ezra into the farmhouse.

Stepping into the front parlor, Jonathan's eyes explored the room. He was somewhat surprised to find it neat and tidy. He saw no sign of anyone, dead or alive. It felt as if the people who lived there had left.

"Hello?" he called. But he was not surprised when he received no answer.

"They must be here!" Ezra exclaimed with emotion. "They *must*! I will not rest until I see their rotting corpses with my own eyes."

Ezra ran up the stairs. Standing in the parlor with his sister, Jonathan could hear his father's frantic footsteps above him.

Ezra ran from room to room. Jonathan then heard

Ezra climb up to the attic. When Ezra returned, he ran past the children as if not seeing them. Jonathan heard him as he explored the large common room, the shed, and the barn.

A few minutes later Ezra returned to the parlor, his face purple with rage.

"Papa, what *is* it?" Jonathan cried.

CHAPTER 4

"They are gone!" Ezra screamed. "A plague has killed everyone in Wickham—*but the Goodes have escaped!"*

Jane Fier ran into the house with Rachel in her arms. "Please, Ezra," she pleaded, tugging at her husband's sleeve. "We must leave this horrible place. The Goodes are not here. We must leave!"

Ezra shook her off. "No," he replied firmly. "We will stay here, Jane. The Goodes lived here not long ago. Somewhere in this house there will be a clue to tell us where they have gone."

He made his way to a desk in the corner and started digging through the drawers.

Jane followed him, weeping. "Ezra, we cannot stay

here! We cannot! We cannot stay here all alone with only corpses for neighbors!"

"Wife—" Ezra started.

"Think of your children!" Jane cried, holding the baby against her chest.

"Silence!" Ezra screamed, pushing her away. He glared furiously at her. Jonathan trembled when he saw that mad gleam in his father's eyes.

"I have heard enough from you, Jane!" Ezra cried sternly. "No more pleading and no more questions! From now on I expect obedience from all of you—obedience and nothing else!"

No one moved. Abigail whimpered softly. Ezra's harsh expression didn't soften.

"I am going to find the Goodes," he said slowly through gritted teeth. "They cannot escape me. I am going to find them. *And nothing will stop me!*"

Jonathan's mother ran from the room, crying. Abigail clung to Jonathan's side, and he put an arm around her tiny shoulders.

Ezra said, "Jonathan, start unpacking the wagon. This house will be our new home."

Jonathan gasped. We are going to live *here,* in someone else's house? he wondered, horrified by the idea. We are going to live here, so near the frightening village of corpses?

"Jonathan—do as you are told!" ordered his father, his voice booming through the house.

"Yes, Papa," Jonathan said.

With a sinking heart, Jonathan hurried outside. His hands trembling, he unhitched the horse and led him into the barn.

We are going to live in their house, he thought. The Goodes' own house, with all their things in it. What if they are not dead? What if they come back—and find us here?

He found a bucket in the barn and carried it outside. There was a pump in the yard. He pumped water into the bucket and took it to the horse.

At least we will have a place to sleep tonight, he told himself. With a featherbed. And a hearth to cook by.

Jonathan sighed. Maybe it will not be so bad here, he thought. He gazed around at the green fields, the apple orchard in the distance, and the cozy house. Smoke was already rising from the chimney. His mother must have started a fire.

Maybe we will be happy here, he thought. If only the Goodes do not come back. . . .

The Fiers found everything they needed in the Goodes' house. Jonathan discovered preserves, smoked meat, and cornmeal in the shed. Abigail found a bolt of linen in the attic. Soon she and Jonathan had fresh new clothes made from the linen.

Their mother kept busy cooking, cleaning, spinning,

and sewing. Abigail helped her mother and took care of Rachel. Jonathan did the heavy chores: chopping wood, drawing water, caring for the horse. When his mother was very busy, he also looked after the girls for her.

As they all settled in to their new life, Jonathan's only concern was for his father. Ezra Fier had only one thing on his mind—where had the Goodes gone?

Jonathan watched his father rummage through storage bins and drawers reading every scrap of paper he could find, studying anything that might give him a clue to their whereabouts.

He thinks of nothing but revenge, Jonathan thought angrily, watching his father read ledgers one day. He wouldn't even eat if Mama didn't put a plate of food in front of him every evening. Nothing distracts him from the Goodes.

Then Abigail ran into the room, shouting, "Papa! Look at me!"

Ezra glanced up from the ledger, and Jonathan saw his father's scowl melt into a smile. "Where did you get that pretty dress?" Ezra asked. "Turn around for me."

Abigail tossed a lock of red hair off her forehead and turned slowly, showing off her new blue dress.

"Mama found it in the back of an old wardrobe upstairs," she explained, her blue eyes twinkling. "It fits me perfectly!"

Ezra held his arms out, and Abigail ran to him for a

hug. Releasing her, he said, "Run along now and help your mama. I have work to do here."

"Yes, Papa," Abigail said. She skipped out of the room.

Papa looks almost happy, Jonathan thought as he watched his father. Abigail is the only one who can do that. She is the only one who can still make Papa smile.

Quickly Ezra's smile faded, and he turned to Jonathan and demanded, "What are you looking at, boy? You have chores to do, have you not?"

"Yes, Papa," said Jonathan. He hurried out of the room.

About three weeks after they had moved into the house, Ezra called Jonathan to him. "Hitch up the wagon," Ezra said. "We are going to call on our neighbors."

There were a couple of farmhouses a few miles down the road. Jonathan knew that people were living in them because he could see smoke rising from that direction every morning.

The Fiers' wagon stopped in front of a large, prosperous-looking farmhouse with red chickens pecking around the yard. Jonathan saw a young woman working in the garden, bending low to pull out weeds. She stood up when she saw Jonathan and Ezra approach.

Ezra took off his hat. "Good day, miss," he said. "Is the master of the house at home?"

The young woman curtsied and hurried excitedly into the house, calling, "Papa! We have visitors!"

A gray-haired man with a big belly topping toothpick legs came out of the front door and introduced himself in a friendly way. Ezra removed his hat to introduce himself and Jonathan.

"We have just moved into the area, Master Martin," Ezra explained. "We are looking for a family named Goode."

At the mention of the name Goode, the older man blinked hard. His face turned pale.

"We thought the Goodes were living down the road, but they are gone," Ezra continued. "Would you happen to know what has become of them?"

The man's friendly expression faded, replaced by a scowl. "I do not know the Goodes," he said gruffly. "I am sorry. I cannot help you. Good day, Master Fier."

Abruptly the man hurried back into his house, shutting the door behind him and his daughter. Jonathan saw the girl's face at the window. The old man pulled her away.

Ezra began to shake with rage. "What can this mean?" he cried. "Why does he refuse to speak to us?"

"Perhaps they know something at the next farm, Papa," Jonathan said softly, trying to calm his father.

They continued on to the next farm, three miles away. This one appeared poorer, a smaller house with rocky fields behind it. A thin old man tilled the field with a single hoe.

"Good day, sir," called Ezra, tipping his hat as he approached. "May I have a word with you?"

The man stopped but made no move toward them. He stared at Jonathan and Ezra suspiciously.

"What is it, then?" he asked in a surly voice.

"My name is Ezra Fier," Ezra told him. "This is my son, Jonathan. We are looking for a family in the region and wondered if you knew what had become of them."

"What family is that?" asked the old man, leaning on the hoe now.

Ezra cleared his throat. "The family of George Goode," he said.

The man's scowl deepened. He remained still for a moment, leaning on the hoe, his eyes studying Ezra. Then he raised himself, turned, and strode quickly toward his barn.

Ezra nodded at Jonathan. "He is going to tell us something," he whispered. They followed the old man across the rocky ground to his barn.

The old man disappeared inside. Jonathan and Ezra waited several yards from the door.

In a moment the man came running out, holding a long knife.

Ezra smiled uncertainly. Then Jonathan saw the confusion on his face.

Before Ezra could move, the man had pressed the knife to Ezra's neck. "I am going to cut your throat," he snarled.

CHAPTER 5

Ezra's body stiffened.

With a low grunt the man tightened his grip and held the knife blade tight against Ezra's skin.

"Stop—please!" cried Jonathan. "We have done nothing wrong!"

"George Goode was the child of a witch!" said the man. "His evil brought the plague to our village—and he escaped it! What do *you* want with George Goode?"

"We are no friends of his, believe me," Ezra choked out. "We wish him nothing but harm."

The man relaxed a little, easing the knife blade back a few inches from Ezra's throat. "Get off my farm," he growled. "Do not come back, ever. And never dare to ask about the villainous Goodes again."

He released Ezra. Ezra and Jonathan hurried to the wagon and drove off.

"Remember this day, son," Ezra said solemnly. "This is further proof of the evil of the Goodes. We are not the only people they have harmed."

The next day Jonathan's father went back to searching the house. "I must have missed something," Jonathan heard him muttering. "What are they hiding? What are they hiding?"

Jonathan carried a stack of firewood inside one morning as his mother sat sewing by the hearth with Rachel on her lap. Abigail stood over a basin full of water, scrubbing the last of the breakfast dishes.

"Mama says I have no more chores to do today," Abigail said happily. "Not until suppertime. I am going to go exploring."

"Watch her, Jonathan, please," said his mother. "Do not let her stray too far."

Abigail tossed the dirty dishwater out the door and wiped her hands on her apron. She pulled on her cap and ran outside, the blue ribbons on her cap flying.

Jonathan followed her. "Shall we go to the creek?" he suggested.

"I have already been to the creek," said Abigail. "I want to go into the village."

Jonathan stopped. "Into Wickham? But why, Abby? There is nobody there."

"I know," said Abigail. "We can go anywhere we like. There is no one to stop us!"

"No," said Jonathan. "Mama said you should not stray too far. The village is too far."

"Are you scared, Jonathan?"

Jonathan bristled. Was his younger sister daring him? "Nothing scares me," he said, although he knew that was not true. His father scared him, for one. And all those dead people in the village . . .

"Come on," said Abigail. "I am going to the village. If you must keep an eye on me, then you will just have to come along."

She ran down the road with Jonathan following close. He felt nervous about going back to the village, but he could not let his younger sister go alone.

The streets were as quiet and empty as before. The silence roared in Jonathan's ears. He heard no dogs barking, no birds chirping, no insect sounds.

"What do you think they were like?" Abigail whispered. "The people who lived here?"

"I do not know," said Jonathan. "Like us, I suppose."

They walked down the dirt road to the village common. Abigail found a small pile of bones lying under a tree.

"Look, Jonathan," she said sadly. "This was a puppy."

Jonathan stared at the grisly little skeleton. Maybe we should not be here, he thought. He glanced around. Were all the people in the town really dead?

"The poor puppy should not have to lie in the sun like this," said Abigail. "I think we should bury him."

"We have no shovel," said Jonathan.

"We can get one," Abigail said, indicating the houses and sheds all around them. "I am sure any one of these sheds will have a shovel in it."

"We cannot just take somebody's shovel, Abby," Jonathan said.

"Why not?" Abigail demanded. "It is not stealing. They are dead."

Yes, Jonathan thought. They are dead. And their bodies are still sitting inside these houses, just as this puppy's bones are lying out here in the sun.

Jonathan shuddered. He did not want Abigail to go into one of the houses to find a dead person.

"I will get a shovel," he said. "You wait here."

He walked up to the nearest house—maybe the house where the puppy had lived, Jonathan thought. It was a little wooden cottage, only two rooms.

Abigail stood right behind him as he gingerly pushed open the door.

"I told you to stay by the tree," Jonathan said gruffly.

"I want to come with you," she said. "I am too scared to be alone."

Jonathan sighed and took her hand.

It was dark inside the cottage. Jonathan's eyes took a moment to adjust to the darkness.

Abigail clutched Jonathan's sleeve. They stood frozen in the doorway.

Then Abigail whispered, "Go get the shovel."

Jonathan stepped carefully across the room. He opened a cupboard beside the back door of the cottage.

Inside the cupboard, something gleamed white with two dark and empty eye sockets glaring out.

A skeleton.

Jonathan leaped back. Abigail screamed.

The skeleton shifted. It toppled out of the closet and clattered to the floor.

Jonathan leaned over it, panting, trying to slow the frantic beating of his heart.

Then he started backing away.

"Wait!" Abigail whispered. "I see a shovel in the cupboard."

Jonathan forced himself to glance back into the cupboard. He saw the shovel. But he did not want to get it.

"Get it!" demanded Abigail. She gave him a shove.

He stepped carefully around the clutter of bones on the floor—all that remained of the skeleton. Then, holding his breath, he snatched the shovel and ran out of the house.

He was glad to be back outside in the bright sunlight. He followed Abigail to the tree and dug a little hole. Then he laid the puppy's bones in the grave. Abigail stood beside him with a branch in her hand.

"Dominatio per malum," she chanted solemnly, waving the branch over the puppy's grave.

"What does that mean?" Jonathan asked.

"I do not know," said Abigail. "Those are the words on that sparkly thing Papa wears around his neck."

Jonathan knew the words, too. The silver pendant with four blue stones had always fascinated him. He had once asked his father what the words meant, but Ezra refused to tell him.

Squinting against the bright sunlight, Jonathan covered the bones with dirt. Then Abigail planted the branch in the ground as a marker.

They were late for supper that evening. Ezra was already seated at the table with his usual preoccupied expression. Jonathan entered the kitchen first, and Ezra barked at him, "Where have you been?"

"Outside" was all Jonathan said.

Abigail came in next, and Ezra smiled. She went to him and gave him a kiss. He played with the blue ribbons on her cap.

"You are keeping an eye on your sister, I hope," Ezra said to Jonathan.

"Yes, Papa," Jonathan replied quietly. He revealed nothing about going into the village. He knew it would make his father angry. Abigail kept it a secret, too.

* * *

A few days later Jonathan saw Abigail skipping past the barn, heading for the road. Alarmed, he chased after her. "Where are you going?" he called.

"To the village," she replied without stopping.

He took her hand and pulled her to a stop. "You cannot go," he said sternly. "I am supposed to be watching you."

"You can watch me in the village," she replied impatiently.

Jonathan sighed and followed after her.

That day they found the skeletons of two small animals—possibly a cat and a chipmunk. Abigail insisted on burying them, too.

"I am going to come back as often as I can," she told her brother as she stuck a branch in the ground by the tiny graves. "I will find all the poor dead animals and bury them all."

The next time Abigail set out for the village, Jonathan didn't try to stop her. He knew it was useless. He was getting used to the village and all its death, and didn't even mind the awful silence so much anymore.

Then one day, when they were playing in Wickham, Abigail came across the remains of a little girl. The skeleton wore a rotting blue dress that once must have been pretty, and a cap like Abigail's.

"I think we should bury her," said Abigail. "She deserves a proper funeral as much as an animal does."

"We will need a coffin," Jonathan said. "We cannot bury a person in the dirt like a dog or a cat."

"Yes," agreed Abigail. "You go find a box, and I will look for a place to bury her."

Jonathan crossed the village common and entered the tavern to search for a girl-size box. He found a wooden crate. It was a little short, but it would have to do.

He hoisted the crate onto his shoulder and carried it outside to Abigail. He didn't see her by the meetinghouse where he had left her.

"Abigail?" he called, immediately worried.

No answer.

After setting the crate on the ground, he walked down the road. He heard high-pitched giggling behind the village magistrate's house.

Jonathan peered around the side of the house. He uttered a low cry of surprise when he spotted Abigail. She was playing with another little girl!

Jonathan stared at the little girl, startled to see another living person in Wickham. She was skinny, with long blond curls poking out from under her cap, and gray eyes. Where on earth had she come from? he wondered.

He started toward his sister. "Abigail—" he began.

At the sight of him, the other little girl darted behind a tree.

"You frightened her, Jonathan!" Abigail scolded. "No need to worry, Hester," she called to her friend. "It is only my brother."

But the little girl did not come out from behind the

tree. "She must be afraid of boys," Abigail said. She hurried behind the tree to look for the girl.

A second later Abigail reappeared, bewildered. "She is gone!" she told her brother. "She disappeared! And we were having so much fun together."

"Abby—who is she?" asked Jonathan.

"She told me her name is Hester," Abigail answered. "She is very nice."

"Where does she live?"

Abigail shrugged. "She did not say. But I hope she comes back. It was so pleasant to have someone to play with."

Jonathan wondered who this playmate could possibly be. Did she live in Wickham? Could there still be living people in the village?

What a mystery!

The next day, as Jonathan was digging a grave for a baby, Abigail had wandered off to find a stick for a marker. When Jonathan finished digging the hole, Abigail still had not returned.

She may be playing with her friend again, Jonathan thought. I think I will watch them for a few minutes and see what I can learn about that strange girl.

He crept over to the big house, but the girls were not there. He found them playing in the graveyard.

Ducking behind a grave slab, he leaned against the cold stone and spied on them.

Hester twirled around and laughed. She has a pretty, bell-like laugh, Jonathan thought. Just then Hester took Abigail's hand, and the two girls wove a path through the gravestones.

Hester stopped before a hole in the ground. She reached down to tug at something in the hole. Up came the lid of a coffin.

Jonathan stood frozen, watching.

Hester stepped into the coffin and reached up for Abigail's hand.

Abigail touched Hester's hand.

With a firm jerk, Hester pulled Abigail into the coffin.

CHAPTER 6

"Abigail—no!" Jonathan shouted. He burst from his hiding place and ran to the grave.

I must get her out of there! he thought, his heart pounding. I must save her.

He stopped at the edge of the hole, stared down, and—

Abigail popped up out of the coffin, laughing.

Furious, Jonathan grabbed her arms and yanked his little sister out of the coffin. "Stop playing foolish games," he scolded angrily. "We have to go home now."

"But, Jonathan, Hester and I—"

Refusing to listen to her protests, he pulled her along behind him.

We must get away from here, he thought, forgetting the other girl.

Abigail dragged her feet and glanced back at Hester. "Why do we have to go home?" she asked. "I was having fun."

"We just do." Jonathan didn't want to admit the truth—he was afraid.

Afraid of what? Of a little girl?

He did not know. But he knew that something was not right.

"Jonathan, you and Abby must stay in today," his mother said. "I need you both to watch Rachel for me."

Abigail groaned. "I wish we could go back to the village," she whispered to Jonathan. "I was looking forward to playing with Hester."

But Jonathan was secretly relieved. He said nothing about it to Abigail, but he was determined not to go to Wickham anymore.

Hester pulled Abby into an open coffin, he remembered with a shudder. I must keep Abby away from her.

Jonathan and Abigail were playing with Rachel in front of the hearth, rolling a ball along the floor to her, when Ezra appeared.

"Hello, Papa," said Abigail brightly.

Ezra flashed her a smile. "Would you like to go for a walk with me? I need a bit of air."

"Mama asked me to watch Rachel today," Abigail told him.

"Jonathan can watch Rachel," said Ezra. "Come along with me. I like your company."

Abigail jumped up and went outside with her father. Feeling a little hurt, Jonathan watched them through the window.

He gasped when he saw her.

Hester.

Jonathan saw her run up to Abigail and Ezra. Curious, Jonathan picked up Rachel and hurried outside to see what would happen.

He could see the surprise on his father's face as Abigail introduced Hester to him.

"Where do you live, Hester?" Ezra asked.

"Nearby," Hester replied shyly.

"And who are your parents?" Ezra demanded.

"Mama and Papa," answered the blond little girl.

Ezra pointed in the direction of the farmhouses a few miles down the road. "So you live there?"

"She is a good girl, Papa," Abigail interrupted, her eyes shining. She was clearly happy to have a playmate.

Hester turned her sparkling gray eyes on Ezra and asked, "Can Abigail come to my house?"

Abigail tugged at his sleeve. "Please, Papa," she begged. "Please?"

Jonathan stepped forward. "Do not let her go, Papa," he said.

Ezra turned sharply to his son. "Why not?"

Jonathan glanced uneasily at Hester and Abigail. "I cannot say, Papa. I just know you must not let her go."

"Please let me go with Hester," Abigail said. "It is so good to have a friend." Tears were forming in her eyes.

Ezra gazed lovingly at his daughter. Jonathan knew his father could deny Abigail nothing. He knew what would happen next.

"All right, Abigail. You may go."

"Papa," urged Jonathan, "let me go with her."

"No," Ezra said firmly. "You will stay here. Someone must watch the baby."

"But, Papa—"

"You heard me, Jonathan," Ezra said, his temper rising. "You are too old to play with little girls. You will stay here."

He turned to Abigail and added, "Run along, but be home for supper."

"I will!" Abigail called back happily. She ran off with Hester, the blue ribbons on her cap flying behind her.

Jonathan stared after his sister, watching her until they disappeared over the hill.

"Jonathan, your mother is calling you," said Ezra. "Do you not hear?"

"Yes, Papa," said Jonathan. He carried Rachel inside to his mother.

The sun had gone down, and Abigail had not returned home.

"Supper is ready, Jonathan," his mother said. "I will take Rachel now."

She picked up the baby and put her into the wooden high chair. Jonathan took his place at the table, gazing at the darkening sky beyond the window.

Supper, and still Abby is not home, he thought anxiously.

His mother took a pot of chicken stew off the fire and called Ezra to the kitchen. Jonathan could see that his father was worried, too. Deep lines furrowed Ezra's brow, and his eyes were dark and troubled. But Jonathan did not dare say a word.

Jane Fier went to the door and called, "Abigail! Supper!"

There was no response.

"Where is that girl?" Jane wondered aloud.

"She went off to play with a friend," Ezra said quietly. "I expect she will be back soon."

"A friend?" said Jane. "What friend?"

"A little girl," Ezra answered. He looked uncomfortable. "A sweet girl. She lives nearby."

Jane glanced at Jonathan. He knew she wanted him to explain to her, but he said nothing. He knew his mother was frightened, too, but she tried to hide it. "The stew is getting cold," she said stiffly. "We shall have to start without her."

She dished out the chicken stew. The family began to eat. No one spoke.

Beyond the window the sky darkened. Still no sign of Abigail.

Jonathan glanced up, and his mother met his eyes. He turned to Ezra, who was carefully cutting the bits of chicken into smaller and smaller pieces, but not eating a single one.

Jane Fier suddenly stood up. "Ezra, I am worried," she said. "What could be keeping her?"

Ezra stared out at the black sky. He wiped his mouth with his napkin and stood up.

"I am going to look for her," he said.

"Let me go with you, Papa," Jonathan asked.

"No!" Ezra snapped. "Stay with your mother and sister."

He threw on his hat. Then he took the lamp from its hook by the fireplace, lit it with a twig, and walked out into the darkness.

I must go with him, Jonathan thought desperately. He does not know where to search. Only I do.

He decided to follow Ezra.

"I do not want to leave you alone, Mama," he said. "But Papa needs my help."

Jane nodded and said, "Go with him."

Jonathan slipped outside, following a few paces behind the glow of his father's lantern. The evening sky was purple, growing darker every second. A crescent moon hovered over the horizon.

"Abigail!" Ezra called. "Abigail!" He began to walk down the road toward the other farmhouses, away from Wickham.

He is going the wrong way, Jonathan thought in frustration. But then he saw his father stop and stand still, as if he were listening to something. Jonathan listened, too.

There was a soft, sweet sound. Laughter. A little girl's laughter.

Where was it coming from?

Ezra turned in confused circles. The laughter seemed to float on the air from all directions at once.

The voice giggled again. Now it sounded as if it came from the village.

Ezra walked toward it, following the sound.

Jonathan trailed his father into the village. He had never seen it at night before. It felt emptier than ever. Ezra's lantern cast eerie shadows on the trees and houses. The shadows made the houses seem to move and breathe.

"Abigail!" Ezra called again, then stopped and listened.

The little laugh chimed on the wind.

"Is that you, Abigail?" Ezra called out. "Where are you?"

The laugh came again, a little louder, like the tinkling of sleigh bells.

That is not Abigail, Jonathan thought. His father seemed to realize it, too.

"Who are you?" Ezra cried. "Show yourself to me!"

The only response was another girlish giggle. Ezra moved toward it, with Jonathan right behind him.

Staying far enough behind not to be seen, Jonathan followed his father to the graveyard. Ezra stumbled among the crooked gravestones, the little laugh teasing him, taunting him, leading him farther into the maze of headstones.

The lantern flashed a ghoulish yellow light on the gray markers. "Abigail!" Ezra cried, his voice cracking now. "Please come out!"

Ezra stopped again to listen, but this time there was no laughter.

Jonathan crept up closer and stood right behind his father. Ezra did not notice.

Ezra was standing at the foot of a grave. He held the lantern out so it illuminated the name on the marker.

It read, "Hester Goode."

Jonathan could hear Ezra gasp.

Goode? Did the marker really say "Hester *Goode*?"

Then a light breeze blew, and on the breeze came the sound of a voice.

Not laughter this time, but words. Words spoken in the same girlish voice that had led them to this spot.

"Can Abigail come to my house?"

Hester!

Hester's grave. Hester was not living, Jonathan realized to his horror.

Hester was dead.

But still she called.

"Can Abigail come to my house?"

Still she called. Called from the grave.

Abby's little playmate, giggling and calling from the grave.

"Can Abigail come to my house?"

Slowly Ezra moved the lantern to the right.

His hand trembled. He nearly dropped the lantern as it cast its light on another grave.

Freshly dug.

With a new headstone.

The light fell across the inscription on the gray stone.

It read: *"Abigail Fier."*

"No!" Ezra tossed back his head and howled.

The lantern slid from his hand and rolled into the dirt.

Ezra dropped to his knees, still howling. "Abigail! Abigail!" he cried over and over, clawing at the dirt, trying to dig her up.

Shuddering in terror, Jonathan bent over his father, reached for his father's heaving shoulders, tried to stop his father's mournful cries.

Ezra pushed him roughly away.

The breeze blew again, and with it came the laughter. And the taunting request: *"Can Abigail come to my house?"*

Uttering animal cries, Ezra tore at the dirt with his fingers. Desperate, Jonathan began to dig, too. Ezra made no move to stop him now.

It was a shallow grave. Jonathan's fingers soon touched the smooth, polished wood of a coffin.

"No!" Ezra shrieked. "No! Please—No!" With a grunt he shoved Jonathan out of the way and tore open the lid of the coffin.

There lay little Abigail, her eyes closed, her lips white, her face a pale, bluish mask.

She was dead.

"Curse them! Curse them!" Ezra screamed. "The Goodes will pay! They will burn again!"

Then his expression changed. The hatred melted into grief and horror. He lowered his face to his hands, sobbing, "Abigail, Abigail."

Jonathan choked back his own tears and helped his weeping father to his feet. Holding each other and sobbing, they stood motionless in the silent darkness.

Hester Goode's gleeful laughter surrounded them, ringing in their ears.

No matter how they tried, they couldn't stop her gleeful chant:

"Abigail came to my *house! Abigail came to* my *house!"*

PART TWO

Western Massachusetts

1743

CHAPTER 7

"And ever since that day, our family has been cursed. The Goodes will not let us live in peace. That is why we must find them and put an end to this horror, once and for all."

Jonathan Fier stopped outside his sister Rachel's bedroom door to listen. Their father, Ezra, was putting Rachel to bed.

Every night Ezra told his daughter a bedtime story. But instead of reciting a fairy tale, Ezra told her the story of the family curse.

Some bedtime story, Jonathan thought sadly. I am surprised it does not give her nightmares.

"I do not want to go to sleep, Papa," Rachel said. Please, let me stay up a little longer. It is still light out."

"No," Ezra replied firmly. "Get into bed and stay there this time. I mean it."

Jonathan smiled as he heard this. Rachel always hated to go to bed before everyone else.

"But Jonathan does not have to go to bed," she whined.

"Jonathan is almost eighteen and you are a little nine-year-old girl," said Ezra. "I do not want to hear any more about it. Shut your eyes. Good night."

Jonathan hurried down the hall before Ezra came out of Rachel's room. He did not want his father to catch him eavesdropping.

It has been six years since we left Wickham, Jonathan thought. Six years since Abby died. And Papa is more obsessed with the Goodes than ever.

Jonathan ran his index finger along the freshly painted wall of their new house. The third house in six years, Jonathan thought bitterly.

Papa promised this would be the last move. We shall see. Every time we move he says he is positive he has found the Goodes—but still we have not found them yet.

Jonathan started down the stairs, his black shoes loud on the wooden steps. He wore white stockings with the buckled shoes and dark green knee breeches. His shirt was white cotton with a plain ruffle.

His mother no longer made his clothes—she had no need to. All the Fiers had their clothes made by a seamstress now.

The Fiers had grown rich in the last six years. Whenever they moved to a new town, Ezra brought with him some goods—tea, spices, fancy silks—to sell to the townspeople. His instinct for selling was uncanny. In each town Ezra knew exactly what the people would need.

Thanks to his ability, the family was now quite comfortable. But their new wealth had not brought Ezra peace.

As Jonathan reached the bottom of the stairs, he heard a knock at the front door.

"I will answer it, Mama," he called. He could hear her in the kitchen, unpacking.

Jonathan opened the front door. There stood a very pretty girl who appeared to be about sixteen or seventeen years old.

She had smooth brown hair pulled back into a knot at the nape of her neck. She wore a simple green dress with white ruffles at the neckline and the sleeves. She gazed at Jonathan with lively brown eyes, and smiled.

"Good evening," said the girl, dropping into a quick curtsy. She held a round dish covered with a cloth in one hand. "My name is Delilah Wilson. I live on the farm down the road."

"Please come in," offered Jonathan.

"I know you moved in today, and I thought you might like something more with your supper," Delilah said. She held out the round dish as she stepped through the doorway. "I have brought you an apple pie."

Jonathan took the pie and thanked her. It was still warm.

"Please come into the parlor, Miss Wilson," he said. "I will tell my mother and father that you are here. I know they would like to meet you."

He showed Delilah into the parlor and took the pie into the kitchen to his mother.

"How kind of her," Jane Fier said. "Go get your father. We can have some pie and invite our new neighbor to share it with us."

Wiping her hands on her apron, she hurried to the parlor to meet Delilah. Jonathan knocked on the door of his father's study.

"Come in," his father called gruffly.

Jonathan opened the study door. Most of his father's books and maps, his business records, and the family Bible were still packed up in crates. Ezra sat at his desk facing the doorway bent over a map.

"What is it?" Ezra demanded impatiently. His black hair was shot through with pewter gray now, and the lines in his face had deepened.

He did not look up from his map of western Massachusetts. Jonathan knew his father was following a new trail that he imagined the Goodes might have taken.

"Papa, a young woman has come to see us. One of our neighbors."

"So?"

Jonathan cleared his throat. "Well, she would like to meet you."

"Not just now. I am busy."

Jonathan stood in the doorway for a moment, unsure of what to do next. The silver pendant his father always wore flashed in the candlelight, the blue stones gleaming. Ezra said, "Close the door behind you."

Jonathan started into the hall on his way back to the parlor. On his way he heard a light step on the stairs. He glanced up.

Rachel, dressed in a light summer nightgown, was creeping down the steps.

"Rachel!" cried Jonathan. "You heard Papa—"

Rachel raised a finger to her lips to quiet him. "Who is here?" she whispered. "One of our neighbors? I want to meet her!"

"Papa will be very angry—"

But Rachel ignored him. She ran quickly down the stairs and slipped into the parlor, Jonathan right behind her.

His mother was talking to Delilah. When she saw Rachel, Jane Fier opened her eyes wide in astonishment and cried out—

"Abigail!"

CHAPTER 8

"What are you doing out of bed, Abby?" Jane Fier cried.

Jonathan watched as Rachel's young face grew solemn. He stepped forward and, putting a hand on Jane's shoulder, gently corrected his mother.

"It is Rachel, Mama. She wants to meet our new neighbor."

A shadow of confusion passed briefly across Jane Fier's face. Then it cleared.

She took Rachel's hand, patted it, and smiled.

Rachel relaxed and sat down.

I suppose poor Rachel is used to it by now, Jonathan thought sadly. Used to Mama's confusion.

Rachel did resemble Abigail, even though she was blond and Abby had had red hair.

Still, it is not their looks that confuses Mama, Jonathan realized. Abigail lives on in Mama's mind. Mama cannot let Abby die.

Delilah nodded toward the little girl and said, "I am happy to meet you, Rachel."

"My father is busy at the moment, I'm afraid," Jonathan told Delilah. "But he is very eager to meet you and your family. Perhaps he will call on you tomorrow."

Delilah nodded.

"Please excuse me for a moment," said Jane. "I will leave my son and daughter to entertain you while I prepare the pie, Miss Wilson."

Jonathan smiled. Somehow Rachel had gotten her way and would stay up to have pie with them.

Delilah, Jonathan, and Rachel took seats. The parlor was not fully furnished yet, just a couch and a few chairs clustered around a small table.

But Ezra had already hung a large painting over the fireplace—a portrait of Abigail. Ezra had painted it himself, from memory.

In the portrait Abigail was dressed as Ezra had last seen her, in a blue dress, wearing her white cap with the blue ribbons.

"You have a lovely house," Delilah said, glancing

around admiringly. The house, large and elegant, was three stories, painted white with black shutters and surrounded by a white fence. It was the nicest house the Fiers had ever lived in.

"Where have you moved from?" Delilah asked.

"From Worcester," answered Jonathan. "And before that, Danbury."

"My goodness!" Delilah exclaimed. "Why have you moved so much?"

Jonathan hesitated. He certainly did not want to explain his father's obsession with the Goode family to this pretty neighbor. How could she ever understand?

But before he could stop her, Rachel blurted out in a low voice, "It is Papa. He says our family is cursed!"

"Rachel!" Jonathan cut in.

Delilah's eyes widened. "Cursed? What do you mean?"

"This is just a little girl's exaggeration," Jonathan interrupted, hoping to end the discussion then.

"No, it is not!" Rachel insisted. "Papa tells me about it every night before bed."

She pointed to the portrait of Abigail and said, "That girl was my sister. She died when I was little. One of the Goodes got her."

"Rachel—" Jonathan warned. But Delilah acted very interested and pressed Rachel to go on.

To Jonathan's dismay, Rachel told Delilah all about the family curse and the feud between the Goodes and the Fiers. Jonathan watched Delilah's face as she heard the horrible details. She turned pale as flour, and her eyes grew wide.

She will never want to see us again, he thought, and was surprised at his disappointment. He already liked this lively girl very much.

At last Jonathan said, "It is all nonsense, Miss Wilson. My father has been filling Rachel's head with these stories, and she takes them too seriously."

"So you do not believe in the curse?" Delilah asked him, locking her eyes onto his.

"There is no curse," Jonathan replied, frowning. "And there would be no feud if Papa would only let it die. This is all of his own making—he brings trouble on himself. Our constant quest for the Goodes has almost ruled our lives, but the Goodes themselves have done nothing to hurt us."

"What about Abigail?" Rachel demanded.

Jonathan paused. He didn't like to think about Abigail.

Abigail would still be alive if it were not for Papa's crazy ideas, he thought bitterly. Papa forced us to live in Wickham when no decent family should have stayed there.

Abigail's death was Papa's fault.

Jonathan tried to shake away his unpleasant thoughts. He turned his gaze on Delilah. She was studying the portrait of Abigail.

"Abigail looks a lot like you, Rachel," Delilah said.

"Most people say that," said Rachel, smiling at Jonathan.

"Perhaps we should talk about something else," Jonathan said uncomfortably.

"Do you have any brothers and sisters, Miss Wilson?" Rachel asked eagerly.

"Rachel, you may call me Delilah," Delilah said. She turned to Jonathan and added, "You may, too."

Jonathan thought he saw her blush slightly.

"I am an only child," she told Rachel. "My mother died when I was born. I live with my father. He is a minister, but his congregation is very small. We live on a small farm."

Jonathan studied her dress, made of homespun linen dyed pale green. For the first time he noticed how worn it was. The lace at the sleeves was frayed, and here and there the skirt was expertly patched.

She probably wore her best dress to come calling on us, Jonathan thought. She must be very poor. It does not matter. She is still the prettiest girl I have ever seen.

Jonathan walked into town a few days later to see the blacksmith. His mother wanted a new pot to hang over the kitchen fire.

He ordered the pot from the blacksmith and left the shop. Just outside he bumped into a pretty, brown-haired girl in a dark blue dress and white sunbonnet.

"Delilah Wilson! How pleasant to see you again."

"I am glad to see you, too, Jonathan." She carried a small basket. Jonathan took the basket to carry for her. It was empty.

"Where are you going?" he asked.

"I am on my way home," she replied. "I have just come from Papa's church. He has been there all morning with nothing to eat, so I brought him a bit of cheese and bread."

"I am on my way home, too, as it happens," said Jonathan. "May I escort you?"

Delilah smiled. "Thank you. That is very kind."

The afternoon sun shone bright and hot as they walked out of town and down the road to Delilah's house. Jonathan could feel himself begin to sweat under his collar.

"How is your family?" Delilah asked. "Your mother and sister?"

"Quite well, thank you," said Jonathan.

"I liked them both very much," Delilah went on. "Your sister especially. She is very sweet."

Jonathan felt a little uncomfortable at the memory of Delilah's visit—his mother's confusion, Rachel's talk of a family curse. Delilah is being polite, he decided. She must think us very strange.

"I must apologize for Rachel's behavior the other

evening," he said. "I hope she did not frighten you—or bore you—with her silly talk."

Delilah laughed. "Not at all. She is only a child, and children love wild stories. I was exactly the same at her age."

"I am sure you were much more sensible than Rachel," Jonathan protested.

"If anything I was sillier. Just ask my father. At eight I was sure that a fox would come in my window in the night to carry me off. I insisted that we keep all the windows in the house shut at night—even when it was quite hot. My father thought I had gone mad!"

Jonathan smiled at her story and offered her his arm. She accepted, and together they walked arm in arm.

That night Jonathan lay in bed a long time without sleeping. An image of Delilah floated before his eyes: her glossy brown hair, her creamy skin, her rosy cheeks, her mischievous brown eyes.

I shall call on her tomorrow, he thought, growing sleepy at last. I will bring a bouquet of flowers. . . .

A sudden noise made him sit straight up.

What was that?

The sound seemed to be far off. Had he been dreaming?

No. There it was again. Closer now.

Jonathan listened. The sound started low but quickly grew in pitch and volume. At first he thought it was some kind of animal shriek, a tortured cry, a scream of agony.

Jonathan shook with fear. He had never heard any animal make that sound.

Was it a bear? A wolf? An injured dog?

It was moving swiftly toward his house, nearer, nearer.

Now it was right in the yard, and coming closer.

It stopped right under his window!

Jonathan's heart leaped to his throat.

A voice in his head screamed, "Help! Please, somebody—help! It is coming to get me!"

CHAPTER 9

His heart thudding in his chest, Jonathan stumbled to the window. The full moon shone on the wide rose trellis—still barren of roses—that climbed the back wall of the house to the second-floor windows.

He could see the backyard clearly—the woodpile, the new iron pump, the stone well, and the woods surrounding them.

What made that horrible sound? Jonathan asked himself, trembling all over. Was it only a dream? A strange wild animal? Or was it something more terrible still?

He pushed that idea from his mind. Rachel's stories are giving *me* nightmares, he scolded himself.

Silence now. The only sounds were the chirping of crickets and the low hooting of an owl. Still shaken, Jonathan climbed back into bed.

He knew he would *never* get to sleep now. He lay awake all night, listening.

Hours later the sky began to lighten. Jonathan heard his mother pass his room on her way downstairs to begin the day's chores. His father and sister were stirring, too.

Yawning and stretching, Jonathan climbed out of bed and sleepily made his way to the washstand. He splashed cold water on his face and ran a comb through his shoulder-length brown hair. After tying his hair back with a black cord, he slipped on his knee breeches.

In the kitchen Jane Fier was setting dishes on the table. "Good morning, Jonathan," she said brightly. "Would you mind kindling the fire for me?"

Jonathan kissed his mother good morning and went to the hearth. He picked up the bellows and puffed air into the glowing embers left over from the night before.

Rachel skipped into the room in a brown dress and apron, her blond curls bouncing. Ezra followed close behind her. As he poked at the fire, Jonathan wondered whether any of them had heard the terrible cries that had awakened him in the night. Rachel appeared to be cheerful and well rested, but Ezra seemed tired.

"Run out to the well and get me a bucket of water, Rachel," said Jane.

"Yes, Mama," Rachel replied. She opened the back door and headed out to the well.

A moment later bloodcurdling cries from the backyard

made Jonathan drop his fireplace poker. It clattered to the hearth floor as he turned to run outside. Jane and Ezra were right behind him.

Rachel stood by the well, screaming hysterically. Her hands, her face, her hair, her clothes were all splattered in red.

"Abigail—what *is* it?" cried Jane. "What has happened?"

Rachel ignored her mother. Her eyes fixed and staring, she pointed at the bucket she had pulled out of the well.

Peering into the bucket, Jonathan gagged.

It was filled with thick, red blood.

CHAPTER 10

Holding his hand over his mouth, Jonathan reeled backward.

Blood! How could the well be full of blood?

Trying not to vomit, Jonathan raised his eyes to his family. Jane was holding Rachel, trying to comfort her. Ezra's eyes were bulging and his hand shook as he clutched his silver pendant.

"The curse!" he cried. "The Goodes have come for us again!"

Swallowing hard, Jonathan gathered his courage and reluctantly peered into the well. To his relief, the well water was clean.

Only the bucket was filled with blood.

What did it mean?

Her arms around Rachel's shoulders, Jane gently guided her inside. Ezra nervously rubbed his fingers over the pendant, as if it would help him somehow.

"It has happened again. They have found us before we could find them," Ezra said. "There must be Goodes living nearby—or buried near here."

"Calm down, Papa," Jonathan pleaded. "There is no curse. Look—we are all safe."

"Foolish boy," Ezra murmured, and he left his son alone.

Still dazed and shaken, Jonathan stared at the bucket of blood. The howl of agony he had heard in the night came rushing back to him.

Who, or what, could have done this? he wondered.

Was it the work of a crazy person? A wild animal?

Or could his father be right after all? Could it really be the curse of the Goodes?

Rachel stayed in her room for the rest of the morning while Ezra paced the house, tense and scowling.

I must get out of here, Jonathan told himself. As long as I sit in this house, I shall keep seeing that bucket of blood.

He decided to pay a call on Delilah.

Jonathan gathered wildflowers as he walked down the road to the little farmhouse. It was very small—only a cabin really—and shabby, made of brown-weathered shingles, with only a few small windows and one chimney.

To the right of the house sat a tumbledown cow shed. A few chickens pecked at the dirt behind a fence. Beyond them were a stand of scraggly fruit trees and an acre or two of stony fields.

Clutching his handful of purple and white flowers, Jonathan knocked on the door. Delilah opened it.

"Hello, Jonathan," she said, smiling. "What a nice surprise."

As he handed her the flowers, he felt his face grow hot.

She invited him in. A man with shoulder-length gray hair sat at a writing table in a corner of the room. He stood up when Jonathan entered.

"Father, this is Jonathan Fier," Delilah said. "Jonathan, this is my father, the Reverend Wilson."

Delilah's father gave Jonathan a friendly handshake. "I am very pleased to meet you, young man," the reverend said. "I plan to call on your parents soon to welcome them."

"They will be delighted," Jonathan said with a polite bow.

"Father is working on a sermon at the moment," Delilah said. "Shall we go for a walk?"

Jonathan agreed. He and Delilah went outside and strolled through the orchard of fruit trees.

In the warm sunlight Jonathan thought Delilah was prettier than ever. Her cheeks glowed pink, and she had a lively spring to her step.

But as she looked at his face, he saw her frown. "You look tired, Jonathan," she said. "Are you feeling well?"

Jonathan started to say, "Yes, of course." But then he thought better of it. Delilah has already heard all about the family history, he thought, and she is not afraid of me. Not in the least afraid. She is an understanding girl. Perhaps I have found someone I can speak with—at last!

"Something disturbed me last night, while I was sleeping," he told her. "A strange and terrifying noise."

"A noise?" she asked, puzzled.

"Yes. It was as if some hideous creature were rushing through the woods, heading straight for our house. It drew closer until it seemed to be right under my window, shrieking. Then suddenly it stopped."

"What was it?" Delilah asked.

"I do not know," Jonathan replied. "When I looked outside, I saw nothing."

"It must have been a dream," Delilah told him.

"That is what I decided," Jonathan said. "But this morning Rachel went to the well for water, and when she pulled up the bucket—" He paused, wondering if he should continue. Should he say such a shocking thing to a young lady he hardly knew?

Delilah stopped walking and faced him. "What happened?" she asked. "What did you find in the bucket?"

"It was full of blood," he told her.

Delilah gasped.

"My father is convinced that it has something to do with the curse," Jonathan said. "I cannot help but wonder if he is right."

Now Delilah turned her face away. "Oh, no," she said, walking ahead of him. Were her hands shaking? Jonathan could not be sure. "He cannot be right about this, can he, Jonathan? There must be some reasonable explanation."

"There must be," Jonathan said. "But I cannot think of one. Do you suppose a wounded animal somehow got into the well? But that does not make sense. There was so much blood—and no sign of an animal. And the well water was perfectly clean."

Delilah stopped again and took Jonathan's hand. "Please, Jonathan," she pleaded. "Forget about this curse. Let it be your father's obsession, not yours."

Jonathan put his hand over hers. Her skin was so soft. Her words echoed in his mind. Forget about this curse, he thought. That is exactly what I would have said—until today.

He and Delilah walked on in silence.

She is a very sensible girl, Jonathan thought. I am glad we have met. It is so good to have someone to confide in.

That night Jonathan went to bed early and immediately fell asleep.

Deep in the night a noise woke him.

Creak.

Jonathan's eyes flew open. He listened, holding his breath.

It was the dead of night. The house lay bathed in darkness.

Creak.

Jonathan's heart began to pound. There it was again.

Creak. Creak.

It came from the hall. His mouth suddenly dry, his temples throbbing, Jonathan slipped out of bed and crept to the door.

He put his ear to the door and listened. I really did hear a noise this time, he thought. I am sure of it.

Creeeeak.

Slowly, silently, he opened the door. The hall was dark. He listened to footsteps quietly coming toward him.

He peered around the door and into the hall.

There it stood.

His blood stopped flowing in his veins.

At the end of the hall he saw a vision in white—floating toward him.

CHAPTER 11

"Who is it?" Jonathan cried. But his voice came out a choked whisper.

The pale figure whispered, "Abigail! Abigail!"

It floated closer. Jonathan could see a white nightgown and white nightcap, long gray hair flowing under it. He heard the floorboards creaking under her bare feet.

It cannot be a ghost, he thought.

The apparition called out softly, "Abigail! Abigail! Come back!"

It is Mama, Jonathan realized, alarmed. What is she doing?

His mother stepped quietly past him, not seeing him. Again she called, "Abigail!"

She is walking in her sleep, Jonathan realized.

She started down the stairs and Jonathan followed.

She made her way to the back of the house, the ghostly white gown trailing along the floor. "Abigail!" she called a little louder this time. "Wait for me!"

She opened the back door. She was going outside.

Jonathan stepped forward and grabbed her arm. "Mama!" he cried in a trembling voice. "What are you doing?"

She turned around, startled. Her eyes were wide open and full of tears.

She is not asleep, Jonathan thought. She is awake. She knows what she is doing.

"It is Abigail," his mother whispered, tears rolling down her quivering cheeks. "She called to me. She is out there, waiting for me."

Jonathan pulled his mother inside and closed the door. "No, Mama," he said, desperate to soothe her. "You must be dreaming."

"I am not dreaming, Jonathan." His mother's voice was firm now. "She is in the backyard. My little girl . . ."

Jonathan opened the door and peered outside. It was a warm, clear night, well lit by the moon. He saw no one outside. No sign of Abigail.

"No one is there, Mama," Jonathan said. "Please, you must go back to bed."

He put an arm around his mother's shoulders and began to lead her back to the stairs. She struggled against him.

"No!" she cried. "Abigail needs me!"

Jonathan was stronger and guided his mother upstairs. "You cannot go outside—you will catch cold. You had a bad dream, Mama. That is all," he said. "Just a bad dream."

But no matter what he told her, Jane refused to believe that her dead daughter hadn't called to her.

She allowed herself to be taken upstairs, but still she was frantic with grief and worry. She went to bed, and at last, exhausted, fell into a deep sleep.

Jonathan shut the door to his room and went to his window to look out. The yard, with the woods behind it, stretched quiet and peaceful in the moonlight.

In the morning the Fier family went about their chores as if it were any other day. Neither Jonathan nor his mother said a word to anyone about what had happened the night before.

It was almost as if it really *had* been a dream. Jonathan knew better.

Mama has been shaken since Abigail died, Jonathan thought. But it has always been a matter of a momentary confusion. She has never gone this far before.

The next night he lay awake, waiting for a noise. Hours passed in peaceful stillness. Jonathan's body began to relax. Then, just as he began to feel drowsy, he heard it.

Creak.

"Abigail! Abigail!" came the whispered cry.

He heard his father's heavier tread on the floorboards.

"Jane, come back to bed," Ezra whispered. "You will wake up the children."

Jonathan heard his father take his mother back into their room and shut the door. He heard their muffled voices, then his mother crying.

Jonathan's mother stayed in bed all the next day, and the next. But at night she roamed the house, calling for her dead daughter.

"I want to do something for her," Rachel told Jonathan. "Something to cheer her up."

Jonathan sighed. He doubted anything he or Rachel could do would make their mother happy.

"What about the trellis?" Rachel suggested. "We could plant roses. Someday they will grow so high they will reach her bedroom window."

"All right," Jonathan agreed. He was glad to get out of the house, at least.

Jonathan took a shovel and Rachel took a spade. They began to dig holes for the rosebushes.

Feeling a light tap on his shoulder, Jonathan whirled around to see who was there.

He found himself staring into Delilah's pretty face.

"Good afternoon," she said.

"Good afternoon," Jonathan answered.

"Hello, Delilah!" Rachel called.

Jonathan wiped his dirty hands on his work pants and wished Delilah had not found him so muddy. But she did not seem to mind.

"Do you two have time for a visitor?" Delilah asked.

"Of course," said Jonathan.

"I need a rest anyway," Rachel said. "I am tired of digging."

"Shall we sit in the shade?" Jonathan suggested.

Jonathan and Delilah sat under an apple tree while Rachel ran off and was soon back with a pitcher of lemon water.

"I have come to see how the two of you are doing," said Delilah. "I have been worried about you."

Jonathan was silent. But Rachel said, "Oh, Delilah—Mama is not well. She walks through the house every night, calling for Abigail. We think she sees Abigail's ghost!"

Delilah's eyes widened, and she raised a hand to her throat. She turned to Jonathan. "Can this be true?"

"It is true that Mama is upset," Jonathan told her. "Every night she cries out for Abigail. She—she says she sees Abigail in the yard, beckoning to her."

Delilah sucked in her breath and shut her eyes. "This is dreadful," she murmured, almost as if she were talking to herself.

Jonathan leaned closer to her. "But I am sure it is not

a ghost," he said to reassure her. "Please do not worry about us, Delilah. Rachel exaggerates sometimes."

"I do not!" cried Rachel.

A bit of color returned to Delilah's face, and she grew calmer.

"She could be dreaming, could she not?" she suggested. "The same dream, night after night?"

Jonathan sipped his lemon water thoughtfully. He studied Delilah's face, and she smiled at him.

She is so brave, he thought. She is trying to make Rachel and me feel better.

Rachel is afraid of a ghost, and I am afraid that my mother is going insane. Delilah does not want us to be frightened, so she assures us it is a dream.

"Jonathan."

Jonathan's eyes flew open. It was the middle of the night.

Another sound.

Mama?

"Jonathan," came the eerie whisper. "Jonathan—beware!"

Jonathan froze as he stared into the darkness.

It was not his mother, but the soft, sweet voice of a girl.

"Who is there?" he whispered.

"Beware, my brother," came the girl's voice. It seemed to be coming from outside the open window. But that was impossible. . . .

"Beware, my brother," the voice said again. "Or your fate will be worse than mine!"

Jonathan sat up. "Rachel?" he called. "Rachel? Where are you?"

"No," whispered the little girl. "No, not Rachel. I am Abigail."

CHAPTER 12

Jonathan jumped out of bed. "Abigail!" he cried frantically. "Abigail! Where are you?"

He froze in the center of the room and listened.

No one answered. The voice was gone.

His hands trembling, Jonathan lit a candle from the smoldering embers in the fireplace. The candlelight made his shadow rise eerily on the wall.

Jonathan searched every corner of the room. He threw open the wardrobe door and peered inside.

No sign of his dead sister. No sign of anyone.

His heart thumping, Jonathan slumped back onto the bed.

Abigail had called to him. Or *had* she?

Had it been another dream?

Perhaps Mama's madness is getting to me, he thought. But he quickly dismissed the idea.

The voice was real. I did hear Abigail calling me, warning me about something. . . .

Then a soft tapping at his door startled him.

He leaped to his feet, staring at the door.

Should he open it?

He had no time to decide. The door squeaked open slowly.

In walked Rachel.

She wore her nightshift and cap, her feet bare. Her eyes in the dim candlelight were round with fear.

"Rachel, what is it?" Jonathan asked, his voice a low whisper.

"I saw her!" Rachel cried. "I saw Abigail!"

CHAPTER 13

Jonathan rushed to his sister and took her by the shoulders. "You saw Abigail?" he said. "Where?"

"I saw her face outside my window. She called to me, 'Rachel! Beware!'"

"But how did you know it was Abigail?" Jonathan asked. "Do you remember what she looked like?"

"She looked like Papa's picture of her," said Rachel. "She wore a white cap with blue ribbons, and she was floating outside my window. Then she disappeared."

Jonathan let go of Rachel. Maybe Mama really had seen Abigail, he thought. Perhaps she saw what Rachel saw. It *had* to be Abigail. Abigail's ghost.

Abigail had come to warn her family.

But of what?

* * *

"I am going to call on the Wilsons, Mama," Jonathan told Jane. She sat by the hearth in the kitchen, too tired to move.

"Let me go with you," Rachel begged. "I like Delilah."

"Not today, Rachel," said Jonathan. "Today I want to see her alone."

Their mother gave Jonathan a basket of sweet rolls to take with him as a gift. "Please send our regards to her father," Jane said. Then she sighed. "We should have had them to tea by now, but it has been so difficult. . . ."

Tears welled up in her eyes, which she brushed away. Misery had aged Jonathan's mother since Abigail's death. The corners of her mouth sagged, and her eyes were dull and almost colorless. Jonathan noticed that the past few days had sharpened the pain in her face.

"Apologize to the Wilsons for me," she went on. "And tell them—tell them I have been ill."

"I will," Jonathan promised. He put a hand on her arm and added, "You will feel better soon, Mama. I know you will."

She nodded absently. Jonathan took the basket and set off down the road to the Wilsons' farm.

The Reverend Wilson was working in a field when Jonathan arrived, but Delilah's lively face lifted Jonathan's spirits. She took the rolls with a smile. "It was so thoughtful of your mother to send them," she said. "How is she?"

Jonathan sighed. "No better," he told her. "She still

sees Abigail at night. But now, at least, she is not the only one."

"What do you mean?"

"Rachel saw her, too. And I—well, I heard Abigail's voice. She called to me."

Delilah dropped the basket and turned her face away. Jonathan saw her shoulders shaking under her faded pink dress.

"Delilah, what is wrong?" Gently he turned her around, put his arms on her shoulders to stop their shaking, and gazed intently into her eyes. But she lowered her face as if she didn't want him to see her expression.

When she finally raised her eyes, they were filled with tears. "I am very worried about you, Jonathan," she said. "About you and your family. I—I would never wish any harm on you, ever."

Jonathan thought she was even prettier than usual with her eyes shining with tears. He wanted to throw his arms around her and kiss her.

"What are you talking about, Delilah?" he asked. "I know you wouldn't wish harm on us. This has nothing to do with you." He paused, feeling guilty. "I should never have burdened you with our problems, Delilah. You are taking them upon yourself."

Delilah closed her eyes. "My father and I are leaving soon," she said quietly. "Perhaps, once we are gone—"

"No!" Jonathan cried. "You cannot leave! Please!"

He was surprised to hear himself speak these words. The idea of Delilah's leaving was painful. He felt as if he had been punched in the stomach.

I am in love with her, he realized right then. Completely, desperately in love with her.

He took her hands in his and demanded, "Why? Why must you leave? Please, Delilah, stay here. . . ."

She lowered her head again. "It is for the best, Jonathan. You must believe me. By the end of the week we will be gone."

"Delilah, I do not understand—"

"Please go now, Jonathan," she said with a tremor in her voice. "Please—you must leave."

Jonathan made his way from the Wilsons' cottage and trudged home with a heavy heart. I love her, he thought miserably. And I know she loves me, too. I know it. So why must she leave? Why can't she explain? Why is she so sad, and so mysterious?

That night Jonathan waited to hear his mother's whispered cries. He tried to force his eyes open, to remain alert.

But after so many sleepless nights, he couldn't stay awake. He drifted off into a heavy and dreamless sleep.

Then, just before dawn, a horrifying scream pierced his sleep-fogged brain.

Jonathan jerked straight up in bed. The scream had come from the backyard.

He hurried to the window. The first pink light of morning was beginning to show on the horizon. Squinting into the yard, he could see nothing unusual.

The scream lingered in his mind, echoed in his ears. None of the horrors of the past few weeks had prepared him for the terrible agony in that scream.

Jonathan heard footsteps on the stairs. He crept to the door. In the gray light he saw Ezra and Rachel heading downstairs. Jonathan followed.

Where is Mama? he thought. Panic rose in his throat. He pushed it down, swallowed it. No time for panic.

Jonathan followed his father and sister outside. The yard was silent now. But they had all heard the scream. They all agreed it had come from the yard.

"Where is Mama?" Jonathan asked his father.

"I do not know," Ezra said. "That scream woke me up, and she was not there. I cannot help but think—" Ezra glanced at Rachel. He did not finish his sentence.

"Do not worry, Papa," Jonathan said. "We will find her."

For hours they searched the house, every inch of it. Jane was not there. The sun was rising above the trees now.

They dressed quickly and returned to the yard, searching around every bush, behind every tree.

Rachel stood at the edge of the woods, calling for her mother. Jonathan felt tired and discouraged.

What could have happened to my mother? he wondered. How could she vanish into thin air?

His mouth felt dry as cotton. He made his way to the well for a drink. As he tugged on the rope to pull up the bucket, the rope felt strangely heavy.

A wave of dread swept over Jonathan.

"Papa!" he called hoarsely. "Come help me pull up the well bucket."

Ezra narrowed his eyes at Jonathan but said nothing. He stepped beside his son. Together, their faces set in hard concentration, they heaved on the rope.

"It is so heavy, Papa," Jonathan said, pulling with all his strength. "I cannot imagine—"

One final tug.

Jonathan gasped in disbelief.

And then he started to scream.

CHAPTER 14

Jonathan's scream roared over the yard.

"What is it? What is it?" Rachel cried shrilly, running to the well.

Jonathan was too horrified to reply. Too horrified to move. Too horrified to pull his eyes away from the gruesome sight before him.

At the end of the well rope, sprawled over the bucket, was the body of his mother.

Her skin was blue and bloated. Her wet hair plastered against her skull and face. Her soaked nightgown clung tightly to her lifeless form.

"No! No! *No!*"

Jonathan's sobs wrenched his throat.

"Mama!" Rachel whispered. "Mama—why?"

Jonathan's father held on to the bucket with both hands. His eyes were shut. His lips moved in a silent prayer.

"No! No!"

Trying to turn his gaze away, Jonathan saw something. Something gripped tightly in his mother's closed fist.

He reached down and pried open the cold, bloated fingers.

"Ohhh!" Jonathan gasped when he saw it.

A white cap with blue ribbons.

"Mama! Mama!" Rachel repeated. She dropped to her knees in front of her mother and began to sob.

Without a word, Jonathan helped Ezra lift Jane's body and set it down on the grass.

Can that really be my mother? Jonathan asked through a blur of tears. Can that really be my mother so cold, so still?

He picked up his little sister and carried her, sobbing, into the house.

There is no doubt in my mind now, Jonathan thought later. The Fier family is cursed. I did not want to believe it. But Papa has been right all along.

The hair prickled on the back of his neck. In a flash Jonathan suddenly understood.

Delilah's strange sadness . . . Her sudden desire to leave, to get away from the Fiers . . . It all fell into place like the pieces of a puzzle.

Jonathan ran past where his father sat slumped at the table, his head buried in his hands, and out into the yard.

Rachel's face appeared in her bedroom window. "Where are you going?" she called down to him.

Jonathan did not answer her. Instead, he started to run. Glancing back, he saw Rachel following him, but he didn't stop to send her home.

Jonathan ran down the road to the Wilsons' farm. Delilah was in the yard, feeding the chickens.

As he came into view, she dropped the sack of feed. He grabbed her hands and held them tight.

"Delilah, my love!" he cried breathlessly. "You must tell me. You must tell me your secret."

She stared at him, startled.

Rachel arrived, panting, holding her side from running so hard.

Jonathan ignored her. He did not care who was there, who heard what he had asked. He had to know if he was right. He had to know *now.*

"I already know your secret," he told Delilah. "Just tell me yourself."

He gazed deeply into her brown eyes.

"Yes," she replied quietly. "I can see it in your face, Jonathan. You know my terrible secret, don't you?"

She shut her eyes, a tear falling onto her cheek.

"I am a Goode," she confessed.

CHAPTER 15

Jonathan stared at her. He opened his mouth to speak, but no sound came out.

"How can you be a Goode?" Rachel demanded. "I thought your name was Wilson."

"We—we changed our name," Delilah explained. "We once lived in another town, near Boston. But when word of the plague in Wickham reached our town, our neighbors drove us out. They had heard rumors that the Goodes were responsible for the plague, so they shunned us. We moved west—and Father changed our name. We became the Wilsons."

Jonathan suddenly felt dizzy. He rubbed his temples with his fingers.

"I wanted to tell you my name was Goode," Delilah

said. "I knew I should be honest. But I liked you both so much. I did not want to scare you away. And I thought that maybe—maybe there really was no curse."

She paused and gazed at Jonathan.

"You did not believe in the curse," she said softly to him. "And you are so smart and kind. I thought that if you did not believe in it, then it could not be true."

"I did not want to believe it," Jonathan said. "I wanted to be happy."

A sad smile crossed Delilah's face. "I am afraid we cannot deny it any longer," she whispered. "There is a curse on your family. A curse on both our families." She swallowed hard. "There is only one way to stop it."

Jonathan's heart pounded harder. "There is a way to stop it?" he demanded breathlessly, hardly daring to hope it was true. "What is it?"

Delilah avoided his eyes. "It involves some sacrifice," she said, blushing. "On your part."

"I will do anything!" Jonathan cried. "Please, Delilah. Tell me how to break the curse."

She took a deep breath. "The feuding families must unite. They must form an unshakable bond."

"How?" Jonathan asked.

"Marriage," Delilah replied, still avoiding his eyes. "A Goode and a Fier must marry."

"But that is very simple," Rachel interrupted. "You two can get married."

Kneeling, Jonathan took Delilah's hand and kissed it joyfully. "How can you call that a sacrifice, Delilah? I am already in love with you. You must know that by now. I love you so much I would marry you even if it brought a *new* curse down on me and my family!"

Tears streamed down Delilah's cheeks. "Jonathan—"

He stopped her. "Please, dear Delilah, before you say another word—I must ask for your hand in marriage."

She smiled through her tears and struggled to speak. "I love you, too, Jonathan," she replied softly. "But I am afraid—"

"What are you afraid of?" he asked. "You are not afraid of *me,* are you?"

"No, I am not afraid of you. I am afraid of the curse. I am afraid that something could happen—something terrible—to stop our wedding."

"Nothing can stop me from marrying you!" Jonathan declared, rising to his feet. "And to make sure of that, we shall marry as soon as possible. Your father can marry us. He is a minister. He can do it *today,* before anything can happen."

Delilah's face lit up. Smiling, she wiped the tears from her cheeks. "He is at the church right now. Oh, Jonathan, I am so happy! I can hardly believe this is happening."

Jonathan smiled at her, but deep inside him a question still burned. Could this marriage really end the curse—once and for all? Could that be possible?

"We will be sisters, Delilah!" Rachel exclaimed. "I will bear witness at the ceremony."

Jonathan had almost forgotten his sister was there. "No, Rachel," he ordered. "Run home and stay with Papa. He will be wondering where you are now—and he must not find you here. Run home—please. Hurry!"

In the tiny clapboard church Jonathan gripped Delilah's hand. Her father, the Reverend Wilson, stood behind a simple altar, facing them, a worn black leather Bible in his hands.

"I, Jonathan, take thee, Delilah . . ."

Jonathan repeated the minister's words, hardly knowing what he said. His heart was racing. His only desire was to get safely through the ceremony—and then to hold his new wife in his arms.

Now Delilah repeated the vows.

Jonathan stole a glance at his beautiful bride. He only wished his mother was still alive to share this moment.

The ceremony was nearly over. In moments I will be married, he thought.

And the curse will be ended. The Fiers and the Goodes will be joined.

The Reverend Wilson cleared his throat. "If anyone knows of just cause why these two should not be united in holy matrimony, let him speak now, or forever hold his peace."

Silence.

Then a startling crash.

Spinning around, Jonathan saw that the doors of the small church had flown open.

Silhouetted against the bright daylight outside, a man came into focus.

What is that in his hand? Jonathan wondered, squinting into the bright rectangle of light.

A rifle?

Ezra!

"Stop at once!" Ezra screamed. He burst into the church and strode up the aisle, rifle in hand.

Rachel burst in behind him. "Jonathan, I am sorry!" she cried, her voice shrill with fear. "Papa made me tell! I am sorry!"

The little girl tugged desperately at her father's arm, trying to hold him back. Ezra pushed his daughter roughly aside and continued down the aisle, his eyes narrowed on Jonathan, his features set in hard fury.

"Stop this wedding!" he demanded. He stopped and raised the rifle to his shoulder. "All Goodes must die!"

Jonathan felt his heart skip. "Papa—no!" he screamed.

With a desperate cry he dived toward his father and grabbed the gun, trying to take it from him.

They struggled.

Delilah raised her hands to her face and screamed.

"Traitor!" Ezra snarled bitterly to his son. "How could you do this to me?"

"Papa—give me the gun!" Jonathan demanded.

The two men wrestled over it, their shoes scuffling over the wooden floorboards.

"Give it to me!" Jonathan pleaded.

He tugged hard and pulled the rifle free.

As Jonathan staggered back with it, the rifle went off.

"Ohhh!" Jonathan uttered a startled cry as the sound echoed through the tiny church.

He heard a sharp cry.

And turned to the altar.

Delilah stood as if suspended by wires, her features twisted in shock and horror.

A red stain appeared on the front of her white dress.

Jonathan stared helplessly as the stain darkened and spread.

I've shot Delilah, he realized.

CHAPTER 16

"Delilah!"

Jonathan screamed her name in a choked voice he didn't recognize, and let the rifle fall.

Before he could run to her, Delilah's eyelids slid shut. She uttered a faint gasp and slumped to the floor.

Jonathan dropped beside her. "Delilah! Delilah!"

He called her name again and again.

But, he knew, she could not hear him now.

The dark blood puddled beneath her white dress.

"Oh, Delilah," Jonathan sobbed, cradling her head in his arms.

Behind him, Jonathan heard a click. He turned.

Ezra had picked up the rifle, which he was now pointing at the minister's head.

"All Goodes will die," Ezra said calmly, hate burning in his eyes.

The Reverend Wilson fell to his knees beside his daughter's lifeless body. "Please do not shoot me!" he cried. "Please!"

Jonathan gently laid Delilah's body on the floor and stepped toward his father. "Papa, please—"

Ezra leveled the rifle at Jonathan. "Do not get in my way again, son," he growled, his voice hard and sharp as a steel blade. "I am warning you."

Jonathan said nothing. Ezra turned back to the minister. "All Goodes will die," he repeated.

Reverend Wilson clasped his hands together as if in prayer. "Please do not shoot me," he begged again. "I am not a Goode!"

"Your lies will not succeed with me," Ezra snapped. "You cannot save yourself. My wife is dead because of you—and now you must pay the price."

Delilah's father shook in terror. "It is true! I swear to you! I am not a Goode. Delilah was not a Goode either!"

He turned to Jonathan and added, "Jonathan—she lied to you!"

CHAPTER 17

"What are you *saying*?" Jonathan cried in disbelief.

"Do not listen to him, boy," Ezra urged coldly. "He is only looking for a way to save himself."

"I am telling the truth!" the minister insisted. "It was all a trick. A fraud! I *swear* it!"

Jonathan ignored his father and the rifle. "A trick?" he repeated weakly, grabbing the front of Reverend Wilson's robe. "A trick?"

"I—I wanted Delilah to marry you, Jonathan," the minister sputtered, his eyes on Ezra's rifle. "We are so poor, you see. And you are so well off. Delilah—she came home and told me the story of your feud with the Goodes. I—I had an idea. I saw a way we could use it—to trick you into marrying her."

"To trick me . . ." Jonathan murmured.

"I made her do it!" the minister cried. "I forced her to." He lowered his gaze to his daughter's body. He stared at it for a moment as if he just realized she was dead. Then, with a shudder, he pulled his eyes away.

"Delilah was a good girl at heart," Reverend Wilson muttered. "A good girl."

"This is all nonsense!" Ezra snarled. "Prepare to die, Goode! I have waited so long, so long—all my life—for this chance. You will not cheat me of my revenge with your desperate lies."

"Please, Papa," Jonathan begged, pushing the rifle aside. "Let him speak."

"I forced Delilah to pretend that she was a Goode," Reverend Wilson confessed sadly. "But I knew you would not marry her just because of that. So she made you think your dead sister was haunting you. She made terrible screaming noises at night. Delilah filled your well bucket with chicken blood. She made a cap with blue ribbons on it, like the one she saw in a painting of your sister. And she climbed your rose trellis to appear in your windows at night."

Ezra lowered the rifle. His face grew red and his jaw trembled as he listened.

"Delilah lured your mother outside with that blue-ribboned cap," the minister continued in a quivering voice. "She threw it into the well. Your mother leaned over to retrieve it. And—she fell into the well. . . ."

He swallowed hard. "Delilah tried to help her, but she couldn't reach her."

He stopped again. He was breathing noisily, his chest heaving under his dark robe.

"Why?" Jonathan asked. "Why did you make Delilah do all this?"

"We had to frighten you, to make you desperate," answered the clergyman. "So desperate you would do anything to stop the horrors. So desperate you would marry Delilah. We were so poor, you see. So poor—"

"But I loved her," said Jonathan. "I would have married her anyway."

He dropped to his knees beside Delilah's dead body. Her mouth had fallen open, and a trickle of blood ran down her chin. Jonathan stared at the body as if it belonged to a stranger.

The minister shuddered violently now. "I know you cannot forgive me," he pleaded with Ezra, "but please, please do not kill me!"

Ezra's face hung slack. The anger faded from his eyes. The rifle fell from his hands and clattered on the church floor.

"My wife—my daughter—" he murmured. "The curse . . ."

His face had become as pale as Delilah's. His thin lips barely moved as he whispered, "The curse. The Fiers are truly cursed. . . ."

His hands flew to his head and he uttered a sorrowful wail and tore at his graying hair. Then he ran from the church, screaming.

Jonathan heard a horse whinny. Then a piercing scream, and finally a sickening crunch.

CHAPTER 18

"What was that?" Jonathan cried, knowing the answer to his question.

He ran outside. A small crowd had gathered around a horse and wagon.

Jonathan shouted, "Papa! Papa!" and pushed through the silent crowd.

"Papa!" Jonathan cried, seeing Ezra sprawled on his back, a dark open wound in his side, blood puddling on the dirt street.

"Get the doctor!" someone cried. "This man has been trampled!"

Jonathan knelt beside his father. Ezra's eyes rolled around blindly for a second. Then they focused on Jonathan.

Ezra lifted his hand and let it fall on the silver amulet.

"Take this," he whispered to Jonathan. He closed his eyes for a moment, gathering his strength. "Jonathan—" His voice grew weak. "The power of the Fiers is in this amulet. You must wear it always. Use it—use it to avenge my death."

Ezra took one last, shuddering breath. Then blood poured from his mouth. His eyes froze in a fixed and lifeless stare.

"Papa—" cried Jonathan. "Papa . . ."

Jonathan buried his face in his hands and sank deeply into his sorrow.

So many people have died, he thought. Abigail, Mama, Delilah, Papa. All because of this dreaded curse.

His father's strange silver pendant glinted in the sun.

The curse dies with my father, Jonathan thought. I will put an end to it, here and now.

No minister would give Ezra a funeral or allow his body to be buried in a church cemetery. He had been insane, a murderer, Reverend Wilson had warned. So Jonathan had Ezra's body cremated. Now all that remained of Ezra was a jar of ashes.

Rachel cried herself to sleep. Jonathan listened helplessly to her sobs, every cry torturing him.

He sat by the hearth, waiting for her crying to stop. At last the house grew still, and he knew she was asleep.

He took Ezra's ashes and poured them into an iron strongbox. Then he picked up the silver pendant.

To Jonathan's surprise, the pendant grew hot in his hand. He saw flames, flames he thought would swallow him up.

But the flames died as quickly as they had appeared. And the jeweled pendant cooled.

Jonathan examined the pendant, felt its weight against his palm.

His father's last words echoed in his mind. "Use it—to avenge my death."

No, thought Jonathan. No more revenge. No more feud. No more curse.

"I am sorry, Papa," he whispered. "But I cannot let our family suffer any longer. There is still Rachel. . . ."

He thought of his little sister, sleeping upstairs in her bedroom. She had already been through so much. But she might have a chance at happiness still. At least, Jonathan hoped so. He would do everything in his power to make her happy.

The first step, he decided, was to get rid of the pendant.

He dropped it into the strongbox. It landed softly on top of Ezra's ashes. Jonathan closed the heavy iron lid and locked it.

Then he took a lantern from its hook by the hearth. He made his way out into the night. He knelt beneath the apple tree. With a spade, he began to dig up the moist earth.

Bitter memories leaped to his mind as he worked

under the tree. He tried to force them away as soon as they arose, but they kept coming back.

He remembered drinking lemon water with Rachel and Delilah one hot day, on that very spot. Delilah . . .

He stopped digging and shoved the iron box in the hole. Then he scooped dirt back on top of the box.

This box is Papa's coffin, Jonathan thought. This shallow hole, his grave. This lonely, secret ceremony is his funeral.

Papa and the cursed pendant will be buried here forever.

Jonathan finished filling the hole and smoothed the dirt. He left nothing to mark the spot.

It is done, Jonathan thought. He stood and wiped the dirt from his hands. That is the end of the horror. The curse is finished. The feud is over.

The Fiers and the Goodes will suffer no more.

Village of Shadyside

1900

Nora's entire body tensed as she listened. She held her breath as the footsteps in the hall came closer and closer to her room. She waited for them to stop at her door. . . .

But they passed by.

She exhaled, then picked up her pen and began to write again.

"Jonathan Fier hoped he could bury the curse along with Ezra's ashes," she wrote. "And it seemed to be true. The evil stayed buried for one hundred years. For one hundred years the Goodes and the Fiers lived in peace.

"In fact, the feud was forgotten. Children grew up hearing none of the horrifying stories. They knew nothing of the curse upon the two families."

But it is not easy to end a curse, Nora thought.

Jonathan Fier's great-great granddaughter innocently unleashed the evil once again. During that hundred years of sleep, the evil power had grown even stronger.

Nora touched the pendant around her neck. Oh, she thought mournfully, if only it had stayed buried forever. . . .

Part Three

Western Massachusetts

1843

CHAPTER 19

It is too bad the old apple tree died, thought Elizabeth Fier.

She was kneeling in her green gardening dress, digging with a trowel in the rich dark soil. Heavy leather gloves protected her hands. The apple tree had died, and her brother, Simon, had chopped it down.

Now there was a bare spot in the backyard. Elizabeth thought it looked empty and a bit sad.

But I will take care of that, she thought, adjusting her straw bonnet over her long, dark hair. This flower garden will be even prettier than the old tree. I will fill it with pansies and snapdragons.

As she worked, she hummed a tune her mother had tried to teach her on the piano. She stopped humming as her trowel hit something hard under the dirt. She lifted the trowel out of the dirt, then poked it into the earth again.

There is something buried here, she thought. Maybe some kind of treasure!

A voice inside her head told her it was most likely a root from the old dead tree. But she would soon find out.

She dug around the hard spot, wiping the dirt away with her fingers. She tapped her trowel against it again. It clanged, metal against metal.

A short while later she pulled up a metal box. It had a heavy lock on it, but the box itself was so rusted the hinges had broken.

"Elizabeth!" her mother called from the kitchen door. "Come in and wash up! Supper is ready."

Elizabeth called back, "I will be there in a minute, Mother."

The rusty box fascinated her. What is inside? she wondered. Maybe it really *is* full of treasure.

Carefully she lifted the rusty lid and peered inside. A coarse gray dust covered the bottom of the box. Elizabeth removed her gardening gloves and dipped her fingers into the dust. She touched something solid and pulled it out.

It was a round, silver disk on a silver chain. A silver claw with three talons seemed to clutch the top of the disk. It was studded with four blue stones. On the back Elizabeth saw the inscribed words: *Dominatio per malum.*

Latin, Elizabeth thought. But she did not know what the words meant. Maybe Simon would know.

What an odd necklace, she thought. But I like it.

She stood up, necklace in hand, and ran inside. Her father, Samuel Fier, and her sister and brother, Kate and Simon, were already seated at the dining room table.

It was a warm evening in late spring, but a fire burned in the old brick hearth. The house was very old; it had been in the Fier family for a hundred years. Samuel Fier and his family lived prosperously there.

"Go wash your hands, Elizabeth," said her mother, Katherine. She was a plump, pretty, round-faced woman with light brown hair piled on top of her head.

Elizabeth poured fresh water into the washbasin and rinsed off her hands.

Her mother set a platter of sliced turkey on the table, adding, "I wish you would not stay out in the garden so late, Elizabeth. It leaves you no time to change for supper."

"I am sorry, Mother," Elizabeth replied, returning to the table. She held up the silver disk. "Look what I dug up," she said. "Isn't it strange?"

Kate gave the pendant a dismissive glance and said, "It is ugly."

Kate was seventeen, a year older than Elizabeth. Her hair was a lighter shade of brown and her eyes a lighter shade of blue than Elizabeth's. But they both had the same pale skin and full, red lips.

Their brother, Simon, who was eighteen, had a very tall, thin body with an angular face, thin lips, and black hair. His eyes, too, were black.

Simon studied the pendant as Elizabeth dangled it before him. "Where did you find it?" he asked.

"In the backyard, where I am digging my new garden. It was buried under the old apple tree."

Samuel Fier touched the amulet lightly. "I have never seen anything like it," he said. "I wonder what it was doing buried there. Someone must have buried it for a reason."

"Maybe it should stay buried," Kate joked

Elizabeth ignored her sister's comment. "I like it," she said. "I am going to wear it as a good-luck charm."

She draped the silver chain around her neck.

Suddenly her neck began to tingle. Elizabeth shuddered and closed her eyes. They burned.

When she opened her eyes, the dining room was gone and she was surrounded by fire!

Hot flames licked at her long curls, at the hem of her dress. Fire singed her eyelashes.

I feel faint, she thought. She shut her eyes again and prepared to be engulfed in flames.

CHAPTER 20

"Elizabeth! Elizabeth! What is the matter?"

Elizabeth heard the alarmed voices of her mother and father as the flames died away. She shook her head and opened her eyes.

The fire disappeared. The room came into focus, as did the platter of turkey, her family. Everything seemed normal.

"Elizabeth, what happened?" her mother asked.

Elizabeth groped for a chair and sat down. "It is nothing, Mother, really," she said. The flames were already fading from her memory. "I just felt faint for a minute. I am all right now."

"You need something to eat," said Mrs. Fier.

"You are probably right," said Elizabeth. "I am very hungry."

For the rest of the evening Elizabeth felt fine. There were no other strange incidents. Soon she forgot all about the frightening sensation of fire.

A few weeks later the flowers in Elizabeth's garden were beginning to sprout. As for the strange pendant she had found there, it was now her favorite piece of jewelry. She never took it off.

The Fiers were sitting down to supper on a warm June evening. Elizabeth was just passing a dish of fresh peas to Simon.

Suddenly they heard a knock on the door.

"Who could that be?" asked Mrs. Fier, filling their glasses with water.

"I will answer it," said Elizabeth. She stood up and hurried to the door.

There, in the fading light, stood a tall, ragged man. The sight of him startled Elizabeth.

His broad-brimmed straw hat was caked with dirt and sat low over his gaunt face. His black jacket and trousers were faded and hung loose on his skeletal frame. His boots were worn thin.

His eyes, hard and glittering, stared at the disk around Elizabeth's neck, but he said nothing.

He must be a poor drifter, Elizabeth said to herself,

collecting her thoughts. But why does he not speak?

"What do you want?" she asked him.

He raised his eyes from the pendant to Elizabeth's face. Then he moved his cracked lips. "Please help me," he pleaded in a weak voice. "I am hungry. Can you spare any food or water?"

As Elizabeth glanced back at her family's bountiful supper, the drifter added, "I will gladly do a day's work in return for a meal."

Mr. Fier came to the door and stood behind his daughter. "Please come in," he said to the drifter. "We were just sitting down to eat, and we have plenty to share."

"Thank you, sir," said the drifter. He smiled through his dry lips and stepped inside.

Elizabeth watched him sit down and take a plate of food. His hands are bony, she thought with pity. And he looks sick. That must be what makes his eyes glitter so. The poor man!

First the drifter drank two full glasses of water. Then he began to eat, rapidly shoveling the food into his mouth.

He said nothing until he had eaten every morsel on his plate. Elizabeth struggled not to stare at him as he gobbled up his food.

When he had finished the first serving, Mrs. Fier took his plate and refilled it. The man thanked her very sincerely.

"My name is Franklin," he told them. "But my friends

call me Frank. I consider you all my friends now."

All the Fiers smiled.

Now that he has eaten a bit, Elizabeth thought, his eyes are warmer and his face is friendlier. To think that I was frightened of a sick, weak, hungry man!

"Do you live around here, Frank?" asked Mr. Fier.

Frank shook his head. "I have no home," he said. "Not anymore."

There was silence for a moment as Frank tore at a slice of bread with his teeth.

"I used to have a family," he continued. "I was one of seven brothers. We lived on a farm with my mother and father. But I lost them all, my whole family, and the farm, too. I am alone in the world now."

He spread a thick layer of honey on the bread.

"Now I roam around, picking up work where I can find it. But sometimes there is no work to be had. And when there is no work, there is no food."

"Why don't you settle down somewhere?" Mrs. Fier asked.

"I would, ma'am," Frank said. "I certainly would. I would settle down anywhere on earth, if I had a good reason to."

His lifted his gaze from his plate. Elizabeth felt a little shiver.

He is looking right at me, she thought.

Frank wiped his mouth and pushed his chair back

from the table. "That was a delicious supper," he said, standing up. "I thank you very kindly for it. Now I feel ready to do just about anything. You name the task, and I will do it for you."

"Oh, no, Frank," Mrs. Fier protested. "We would not think of making you work for your supper. We were glad we could help."

"Nevertheless, ma'am," Frank said. "I would feel better if I could do something for you."

"We do not need anything done," said Simon. "But you could use a good hot bath, I bet."

"Oh, no," said Frank. "I could not trouble you."

But the Fiers insisted, and Frank had to accept. While their mother cleaned up the supper dishes, Kate and Elizabeth got the wooden bathtub out of the pantry and set it on the kitchen floor. They boiled water and poured it into the tub.

Then the women left the room so Frank could take a bath. Simon left a clean suit of clothes for him on a chair.

Elizabeth paused at the door on her way out of the kitchen. She turned around just as Frank was taking off his dirty, tattered shirt. The movement of his arms made the muscles ripple through his back.

Embarrassed, Elizabeth hurried out. She hoped Frank did not know that she had had a glimpse of his bare back. It was not a proper sight for a young lady.

All the Fiers waited for Frank by the fire in the parlor.

Kate bent over her needlepoint, and Elizabeth worked at her knitting. Kate's birthday was coming up, and Elizabeth had decided to knit a scarf for her.

Elizabeth glanced up, startled by a noise at the parlor door.

There stood Frank, fresh from his bath. Elizabeth had to stop herself from gasping out loud at the change in him.

She realized that he was probably ten years younger than she had thought at first, closer to twenty than thirty. His face had taken on a new warmth, now that he was clean, fed, and rested. His hair was neatly combed, and Simon's borrowed clothes fit him elegantly.

He is handsome, Elizabeth realized. Very handsome.

She suddenly became aware of the weight of the amulet hanging from her neck, and the coolness of the metal against her skin. She held it in her palm, and it grew warm.

Frank says he is just a drifter, Elizabeth thought as she watched him take a seat by the fire. But there is more to him than that. He did not tell us much about his family, or say where he comes from. Who is he, really?

She would soon find out.

Frank leaned back against the cushioned chair by the fireplace, grinning at the Fier family gathered around him.

They are all smiling at me, he thought. They are so welcoming to the poor, starving drifter in their home. They are being so kind, so good-hearted.

They will take me in, he mused, and they will nurse me back to health. As I get stronger, I will help them out around the house, entertain their sweet daughters and their lonely son.

Soon they will begin to trust me, and before they know it, depend upon me. They will all love me, all five of them, like a brother and like a son.

Frank warmed his hands over the crackling flames in the hearth. Mrs. Fier offered him a cup of hot coffee.

It is beginning already, he thought. I can see the warmth shining in their eyes. They want to help me. They are beginning to love me.

I will wait. I will wait until they all love me as much as they love one another. I will wait and endure it all.

Then I will turn on them—and that will make it all worthwhile. I will enjoy the shock and terror in their faces. It will make up for everything my family suffered at their hands and all the pain I have endured to find them.

I, Franklin—the last of the Goodes.

CHAPTER 21

Frank finished his coffee. Then he stood up, stretched, and smiled at the Fiers.

"Thank you all, for everything," he said. "You were very kind. But you must be getting tired, and I am keeping you up. I will be moving on now, so you can go to sleep."

"You are leaving?" said Kate.

Oh, no, Elizabeth thought. He cannot leave. Not yet.

"I have imposed on your hospitality long enough," Frank said modestly. "You had better be careful—if you are too kind, you will have ragged drifters like Franklin Goode at your door every night!"

Mr. Fier chuckled at that. He put a hand on Frank's shoulder and said, "We cannot let you go off into the night this way. You must spend the night here, with us. I insist."

"Please, Frank," said Mrs. Fier. "I will not get a wink of sleep if you leave now. I will worry about you all night."

"Well . . ." said Frank, pretending to think it over. "I would not want to interfere with your sleep, Mrs. Fier. I will be glad to stay. But just for tonight. Then I will be on my way."

Hurray, Elizabeth thought to herself, secretly. He is staying!

Mrs. Fier sent Elizabeth to get the guest room ready.

He is so brave, Elizabeth thought as she tucked a fresh linen sheet under the pillow. He is strong and self-reliant.

She paused, remembering the ripple of muscle she had seen on his back. The memory gave her goose bumps.

Franklin Goode, she thought. And then—she could not help herself—"Mrs. Franklin Goode." She turned the sound of it over in her mind.

It is a nice name, Elizabeth thought. A very nice name indeed.

Elizabeth heard the heavy blows of an ax in the backyard as she made her way to the kitchen window to peer out.

There was Frank, wearing Simon's work clothes, chopping wood. When he raised the ax above his head, the metal glinted in the sun.

It is a warm day, Elizabeth thought. Frank must be very thirsty. So she poured a glass of cool water and took it to him.

Frank smiled at the sight of her. He gave the log one last blow, then set down the ax. He took the glass from Elizabeth's hand and drank down the water without a word.

Then he returned the empty glass to her, saying, "Thank you very much, Elizabeth. You must have read my mind."

"I just thought you might be thirsty, that is all," she replied.

Frank sat down on the pile of logs and gazed up into Elizabeth's face. She found herself blushing.

"Have you ever seen the sea, Elizabeth?" he asked.

She shook her head. "I have never been out of this town. Well, I have been to Worcester once or twice—"

"Someday soon, Elizabeth, you must see the ocean. If you have not seen it yourself, you cannot imagine it. It is so wild, and so beautiful. On a clear day the ocean is a dark blue-green color that is so hard to describe. But—your eyes—"

He stared intently at her face. Elizabeth's eyes were locked onto his. His gaze was hypnotic.

"But what?" she asked him. "What about my eyes?"

"Your eyes," Frank said. "Your eyes are the only thing I have ever seen that are the same wild color as the ocean."

Elizabeth's heart fluttered. She had never heard anyone speak that way before.

It is as if he is speaking directly through his heart, she thought.

"I am just about finished chopping wood," Frank said. "I would like to take a walk to look around. Would you do me the honor of accompanying me, Elizabeth?"

"I would love to," she replied. "Though I warn you, you will be disappointed. There is not much to see in town."

"I am not interested in towns anyway," said Frank. "I would rather take a walk through the woods."

She set the glass on top of a log. He offered her his arm, and she accepted it. They walked across the grass of the back lawn to the woods that stood at the edge of the Fier property.

The woods were magical that day. Rays of sunlight streamed through the tall pine trees, and the brown needles made a soft, fragrant carpet on the ground. Elizabeth led Frank to a clearing where two large, flat stones sat side by side like chairs.

"Kate and Simon and I loved to play here when we were children," she explained. "We used to pretend this clearing was the throne room in a castle. Simon sat on that big stone there, and Kate on the smaller one."

She sat down on the smaller rock, leaving the larger one to Frank. "Simon was the king, and Kate was the queen. I usually had to be the princess."

Frank smiled and sat down on his rock. Elizabeth paused and listened. She heard only the rustling of the squirrels and the chirping of the birds. There were no people around, she felt sure.

Still, she lowered her voice as she said, "There is an old woman who lives in these woods. She hobbles through the pines with a cane, all stooped over. She has white hair and wears black clothes. Simon and Kate and I used to see her when we played in this very spot. We ran if we saw her coming."

"Why?"

Elizabeth shrugged, feeling slightly silly. "All the children were afraid of her. We called her Old Aggie. People said she was a witch."

"I am sure they were just trying to frighten you," said Frank. "Your parents were probably hoping a story like that would keep you from wandering too far off."

Elizabeth smiled. "I suppose you are right. Still, I always believed that Old Aggie really was a witch. One boy I knew said that if you got close enough, Aggie's cane turned into a live snake."

Elizabeth could not stop herself from shivering. "I often wonder if she is still alive."

"I am sure she is not," Frank said in a comforting voice. She smiled. She felt safe with him there.

A ray of sunlight fell on the silver pendant around Elizabeth's neck. Frank reached for it.

"Where did you get this necklace?" he asked.

"It is a strange piece of jewelry, is it not?" said Elizabeth. "I found it in our backyard. It was buried in a rusty old strongbox."

Frank studied the pendant, turning it over in his hand, rubbing his fingers over the blue jewels. "What do the words mean?" he asked her. "Do you know who it belonged to?"

Elizabeth shook her head. "I do not know anything about it. But I like it. I wear it for good luck."

Frank nodded absently and studied the amulet for another long minute. Elizabeth found it odd that he was so interested in her charm.

Frank seemed to read her thoughts. He let the amulet fall back against her chest and smiled at her.

"I am curious about it," he said, indicating the amulet, "because it belongs to you. I only hope that this good-luck charm has enough power to keep you safe. Someday you might need a real protector. The world is full of danger, Elizabeth."

His eyes were shining as he said this, and Elizabeth's heart swelled at his words.

He is talking about himself, she thought happily. He wants to protect me. Could it be true? Could he really be falling in love with me?

They strolled silently back to the house, arm in arm. Occasionally Elizabeth glanced at his face and found him watching her, a warm smile lighting up his face.

"That dog followed me all the way to Boston!" Frank said, and all the Fiers laughed. Elizabeth and her family were sitting around the supper table while Frank told them about his adventures. Elizabeth watched the rapt faces of her parents as they listened to Frank's stories.

They like him, she thought happily. She wanted them to approve of him. She had an idea in the back of her mind that they wanted her to marry someone with property and money—and Frank was penniless.

But character is more important than money, Elizabeth told herself. Surely Mother and Father can see that.

"You are not much older than I am," Simon said wistfully, "but you have seen and done so much."

Simon envies him, Elizabeth thought, suppressing a smile. She could not help being pleased at seeing her older brother humbled a bit. As the eldest Fier and the only boy, Simon sometimes acted as if he were a prince.

"Do not envy me, Simon," Frank said. "If I still had a wonderful family like yours, I would never have left home."

Frank's eyes paused on Elizabeth, and she smiled at him.

"What exactly happened to your family, Frank?" Mrs. Fier asked. "You have not told us."

Frank set his fork and knife on his plate and wiped his mouth with his napkin. The Fiers watched him, waiting to hear the tragic story he would tell.

"My family died mysteriously," Frank began. "One by one. First my parents, then each of my brothers, until only I, the youngest, was left. They showed no sign of sickness, just died very suddenly, one at a time."

Mrs. Fier clucked her tongue, and Mr. Fier slowly shook his head.

"Each time someone died we called the doctor, but he never knew what had happened. No one understood it. All doctors were at a complete loss."

Frank paused and took a breath. "At any rate, the day came when I was the last Goode left. I was twelve years old. No one wanted to take me in, for fear they would catch whatever it was my family had. So I went off on my own. To this day, I wonder why I alone was spared. I am still waiting for the curse to come and strike me dead."

Elizabeth felt her eyes fill with tears. My poor Frank, she thought. She wished she could reach across the table to comfort him, but she knew her mother would think her too forward.

She glanced at her sister Kate. Kate's eyes, too, were shining with tears. Her face glowed as she listened to Frank, hanging on his every word.

Kate's expression made Elizabeth suddenly feel uncomfortable. Why was Kate gazing at Frank that way?

Elizabeth did not want to think about it, so she turned away. Soon she forgot about it, caught up in the story of Frank's first night alone.

After supper the family gathered in the parlor. Mrs. Fier sat at the piano and played. Simon and Frank began a game of chess. Elizabeth picked up her knitting needles, and Kate focused on her needlepoint.

The fire crackled and sputtered; the gaslights hissed; the clock ticked on the mantel.

Elizabeth could not concentrate on the scarf she was knitting. She glanced over at Simon and Frank to be sure they were not paying attention to her. Then she leaned across the couch toward Kate.

"I like Frank very much," she confided to her sister in a whisper. "Don't you?"

Kate glanced up from her work, her eyes startled and wide. Her hands fidgeted nervously.

"Of course I like him," she whispered back. "We all do. Why are you asking me this?"

"I was just making conversation," whispered Elizabeth.

Kate seemed to be embarrassed as if she had been caught in a lie. She put down her needlepoint and left the room, her full skirts rustling as she walked.

Frank glanced up from the chess game when Kate left the room. He forced himself not to look at Elizabeth. Instead, he turned his head toward the fire so she would not see the smirk on his face.

This is going to be easier than I imagined, he thought with satisfaction.

"Your move, Frank," said Simon.

Frank tried to concentrate on the game. He could

not let Simon beat him, not the first game. He would let Simon take the third one, maybe.

Simon was staring at the chess pieces with total concentration. A lock of black hair hung over his forehead.

He is just a boy, Frank thought. He does not understand what is happening.

My plan is working, Simon, Frank told him in his mind. Your family likes me better with every passing day. Even you enjoy my company, do you not, Simon?

I am winning your trust, all of you. Soon you will believe anything I say.

As soon as I have that perfect trust, I will act.

I watched my brothers die, one by one. You will soon know what that feels like, Simon.

I will become your sisters' only hope. Then I will watch them die, one by one.

Frank slid his queen across the board. "Checkmate," he said, grinning.

CHAPTER 22

"Put that watering can down."

Elizabeth glanced up from her garden, startled by the sound of a deep, booming voice. Then she broke into a laugh. It was only Frank, teasing her.

"It has not rained all week," she protested. "My flowers are thirsty." She straightened her straw bonnet and continued watering the garden.

Frank stepped closer to her. "All right, water them," he teased. "I will go for a walk in the woods by myself."

She pouted. "I am almost finished. There." She set the watering can down. "Let me come with you. I would not want you to get lost."

She took off her sunbonnet and left it on the grass. Her hair was tied back with a red satin ribbon. Frank took her hand and they started off through the woods.

Every day, when the weather was fair, Frank and Elizabeth walked through the woods to the clearing with the two flat rocks. Elizabeth looked forward to their walks more and more. No one else in the family knew about them.

I am not keeping our walks a secret, exactly, Elizabeth thought. I just have not mentioned them.

Elizabeth knew that her mother would want to come on the walks—but that would ruin them. They would not be the same with her mother—not at all.

Anyway, Frank has never done anything improper, she thought. I have no reason to worry.

Now they had reached the clearing. Elizabeth sat down on her rock, the smaller one. But instead of sitting on his rock, Frank lingered behind her.

Elizabeth felt a gentle tug on her hair, and then felt it fall loose about her shoulders. She sighed. Frank had untied the ribbon from her hair.

She leaned back against him. Frank playfully draped the red ribbon across her throat. She giggled. He tugged on it lightly. She giggled again.

Then Elizabeth sat still, quivering with excitement, waiting to see what would happen next.

Behind her, just out of her sight, Frank held the two ends of the ribbon in his hands.

He wound each end around his index fingers.

Elizabeth sat in front of him, trusting her fate to him, completely in his power.

He smiled.

Then he tugged on the ribbon, preparing to strangle her.

CHAPTER 23

A twig cracked nearby. Frank froze.

Elizabeth's body tensed.

She heard the snap of another twig. Then the shuffle of someone moving through pine needles.

Someone was close by.

The ribbon fell from Frank's hand.

Elizabeth climbed to her feet and clutched at his arm, her eyes scanning the woods.

The shuffling noise moved closer. Then Elizabeth saw a stooped figure walking slowly and steadily their way.

A white-haired old woman, dressed all in black, hobbled through the pine needles, a cane poking the ground in front of her.

Elizabeth gasped. "Aggie!"

She grabbed Frank's hand and pulled him through the woods, back toward the house. She did not look back, and she did not stop until they were safely in her yard.

"That was the old woman," Elizabeth said, panting. "Old Aggie. She is still alive!"

"She appeared to be a harmless old woman," Frank told her.

"No, she is not!" Elizabeth cried breathlessly. "Somehow I know she is *not* just a harmless old woman. There is something different about her . . ."

Frank took Elizabeth in his arms and held her tight. She closed her eyes and rested her head against his chest, catching her breath.

She felt safe now. I will always feel safe with Frank, she thought.

Calm at last, she lifted her head and smiled. "It is too bad Old Aggie came along," she whispered. "She spoiled such a lovely afternoon."

Frank hesitated a second, then smiled.

He is embarrassed, Elizabeth thought fondly. He was going to kiss me. He was going to ask me to marry him, and he wanted to surprise me. But now he knows that I know.

Oh, well, she thought as she and Frank started back toward the house. He will ask me soon. And I will not disappoint him. I plan to say yes.

Elizabeth opened the back door, and she and Frank

stepped into the kitchen. They found Kate stirring a pot of soup.

Kate glanced at her sister and Frank when they walked in. Elizabeth smiled at her and said, "How is the soup coming?"

Kate did not answer. Her mouth fell open, but no sound came out. She dropped the soup spoon and ran from the room.

Elizabeth stared after her, shocked. She suddenly felt aware of her hair hanging loose about her shoulders. She turned to Frank, who had a strange, thoughtful expression on his face.

"What could be the matter?" Elizabeth asked him. "Do you think Kate is all right?"

"I am sure she is fine," Frank replied. "Perhaps she burned her hand on the pot."

"I had better make sure she is not hurt," said Elizabeth. She started to follow Kate, but Frank caught her by the wrist and held her back.

"Do not worry about her," he said. "Your mother is upstairs. I am sure she is taking care of Kate."

"I suppose you are right," Elizabeth said doubtfully. She felt she should go after her sister, but Frank seemed to want her to stay with him.

The soup began to boil. Elizabeth picked up the spoon to stir it.

I cannot go running after Kate, she reasoned as she

felt Frank run his hand through her hair. Someone has to stay here to watch the soup, after all. If it boils over, we will not have any supper tonight, and I am sure Kate does not want that.

A few weeks later Elizabeth paced the house impatiently, searching for Frank.

Where *is* he? she wondered. It was time for their walk, and she could not find him anywhere. She sighed and sat down on a chair in the parlor and picked up her knitting.

I might as well work on Kate's scarf while I am waiting for him, she thought. I might as well make myself useful, as Mother would say.

The back door slammed. Here he is at last, she thought.

She stood up, waiting to greet him. But it was not Frank who burst into the parlor. It was Kate.

Kate's face was flushed, and she carried a basket of mulberries in her arms.

"Oh, Elizabeth!" she cried, letting the basket fall to the floor. She ran to her sister and threw her arms around her neck. "The most wonderful thing has happened!"

"What on earth is it?" asked Elizabeth. She had never seen Kate so excited.

"You will be so happy for me!" Kate gushed. She took Elizabeth's hands in hers, knitting and all, and danced her around the room. "Mother will play the organ, and you can decorate the cake!"

"The cake?" asked Elizabeth. "Kate, what are you *talking* about?"

"Haven't you guessed by now?" cried Kate. "Frank and I are going to be married!"

CHAPTER 24

"Married!" Elizabeth uttered, unable to hide her shock. "You—and Frank?"

"What is all the commotion in there?" Simon and Mr. Fier came hurrying in from the front porch, and Mrs. Fier appeared on the stairs. "What is going on, girls?"

Elizabeth stood frozen in place, trying to stop her knees from shaking, while she watched Kate run into their mother's arms. "Mother! Frank has asked me to marry him!"

Elizabeth stood aside to watch the happy uproar that followed this announcement. Mrs. Fier's kind face lit up, and Mr. Fier clapped his hands delightedly.

Finally Elizabeth could not help herself. She could not keep the words from bursting from her lips. "It cannot be!" she cried in a trembling voice. "Frank loves *me*!"

No one seemed to hear her.

Simon asked, "Where is Frank? I want to congratulate him."

How can this be? thought Elizabeth. Is this really happening? Kate and Frank?

She wanted to scream. She wanted to fly out of the room. She wanted to disappear forever.

How can this be? *How can this be?*

She uttered a sob of grief, of anger, of disbelief.

Kate and Frank?

Elizabeth remembered just then all the times that Kate had acted strangely around her and Frank. When Elizabeth told Kate that she liked Frank, and when Elizabeth and Frank had come in from the woods and found Kate stirring soup. Kate had seemed upset those times. Now it all made sense.

Kate had loved Frank all along.

And Kate had *stolen* Frank from her!

"How *could* you?" Elizabeth shrieked at the top of her lungs.

Her new outburst made everyone fall silent, and they all turned to stare at Elizabeth.

"How *could* you?" she raged at Kate again. "My own sister!"

"What?" Kate gaped at her, bewildered. "Lizzie—what are you talking about?"

"I—I—I—"

Elizabeth found herself speechless now.

Afraid of the intense anger she felt, afraid she might explode from rage, she tightened her fists around the knitting needles and ran from the room.

I must find Frank! I must find Frank! she told herself as violent sobs escaped from her throat.

She pushed blindly through the kitchen, out the back door, and into the woods. Behind her, she could hear Kate calling her name.

Elizabeth ignored her. Frank was all that mattered. Kate could not be trusted.

"Frank!" she screamed. "Frank!"

Her feet padded over the brown carpet of pine needles. Sharp branches tore at her skirt, but she barely noticed.

Elizabeth had almost reached the clearing when she realized she was still clutching Kate's unfinished scarf and her knitting needles. She tossed them onto the ground and kept running.

"Frank!" she called.

Far behind her, she could still hear Kate's worried call: "Elizabeth! Elizabeth!"

Simon and his parents were left standing in the parlor in a daze. None of them understood what had just happened.

Wasn't Kate's announcement a joyful one?

At last Mrs. Fier said, "Simon, run after the girls and see what this is all about."

Simon nodded and started after his sisters. He heard voices ringing through the woods. They were his sisters' voices.

No sign of Frank. Simon could not help wondering where Frank was all this time.

He tried to follow the voices, but they seemed to come from all directions in the thick woods, like birdcalls.

Then, suddenly, there was a bloodcurdling scream.

Simon froze. The woods fell silent.

Silent as death.

What was that? Where had it come from?

He ran in the direction of the scream. Soon he found himself in a clearing. He recognized it as the place where he and his sisters had played as children.

Simon's eyes frantically searched the clearing.

Who screamed? Why?

Behind the bigger of the two rocks he saw something dark. Simon squinted hard until it came into focus.

A pair of dainty black high-button boots.

He took a step closer, his heart beating wildly. The ground seemed to tilt under him.

Taking a deep breath, Simon peered behind the rock.

"Ohh." He gripped the top of the rock as his eyes landed on Kate's body. She lay sprawled on her back, her light brown hair spread out around her head like a halo.

Her pale blue eyes were open, reflecting the sky.

Simon gripped the rock till his hand hurt. "Kate?"

She did not answer. She stared up lifelessly, a knitting needle plunged through her heart.

CHAPTER 25

Elizabeth sat in the rocking chair by the fireplace. Her hair fell in tangles down her back. Her eyes, red-rimmed and bloodshot, stared out from her tear-stained face. She rocked back and forth, back and forth, hugging her knees under her torn blue dress.

"Kate was a liar," Elizabeth murmured, rocking. "Kate was a liar. Kate was a liar."

Mrs. Fier stood over the rocking chair, helplessly wringing her hands. Mr. Fier stared at his daughter in horror and disbelief.

Frank sat tensely on the couch, his eyes darting from face to face. Simon paced the room, lost in his own unhappy thoughts, not seeing anyone.

"Kate was a liar," Elizabeth murmured. "Frank did not love Kate. Frank loves Elizabeth."

She lifted her head to search for Frank. Her eyes met the horrified stares of her parents instead.

"Why are you staring at me that way!" she screamed. "I did not kill her! I swear it!"

Her mother and father said nothing. Elizabeth rocked again.

They do not believe me, she thought bitterly. It is written all over their faces. They think I killed my own sister. They think I stabbed Kate with a knitting needle.

Frank was at her side now, kneeling beside the rocking chair. He took her warm, sticky hand in his. His hands were so cool, so calm and soothing.

"Elizabeth is the gentlest creature I know," Frank said to her parents. "She could never kill anyone."

Still her parents said nothing. Her mother's face was twisted in grief, fear, and confusion.

Elizabeth focused on Frank only.

Frank's handsome face was calming. He gave her a tiny, encouraging smile. At once she felt better.

I would be all alone in the world without Frank, she thought.

Then she said to her family, "Frank believes in me. He knows I am innocent. Why don't *you* believe me?"

No one said a word, but Elizabeth could see it on their

faces. They blame me for Kate's death, she thought. They blame me *and* Frank.

Mr. Fier stormed out of the room. Mrs. Fier hurried after him. Then Simon, too, strode out, disgust registered on his face.

Elizabeth dissolved into tears and continued to rock back and forth, back and forth, crying.

"Hush," Frank whispered. "Hush, Elizabeth. Forget about them. There is nothing you can do to make them believe you."

He gave her a white handkerchief. She dried her eyes. "My own family," she whispered. "They will never believe me. They will never speak to me again, I suppose."

"You are too hard on them," Frank said. "They do not want to accept the truth. They *cannot* accept it. That is why they will not believe you."

Now he took both of her hands in his. "But I believe in you, Elizabeth. I always will."

She stopped rocking and smiled at him gratefully.

"It is hard for a mother and father to imagine their own child killing herself," Frank went on. "But I know that is what happened. Kate killed herself. Your parents did not see it, Simon did not see it, but you and I could see it. Kate was going mad."

Elizabeth nodded. All that strange behavior. It was the only logical explanation.

"Kate was jealous of you," Frank said. "You know I never told Kate I would marry her. How could I? I am in love with you."

He kissed her hands. Elizabeth drank in every word he said.

"Kate made it up," said Frank. "She made up that whole story about our engagement. She ran right to you to tell you first. I think she really believed it was true. She was mad, truly mad, the poor girl."

"Poor Kate," Elizabeth whispered.

"She was capable of anything," said Frank. "No one could help her."

Elizabeth knew he was right. She sighed and started rocking again. "Frank, I cannot stay here. They all hate me." She gestured toward the second floor, where her parents and Simon had gone. "I must get away."

"I know what to do," Frank said. "We can run away together. We shall elope."

He gently took her chin in his hand and turned her face toward his. "Elizabeth Fier, will you marry me?"

They were the most wonderful words Elizabeth had ever heard. She felt a little of her old spirit come back.

"Yes," she said, throwing her arms around Frank's neck. "Yes. We will leave tonight."

Elizabeth's touch gave Frank a cold chill, but he did not let it show.

Yes, he thought to himself. We shall elope. We shall leave this house tonight, Elizabeth and I.

But only one of us will return. And it will not be Elizabeth.

This trusting girl will pack up all her belongings, he thought gleefully, and follow me wherever I go. I will take her into the woods to kill her, just as I killed her sister.

Kate's face was so wonderfully surprised at the end, he thought. When she saw me coming, she smiled. She opened her arms to me. Even when I raised the knitting needle over my head, she did not understand. She had no idea what was happening—not until the very last second.

Then she understood it all. It came to her in a flash.

The horror of betrayal.

The Fiers need to learn what that feels like. They will all know soon enough.

CHAPTER 26

Simon paced the house as if in a daze, weighted down with grief and sadness, his mind whirring with thoughts of Kate's death.

His parents were locked in their room. Through the door he could hear his father's heavy boots on the floor, his mother weeping and wailing for her daughters.

Elizabeth, too, was shut in her room. Simon put his ear to her door. He heard her scurrying around.

What could she be doing? he wondered. He was afraid she had lost her mind.

Evening fell. No one prepared supper, no one thought of eating. Simon's grief gave way to uneasy restlessness.

I *have* to get out of this house, he thought, or I will go mad!

The sky was still hovering over the trees as Simon made his way out of the house, but once in the woods the darkness surprised him. It was midsummer, and the leaves were at their thickest. They blocked out most all of the fading sunlight.

Simon found the woods unusually still. The daytime animals had already hidden away for the night. The nocturnal creatures had not yet crept out of their dens to hunt.

Simon walked on, deeper and deeper into the woods. All he wanted was to put his house and family behind him.

He found himself at the clearing with the two flat stones. The woods were almost completely dark now. Simon sat on the bigger stone, the one that had once been his throne. He patted the smaller stone beside it. That had been Kate's.

Kate was dead now.

Kate is dead.

He realized he could not escape from his grief.

Simon peered through the darkness, staring at the spot where he had found Kate's body. A cold chill ran down his back as the ugly sight returned to him: Kate's eyes, so glassy, so empty. The needle poking out of her chest. The blood had spread across the front of her dress.

The blood had spread like evil, Simon thought. And now there is evil everywhere. It lives inside my family's house, right now. Evil lives inside Elizabeth and Frank. It lives in these woods, in the air around me.

He took a big gulp of air, then exhaled.

It lives inside me, too, he thought. I feel it. There is evil living inside me.

Then the deep silence of the woods was broken. Simon heard a noise. The snap of a twig, somewhere nearby.

Simon froze. He listened.

Was it an animal? A deer?

Snap. The noise was behind him.

How had it moved so quickly, so quietly?

Simon wanted to turn, to look. But he was paralyzed with fear.

Something grabbed him from behind.

A claw!

Pain shot through his shoulder. The claw dug deeper.

Simon turned at last. He took one look at his attacker, and the blood drained from his face. He screamed.

CHAPTER 27

Old Aggie!

Simon felt the blood throb at his temples. He had never seen the old woman so close up.

Her face was hidden by a black hood. In one wrinkled hand she held the cane she always carried. The fingers of the other hand were covered with rings. They dug into Simon's shoulder. Aggie was so stooped that her head was even with Simon's as he sat before her.

Simon tried to stand.

But with one wrinkled hand, the old woman held him in place. The pain in Simon's shoulder deepened.

"Do not go," she commanded in a gravelly voice.

Shaking, Simon tried to calm down. It is only an old woman, he told himself. Only an old woman.

"S-sorry I screamed like that. You startled me," he stammered.

Old Aggie slowly let go of his shoulder. Simon felt her long fingernails pull out of his skin.

She held out her bony, jeweled hand. "Give me your hand," she croaked.

Simon hesitated. He saw her black eyes glowing like coal under her hood.

"Your hand," she repeated in her deep, raspy voice.

Simon obeyed. He offered her his trembling hand.

She took it firmly in her own and bent close to his palm, her long, crooked nose almost grazing his hand.

Finally she released his hand and trained her eyes on his face. Simon's heart pounded as he waited to see what would happen next.

The children said she would kill us and eat our hearts, he thought, remembering his childhood fears of Old Aggie.

But that had to be a foolish childhood tale.

Aggie cleared her throat. "Hear me, Simon Fier, and hear me well."

How does she know my name? Simon wondered. He did not dare to ask her.

"You have allowed a man named Franklin Goode into your home. Am I right?" croaked Old Aggie.

Simon nodded.

"That was foolish of you. He will destroy you all. You must stop him."

Simon swallowed.

Old Aggie continued. "Franklin Goode killed your sister Kate. At this very moment he plots the death of Elizabeth."

Simon was shaken. Could the old woman be speaking the truth?

"Fier," Old Aggie murmured. "Fier. Fier. A terrible name. A cursed name."

"What do you mean?" Simon demanded. "Why do you say that, old woman?"

"Your fate lies in your name," Old Aggie replied, her face hidden in the darkness of her hood. "The letters in your name—they can be rearranged to spell *fire.* Fier. Fire. Fier. Fire." She repeated the two words several times in her croaking voice, chanting them to sound like curses.

"I do not understand," Simon confessed.

"That is how your family will come to its end," Old Aggie rasped.

"What? How?" he demanded. "How?"

"By fire," she murmured. "Fier. Fire. You shall meet your end by fire."

Simon gasped as Old Aggie pointed a long, terrible finger in his face. "You are under a curse!" she cried. "A curse cast by the Goodes, and by your own evil history. Now you have allowed a Goode into your home, into your family. Your suffering will know no end, Simon Fier."

"But wh-what can I do?" Simon choked out in a shrill, tight voice. "What?"

The old woman reached into the folds of her long black robe and pulled out a small silver dagger, its handle studded with dark rubies.

"Take this dagger," she whispered. "Its tip is poisoned. You have only to scratch the skin of your enemy with it, and he will die."

Simon took the dagger from her with a trembling hand.

"Be careful," she warned him. "The dagger will only work once. Do not waste the poison."

"I—I will not," Simon promised, gazing at the dagger as if it were alive.

Old Aggie nodded. "Go now. Hurry, before it is too late."

Simon jumped up and began to run through the dark woods.

When he glanced back at the clearing, the old woman had disappeared.

Had she told him the truth?

Was the rest of his family in danger? In danger from Frank Goode?

Or was the old woman as crazy as the children always claimed?

A yellow glow led him back to his house. He emerged from the woods and saw the kitchen ablaze with light. The rest of the house was in darkness.

Simon burst into the kitchen doorway and stopped.

He stared down and saw his mother sprawled in a dark puddle of blood on the floor.

Simon's father was slumped over the kitchen table. Bright red blood had flowed from a wound in his side and lay pooled on the floor.

"Simon!"

Elizabeth's voice.

Simon raised his eyes from the horrifying sight of his murdered parents.

Elizabeth was cowering in a corner by the hearth. Frank Goode stood before her, an ax raised over her head.

The ax that he had used to murder Simon's parents.

The blade was stained bloodred in the firelight.

Simon cried out as Frank let the ax fall.

CHAPTER 28

Simon tried to cry out, but the sound caught in his throat.

Elizabeth uttered a high-pitched howl.

The ax blade made a whistling, slicing sound as it fell.

It grazed Elizabeth's head, chopping off a clump of her hair.

As she began to sob, Frank tossed his head back and laughed.

"Just teasing you, Elizabeth," he said. "But the next one is for real."

Elizabeth pressed herself against the wall and panted. Without realizing it, she had wrapped her hand around the pendant she had found in the garden.

Frank turned to Simon and smiled.

"The Fiers nearly won," he said. "Your family nearly managed to destroy the Goodes forever. That is what your ancestors wanted, is it not? To wipe us from the face of the earth?"

Gripped with the horror of the scene he had walked in on, Simon struggled to breathe. The last trickles of his father's blood onto the floor roared like a rushing waterfall in Simon's ears.

Frank took a step toward him.

"In the end, though," Frank continued slowly, calmly, "the Goodes will survive. I am the last of my family—but that is enough. I have served my ancestors well. I have lived to destroy the Fiers."

He took another step toward Simon, the ax blade red and gleaming in the firelight.

Simon's trembling hand squeezed the handle of the silver dagger, hidden under his coat. He hoped Old Aggie had been telling the truth about the dagger's power.

Frank hoisted the ax high. With a loud grunt, he swung the ax down toward Simon's head.

Elizabeth's scream pierced the air.

Simon ducked out of the way as the ax blade dug deeply into the tabletop.

Simon had the advantage and drew the dagger from under his coat, lunged forward, and scratched the blade across Frank's arm.

A tiny red line, as thin as a hair, appeared along

Frank's forearm. He stared at it, then at Simon. He burst out laughing.

"Is that how you hope to stop me, Simon?" he cried. "With a scratch from a dagger?"

Simon stood panting, his chest heaving.

Frank laughed.

With every sound Frank uttered, Simon felt his heart grow colder. He raged with hate for Frank and for every Goode who had ever lived.

Frank turned back to Elizabeth. "If you are going to fight me, Simon, I will have to take care of your little sister first," he said.

Elizabeth had darted away from the corner. But there was nowhere for her to run.

Frank easily pulled the ax blade from the tabletop and took a step toward Elizabeth. Then another.

"Simon—*help me!*" Elizabeth cried. *"Help me!"*

Frank took another step toward her. He started to raise the ax.

The old woman's magic—it hadn't worked! Simon realized.

I am not strong enough to pull the ax from Frank's grip. I am not strong enough to fight him.

I foolishly counted on Old Aggie's magic.

And now Elizabeth and I are going to die.

Across the room Frank uttered a triumphant roar as he moved in on Elizabeth, his ax blade raised high.

CHAPTER 29

"Simon—*stop him!*"

Elizabeth's terrified cry rang in Simon's ears.

He started to leap at Frank, hoping to pull him down from behind.

But Simon stopped halfway across the kitchen.

And stared in amazement as the ax fell from Frank's hand, ringing against the stone hearth.

Frank's eyes rolled back in his head. He uttered a startled cry and crumpled to the floor.

Elizabeth's eyes flew open. Her entire body was trembling.

Simon bent over Frank's body and examined him.

Dead. Frank was dead. The poison had worked.

Simon ran to comfort his sister. He wrapped his arms

around her and held her until she stopped shaking. "We are safe now," he whispered. "We are both safe."

Elizabeth nodded, crying softly, and buried her head in his chest.

Simon gazed over her shoulder at the gruesome scene in the kitchen. His mother and father lay in congealing pools of blood.

They had always been kind, good people, Simon knew. They were kind and took in a starving drifter—and he murdered them in return.

Kate had never harmed anyone in her life. And she had been brutally, coldly murdered, too.

Goodness is weakness, Simon told himself. That is clear to me now.

Goodness is weakness.

Only evil can fight evil.

Elizabeth and I will leave this house, he decided, holding his sister, letting her cry. This house holds only memories of horror for me.

Elizabeth's tears slowed. "Simon," she said, "you saved my life." She touched the silver amulet again. "We are orphans now. You and I are the only ones left alive. I—I cannot help feeling that this amulet had something to do with saving us."

The silver disk flashed in the firelight. The deep blue stones glowed like human eyes.

Elizabeth pulled the pendant over her head. She gazed at it, then held it out to Simon.

"I want you to have it," she said. "Please—take it. Its power saved me. From now on, that power must be yours."

Simon bent forward, and Elizabeth slid the silver chain over his head.

Immediately he felt warm. He closed his eyes, but instead of darkness he saw flames, hot red fire.

The flames faded quickly, and then Simon saw only Elizabeth's tear-stained face, watching him.

He led his sister away from the scene of horror, out of the kitchen, into the cool night air. He thought of the flames, and Old Aggie's words echoed in his mind.

"The letters in your name spell fire—and that is how your family will come to its end. By fire."

I will not let it happen, Simon thought grimly as he and Elizabeth stared at the full moon rising. Old Aggie's prediction will not come true.

I have the power to stop it. I can change the future.

The last Goode is dead, he thought with satisfaction. The feud is over now. The curse has been erased. All except for the fire, the fire in my name . . .

The amulet burned against his chest as he thought about the fire, the letters in his name. And then, suddenly, he knew—he knew exactly what he had to do.

It is simple, he thought. I will change my name.

I will change the letters, so that they will no longer spell *fire.* That will end the curse once and for all.

Elizabeth gripped his hand tightly. She is still afraid, he thought sadly. She does not understand that there is no need to be afraid anymore.

There are no more Goodes. No more feud. No more curse. We are safe. This time, it really is over.

I am the one who can beat the ancient curse. I am powerful. I will change the future, beginning with my name.

I am no longer Simon Fier.

Now and forever I will be known as *Simon FEAR.*

The Burning

THE FIER FAMILY TREE

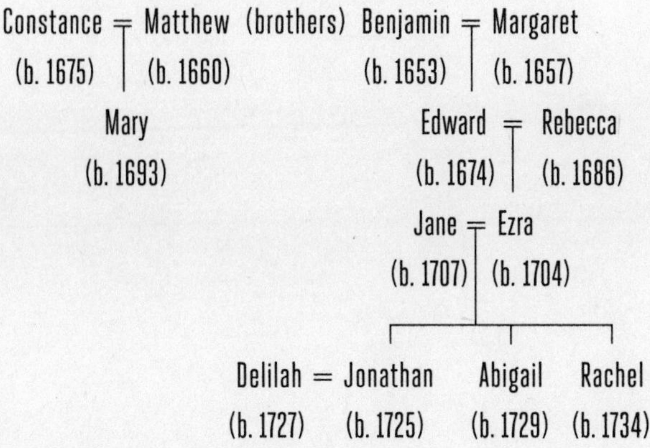
Constance = Matthew (brothers) Benjamin = Margaret
(b. 1675) (b. 1660) (b. 1653) (b. 1657)
Mary
(b. 1693)
Edward = Rebecca
(b. 1674) (b. 1686)
Jane = Ezra
(b. 1707) (b. 1704)
Delilah = Jonathan Abigail Rachel
(b. 1727) (b. 1725) (b. 1729) (b. 1734)

(100-Year Break)

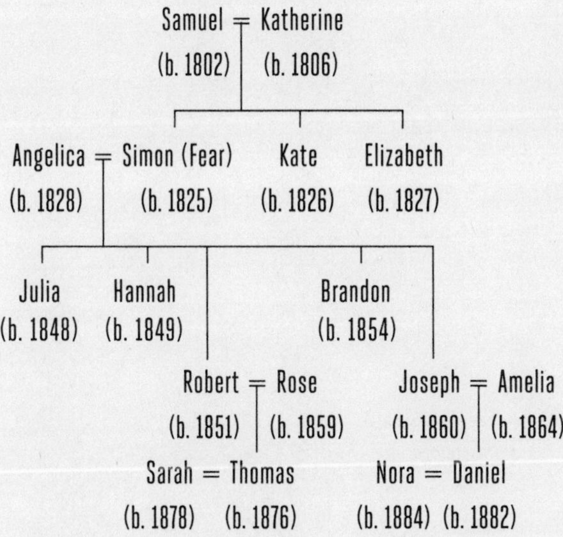
Samuel = Katherine
(b. 1802) (b. 1806)
Angelica = Simon (Fear) Kate Elizabeth
(b. 1828) (b. 1825) (b. 1826) (b. 1827)
Julia Hannah Brandon
(b. 1848) (b. 1849) (b. 1854)
Robert = Rose Joseph = Amelia
(b. 1851) (b. 1859) (b. 1860) (b. 1864)
Sarah = Thomas Nora = Daniel
(b. 1878) (b. 1876) (b. 1884) (b. 1882)

Village of Shadyside

1900

The candle flickered low. Candle wax puddled on the narrow wooden tabletop.

Nora Goode set down her pen and stretched. Her shoulders ached. She rubbed her tired eyes.

Shadows cast by the single candle danced around the small room. Nora raised her eyes to the small window. Pale gray light seeped in between the bars.

The first light of morning, Nora thought. She felt a stab of panic in her chest.

The first light of morning, and I still have so much to write.

She flexed her aching fingers, then picked up the pen. "I must finish my story before they come for me," she murmured.

The story of the two families—the Fears and the

Goodes. The story of the evil curse that followed them through time.

So much to tell.

She had been writing all night, but she knew she had to continue. Nora swept her dark hair back over her shoulders. Then gave a start.

What was that darting shadow against the wall?

Nora turned to see a scrawny rat scamper across the bare floorboards toward her feet.

Ignore it, she told herself. Do not be distracted, Nora. This story is too important.

It must be told. It must be written.

If I do not finish the story of the Fears, no one will know how to stop the evil. Then the horrors will continue forever.

Nora hunched over the table and started to write again. I must now tell the story of Simon Fear, she decided.

To try to avoid the family curse, Simon changed his name from Fier to Fear. As a young man of twenty-one, he moved to New Orleans to seek his fortune.

Nora shook her head bitterly. Did Simon really believe he could leave two hundred years of evil behind him?

Ignoring the scratching of the rat, ignoring the sputtering of the dying candle, Nora dipped her pen in the inkwell and continued to write. . . .

PART ONE

New Orleans, Louisiana

1845

CHAPTER 1

Simon Fear stopped in front of the white picket fence that stretched the length of the sprawling white mansion. Through the enormous front window he could see the partygoers in fancy dress.

It was brighter than day inside the ballroom. The light from the window swept over the front lawn. Horse-drawn carriages waited in line by the entrance to let off their passengers. A row of servants in uniform stood ready to assist them.

Simon hesitated. He pulled at the cuffs of his jacket. The sleeves were too short. His shirt cuffs were frayed. He had no ruffles on his shirtfront.

These are the wealthiest society people in New Orleans, he told himself, watching a woman in a full, three-tiered pink ball gown enter the white-columned mansion. Do I really have the nerve to enter this party without an invitation?

The answer, of course, was *yes.*

Before dressing for the party, Simon had made a mental list of his assets:

I am good-looking.

I can be very charming and witty if I desire to be.

I am as smart as anyone in New Orleans.

I am determined to do anything it takes to be a success.

Taking a deep breath, Simon straightened his black cape with the purple satin lining and strode up to the gate, his eyes on the entrance.

I am sure that Mr. Henry Pierce and his charming daughter, Angelica, would have invited me to their debutante ball if they had known me, Simon told himself.

Well, tonight I will give them a chance to get to know me.

And I will take this opportunity to introduce myself to as many wealthy young ladies as I can. After tonight I will not have to sneak into parties. The invitations will pour in.

Simon stopped at the gate. From inside the open double doors he could hear laughter, the clink of glasses, and the soft music of a string quartet.

These sounds were being repeated all over the town. It was Mardi Gras, and all of New Orleans was celebrating with masked balls, debutante parties, and wild, noisy street parades.

The fancy-dress ball Henry Pierce was throwing for his daughter, Angelica, was the most exclusive party of them all, which was why Simon had selected it.

But now, gazing at the line of servants that blocked his way to the entrance, Simon began to lose confidence.

Can I really get past them? he wondered, pulling nervously at his jacket cuffs. Have I come this far only to be turned away?

No. I cannot deprive the beautiful and wealthy young women of my company.

Without any further hesitation Simon swept his cape behind him and moved through the gate and up the wide stairs.

"I beg your pardon, sir." A white-haired servant wearing a tailcoat over old-fashioned knee breeches and a red satin waistcoat stepped forward, his hand outstretched. "May I see your invitation?"

"My invitation?" Simon smiled at the servant, his dark eyes flashing in the bright gaslight. "Why, yes, of course," he said, stalling for time.

Reaching into his coat pocket, Simon dipped his head and deliberately caused his black top hat to fall off. The hat bounced onto the wide porch.

Pretending to reach for it, Simon kicked it toward the door.

"Allow me to get that for you, sir," the servant said, moving quickly toward the hat.

But Simon was quicker. He scooped up the hat by its brim, then threw his arm around the shoulders of a smartly dressed gentleman just entering the house.

"Why, George, old fellow! How good to see you again!" Simon declared loudly, keeping his arm around the man's shoulders and entering the house with him.

"Do I *know* you?" the startled man cried.

"So sorry. My mistake," Simon replied with a curt bow.

The servant stepped into the doorway to search for Simon. But he had already lost himself in the crowd.

He was breathing hard, excited by his daring entrance. His smile remained confident as he handed his cape and hat to a servant and moved into the ballroom.

Crystal chandeliers hung low from the ceiling, sending a blaze of yellow gaslight over the crowded room. The vast floor was an intricate pattern of dark and light inlaid wood. The walls were covered in brocade.

Simon studied the young women, such beautiful young women, with sausage curls framing the sides of their glowing faces. Their long hooped ball gowns swept across the shiny floor. Their voices chimed brightly. Their laughter tinkled like the clink of champagne glasses.

The men strutted about in their dark tailcoats and taper-legged trousers. Simon scoffed at their flowing white cravats and ruffled white shirts, scoffed and envied them at the same time.

It takes more than a ruffled shirt to make a gentleman, he reminded himself.

I am as much a gentleman as any of these peacocks. And some day I will have a wardrobe full of ruffled shirts, shirts to put all of these dandies to shame.

In the far corner a string quartet played Haydn. Simon started to make his way toward the center of the room, but a servant lowered a silver tray in front of him. "Champagne, sir? It arrived from France only this morning."

"No, thank you." Simon stepped past the servant, his eyes on two young women in silk ball gowns against the wall. I have more serious business here than drinking champagne, he told himself.

Turning on his most charming smile, he slicked back his dark hair, tugged at his coat cuffs, and made his way to introduce himself to the two young women.

"Good evening," he said with a polite nod of his head.

The two young women, pale and blond with sparkling blue eyes, turned briefly to stare at him. Then, without replying, they returned to their conversation.

"Wonderful party," Simon offered, standing his ground, continuing to smile.

They ignored him.

"Allow me to introduce myself," he said, refusing to give up.

They walked away without another glance at him.

Such snobs! Simon sneered. There are so few wealthy

people in this town that they all know one another. They stick together and do not allow any newcomers in. Especially newcomers with a northern accent.

The Haydn piece ended. After a brief pause the quartet began to play a reel. The room erupted excitedly as the young men and women quickly formed two long lines across the floor and began to dance.

Simon stepped into the line. He didn't know how to do this reel. But he was confident he could pick it up.

Confidence. That was the key, Simon knew. That was the key to being accepted by these wealthy New Orleans snobs.

As he picked up the rhythm of the dance, Simon attempted to catch the attention of the dark-haired girl across from him. She glanced at him briefly, then deliberately avoided him, keeping her eyes to the floor until the dance had ended.

I will triumph here eventually, Simon reminded himself. Young women will be begging me for a dance!

He made his way across the crowded, noisy room toward the central hall—and then stopped short in the doorway. A wide stairway, its banister festooned with yellow and white daisies, stretched up to his right. And standing on the bottom step, facing him as she leaned over the flowers, was the most beautiful girl Simon had ever seen.

She had black hair, lustrous in the gaslight from the chandelier above her head. Curls tumbled beside her face with clusters of flowers holding them in place. Simon could see her flashing green eyes, catlike eyes above a perfect, slender nose, dark full lips, high, aristocratic cheekbones, and the creamy white skin of her shoulders revealed above the lace-edged top of her blue ball gown.

A blue ball gown. Most of the other young women had selected pink and white and yellow. This one stood out boldly in satiny blue.

Simon moved closer, staring intently at this striking vision. He suddenly realized that his mouth was dry, his knees weak.

Is this what the poets call love at first sight? he wondered.

It was a feeling Simon had never experienced.

The young woman was still leaning against the banister, talking to another young woman, tall and frail-looking in a gown of pink satin.

Look up. Look up. Please . . . look toward me, Simon urged silently.

But the two kept chattering, seemingly unaware of Simon's existence.

I must speak to her, Simon decided.

"What is her name?" He was so smitten, so stunned by the feelings sweeping over him, that Simon didn't realize he had spoken the question aloud.

"That is Henry Pierce's daughter, Angelica," an elderly

man with a white mustache replied, eyeing Simon suspiciously. "Are you unfamiliar with our host and his family?"

"Angelica Pierce," Simon muttered, ignoring the man's question. "Thank you. Thank you so much."

Angelica Pierce, you do not know me, Simon thought, dizzy with excitement, a kind of excitement he had never felt before. But you shall. You and I are meant for each other.

I shall introduce myself now, Simon decided, his heart pounding. He straightened his tailcoat and cleared his throat.

Continuing to stare intently at Angelica Pierce, he took two steps toward the staircase.

But he was stopped by firm hands on his shoulders.

Two grim-faced young servants had blocked Simon's path. "I am sorry, sir," one of them said coldly, a sneer contradicting his polite words. "But if you haven't an invitation, we must ask you to leave."

CHAPTER 2

"President Polk? He isn't here tonight—is he? You are teasing me, are you not, Angelica?" Liza Dupree gaped openmouthed at her cousin.

Angelica laughed. "You are so gullible, Cousin Liza. What if I told you that the King of France were here? Would you believe that, too?"

Liza's cheeks reddened. "You are always teasing me, Angelica. You have such a cruel sense of humor."

"I do, *don't* I!" Angelica exclaimed, toying with a shiny black curl.

"You should have known President Polk wasn't here," Angelica told her cousin. "This party is much too exclusive. He would never get through the door!"

Both girls laughed.

"Did you see the gown Amanda Barton is wearing?" Angelica asked cattily.

"No. Is it charming and wonderful?" Liza asked.

"About as charming and wonderful as our window draperies," Angelica said with a sneer. "In fact, I believe it is made of the same fabric!"

Both girls laughed again. "I think this is the most wonderful party," Liza gushed. "I just adore—" She stopped when she saw she didn't have Angelica's attention. Angelica's gaze had flitted away for a second.

"Angelica, what did you see?"

"Who *is* that young man?" Angelica asked finally.

"Who? *Which* young man?" Liza asked.

"The one in the plain shirt and old-fashioned tailcoat," Angelica replied. "Don't allow him to see you looking. He is staring hard this way with big dark eyes."

Liza searched until she found him. "What an expression!" she declared, raising a hand to stifle her laughter. "Those brown eyes. He looks so sad and forlorn, like one of your father's hunting hounds!"

Liza expected Angelica to laugh, but she didn't. "Why is he staring at me like that?" Angelica demanded, stealing quick glances at him. "Do I know him?"

"I think I have seen his clothes on a scarecrow in one of my father's cotton fields!" Liza joked. "But I have never seen *him*!"

"He . . . he is frightening me," Angelica stammered.

Her face suddenly appeared pale. The color faded from her eyes.

"Don't let him see us stare at him. He will surely come over here," Liza warned. "Shall we go upstairs for a rest?" She knew that Angelica was fragile, not as robust as she appeared.

"No. I—*Look!"* Angelica cried.

Both girls peeked as two solemn-faced servants stepped up to the young man. There was a brief argument. Then each servant grabbed an arm and forcefully pulled the young man toward the door.

"Oh, my! Oh, my!" Angelica cried, raising her hands to her pale cheeks.

Liza placed a hand on her cousin's shoulder. "It's all right."

A few girls cried out in alarm. Angelica heard a rush of murmured questions throughout the room. The string quartet stopped playing.

"He is leaving. It is all right," Liza assured her cousin.

Angelica watched as the young man moved toward the door, taking long strides, not turning back. As soon as he had disappeared, the music started up again.

"Just an intruder," Liza said. "I wonder how he got past the servants."

Angelica's expression was thoughtful. Her emerald eyes began to sparkle again. "That young man was rather interesting," she told her cousin. "There was something about him. . . ." Her voice trailed off.

"Angelica Pierce, I am ashamed of you!" Liza protested. "How can you be so selfish?"

"Selfish?" Angelica asked, raising her long skirt as she stepped down to the carpet.

"You already have not one but *two* handsome young men eager for your attentions. James Daumier and Hamilton Scott are two of the best-looking, wealthiest young men in all of New Orleans. And they would both *die* if they knew you found that shabby intruder interesting."

Angelica sighed. "Speak of the devil," she said, rolling her eyes. "Here comes James. It must be his dance."

"Well, go!" Liza urged, giving her cousin a gentle shove. "And *smile*! This is *your* party—remember?"

Angelica forced a smile and raised her eyes to James. James grinned at her, showing off about eight hundred teeth.

Does he have to grin at me like that? Angelica wondered unhappily. I am always afraid he is going to bite me!

Most girls would probably consider James Daumier good-looking, Angelica realized. He was tall and broad shouldered and had intense silver gray eyes beneath white blond hair.

If only he wouldn't grin like a dog that's just tucked away a juicy bone! Angelica thought.

"I have been looking all over for you. Were you and your cousin Liza gossiping about me?" James teased.

"We might have been," Angelica replied coyly. She

took his arm and allowed him to lead her to the dance floor.

He danced stiffly, standing three feet in front of her, his grin frozen on his face, his silver gray eyes staring into hers. "Are the musicians going to play that new dance?" he whispered, leaning closer. "The waltz?"

Angelica gasped and narrowed her eyes coyly at James. "James Daumier!" she cried. "You *know* my father would never allow evil waltz music to be played in this house! What a scandalous thought!"

James frowned in mock disappointment. "I have heard that it is quite an enjoyable dance."

Angelica started to reply. But James turned away as another young man tapped his shoulder. Angelica immediately recognized her other young suitor, Hamilton Scott.

"I believe this is my dance," Hamilton told James with a polite nod. James made an exaggeratedly formal bow and, flashing Angelica one last grin, backed away.

Hamilton had curly red hair and a face full of freckles. Angelica thought he looked about twelve. But he was nineteen, a serious young man with strong political feelings.

While James liked to talk to Angelica about fashion and friends and the sleek thoroughbred racehorses his father raised, Hamilton lectured her on the morality of slavery and the trade policies of the French.

"I wish you could dance every dance with me," Hamilton told her.

"I do not think my feet would survive it," Angelica teased.

She spent the rest of the evening dancing with James and Hamilton. She knew she should be having the time of her life. After all, it was Mardi Gras, and after this party there would be another party, and then another. But she found her mind wandering.

Something was troubling her.

When the party had ended and the last carriage clattered off into the night, Angelica walked past the servants busily cleaning up the ballroom and stepped through the French doors into the garden.

It was a cool night, the air soft and sweet-smelling. Paper lanterns with oil lamps inside cast pale yellow light at her feet. A heavy dew made the grass glisten. Angelica bent and pulled off her satin party slippers. Holding them in one hand, she let her stockinged feet sink into the cool wet grass.

I should be thinking of James or Hamilton, she scolded herself. Then why does that intense-looking stranger keep filling my thoughts?

I am eighteen, Angelica thought. Father wishes me to marry soon. He is impatient for me to decide between James and Hamilton. He will make me marry one of them.

Do I love James? Do I love Hamilton?

I *like* them both, she told herself.

I like them both for different reasons. James for his

good looks, his charm, his mischievous sense of humor. Hamilton for his intelligence, his seriousness, his caring.

But do I *love* them? Do I want to marry either of them?

Deep in thought, gazing into the soft lantern light, listening to the rustle of the breeze through the magnolia blossoms, Angelica took a few steps into the garden.

She was too stunned to cry out when strong hands grabbed her from behind.

CHAPTER 3

Angelica gasped and spun out of her attacker's grasp.

"Do not cry out!" he whispered.

"Y-you!" Angelica stammered, her heart pounding. "Who *are* you? What are you *doing* here?"

"Do not be afraid. I will not harm you," Simon Fear whispered.

"But how did you get into my garden?" Angelica demanded, her fear turning to anger. "Who *are* you?"

"My name is Simon Fear," he told her, his dark eyes locked on hers.

Angelica bent to pick up her shoes, which in her alarm she had allowed to fall. But she kept her eyes trained warily on Simon. "You entered my party uninvited," she said, standing up. "Now you attack me in my garden. Are you a thief? Are you *mad*? What do you *want*?"

"I want you to marry me," Simon replied without hesitation. He pulled off his top hat and held it in front of him with both hands. His dark hair fluttered in the breeze.

Angelica started to reply, but only a startled laugh escaped her throat. "The answer is that you are *mad*!" she declared. "Will you turn and leave the way you came? Or do I have to call the servants to usher you out once again?"

"I saw you at your ball," Simon said, ignoring her questions, determined to tell her what was in his heart. "I saw you standing on the staircase. And I knew that I was in love with you."

"From one glance?" Angelica scoffed. "And how much champagne had you drunk, Mr. Fear?"

"Angelica, I knew at that moment," Simon continued, "that you would be my wife."

Angelica laughed again, but her laughter was tinged with fear. "Have you escaped from an asylum?" she demanded. "Are you dangerous? Can you hear a word I say?"

"You *will* be my wife, Angelica," Simon insisted, his dark eyes glowing in the lantern light.

"I am going to call for help now," Angelica told him,

shivering. The hem of her long ball gown was wet. The wet grass had chilled her feet, and the cold ran up her body. "Please—"

"I will leave," Simon offered, still holding the top hat in front of him. "I did not mean to alarm you. But I *had* to come back. I had to see you. To talk to you."

"You have said more than enough," Angelica told him dryly.

Simon replaced his hat and began running toward the back fence, the fence he had climbed to enter the garden. Halfway there he turned back to her. "You will marry me, Angelica Pierce. Mark my words!"

As he climbed the fence and vanished from the garden, her scornful laughter rang in his ears.

Simon wandered dizzily through town. The Mardi Gras parade had ended, sending hundreds of costumed revelers into the streets. Lively dance music, the *strump* of banjos, and the happy cries of fiddles and harmonicas poured from every doorway.

Torches floated by, casting a wash of eerie yellow light over the shouting, laughing faces. A group of masked partygoers rolled a barrel-size keg of beer along the side of the street. Several bare-chested men, weaving arm in arm ahead of Simon, sang a sad song at the top of their lungs.

Simon didn't see any of it.

As he made his way aimlessly through the whooping,

laughing crowds of the French Quarter, all he could see was Angelica Pierce.

Dazed and nearly delirious with happiness, he wandered until he left the noisy crowds behind. All torchlight disappeared. This old section of town was dark, lit only by the sliver of moon overhead.

Where am I? Simon asked himself, noticing for the first time the low wooden buildings, all dark and silent. I seem to have wandered down by the docks.

The darkness brought darker thoughts to his mind.

Angelica, he had seen, already had suitors. *Two* suitors, to be exact.

After he had been removed from the party, Simon had doubled back and found a hiding place in front of the house. From his vantage point he had spied into the ballroom window.

Staring into the brightness, he had watched Angelica dance. He had seen the two young men who were her partners. Simon didn't know their names, but he would make it his business to find out.

Two worthy young gentlemen, Simon thought bitterly. But I am more worthy! I may not have their money or breeding—but I shall have Angelica!

His heart still pounded with the excitement of meeting Angelica. The dark streets appeared to tilt up to meet him. The low buildings grew darker. Behind the buildings he could hear the rush of water.

The docks must be on the next block, he realized. I have wandered into an unsafe neighborhood.

Just as he had this thought, he felt a heavy arm take hold of him. He felt a sharp pain as something sharp was pressed against his throat.

CHAPTER 4

Simon tried to cry out, but the pressure against his throat made him gag. It took him a few seconds to realize it was the blade of a knife pressed against his neck.

"I'll be taking your purse," a raspy voice whispered close to his ear, so close Simon could smell the whiskey on his attacker's breath. "Or I'll be cutting your throat."

Simon croaked out a helpless protest.

"A fine gentleman like you doesn't want his throat cut," the man rasped. *"Does he?"* Then the attacker eased back the knife blade just enough to allow Simon to speak.

"I-I'll pay you," Simon managed to choke out.

I cannot die on this lonely dark street, Simon thought,

his legs trembling, his heart thudding loudly. I can't die now—I have just met Angelica.

"I have but little money," Simon said in a trembling voice. "But I will give it all to you."

"Yes, you will—and quickly!" the thief ordered. He loosened his hard grip on Simon, then gave him a hard shove in the back.

Startled, Simon cried out and stumbled to his knees on the hard cobblestones. He glanced up to see his attacker, a dark-haired young man with a red bandanna tied across his forehead. He was swaying drunkenly, squinting hard at Simon.

"What are *you* looking at?" he rasped angrily at Simon. "Your purse, or I'll cut you now!" He waved the knife.

"I-I'm getting it," Simon stammered.

As he pushed his cape out of the way, a stud fell out of his shirtfront and Simon's silver pendant dropped into view. Simon never removed the pendant since his sister Elizabeth had given it to him back home in Wickham two years before.

With its three silver claws and mysterious blue jewels, the disk-shaped pendant had been in the Fear family for generations. A strange old fortune-teller named Aggie had told him all about the pendant and its powers. But Simon had resisted using it. He had no use for evil magic.

Climbing to his feet, Simon quickly grabbed the chain and started to tuck the pendant back into his dress shirt.

But the thief had spotted it. He raised his knife menacingly, the long blade gleaming in the moonlight. "Do not try to hide the silver coin, mate," the man growled. He stretched out his free hand. "I will take it, too."

"It is not a coin," Simon protested. "It is a family memento. Worthless to anyone except me."

"Give it up!" the thief shouted impatiently.

Simon reluctantly stepped forward. Holding the silver disk tightly in one hand, he struggled to remove the slender chain from around his neck.

The silver disk felt warm in his hand and vibrated as he gripped it.

A gust of wind blew down the street, fluttering Simon's cape. He reached to hand the pendant to the thief.

But instead of dropping it, Simon suddenly shoved the disk hard into the man's face. The four dark jewels dug into his cheek.

The thief cried out, more startled than hurt.

"Hey—you *die* for that!" he cried, brandishing the knife.

Still gripping the silver pendant, Simon jumped back.

Dark blood trickled down the man's cheek from small puncture holes. With an angry snarl he came at Simon.

Simon dodged the knife.

The thief swayed, squinting hard, trying to keep his balance, cursing under his breath. He leaped forward again, forcing Simon back against a building wall.

A pleased grin slowly formed on the man's face as he realized he had Simon trapped.

He stepped forward, watching Simon's helpless attempts to move away from the wall.

And then he stopped.

A howl of pain escaped his lips. He let the knife drop to the ground and grabbed the sides of his face with both hands. "Help me! My face—it's on *fire*!" he screamed.

Even in the pale moonlight Simon could see the man's face darken, as if badly sunburned.

"Help me!" the man shrieked. "Oh, please!"

His back pressed against the wall, Simon stared in helpless horror as the man's face darkened more. Then blistered. The blisters popped open and began to seep.

The man's eyes rolled around. His hands flailed. His shrieks faded to whimpers as the blistered skin burned away.

Chunks of skin melted off, revealing gray bone underneath. Gasping in agony, the man continued to whimper until no skin remained. A gray skull, locked in a hideous grin of horror, stared pitifully at Simon.

And then the body crumpled to the ground.

His chest heaving, the blood throbbing at his temples, Simon swallowed hard, forcing back his horror at the gruesome sight.

Then he carefully slipped the chain around his neck and tucked the ancient pendant under his dress shirt.

I have used the power of the ancient amulet, he realized. The Fear family has long had powers, powers it has used for evil, powers it has used for so many generations in its battle against the Goodes.

Dominatio per malum. Those were the Latin words engraved on the back of the silver disk. *Power through evil.*

Simon had long resisted the evil power of the Fear family. He had vowed never to use the ancient power of the pendant. The Goode family had been defeated. The centuries-old feud between the Goodes and the Fears was over.

Aggie, the fortune-teller, had told Simon his family would end in fire. The family name had been Fier then. "Rearrange the letters in Fier and you've got *Fire*!" the old woman had exclaimed.

Simon was determined that this prediction would never come true.

So he had changed his name from Fier to Fear. He wore the ancient evil pendant—but never used it.

Until this dark Mardi Gras night.

Wild thoughts raced through Simon's mind as he stared down at the dead figure crumpled at his feet.

I have the powers of the Fears, he realized. I have the power to get what I want. And what do I want most in the world?

I want Angelica Pierce. Beautiful Angelica.

Two obstacles stand in my path, Simon thought

excitedly. Two obstacles—the two young men I saw dancing with her.

It shall be easy to get them out of my way, he decided, feeling the warmth of the pendant against his chest.

The two young men have wealth and breeding. But I am a Fear. And what good are wealth and breeding *if you are dead!*

Having decided on his course of action, Simon swept his cape around himself. Then, stepping over the thief's body, he started toward home, humming happily to himself.

CHAPTER 5

"I love being up so high," Angelica told her cousin. "You can see everything from here."

"You can see everyone come in," Liza agreed, peering down at the orchestra seats through the ivory-plated opera glasses. "You can spy on everyone and gossip about them—and no one can hear you!"

Angelica laughed and tried to snatch the opera glasses from her cousin. James Daumier tugged at his cravat and shook his head disapprovingly. "The opera house is a place for beautiful music. Surely you do not come here to gossip."

"Look at that scarlet cape Margaret Fletcher is wearing!" Angelica exclaimed, ignoring James's comment. "It looks like something she should wear to the Mardi Gras parade."

"The color scarlet becomes Margaret Fletcher. She should wear it always," Liza said cattily.

James turned to Angelica. She could feel his silver gray eyes studying her. "Angelica, you look beautiful tonight."

"Oh, James, you're so sweet," Angelica replied. She squeezed his hand, but her attention was on the crowd filing into their seats in the orchestra below.

James leaned close. "Maybe some day you and I shall have an opera box of our own," he whispered.

"Why, James—what on earth for?" Angelica declared. "We can always use Father's. He *hates* the opera!"

"I meant—" James started, but stopped. Out of the corner of her eye Angelica saw his face go red.

Why is James so serious tonight? she wondered. Is he getting ready to propose to me? Is that why he seems so nervous and uncomfortable? Or is his cravat too tight?

If he *does* propose to me, what will be my reply? Angelica asked herself. She pulled up her long lacy white gloves and turned back to her cousin. "Liza, who are you looking at?"

"That young man from Biloxi," Liza replied without lowering the opera glasses. "The tall one with the charming smile and those devilish blue eyes. Remember, Angelica? You promised to introduce us?"

"Do you mean Bradford Diles?" James asked Liza. "You wouldn't like him. He is not your type. He is witty and charming."

"What?" Liza's mouth dropped open in mock outrage.

James and Angelica laughed.

"I do not find your sense of humor at all amusing," Liza replied, making a sour face.

"I know you well," James continued. "You like the strong, silent type."

"I would like *you* better if you were silent!" Liza declared.

Angelica leaned over the velvet-covered railing to watch the people below. Rows of gaslights flickered brightly along the wall. The orchestra tuned up in the wide pit beneath the shimmering royal blue curtain. Dark-uniformed ushers led the lavishly dressed opera patrons to their seats.

Two weeks had passed since Angelica's ball. Two weeks of nonstop celebration and Mardi Gras parties.

One party with James, then one party with Hamilton, she thought. Then one party with both of them competing for her attention, for her smiles. James and Hamilton. Hamilton and James.

Who will it be? The question troubled Angelica, lingered in her mind like a headache that refused to go away.

On two occasions that strange, dark-eyed young man, Simon Fear, had come to call on her at her house. The first time she ordered the servants to send him away. The second time she agreed to see him—but made sure that Liza was in the room.

Simon had burst into the sitting room eagerly, a triumphant smile on his handsome face—as if being admitted to the house were an important victory for him.

He strode confidently up to Angelica, took her hand, and kissed it. Angelica heard Liza gasp, shocked by the young man's bold behavior.

The visit had been a short one since there was no adult available to chaperone. Angelica introduced Simon to her cousin. Simon greeted Liza warmly, then ignored her, rudely staring the whole while into Angelica's eyes.

As they talked of the weather and the Mardi Gras and other acceptable topics, Angelica remembered their brief but heated conversation that night in the garden.

"You will *be my wife,"* Simon had told her.

Every time the words repeated in her mind, every time she thought of his intense dark eyes and the confidence, the arrogant confidence in his voice, Angelica felt a chill of excitement—and fright.

When Simon had left, Liza tossed back her head and laughed. "What an absurd young man!" she declared scornfully. "Did you see the way he looked at you?"

"He has lovely eyes," Angelica replied.

Liza cut her laughter short, her expression suddenly serious. "Angelica, you cannot possibly be thinking about Simon Fear. Your father would have a *fit* if he knew you allowed Simon in this house! He would have the boy horsewhipped and sent back North to his home. Your father would never approve of Simon Fear—and neither should you."

Liza's words brought a smile to Angelica's face. "I do *not* approve of him," she told Liza. "I do not approve of him at all. . . ."

The orchestra stopped tuning up and fell silent. The gaslights were dimmed.

The Pierce family box was near the stage, high above the orchestra. It was the perfect place to see and be seen, which in Angelica's mind was the main reason to attend the opera.

James smiled at her. "It is about to begin. You and your cousin will have to stop gossiping for a while."

"Oh, good heavens! Look who is here!" Liza exclaimed. She handed the opera glasses to Angelica, then pointed below them.

"Who is it?" Angelica asked, raising the glasses to her eyes. "Oh!" Angelica uttered a soft cry of surprise as in the dimming light she spotted Simon Fear. He was in a seat beneath her box—staring up at her!

Realizing that her glasses were trained on him, Simon smiled wide and waved up at her.

Angelica lowered the glasses and sank back in her seat. "Such arrogance!"

Liza tossed her head. "The opera is supposed to be for society people," she said snootily.

"Who is it?" James asked Liza. "Have you found yourself another young man from Biloxi?"

"It is just someone I know," Angelica replied.

Something about Angelica's tone of voice roused James's curiosity. "Someone you know? A boy?" He leaned forward and peered down, his hands on the railing.

"James, please," Angelica whispered. "The opera is about to begin." She reached out to pull him back.

But to her surprise James rose to his feet, still leaning over the railing.

"James—what on earth—!" Angelica whispered.

James turned to her, his silver gray eyes wide in an expression of terror. His hands came off the railing. They rose stiffly in front of him, and he turned and started climbing onto the box railing.

"James—come down!" Liza shrieked. "James—get *off* there!"

James balanced awkwardly on the balcony railing for a moment, his mouth open in a silent scream. His arms began thrashing wildly at his sides. His legs trembled.

"James, you're going to *fall*!" Angelica cried.

She grabbed for him with both hands.

Too late.

Without uttering a sound, he toppled over the rail.

"James! James!" Angelica shrieked, her arms still outstretched.

She called his name again and again, not believing her

eyes. Not believing that he was gone. Not believing the empty space beside her.

And then her high-pitched screams blended in with the other startled cries and shrieks of horror that filled the darkened hall.

CHAPTER 6

Simon watched the body plunge from the box. It hit with an echoing *thud* in the aisle.

Then, as horrified screams rose up in the darkness, Simon tucked the silver pendant under his dress shirt and quickly made his way to the aisle.

A few moments later he entered the private box to find Angelica and her cousin comforting each other, their tearstained faces filled with disbelief.

Liza's shoulders heaved as she sobbed. Her face was buried in her gloved hands.

Angelica gazed up, startled to see Simon. She brushed away the tears from under her eyes.

"I am so sorry for you, Angelica," Simon said softly,

his dark eyes locked sympathetically on hers. "So sorry . . . so sorry."

"Did you—did you *see* him fall?" Angelica asked Simon. "Is James alive? I cannot bear to look."

Simon lowered his head sadly. "I am so sorry, Angelica. Your friend is dead."

"Nooooo!" Angelica uttered a wail of horror.

"He fell so far, so rapidly," Simon reported in a whisper. "I saw him land on his head. I am sure he died instantly."

Angelica shuddered and shut her eyes.

"He did *not* jump!" Simon heard Liza cry in a shrill, frightened voice. "Why would James jump? Why did he climb onto the railing?"

"If I can be of any help . . ." Simon offered Angelica, his hand placed lightly on her trembling shoulder. "Please know that you can always rely on me."

Angelica leaned against her father and allowed him to lead her into the sitting room. As they walked, she pulled off her black bonnet and tossed it onto a chair.

"It was a good funeral," Henry Pierce said in his gruff rumble of a voice. He was a burly, red-faced man with a thick black mustache, and his appearance was as gruff as his voice. "Until the horse pulling the hearse cart tossed a shoe. I cannot understand why they do not inspect these horses before a funeral starts."

"Yes, Father," Angelica replied weakly. She made her way to the long couch and sat down.

"You look very pale," her father muttered, narrowing his blue eyes as he studied her. "I wish you were stronger, Angelica."

"Yes, Father."

"You have stood up very well under this tragedy," he remarked, shaking his head sadly. He tsk-tsked, his mustache rolling up and down. "James Daumier was a fine young man."

Angelica sighed. She wished she could change her dress. The heavy black wool was hot and uncomfortable.

"Hamilton Scott will be a very suitable husband for you," Mr. Pierce said, striding to the window. "I have spoken to his father, who approves the match wholeheartedly."

"Father, please do not force me to think about marriage now. Not on the day of James's funeral," Angelica said in a quivering voice. "I feel so light-headed and fluttery. I am afraid I may swoon again."

"Save your strength, daughter. We will discuss it when you are feeling stronger." Mr. Pierce pulled back the window curtains. Bright yellow sunlight streamed into the room.

Angelica blinked, waiting for her eyes to adjust to the brightness. "Ah, Liza—here you are!" she cried, turning to the door.

Liza entered the room unsteadily, her black bonnet

still covering her head, the hem of her black dress grazing the floor. "Funerals are so sad, Angelica!" she wailed.

"The funeral of a fine young man is especially sad," Mr. Pierce agreed solemnly. "Would you girls care for tea? I shall alert the staff."

Angelica watched as her father left, her hands folded tightly in her lap. "It—it was a pretty funeral," she stammered, motioning for Liza to sit down beside her. "All those flowers."

Liza pulled off her long black gloves and let them fall to the floor. She sat down beside her cousin and put a hand gently on her arm. "How are you, Angelica?"

"I feel better now that Father has left my side," Angelica admitted, covering Liza's hand with hers. "He means well, but he cannot stop talking about Hamilton Scott."

"You mean—"

"I mean with James *dead*—" The word caught in Angelica's throat. "With James dead," she started again, "Father is urging me to accept Hamilton. Father thinks it best that Hamilton and I announce our betrothal and marry as quickly as possible."

"But do you *care* for him, Angelica?" Liza asked.

Angelica replied with a pained sigh. She squeezed her cousin's hand. "Simon has been such a comfort these past few days," Angelica offered, focusing on the window. "He has been so considerate, so understanding."

"Angelica!" Liza exclaimed, unable to conceal her disapproval. "I had no idea you were seeing Simon Fear."

"He has paid me visits," Angelica said, still avoiding her cousin's stare. "He has been very kind. I do not know why you are so suspicious of Simon, Liza. Just because he is a northerner and does not come from wealth—"

"I do not trust him. That is all," Liza replied sharply. She shifted her weight on the couch. "You avoided my question about Hamilton. How do you feel about Hamilton, Angelica? Do you care for him?"

Before Angelica could reply, the butler appeared in the sitting room doorway. "Mr. Hamilton Scott is here," he announced. "Shall I show him in, miss?"

Simon Fear leaned against the white picket fence and stared at the sprawling mansion. From his vantage point Simon could see clearly into the sitting room window.

How considerate of Mr. Pierce to pull the curtains back for me, Simon thought.

A carriage came clattering by, pulled by two handsome black horses. Simon bent and pretended to clean something off his boot. When the carriage had passed, he took his place again beside the fence.

He saw Hamilton Scott enter the room and make his way to the couch where Angelica and Liza were seated. Hamilton bowed low and kissed Angelica's hand.

How very gallant you are, Hamilton, in your boyish

way, Simon thought cruelly, feeling the three-clawed pendant heat up under his shirt.

How unfortunate for you, Hamilton, that the next funeral will be yours. And then *I* shall be the one in the sitting room, bowing low to kiss dear Angelica's hand.

CHAPTER 7

One month later Angelica was holding on to Hamilton's arm as they pushed their way through the laughing, celebrating crowd. "Wait for me! My shoe is caught in a plank!" Liza called.

Angelica called impatiently back to her cousin. "Hurry! We don't want to miss Aunt Lavinia!"

"And I want to get a good look at this paddle-wheel boat!" Hamilton declared.

Liza managed to get her shoe free from the dock and moved quickly to her cousin, holding up the hem of her long gray dress.

"Do you see Aunt Lavinia?" Angelica asked. "There are so many people here to see the boat off, it looks like Mardi Gras all over again!"

As they moved closer to the boat, Angelica could see that a red carpet had been spread down the gangplank. Smiling passengers, their arms loaded with farewell presents, stopped on deck to wave good-bye to friends and family on shore.

A brass band played march music beside the gangplank. White and yellow streamers had been strung along the top of the pier. Horse-drawn taxis pulled up to let off more passengers.

"There she is!" Liza exclaimed. "Aunt Lee! Aunt Lee!"

Angelica and Hamilton pushed past a man pulling an enormous black steamer trunk and hurried up to greet Angelica's aunt Lavinia.

"Why, *there* you are!" Aunt Lavinia cried happily. "My goodness. I thought I missed you!"

Angelica's aunt was a large, robust-looking woman. Her blue traveling bonnet matched the blue of her eyes. Her round cheeks were flushed with excitement. She had traveled to New Orleans for Mardi Gras, but now was returning home to Memphis.

There were hugs all around. Angelica introduced Hamilton, who said something, but his words were drowned out by an ear-shattering blast from the boat whistle.

"Oh my, I had better be boarding!" Aunt Lavinia exclaimed. "It was so nice of you to see an old aunt off!"

More hugs. Then Angelica's aunt gathered her belongings

in her arms and started toward the gangplank.

"She is a dear," Liza said, waving to her aunt.

"This boat will make it upriver to Memphis in no time," Hamilton remarked. "Look. It has *two* paddle wheels. That should double its speed."

Another blast of the whistle made Angelica cover her ears. She tugged on Hamilton's arm. "There is no one on that pier," she said, pointing. "Come on. We can get a better view when the boat pulls away. We shall be right on the water."

Liza hesitated. "That pier is roped off, Angelica. I do not think they want us to stand there."

"We can stand there if we want," Hamilton said. "Come on. I want to be as close as I can when the boat starts to move."

With Hamilton in the lead, the three of them ducked under the rope and stepped out to the edge of the pier. Below them the water lapped against the wooden pilings, the water green and golden, shimmering in the bright afternoon sunlight.

"I can see fish down there. Look. A whole school of them," Hamilton said, bending over the edge of the pier and pointing into the gently rocking water.

"I—I don't think we should be here," Liza stammered. She glanced around uncomfortably.

"No one cares if we watch from here," Angelica told her cousin.

The last passenger had boarded, Angelica saw. The gangplank had been pulled on board. Two young sailors in white suits were rolling up the red carpet. The band started braying out another march.

Angelica shielded her eyes with one hand and searched the deck for her aunt. She felt a tap on her shoulder. "Turn around," Liza instructed in a hushed voice. "Look who is here."

Confused, Angelica followed her cousin's gaze. To her surprise, Simon Fear was standing at the edge of the crowd. He had a hat pulled down over his forehead. His hands were stuffed into the pockets of a gray coat.

How strange, Angelica thought, staring intently at him. Why is Simon here? He doesn't appear to be seeing anyone off.

With two short blasts of its whistle, the paddle boat began to pull away from the dock, its wheels spinning slowly, churning the water.

Peering back toward the crowd, Angelica saw Simon pull something from his coat pocket. The silvery object caught the light of the sun. Simon raised the object high.

Angelica shook her head, then turned to watch the boat depart. What a strange young man he is, she thought, an amused smile spreading across her face.

Another blast of the whistle. The boat began to pick up speed. Behind Angelica the crowd waved and cheered.

Angelica watched the twin paddle wheels turn,

creating two frothy waterfalls as the boat pulled away. She glanced back. Simon hadn't moved. He still held the silvery object high in one hand.

"Hamilton, this is exciting, isn't it?" she asked. "Hamilton? Hamilton?"

He had been standing by her side at the edge of the pier.

Where had he disappeared to?

"Liza, have you seen Ham—" Angelica started.

But her voice caught in her throat as she glanced back at the boat.

And then she started to scream.

CHAPTER 8

"Did he fall?" Liza cried. "Did he fall?" She grabbed Angelica, repeating the question. "Did he fall?"

"Hamilton! Hamilton!" Angelica screamed, raising her hands to her cheeks.

She watched Hamilton disappear under the golden green water.

And then she saw him rise up again as if floating on air.

"Hamilton! Hamilton!"

As Angelica gaped in horror, she saw that Hamilton was caught in the blades of the paddle wheel.

"No! Oh, please—no!" she shrieked.

His limp body rose up, then made a loud crunching sound as it was crushed between the wheel and the boat. It plunged back into the water, then was dragged up again, only to be crushed with another loud *crunch.*

"Did he fall? Did he fall?" Liza repeated the question breathlessly, crazily, strands of her brown hair loose and blowing wildly about her head. Tears streamed down her face.

Hamilton disappeared under the water. Then his lifeless body rose again. His arms waved helplessly. His head, the skull crushed beyond recognition, rolled back, then forward as the wheel carried him into the boat again.

The water pouring off the big paddle wheel was pink, stained with Hamilton's blood.

"No! Oh, no. Please, no!" Angelica moaned, unable to take her eyes off the gruesome scene of horror.

"Did he fall? Did he fall?" Liza continued her stunned refrain, her eyes rolling crazily in her head.

Suddenly Angelica felt a firm arm around her waist.

Uttering a soft cry of surprise, she turned to see Simon at her side. "Simon!" she cried in a high voice she didn't recognize. "Simon, he—he—" She pointed to the boat.

"Poor Angelica," Simon said softly, holding her tightly. "Poor Angelica. You have suffered so much."

"Angelica, it is a pleasure to see you out of your mourning clothes," Henry Pierce said, smiling beneath his dark mustache. He gently placed a hand on her shoulder in passing. "You are feeling better?"

Angelica nodded but didn't return his smile. She smoothed her shiny black hair. "Two months have passed, Father. I felt it proper to end my mourning for Hamilton."

Mr. Pierce made his way to the window and peered out into the evening darkness. "An unhappy time," he muttered, more to himself than to her. He turned back to Angelica. "You are so pale, Daughter."

"I am feeling better," Angelica told him. "At least the dreadful fainting spells have ended."

"You have been considering my advice?" he asked, keeping his gruff voice soft. His eyes searched hers, as if seeking her true feelings. "I really do believe that traveling abroad is a good idea for you now."

Angelica sighed. "I haven't had much time to think," she replied with some sadness.

"I hope you have not been too lonely since Liza returned home to Virginia?"

"I needed this time by myself," Angelica said, toying with her hair.

"Simon Fear has visited you often," her father remarked, frowning.

"Simon has been a true comfort," Angelica replied.

Mr. Pierce nodded thoughtfully. "I hope you have not encouraged that strange young man in any way." He took one more glance out the front window, then made his way back to where Angelica was sitting. "I am feeling quite tired this evening. I believe I shall retire."

"Good night, Father," Angelica said. She rose and planted a kiss on his broad forehead.

Startled by this unusual show of affection, Mr. Pierce turned bright scarlet. He smiled, wished her good night, and strode quickly from the room.

Smiling to herself, Angelica moved to the sideboard against the wall and bent to pull two silver goblets from the cabinet. She busied herself there for a few moments, then returned to the couch.

About half an hour later the butler entered the sitting room, carrying a small white card on a silver tray. "Mr. Fear wishes to see you, miss," he said, presenting Simon's card to her.

Angelica took the card and glanced at it quickly, unable to suppress a smile. She nodded to the butler. "I will see him."

Simon entered, holding his hat in one hand, his dark hair slicked down, a look of concern on his face. But his expression softened to happiness when he saw that Angelica had traded her black mourning dress for a light-colored gown.

Smiling at her, his dark eyes glowing in the soft light of the gas lamps, he crossed the room quickly, then bent and kissed her hand.

She motioned for him to sit beside her. Raising his coat-tails, Simon lowered himself to the couch. "Angelica—" he started.

But she raised a hand to silence him.

Her emerald eyes burned into his. "Simon, I will marry you," Angelica said.

He stared at her blankly. He swallowed hard.

"Simon, did you not hear me?" Angelica demanded. "I said that I will marry you!"

"I—I am so—so—" he stammered.

Angelica tossed back her head and laughed. "Why, Simon, I have never known you to be tongue-tied!"

Simon blushed. "My dear Angelica, I am so overcome with happiness that I am speechless!" He took her hand in both of his. "I am thrilled, Angelica. I am the happiest man in all of New Orleans! I am *bursting* with happiness, I swear it!"

Angelica jumped to her feet and walked quickly to the sideboard. "Simon, let us have a toast," she said happily. "A toast to our marriage, to our happiness."

She filled the two silver goblets from a silver pitcher. Simon crossed the room and took one of the goblets from her hand. "To years and years of wedded happiness!" he proclaimed, beaming at her.

The silver goblets clinked.

They stood in front of the sideboard, their goblets raised, their faces glowing in the soft gaslight.

Then, to Angelica's surprise, Simon's expression darkened. "I must tell you something now, dear Angelica," he said, lowering his voice to a whisper.

She gazed back at him expectantly, her eyes locked on his.

"I love you so much," Simon said. "So much . . . I would do anything for you." He hesitated.

"Yes, dear," Angelica replied impatiently. "What is it?"

"I was so determined to have you. Nothing . . . no one could stand in my way." Simon continued, his eyes sparkling now.

"Yes?"

He took a deep breath, then let it out. "I love you so much—so much—that I *murdered* James Daumier and Hamilton Scott to win you!"

CHAPTER 9

Simon stared hard at Angelica, waiting for her reaction to his words.

She gaped at him in stunned silence, the silver goblet trembling in her hand.

"Angelica," he said, his voice quivering with emotion, his eyes pleading with her not to be repulsed by his news, not to reject him because of what he had done. "Angelica, I murdered them for *you*. That is how powerful my love is. My love for you is so overwhelming that I was driven to *kill* for you! I beg you to understand!"

Angelica didn't reply. She raised the goblet to her mouth and took a sip. A drop of the dark wine trickled down her lip.

Finally she spoke. "You—you *killed* them?"

Simon nodded solemnly.

"But how?" she demanded in a tiny voice.

He hesitated. "I have powers," he said simply. His hand tightened nervously around the goblet. Holding his breath, he stared at her, waiting for her to react.

To his surprise, Angelica's cat eyes narrowed and she uttered a scornful laugh.

"Angelica—?" he cried.

"You?" she cried. *"You* killed them?" She laughed again, laughed until tears rolled down her cheeks. "You fool!" she declared, shaking her head. "It was not *your* powers that killed those two oafs! It was *mine*!"

"What?" It was Simon's turn to gape.

"I killed them!" Angelica exclaimed through her tears of laughter. "I did it, not you! I have practiced the dark arts since I was a child. I knew I would never be allowed to marry you while James and Hamilton were around. And I knew that night at my party that you and I belonged together!"

"But, Angelica—!"

She raised a hand to silence him. "I could not marry James or Hamilton. They were both innocents, both lacking in imagination, both lacking the evil it takes to enjoy this world. So I cast spells. I murdered them both, Simon. I made James leap off our opera box railing. I made Hamilton fly off the pier into the paddle wheel. I murdered them for *you*—for *us*!"

Simon swallowed hard in stunned silence. "I—I do not *believe* it!" he finally managed to choke out.

"We will combine our powers," Angelica declared, raising her goblet.

"Yes, yes!" Simon agreed, quickly recovering from his shock. "Yes, Angelica, my dear. Together, nothing can stop us from getting what we want!"

Angelica's smile faded. "Only one thing can stop us, Simon, my love. One very powerful thing—my father. He will never approve of you. He wants to send me to Europe to get me away from you."

"Come! Let us see him at once!" Simon cried, his dark eyes sparkling with excitement. He grabbed Angelica's hand and began to pull her.

"Simon, stop! Where are you taking me? We cannot see Father yet. We have no plan. Simon, we need a strategy!"

Ignoring her pleas, Simon pulled Angelica toward her father's bedroom. They stopped short in the doorway when they saw Henry Pierce lying sprawled on his back on the bedroom carpet.

His face was bright purple. His mouth was frozen open. His lifeless eyes gazed up at the ceiling like clouded glass marbles.

"Simon . . . I—I—" Angelica gripped Simon's sleeve. "Is he—dead?"

"The doctor will believe it was his heart," Simon said

softly, unable to keep a smile from forming on his handsome face.

"No!" Angelica cried, dropping to her knees beside her father's dead body. "Father!" She raised her eyes slowly to Simon. "*You* did it? You did it for me?"

"For us, my darling," Simon replied. "I murdered your father before I came into the sitting room. I knew it was the only way we could be together."

"Oh, thank you!" Angelica cried, jumping up and throwing her arms around him. "We are wealthy now, Simon. We are wealthy—and free!"

They hurried back to the sitting room and raised their silver goblets. "Let us drink!" Angelica urged. "To us!"

She clinked her goblet against his. They both drank.

"Delicious," Simon declared. "So bitter and sweet at the same time." He smiled at her knowingly. "It isn't wine—is it?"

"No," Angelica replied, returning his grin. "It isn't wine. It is blood."

Simon snickered and stared into the goblet. "You are full of surprises tonight, Angelica."

He wrapped an arm around her slender shoulders. Then they tilted the goblets to their lips and drank, allowing the rich, dark liquid to flow down their chins.

Village of Shadyside

1900

Nora Goode dropped the pen and tried to stretch the cramps from her aching fingers. Yawning, she stared at the narrow window on the bare gray wall.

Morning sunlight cast a small yellow rectangle over the dark floorboards.

Soon they will be coming, Nora thought, turning her eyes to the door.

I must finish my story before they come. I must leave this written record for all to see.

The evil that has followed the Fear family through the generations must be known. Otherwise it will never stop.

She raised the crust of bread from the metal pan of food that had been left for her and dipped it into the cold, yellowish gravy. Stuffing it hungrily into her mouth, she glanced at the stack of pages on the small desk.

So much more to write, she thought, picking up the pen and dipping it into the half-empty inkwell. The story of Simon Fear is so long and so frightening.

Simon and his precious Angelica were married in 1846. Now I must move my story to nearly twenty years later.

It is the year 1865. The War Between the States is drawing to a close.

Simon and his bride have moved North to Shadyside Village, where they built an enormous mansion in the woods, away from prying eyes. They used Angelica's money, of course.

They lived there with their five children: two daughters, Julia, seventeen, and Hannah, sixteen, and three sons, Robert, fourteen, Brandon, eleven, and Joseph, the youngest at five.

The family seemed happy and prosperous for a while. But with so much evil lurking within the walls of the Fear mansion, their happiness could not last.

Nora scraped the last of the yellow gravy from the pan. Then she picked up her pen, bent over her pages and began writing feverishly. . . .

PART TWO

Shadyside Village

1865

CHAPTER 10

"Whom will I be seated next to at the party tonight, Father?" Julia asked her father.

Simon Fear glanced up from the documents he had been reading. "Hmmm. I believe I have you seated next to the mayor, Julia."

"Oh, no!" Julia leaped up from her chair by the fireplace and marched purposefully to her father, who sat behind his small writing desk. "Please, Father. Must I sit next to Mayor Bradford? You know the man is completely deaf! He cannot hear a word anyone says to him!"

"Then that makes him the perfect dinner companion for you, my dear Julia," Simon replied cruelly, frowning over his square spectacles. "You never utter a word at our dinner parties. You always sit in complete silence. So you and the mayor should be perfectly content!"

"Father!" Julia uttered an exasperated cry.

Simon studied his oldest daughter with some sadness. She had her mother's beautiful black hair. But Julia's face was plain, her jaw too wide, her nose too long, her tiny gray eyes set too close together.

She was quiet, withdrawn, and shy, with little personality. A disappointment to Simon. He had hoped that moving to Shadyside Village, where the Fear family was the wealthiest and most prominent family, would help pull Julia from her shell. But she had become even more awkward and shy since the move.

She is only happy at her potter's wheel, Simon thought. Making vases and clay sculptures—that is the only time she smiles or shows any sign of enthusiasm.

"Father, I think you are being unfair to my sister!" Hannah came bursting in from the back parlor. "Julia can have my seat next to Mr. Claybourne. I am sure that she and that charming old man will find plenty to chatter about, if that is what concerns you."

Simon set down his papers and climbed to his feet. His back ached as he stood. He realized he was getting older.

He unfastened his stiff collar and pulled it off. "No, I am sorry. I want *you* to sit next to that windbag Claybourne," he told Hannah. "I want you to charm him, Hannah, as only you can. I need Claybourne's support for the library I wish to build."

With his eyes trained on Hannah, Simon didn't see Julia's hurt expression.

"I am sure that Julia could handle Mr. Claybourne as well as I," Hannah insisted, stepping behind her father's desk to give him a playful hug.

No, Julia could *not,* Simon thought. Hannah, he knew, was the charming sister. At sixteen she was tall, slender, and graceful, with wavy golden hair and lively brown eyes. She was as outgoing and lively as Julia was shy.

Simon needed his younger daughter at his dinner parties. He relied on Hannah to charm and delight the guests and to keep the conversation lively.

"The table is already set," he told the girls. He removed Hannah's arms from around his waist and straightened the papers on the little desk. "There will be no more discussion of this matter."

"Oh, Father!" Hannah complained with an exaggerated pout.

"I do not understand why we have so many of these endless, boring dinner parties, anyway," Julia said bitterly. "Can you not build all your libraries and museums and parks without so many dinner parties?"

"We have discussed this before," Simon replied impatiently. "I need the support of the important citizens of Shadyside. Why must I say all this again, Julia?"

Julia took a deep breath, struggling to keep back her tears. "Well, if you do not believe I have the personality to grace your table, if you really believe the only place for me is to be seated in the corner next to a deaf man, then perhaps I shall stay in my room tonight!" she cried.

Simon opened his mouth to reply, but a sound in the doorway interrupted him. He and the girls turned to see Mrs. MacKenzie, the housekeeper, enter with a short, red-haired girl in a maid's uniform.

"I am so sorry to be interrupting, sir," Mrs. MacKenzie said, rolling her white apron in her hands. "But I am training Lucy here on the procedure for dusting. Lucy is the new maid. She just started this week. She is helping us tidy up and get ready for the dinner party tonight."

Lucy blushed and lowered her eyes. She was a tiny girl, Simon saw. No more than eighteen. She had orangey red hair pulled back into a tight bun, pale green eyes, and a tiny, sharp nose like an upturned V.

"Go right ahead and dust, Mrs. MacKenzie," Simon said, happy that his discussion with Julia had been interrupted. "I am going upstairs now to speak with my wife about tonight."

"Now, Lucy, you be careful of Miss Julia's fine pottery here," Simon heard the housekeeper instruct as he nodded good-bye to his daughters and made his way to the front stairs.

"Father, I wasn't finished!" Julia called shrilly.

Simon ignored her and continued down the long marble-floored hallway. As he reached the stairway, his three sons, Robert, Brandon, and Joseph, came bounding down, dressed in their riding outfits.

"And where might you be going, as if I could not guess?" Simon asked.

"I am taking the boys for a short ride," Robert replied, straightening little Joseph's cap.

"My pony is waiting for me," five-year-old Joseph told his father.

"Be watchful in the woods," Simon warned Joseph. "My horse balked at a snake yesterday afternoon. Nearly threw me. I killed the snake, but there might be more."

"I'm not afraid of snakes!" Brandon declared. "I step on them!"

Robert gave his younger brothers a gentle shove toward the door. "Don't worry, Father. I will take care of them."

They went on their way, and Simon climbed the stairs, his mind on the dinner party just a few hours away.

At the top of the stairs a maid was polishing the mahogany banister. Simon stepped past her and hurried toward his wife Angelica's room.

"Angelica!" he called eagerly from the hallway. "Angelica, I have several matters to discuss with you, my dear."

He stopped in her doorway, his hands on the doorframe—and gasped.

"Angelica!"

Simon stared down at her. She was sprawled on the floor on her back, her black hair in disarray around her head, her green eyes staring blankly at the ceiling, her mouth open.

Angelica. Not breathing. Lifeless.

"Angelica!" Simon cried. *"Oh, Angelica!"*

CHAPTER 11

Simon's frightened cries aroused Angelica, and she sat up. She blinked once, twice, and smiled at him, her emerald eyes shining.

"Simon—where am I? What is happening?" she asked groggily.

"I—I found you on the floor, Angelica!" Simon replied, greatly relieved. "I thought you were—"

"The spirits," Angelica whispered, sitting up. "The spirits called me, Simon. I must have swooned, fallen into a trance."

"I was frightened," Simon said, taking Angelica's slender white hands and pulling his wife to her feet.

Angelica squeezed his hand affectionately. "I slip in and out of my trances and cannot control them as I used to."

She lowered herself to the edge of the bed, straightening her black hair with both hands. She looked tired. In the sunlight from the window he could see that her once smooth face was lined, the skin tight and dry. Only her eyes retained their youthful glow.

"Angelica, perhaps it is time to put away the magic, to retire your dark arts," he said softly, standing over her.

She gazed up at him in surprise. "Simon, my powers have served us well," she said. She gestured around the luxurious bedroom. "We have become even more wealthy, the wealthiest people in Shadyside. We have five wonderful children. We have succeeded because of our powers, yours and mine. I cannot give up now."

"But to enter your room and find you lying unconscious on the floor—" Simon started.

Angelica raised a hand to silence him. "When the spirits call, I must follow." She muttered a chant.

"Angelica—"

"Simon, hush. The spirits will hear you. I will have to cast a cleansing spell to rid the house of your negative words."

He sighed and paced the carpet in front of her. "Let us change the subject," he said finally. "Let us discuss the dinner party tonight. I have spoken to Hannah and Julia and—"

"I cannot attend the party. I am sorry, Simon," Angelica told him abruptly, climbing to her feet.

He turned, startled. His face reddened. "What?"

"I read the cards this morning," Angelica told him with a shrug. "They advised against any kind of celebration."

"Angelica, I beg of you," Simon said heatedly. "I need you this evening. As you know, this dinner party is most important."

"I am sorry," she replied, taking his arm. "I cannot go against the cards. I cannot take that risk. I cannot tempt the vengeance of the spirits. I must always obey. Ask one of the girls to act as hostess, Simon. I will stay in my room tonight. The cards have instructed me."

Simon sighed. He knew there was no point in arguing with his wife. He gazed at her with concern. Her dark powers had taken over her life, he realized. Her chants, her spells, her cards—they kept Angelica in her room for days at a time.

The children worried about her and missed her. And now Simon realized that he, too, was worried.

"Give the cards another reading, Angelica," he urged, handing the deck of strange, colorful cards to her. "Perhaps they will advise you differently this time."

"Very well," she replied softly, "but I know what they will tell me." Smiling, she gave Simon a gentle shove toward the door. "Go now, husband. Go ask Hannah to serve as your hostess. She will charm your guests even better than I."

Reluctantly Simon bid her farewell and made his way

from her room. He could hear her murmuring over the cards as he walked along the long hall to the front stairs.

Simon was halfway down the stairs when he heard a loud, shattering crash from the parlor.

CHAPTER 12

"My favorite bowl!" Julia was screaming as Simon rushed into the parlor. "That was the best bowl I ever made!"

"I'm so sorry, miss," Lucy, the new maid, said quietly, staring down at the shattered pieces on the carpet. "It—it just slipped from my hand." She covered her face with her hands.

"What has happened here?" Simon demanded.

Julia bent to pick up the largest piece of her bowl. "Shattered," she said sadly, shaking her head.

"I *told* you not to hold it in one hand like that!" Mrs. MacKenzie scolded Lucy.

"Lucy has dropped Julia's favorite pottery bowl,"

Hannah told Simon. She walked over to Lucy and Mrs. MacKenzie. "I am sure you did not do it on purpose, Lucy. Go get a broom and clean it up."

"I *told* her not to hold it like that," Mrs. MacKenzie repeated fretfully. She gave the trembling maid a shove. "Well, go on, girl. Let's be cleaning this mess up. And no more accidents, hear? We have a lot to do before the guests start to arrive."

Simon shook his head fretfully at Julia. "I am certain you can make another bowl just like it," he said impatiently. "We really have no time to worry about your pottery today."

Hurt, Julia started to reply. But Simon turned quickly to Hannah. "I will need you to be hostess tonight, Hannah. Your mother is . . . not feeling well."

The girls exchanged glances.

Hannah took her father's arm. "I shall be glad to take Mother's place tonight," she said. "But shouldn't Julia act as hostess? She is the oldest, after all."

Simon pulled away from her impatiently. "Please!" he cried sharply. "Enough arguments and discussion for today! I asked *you* to be my hostess tonight, Hannah. I do not believe any further discussion is necessary!"

Before either of his daughters could reply, Simon stormed out of the room.

Hannah turned to Julia, who still held a shard of pottery in her hand.

"Father has no confidence in me, I am afraid," Julia remarked sadly. She let the piece fall to the carpet.

"Julia, I feel so bad," Hannah said with genuine feeling. "But you know how Father is, so headstrong and stubborn."

Julia forced a smile. "Dinner parties make me so nervous. But perhaps I can be a success tonight. Perhaps I can force Father to change his mind about me."

In the kitchen Mrs. MacKenzie continued to scold Lucy. "Be careful, my girl," she warned. "You don't get many chances in this household."

"I will. I promise," Lucy replied meekly.

Mrs. MacKenzie handed the maid a long sheet of paper with several names scrawled on it. "Here, Lucy. You must sign the servants' list."

Lucy hesitated. "But I cannot write, ma'am," she said, blushing.

Mrs. MacKenzie took the paper from her. "Very well, then. Tell me your complete name, child, and I will scribble it for you."

"My name is Lucy Goode," the maid replied quietly.

Mrs. MacKenzie started to write, then stopped. Her eyes narrowed as she trained them on the girl. "Goode, did you say?"

Lucy nodded.

"Well, I wouldn't be repeating that name around here

if I was you," the old housekeeper advised. "Mr. Fear is always talking about some family named Goode that done him wrong. Keep the name to yourself, girl. If you wish to keep your job."

"Don't worry," Lucy replied, her eyes suddenly cold and hard. "I won't be telling a soul."

As the guests arrived that evening, Hannah stood beside her father, her lively brown eyes reflecting her excitement. Her gown was made of delicate white lace over green satin. A hoop underneath made the wide skirt hold its shape. The skirt was three-tiered, the hem of each green tier trimmed with white lace.

Hannah wore short white lace gloves, and her gown had ruffled short sleeves. Her blond hair was tied to one side in a tight bun, held in place by a corsage of yellow and white flowers.

Julia's dress was simpler, white lace over pink velvet. The neckline dipped low, revealing her shoulders. Her shiny black hair, parted in the middle, fell gracefully in ringlets beside her face.

"You look wonderful tonight," Hannah whispered to her sister. She could see that Julia had taken extra care with her appearance. "Father is sure to notice," Hannah whispered, doing her best to encourage Julia.

Julia will never be a beauty, Hannah thought with some sadness. *But when she dresses up, she looks quite* lovely. If only she would smile more and not clasp her hands so tightly in front of her.

Wine was served in Simon's library. The large square room, furnished in dark wood furniture, with its four walls of bookshelves, seemed to be the perfect setting for an evening devoted to discussing the Shadyside village library.

Working hard to be a good hostess, Hannah moved from guest to guest, her eyes sparkling, her smile warm and genuine. She chatted and joked with Harlan Claybourne. She even managed to get a smile from sour old Mayor Bradford.

A short while later Simon led everyone to see his new collection of weapons and uniforms from the War Between the States. Simon had been collecting swords and rifles from both the armies of the North and the South. After admiring Simon's collection, they were all summoned to the formal dining room for dinner. Simon led the way with Hannah on his arm.

The majestic room was lighted entirely by candles. Silver candelabras glowing with tall, slender candles were placed every few feet along the center of the white Irish linen tablecloth. The silver dinner plates and delicate wineglasses shone in the soft, flickering light.

"You set a fine table, Simon," Harlan Claybourne declared grandly, taking his place next to Hannah.

"I have fine guests," Simon replied graciously.

Father is certainly in a good mood tonight, Hannah thought gratefully. She had seen him become sullen and silent at parties that weren't going as planned.

I do wish Mother were here, Hannah thought. She is ill so often lately. She spends so much time upstairs in her room that I am actually lonely for her.

Hannah watched as Julia helped the old mayor into his chair at the far end of the table. Then Julia took her lonely place beside him. The mayor immediately reached for the loaf of bread. He took a piece for himself, Hannah saw, and didn't even offer the bread to Julia.

Poor Julia, Hannah thought, lowering herself into her seat. Father can really be unfair at times.

She turned her attention to Mr. Claybourne and began chatting with him about his horses.

A few moments later Lucy entered in a starched black uniform with a lacy white apron over it, carrying a large china tureen of soup. Starting at the head of the table, she served Simon Fear first, dipping a long-handled silver ladle into the tureen and filling his bowl with the soup.

"Very good, Lucy," Simon said approvingly. "That is a very big tureen. Are you sure you do not need help with it?"

"No, sir," Lucy replied meekly. "Mrs. MacKenzie said I can do it on my own."

She continued down the table, ladling the rich orangey-red soup into bowls.

"What *is* this marvelous soup? Is it tomato?" Mrs. Graham, the reverend's wife, asked as Lucy continued down the table.

"It is lobster bisque," Hannah replied, "in a tomato base."

"It certainly is hearty," Reverend Graham remarked.

Hannah started to say something about the recipe but was interrupted by a high-pitched shriek from the end of the table.

It took Hannah a moment to realize that it was Julia who was screaming frantically at the top of her lungs.

CHAPTER 13

"My shoulder! Ohhhhh, my shoulder!" Julia shrieked.

Several guests cried out as Julia leaped to her feet, sending her chair clattering to the floor.

"I'm so sorry, miss!" Lucy cried, struggling to hold on to the big soup tureen.

"Owww! My shoulder! And look at my dress!" Julia wailed.

"My arm was bumped. I didn't mean to spill it!" Lucy backed timidly against the sideboard.

Julia grabbed up her white linen napkin and began dabbing frantically at her shoulder and the neckline of her dress. "Ow, it burns!" A dark orange stain ran down the white lace shoulder of the gown onto the pink velvet bodice.

"Julia, dear, you may be excused to freshen yourself up," Simon called from the head of the table.

He intended to be understanding, Julia knew, but she heard only disapproval in his voice.

I have done something clumsy once again, Julia thought unhappily. Hannah would never have behaved so badly.

Hannah wouldn't have screamed and knocked her chair over, Julia knew. Hannah wouldn't have made such a commotion.

But what could she do? That steaming-hot soup really *burned*!

"Are you hurt, Sister? Do you need help?" Hannah called from the other end of the table.

"No, I do not need help," Julia replied through clenched teeth. Disgusted with herself, she tossed the napkin onto the table, muttered "Excuse me," and started for the door. She could feel her face burning and knew she was blushing.

She glanced at the doorway and stopped short when she saw the expression on Lucy's face.

Was that a smile? A pleased smile?

Late that night, after the guests had boarded their carriages and headed home, after the servants had cleaned up, Hannah and Julia met in the secret room only they knew about.

It was a long, narrow room without windows, hidden behind the second pantry. Heat from the kitchen stove on the other side of the wall kept the small room cozy and warm. A small gas lamp cast a dim light.

The two sisters had discovered the room when they were small children and had used it as a secret meeting place ever since. They had sneaked blankets and feather pillows in and sometimes pretended they were girls hiding in a faraway cave.

That night Julia did not feel like discussing "little girl" things. Her back resting on a pillow propped against the warm wall, her hands clasped tightly in the lap of her wool nightdress, Julia sighed unhappily.

Beside her, Hannah yawned and tugged at a strand of fine blond hair.

"Did you not see Lucy's expression?" Julia demanded in a low whisper. They always whispered in this secret room, even though no one could hear. "Did you not see the smile on the maid's face?"

Hannah shook her head thoughtfully. "My eyes were on you, Sister. It took me a while to see what all the commotion was."

"But afterward," Julia insisted impatiently. "After I jumped up and knocked my chair over, did you not see Lucy smile as if she were pleased about what she had done to me?"

"No," Hannah replied softly. "I only heard Lucy apologize."

"I *saw* her smile!" Julia exclaimed, raising her voice

angrily. "She spilled the soup on my bare shoulder *deliberately*!"

"Why?" Hannah asked, gesturing for her sister to lower her voice. "I do not understand, Julia. *Why* would Lucy do such a thing? She has no reason to harm you."

Julia ignored her sister's question. "First she broke my finest work of pottery. She apologized for that, too, as I recall," Julia said bitterly. "And then she embarrassed me in front of Father, when I was trying so hard to . . . to act the way he wants me to. Did Father say anything to you? About *me*? About what happened?"

"He seemed displeased that there was a disturbance," Hannah replied, yawning again. "But I think Father was very happy about the dinner."

"Happy about *you*," Julia muttered.

"Being hostess is such hard work," Hannah said. "I thought my smile would freeze on my face."

Lost in her own thoughts, Julia didn't appear to hear her.

"I am so tired," Hannah said, sighing. "I think we had better go up to our rooms."

"Yes," Julia agreed.

The two sisters climbed to their feet, leaving the pillows against the wall. Silently they started toward the door.

In the dark, empty pantry Julia stopped and grabbed Hannah's hand. "Just heed my warning, Sister. Keep an eye on the new maid. Something about Lucy is not right."

Too tired to argue, Hannah muttered her agreement, and the two sisters proceeded up the dimly lit stairway to their rooms.

A single gaslight on the hallway wall provided the only light in the long corridor. As Hannah made her way to her bedroom, she saw Lucy silently slip out her door and vanish into the shadows.

How strange, Hannah thought, feeling chilled and afraid.

The servants have all retired. Why was Lucy in my room at such a late hour?

Curious, she stepped into the bedroom. Logs crackled pleasantly in the fireplace. Hannah's party dress had been removed from the chair on which she had tossed it. The bedclothes were neatly turned down.

How nice of Lucy, Hannah thought, sliding into the linen sheets. She felt a momentary pang of guilt for talking about the new girl with Julia.

I mustn't listen to Julia's wild accusations, she scolded herself.

Hannah pulled the goose-down comforter up over her shoulders and let her head sink into the pillow. Smiling to herself, she listened to the soothing crackle of the fire.

"Oh—!" she whispered when she felt something move against her bare leg.

It must be a wrinkle in the sheet, she told herself.

She shut her eyes again. She was so sleepy. She hoped she could fall asleep quickly.

"Oh—!" Hannah froze.

What was that?

Did something move? Is something in my bed?

She tried to cry out, but her voice caught in her throat as she felt something slither up her leg.

CHAPTER 14

Too frightened to scream, Hannah felt the warm creature slide over her leg. She forced herself not to move. Not to breathe.

It curled itself around her ankle. Then she felt it uncoil.

"Ohhh." She uttered a low, terrified moan and leaped from the bed.

In the flickering light from the dying fire she tossed back the bedclothes and searched the shadows of her bed.

She heard a *hiss,* then saw the flash of dark eyes.

"A snake!" she cried in a tiny, frightened voice.

Rising up on the wrinkled sheet, the snake arched its head and bared its pointed fangs, preparing to attack.

Hannah stood frozen in terror. "How did a snake get into my bed?" Hannah asked aloud. "How?"

Then, with a short cry, Hannah sprang into action and threw the covers over the hissing creature. And started to scream for help.

Hannah's brothers were blamed for the prank. They had been riding in the woods. They must have captured the snake and hidden it in Hannah's bed.

They all denied it. But Simon ignored their protests and punished them. He had little patience for jokes and pranks. "They do not lead anyone closer to success," he warned sternly.

The next evening Hannah was in her room dressing for dinner. Having pulled on a simple white linen frock, high-collared with a delicate red velvet ribbon at the throat, she brushed her long blond hair and tied it back with a matching red ribbon.

She heard a scrabbling at the door and turned to see Fluff, her tiny white terrier, prance into the room, a red ball clamped in his teeth.

"Not now. No ball playing," Hannah told the dog. "You will make me late for dinner, Fluff." She gave the disappointed dog a gentle shove toward the door.

Then she pulled open her wardrobe door to search for her white shoes. "Where *are* they?" she said, bending to search the bottom shelf.

Lucy had straightened Hannah's room that afternoon. She must have moved the shoes, Hannah thought.

She finally found them on the floor at the foot of her bed.

Holding on to the bedpost, Hannah balanced on her left foot and slid her right foot into the low pump.

"Ohhh!" she cried out as a sharp pain shot up her leg.

Looking down, Hannah was horrified to see bright red blood trickling over the white heel of the shoe.

As the sharp pain shot up from her foot, Hannah dropped to her knees on the bedroom floor and pulled off the shoe. Blood had already stained the inside of the shoe.

Hannah bent to examine her foot. Wiping away the bright trickling blood with her fingers, she found a deep cut nearly an inch long on her heel.

Stuck in the cut was a shard of clear glass.

"Oh!" Grimacing with pain, Hannah pulled the piece of glass from the cut with trembling fingers.

The blood flowed more rapidly from the open cut. Balancing on one leg, Hannah screamed for help.

Mrs. MacKenzie appeared a few seconds later. She guided Hannah to the bed. Hannah hopped on one foot, leaving a trail of blood. Then the housekeeper hurried out for gauze bandages.

"Hannah, what has happened?" Julia entered the room breathlessly, a frightened expression on her face. Seeing the trail of blood across the floor, Julia gasped.

"I'm all right, I believe," Hannah told her, watching the blood flow from her heel. "I—I cut my foot."

"How?" Julia demanded, stepping over the blood-covered shoe to get to Hannah's bedside.

Hannah held up the piece of glass that she had kept tightly gripped in her hand. "It was in my shoe," she said, grimacing from a shot of pain that traveled up her leg.

"How dreadful!" Julia declared, staring at all the blood.

"Lucy cleaned my room today," Hannah added darkly. "I believe you may be right about her, Julia. She—" Hannah stopped as Mrs. MacKenzie returned with the gauze bandages.

Julia watched as the housekeeper expertly cleaned and then bandaged Hannah's injured foot. "The bleeding will stop soon," Mrs. MacKenzie assured Hannah, patting her shoulder as if she were still a little girl. "You will be able to come down to dinner in a few minutes. But I would not advise any long hikes for a few days, Miss Hannah."

Hannah thanked Mrs. MacKenzie. As soon as the housekeeper had left the room, Hannah turned back to Julia. "Lucy cleaned my room and moved my shoes. I believe you were right about her. She deliberately—"

Julia raised a hand to stop her sister's accusation. "Are you really sure that Lucy put the glass in your shoe?"

"Who else could have done it?" Hannah demanded impatiently, staring down fretfully at the bandaged foot. "We must tell Father at once. That girl must go. She must be dismissed today. She is a menace! Ow!" She cried out, feeling another stab of pain.

Julia lowered herself to the bed beside her sister and put a comforting arm around Hannah. "Try to calm yourself, Sister," she said in a whisper. "We do not want to accuse Lucy if she is innocent."

"Innocent?" Hannah cried shrilly.

"We have no proof," Julia said, playing with Hannah's blond hair, soothingly braiding and unbraiding it as she had done when they were younger. "We do not know that Lucy put the glass in the shoe."

"No one else was in my room!" Hannah exclaimed.

"But the glass may have fallen from Lucy's dustpan," Julia said. "It may have been an accident, a bit of carelessness."

"But, Julia—"

"I have my own suspicions about Lucy, as you know," Julia continued, ignoring her sister's protest. "But I do not think we should accuse her in front of Father until we have proof."

Hannah stared hard at her sister. Father is right about Julia, she thought with some sadness. Julia is too timid. She has no backbone. She is reluctant to stand up even to a servant girl.

But Hannah decided to back down. "Very well," she said softly. "I will give Lucy one more chance."

"Can you walk down to dinner, or will you need help?" Julia asked, getting to her feet.

"I can walk," Hannah replied softly. "Go ahead. You

know Father hates to be kept waiting for his dinner."

"Mother has actually left her room and is joining us tonight," Julia announced.

"How nice!" Hannah declared. "I shall be right down. Give me a few moments to brush my hair and straighten my dress."

As soon as Julia had left the room, Hannah gingerly climbed to her feet. She found that if she stepped lightly on her cut foot, standing nearly on tiptoes, she could walk with little pain.

Putting most of her weight on the uninjured foot, she made her way across the room to her small dresser mirror and began to brush her hair.

She had finished and set down the brush when she felt another presence in the room—someone to the side of her, staring at her.

Hannah spun around quickly and cried out in surprise.

Lucy was standing in the room, her cheeks bright red, a frightening wild-eyed expression on her face.

As Hannah shrank back against the dresser, Lucy darted forward quickly to attack her.

CHAPTER 15

Her cheeks scarlet, her eyes wild, Lucy stopped a few feet in front of Hannah, breathing hard.

What is she going to do to me? Hannah wondered, pressing against the dresser, her hands raised as if to shield herself from the maid's attack.

"Mrs. MacKenzie t-told me—" Lucy stammered, pointing down. "About your foot, I mean."

"Yes?" Hannah managed to utter in a tight, frightened voice.

"Well, I came up to see if there was anything I could do. To help, that is."

"I think you've done *quite* enough," Hannah replied coldly.

Lucy appeared stung by Hannah's words.

Hannah immediately felt sorry.

Lucy was red-faced and breathing hard because she had hurried up the stairs to help me, Hannah realized. I have become so frightened of her, so suspicious of her, that I really believed she had come to attack me!

"I am sorry you are in pain, miss," Lucy said, lowering her eyes to the floor. "If there is anything I can do for you . . ."

"Thank you, Lucy," Hannah replied, softening her tone. "You may clean up the floor. There was quite a lot of blood. Then take that shoe down to Mrs. MacKenzie. Ask if there is any way it can be cleaned."

"Yes, miss," Lucy said, still avoiding Hannah's gaze.

Limping gingerly, Hannah made her way past Lucy and headed downstairs to dinner.

The picnic was Hannah's idea. She had been cooped up in the house for three days nursing her injured foot. Now the foot was nearly healed, and she was walking normally.

"What an excellent idea," Julia said brightly. "I shall have a basket lunch made up. We shall go out to the woods and enjoy this beautiful day."

Joseph, Brandon, and Robert begged to come along. "I promise we won't be any trouble," begged Robert. "And I shall watch Brandon and Joseph carefully."

Fluff also seemed excited by the idea. The little dog leaped eagerly at the pantry door, whimpering to go out into the sunshine.

"Go get dressed," Julia instructed her sister. "I shall go speak to Lucy about preparing our lunch basket."

The mention of Lucy's name gave Hannah a chill. She had avoided the maid for three days. Hannah realized that she was perhaps being unfair. Lucy *couldn't* be deliberately trying to hurt the two Fear sisters. What reason could she have?

Just the same, Hannah had decided to avoid Lucy and to have as little to do with her as possible.

Pushing Lucy out of her mind, she hurried upstairs to get changed for the picnic.

"Why do they call it Indian summer?" Brandon asked.

"I am not sure," Hannah told him. "But today is certainly the most beautiful Indian summer day."

The sun was high, seeming to float above tiny puffs of white cloud. Leaves shimmered brightly on the tall trees at the back of the lawn. They were still summer green although autumn was here.

Despite the sunshine, the air carried a chill. Hannah wrapped her light blue shawl around her as she watched Fluff scamper through the tall grass.

"Joseph, don't chase Fluff!" Julia ordered. "You're getting the poor dog all excited!"

"I am afraid that Fluff is already excited," Hannah told her, laughing as the dog rolled onto its back and frantically kicked at the air with all four paws. Joseph rolled on the ground, imitating the dog.

"Robert, hold the picnic basket straight. You are going to spill everything!" Julia cried.

"But it is so *heavy*!" Robert complained. "What did Lucy pack in here—an elephant?"

"The flowers are beautiful," Hannah said, pleased to be out of the house. "Look, Julia, we still have roses."

Julia didn't reply. She was distracted by Fluff and Joseph. "Joseph!" she called. "Look out! Do not let the dog fall into that hole!"

At the edge of the woods they all stopped to watch Fluff as he neared a burial plot.

With Joseph close behind, the dog ran to the edge of the freshly dug grave, sniffed along the sides at the moist, dark dirt, then came trotting back toward Robert, Brandon, and the girls.

"Why is there a new grave?" Robert asked, shifting the heavy picnic basket to his other hand, his eyes on the deep hole.

"Did you not hear about Jenkins, the gardener?" Julia asked. "He passed away in his sleep two nights ago. He is to be buried this afternoon."

"Such a kindly man," Hannah said softly. "And look at his fine work all around." She gestured to the flower garden that stretched along the back of the house, bordered on one side by tall rose trellises.

Hannah stepped closer to the grave, staring down into the deep rectangle of dark earth. How strange to think that Jenkins was walking around in our yard just two days ago, she thought with some sadness. And in a short while he shall rest in this underground hole—forever.

"Remove that solemn frown from your face, Sister," Julia urged, stepping up beside Hannah. "Let us not allow this to spoil our fun today."

Hannah forced a smile and turned away from the grave. "Yes, you are right. Into the woods, everyone!" she called brightly and started to run toward the trees, her blue shawl flapping behind her gingham dress.

The woods behind the Fear mansion seemed to stretch on forever. The five picnickers ran into the shadows of the tall trees. Their heavy shoes made the twigs on the ground crackle and snap.

"It's almost cold here under the trees!" Hannah exclaimed.

"How far do we have to walk? This basket is heavy!" Robert complained.

"We can set it down when we come to a clearing," Julia told him.

"Look at Fluff!" Joseph cried, pointing.

The dog had chased a squirrel up a tree and was now trying to climb the trunk after it.

"Does he not know that dogs cannot climb trees?" Julia asked her sister.

Hannah laughed. "Fluff does not know that he is a dog," she replied.

They continued through the woods, enjoying the cool pine-scented air, watching for squirrels and chipmunks. Joseph chased after Fluff, running and jumping and barking as if he, too, were a dog. Robert shifted the basket from hand to hand, complaining about its weight. Brandon picked up stones and threw them on the path.

"Does Father know we are having a picnic in the woods?" he asked Julia.

"I wanted to tell him," she replied, brushing a white burr from the front of her long gingham skirt. "But he was upstairs in Mother's room. She was having another one of her spells, I am afraid."

"Mother and her spells," Hannah said, rolling her eyes.

"Here is a nice clearing," Robert said happily. A circle of tall grass appeared like an oasis among the trees. "Can we have our lunch here?"

"Very well," Julia agreed brightly. "This shall do fine."

"Freedom!" Robert cried, setting the basket down, then stretching his arms.

Julia and Hannah spread a red wool blanket over the grass. Fluff immediately leaped onto the blanket, tracking dirt and leaves over it. Hannah brushed the little dog away. Julia opened the lid of the basket and began to pull items from it and set them down on the blanket.

"Look! Is that a deer?" Robert cried.

"Where?" Joseph spun around wildly, searching all directions at once.

"Follow me," Robert instructed his brothers. "But keep silent. Let's track him!"

The boys headed off at a run toward the trees. "Do not go far!" Julia called after them. "It is almost lunchtime!"

"Mmmmm. Those little pies look good," Hannah told her sister, dropping to her knees on the blanket. "I am suddenly starving."

"Fresh air makes me hungry, too," Julia replied. "Let's see . . . Lucy packed a little meat pie for each of us. And there are raisin cookies and a jug of fresh lemon water." She handed a meat pie to her sister. "Let's eat. We need not wait for the boys."

Hannah raised the small doughy pie to her mouth and was about to take a bite when Fluff leaped into her lap. "Oh!" she cried out, startled.

The dog raised himself on his hind legs and sniffed the pie in Hannah's hand noisily.

"You little beggar!" Hannah cried, laughing. "Down, down! Get off me, and I shall give you a taste!"

Ignoring her, Fluff leaped high, trying to get his teeth on the meat pie.

"Here. Here is a piece for you," Hannah said, using one hand to shove the dog off her lap. She broke off a tiny wedge of pie and held it out to Fluff.

The dog yipped and slurped it up eagerly, licking Hannah's hand clean. "Stop! Stop! You're *tickling* me!" she cried, laughing. "What a scratchy tongue you have, doggy!"

"You *do* spoil that dog," Julia grumbled good-naturedly.

Hannah gave Fluff another piece of the pie.

"Where are the boys?" Julia asked. She climbed to her feet, shielding her eyes with one hand, and searched the woods for them.

"I hope they have not wandered far," Hannah said, following her sister's gaze. "Robert has no sense of direction at all. He can get lost inside the house!"

Hearing a strange sound, Hannah turned back to Fluff.

To her surprise, the dog was whimpering loudly, his head lowered, his tail tucked tightly between his legs.

As Hannah watched in alarm, the dog's entire body began to convulse. Fluff coughed, then his stomach heaved, and he began to vomit, his legs trembling, his entire body quivering.

Then all at once the dog crumpled to the blanket, dropped onto his side, and was still.

"Fluff!" Hannah cried. "Fluff! Fluff! Oh, Julia—what has happened?"

CHAPTER 16

Hannah carefully lifted the dog from a puddle of dark vomit and held him tightly against the front of her dress. "He's dead," she muttered.

"No!" Julia cried in horror. "Hannah, he *cannot* be! He—" Tears formed in the corners of Julia's gray eyes.

"Poor Fluff. Poor Fluff. Poor Fluff," Hannah repeated quietly, still hugging the dead animal to her.

"No. I do not believe it!" Julia cried, shaking her head. "The dog was perfectly fine until—until—"

Both girls had the idea at the same time.

"The meat pies!" Hannah cried. Her eyes widened in horror, and she gaped at her sister. "Julia, did you—?"

Julia lowered her eyes to the pie beside her on the blanket. "No. I did not touch mine. You?"

Hannah shook her head. "Only Fluff. He was the only one to eat. And now the poor dog is dead."

"Poisoned," Julia muttered.

Hannah gasped. *"What* did you say, Sister?"

"Poisoned," Julia repeated the word as she wiped the tears from her eyes. "Lucy. She poisoned the pies. She *had* to."

"No!" Hannah cried, lowering the dog to the blanket, her features set in horror. "You don't think—"

"Lucy," her sister repeated, shaking her head. "She almost murdered us all."

Hannah swallowed hard, her heart thudding wildly against her chest. She climbed quickly to her feet, her expression frightened. "Where are the boys?" she asked, searching the woods. "Julia, go fetch the boys and bring them home. I shall run to tell Father. He must know what Lucy has done—at once!"

As Hannah ran through the woods toward the house, tears rolled down her cheeks.

Poor Fluff, she thought. That poor, innocent dog. He looked so frightened, so confused.

Poisoned.

Poisoned by that villainous maid.

If only Hannah had told her father her suspicions about Lucy after finding the shard of glass in her shoe. Then Fluff would still be alive.

I'll tell Father everything now, Hannah told herself. And the maid will be gone before—before she can kill again.

The back of the rambling Fear mansion came into view. Hannah slowed a little as she passed the burial plot. A closed pine coffin had been set down at the edge of the fresh grave.

Jenkins must be inside it, Hannah realized. The funeral will be held in a few moments.

Thinking of Fluff, a loud sob escaped her throat. Hannah turned away from the narrow coffin and ran the rest of the way to the house.

She burst through the door to the back pantry. "Father! Father! Are you downstairs?" she called breathlessly.

No reply.

In the kitchen bright sunlight streamed across the floor from the back window.

"Father? Father?"

No one there.

Frantically, Hannah started toward the hallway.

But a black-uniformed figure moved quickly to block her path.

"Lucy!"

CHAPTER 17

The sunlight washed over Lucy as she stepped toward Hannah. Her orange hair was secured tightly in a bun. Her eyes locked on Hannah's.

"Lucy—why did you *poison* us?" Hannah blurted out, panting for breath. "Why?"

"What?" Lucy's mouth dropped open.

"Do not play innocent!" Hannah cried angrily. "Why did you poison our lunch?"

"I have no idea what you are talking about, miss," Lucy replied, turning up her sharp nose.

"You murdered my dog!" Hannah shrieked.

"What is all the noise in here?" Mrs. MacKenzie bustled in from the hallway. "Hannah, what is the matter?" the housekeeper asked with concern.

"Lucy tried to poison us!" Hannah cried, pointing at the maid, who took another step back. "She poisoned the meat pies!"

"What?" Mrs. MacKenzie narrowed her eyes at Hannah. "What are you saying about meat pies? The meat pies for your picnic?"

"Yes," Hannah cried. "They were poisoned! Lucy has been trying to harm us since she arrived. And today—"

"No!" Lucy screamed, interrupting. "No! You are telling lies, miss!"

Ignoring her protests, Hannah turned to Mrs. MacKenzie. "I must get my father. He must know at once. Lucy poisoned the pies!"

"No, she did not," Mrs. MacKenzie said firmly, placing her hands on the sides of her long apron.

"What?" Hannah had started to the door but stopped short.

"As I am a witness, Lucy did *not* poison the pies," Mrs. MacKenzie repeated, frowning, her round cheeks a bright pink. "Lucy had nothing to do with your lunch, Miss Hannah. Your sister Julia prepared the lunch."

Hannah felt dazed. The room suddenly tilted. The bright sunlight washing over her made everything go white. "Julia?"

"Miss Julia made the pies," Mrs. MacKenzie insisted. "Lucy asked if Julia needed help. But Miss Julia ordered Lucy to stay out of the kitchen."

"Julia?" Hannah gasped weakly. "No. Please. Not Julia. Not Julia."

"Miss Hannah, are you feeling ill?" Mrs. MacKenzie demanded, tugging on the sides of her apron. "Perhaps I should summon your father?"

But Hannah was already running through the back pantry and out the door.

Her heart pounding, her head spinning from what she had just learned, she ran past the flower garden and across the lawn. She saw her brothers first, coming out of the woods. Their faces were drawn. Julia must have told them about Fluff. The boys nodded solemnly at Hannah, then continued on in silence toward the house.

Julia appeared next. As she stepped out of the woods, she stopped a few yards from Jenkins's coffin.

She was carrying the picnic basket, but set it down when she saw Hannah hurrying toward her. "Hannah, did you find Father? Did you tell him about Lucy?"

Panting hard, struggling to catch her breath, Hannah stared intently at her sister, studying her face, searching for the truth in Julia's small gray eyes.

"Julia—it was *you*!" Hannah finally managed to choke out.

As she stared back at Hannah, Julia's eyes turned cold. She nodded.

"*You* tried to poison me," Hannah accused, her voice just above a whisper.

Julia didn't deny it. She stared back, emotionless, her expression a blank.

"Why, Julia?" Hannah demanded. "Why?"

"I hate you, Hannah," Julia replied quietly, calmly. "I want you to die."

"But why? Why? Why?" Hannah shrieked. She realized she was more horrified by Julia's coldness than by her action.

"Why should *you* be the hostess?" Julia demanded, her black curls falling forward. She made no attempt to push them back. "Why should I not be the pretty one? The charming one? Why should *I* not be Father's favorite? Why should I not take Mother's place? I am the oldest—and the smartest. And—and—"

Her normally pale face was scarlet now. Her eyes burned into Hannah's. Her shoulders trembled. Julia's hands were balled into tight, angry fists at her sides.

Hannah shrank back, suddenly frightened. "Julia, you—*you* put the snake in my bed! *You* put the glass in my shoe. *You*—" Hannah's terrified voice caught in her throat.

Julia didn't deny it. "I wanted you to be scared. I wanted you to bleed. I want you to *die*!"

With a furious cry Julia attacked Hannah, leaping onto her, wrapping her hands around Hannah's throat.

Startled, caught completely off guard, Hannah stumbled and fell backward. She landed hard on her elbows and cried out from the pain.

Julia landed on top of her, her hands still at Hannah's throat.

Crying and groaning, the two girls wrestled on the ground—until Hannah broke free, climbed to her feet, and started to run.

But Julia was faster and tackled her sister hard from behind.

Hannah landed on her stomach on top of the pine coffin. She groaned and tried to pull herself up.

But Julia was on top of her again, pressing her down onto the hard coffin. And again Julia's hands wrapped around Hannah's throat.

"Die! Die! Die!" Julia shrieked at the top of her lungs as her hands tightened viciously around Hannah's throat.

Hannah struggled to roll free, to get off the coffin.

But Julia held tight as she choked off Hannah's air.

CHAPTER 18

Hannah gasped for breath, thrashing her arms frantically, trying to grab Julia, to push her away.

But Julia was too strong, too determined.

Hannah felt herself weaken, felt her muscles go slack, felt her body surrender.

Everything went bright red. Blood red. Then bright white. Hannah felt herself sinking, sinking into the white nothingness.

And then—miraculously—Julia's hands slipped away from Hannah's throat.

Hannah stared up at the white, white sky. Color returned slowly.

She took a short breath. Then another. The air made a whistling sound as it entered her lungs.

Julia thinks I am dead, Hannah realized. She believes she has murdered me. That is why she has released my throat.

Hannah sucked in another breath of air.

A sound in the woods behind them caused Julia to turn her back. Was there someone there? Had someone seen them?

No, it was only a deer scurrying in the underbrush. Julia bent over, hands on her knees, panting loudly.

She thinks she has murdered me.

The words repeated in Hannah's mind, turning her fear to anger. With a burst of strength she rolled off the coffin and landed on her feet.

Hannah stood unsteadily, the ground swaying beneath her.

"You—you're alive?" Julia cried breathlessly, spinning around, her eyes wide. She recovered quickly and lunged at Hannah.

Hannah grabbed the first thing she saw—the heavy iron shovel that had been used to dig Jenkins's grave.

As Julia leaped at her, Hannah cried out and swung the shovel.

It made a metallic *clang* as it slammed against Julia's head.

Julia's eyes bulged wide. Then they rolled up in her head as she dropped to her knees. Blood spurted from her nose, flowed down her chin. Finally she dropped face-down into the grass.

Hannah stared in horror, shaking all over, the heavy shovel still gripped tightly in both her hands. She watched the bright blood, Julia's blood, puddle on the grass.

I have killed her, she realized. *I have killed Julia.*

The shovel fell at Hannah's feet. She wrapped her arms around herself, trying to stop her body from trembling.

Now what?

She couldn't think clearly. Everything kept turning red, then white. Flashing crazily in front of her. The clouds overhead appeared to race. The sun dipped, then rose again.

Crazy. All too crazy.

Julia is dead.

Now what?

Before Hannah even realized what she was doing, she had pulled open the pine lid of the gardener's coffin. The stale aroma of his corpse floated up to greet her.

The old man's purple face stared blankly up at her. The eyes had sunk deep into Jenkins's skull. The lips were pulled tight in a hideous death grin.

Sobbing loudly, struggling to hold back her disgust, Hannah frantically grabbed her sister's body under the arms and pulled it to the coffin. Lifted. Lifted Julia's body, so heavy in death.

Shoved it into the coffin. On top of the rotting gardener.

Shoved it. Sobbing. Trembling. Shoved it. Shoved it in.

One arm draped itself over the side of the coffin.

Hannah grabbed the arm with both hands and bent it into the coffin.

And slammed the lid shut. And clasped it.

And ran blindly to the woods to vomit. To spew up the horror. The horror of having killed her only sister.

Her only sister, who had hated Hannah enough to try to murder *her.*

Choking and sobbing, Hannah clung to the cool trunk of a tree. And waited for her mind to clear, for the ground to stop swaying, for the lights to stop flashing in her head.

Hannah was still at the edge of the woods, still clinging to the solid tree trunk, when the small party of mourners gathered around the freshly dug grave to bury Jenkins.

Her cheek pressed against the smooth bark, Hannah watched the dark-coated minister, Bible in hand, say a few words over the coffin. The mourners, servants from the house and a few people from the village, bowed their heads as the minister spoke.

Then Hannah saw the strongest of the men step forward to lift the coffin into the grave. They struggled for a moment, surprised by the weight of it. Then, working silently together, they lowered the box into the ground and covered it with dirt, using the same shovel Hannah had used to kill Julia.

Julia is in the ground now, Hannah thought, watching the members of the small funeral party walking slowly toward the house. Julia is in the ground with Jenkins.

Hannah stayed in the woods a long while. When the sun began to lower itself behind the trees and the air grew evening cool, she wiped the tearstains from her cheeks. Then she straightened her dress and slowly walked back to the house.

"Where is Julia?" Simon asked.

Hannah pretended not to hear the question. She was slumped in a chair in a corner of the sitting room, watching Brandon and Joseph toss a small ball back and forth in front of the fire.

"Has anyone seen Julia?" Simon repeated impatiently from the doorway, his eyes on Hannah.

"I have not seen her, Father. Not since our picnic in the woods behind the house," Brandon replied, bouncing the ball gently to his little brother.

"Maybe she is still outside," Joseph said, missing the ball and scrambling after it.

"Can you two not find a better indoor activity?" Simon scolded sharply. He disappeared before the boys could reply.

Hannah shivered in spite of the heat that filled the room from the glowing fireplace. She stared at the boys but didn't really see them. Instead she saw the pine box. She saw Julia's arm hanging over the side of it. Then she saw the heavy pine box being lowered into the ground.

"Julia? Julia, are you upstairs?" Hannah heard her father shout up the stairs.

No. Julia is not upstairs, Hannah thought dully. Julia is not in the house, Father. Julia is in the ground.

"Julia? Where is Julia?" She heard her father calling. "Has anyone seen Julia?"

CHAPTER 19

Muttering to himself, Simon Fear pulled his cloak around himself as he stepped into the evening darkness. Having searched the entire house for his daughter, he decided to try the garden.

Sometimes Julia would completely lose track of the time, and Simon would find her on a bench in the garden, dreamily poring over a book of romantic poetry.

A pale crescent moon rose above the woods at the end of the back lawn. The sky was still a royal evening blue. A cool wind picked up and blew against Simon as he crossed the yard.

"Julia? Are you out here?" The wind threw his voice back to him. He pulled the cloak tighter.

The roses on the tall trellises bobbed in the gusting

breeze. The wind howled through the trees.

Or *was* it the wind?

Simon stopped and stood perfectly still, holding his cloak in place, his head tilted as he listened intently.

What was that horrible howl? That pained cry?

Simon took a few steps toward the frightening sound. He stood near the family burial plot, his eyes narrowed, listening.

There it was again.

A frightening shriek. Like the cry of a trapped animal.

Another shriek, high-pitched. A moan.

Simon turned toward the gardening sheds at the fence. Has a wild animal gotten itself trapped in one of the sheds? he wondered.

Another mournful howl.

No. The sound was too close.

So nearby.

Simon grasped his cloak as another shrill cry rose on a gust of wind.

He stared down at the ground. It seemed as if the sound was at his feet.

"But that's impossible!" he cried.

And then he realized that he was standing beside a freshly dug grave, the dark earth still mounded loose over the coffin.

Mr. Jenkins's grave.

Another pitiful cry, a desperate animal shriek.

From the ground. From the grave.

Someone crying out from the new grave.

A girl.

Julia!

"No!" Simon uttered, terror choking him.

Before he realized what he was doing, he had picked up the shovel and begun digging into the earth.

His heart pounding, Simon frantically shoveled, the blade cutting easily into the soft dirt. Working feverishly, he tossed the dirt over his shoulder, digging down, down—until finally, when he felt his chest was about to burst, the shovel hit something solid. The lid of the coffin.

"Yes!" Simon cried and began digging wildly, scraping and shoving the dirt out of the hole.

So close! So close!

"I'm coming!" he screamed in a panic-filled voice he didn't recognize. "I'm coming! I'm coming!"

He didn't try to lift the coffin. Instead he tossed the shovel aside and leaped down into the hole.

With trembling hands he lifted the latch. Then, gasping loudly, his heart thudding against his chest, he pulled up the coffin lid.

CHAPTER 20

"Julia!"

Simon cried out when he saw his daughter sprawled on top of the gardener's corpse.

Her black hair had fallen over her face. He brushed it back gently, his hand trembling, loud sobs escaping his throat.

Dead. She was dead.

So pale. Her face was locked in a grimace of terror, her lifeless eyes wide. Dried blood was caked over her nose and chin.

"Nooooooo!" The howl erupted from Simon. It echoed against the dark walls of the grave he had opened.

He gaped in horror at his daughter. Her fingernails were torn and bloodied. Simon saw long scratch marks along the inside of the coffin lid.

Buried alive, he realized. *Julia was buried alive.*

The wind howled above him. He gazed up at the sliver of pale moon. He couldn't bear to look at her any longer.

"Who?" he cried, scrambling out of the hole, scrabbling over the soft dirt, his arms thrashing wildly. "Who did this? Who?"

Back up on solid ground, he staggered toward the house. "Who did this? Who murdered my daughter?"

He tossed the cloak to the ground and began to run.

The house loomed ahead, a dark blur. The whole world had become a dark blur.

Moments later he stood in the kitchen, struggling to catch his breath, struggling to stop the painful pounding of his heart.

"Mrs. MacKenzie! Mrs. MacKenzie!" he screamed frantically. Where was she? Where was everyone?

He grabbed on to a sideboard to keep himself from collapsing.

Something near his hand caught his attention.

A long sheet of paper with scribbled words down one side. Scribbled names.

The servant's list.

The newly written name at the bottom of the list, the ink still dark and fresh.

LUCY GOODE.

"Nooooooooooo!" A wild animal howl erupted from deep inside him. "Not a Goode! Not a Goode in my house!"

Simon truly believed the Goodes had vanished from the earth. He believed he had killed the last of them—Frank Goode—back in Wickham when he was still a boy.

He believed that the curse had ended that long-ago day. That no member of the Goode family could ever threaten the Fears again.

And now here was a Goode hiding in his own household, carrying on the evil of the Goodes against the Fears—*murdering his Julia!*

"Nooooooo!" Simon grasped the silver pendant tightly in one hand. He felt its warmth, felt its power.

His rage carried him into the front parlor.

He picked out a sword from the new collection of war relics. He waved it high. It gleamed in the light from the gas lamps.

He followed the sword's gleam.

Running frantically, bellowing his rage, Simon followed the glow of the sword through the house.

I will find her. I will find Lucy Goode!

I will put an end to the evil she has brought to my house, to my family!

"Simon! What are you *doing*! Simon!"

Was that Angelica calling to him from the stairway?

He did not slow down. He followed the glowing sword. Glowing like a torch now. Glowing with the heat of his vengeance.

"Simon—stop!"

Angelica sounded so far away.

I will find her. I will find the maid—

There she stood!

A bright blurred figure walking toward him, beyond the blinding glow of the sword blade.

Yes! He had found her!

Yes!

The maid. The Goode. A Goode walking in his very own hallway.

"Simon—*stop!"* Angelica called.

But Simon could not stop.

He lowered the gleaming sword.

The girl shrieked and threw her hands up in terror.

He had her. He had her now.

The sword glowed so brightly, so brightly he could see only its light.

"Simon—*stop*! *Stop!"* Angelica screamed.

But Simon plunged the sword deep into the maid's chest.

CHAPTER 21

The light shimmered around Simon, blinding white light.

As he thrust the sword into Lucy Goode and she uttered a choking gasp of pain, the light grew even brighter.

A small round dark spot formed in the center of the light. The spot grew, spreading its darkness.

It took Simon a while to realize that the spot was blood, blood staining the front of the girl's dress.

Darker, darker. The spot expanded until it blocked out the light.

And as the darkness grew and the shimmering light faded, Simon's vision was restored. He could see clearly once again.

Still holding the long ebony handle of the sword,

staring at the blood as it stained the dress, Simon could see. Could see that he hadn't stabbed Lucy Goode.

He had thrust the sword deep into his own daughter's chest.

"Simon! Simon!" Angelica's shrill cries repeated in his ears, shutting out all other sounds, shutting out his own horrified thoughts. "Simon! Simon! Simon!"

Then Hannah fell forward and slumped into her father's arms, as his sword clanged heavily to the floor.

Warm blood poured over Simon's evening shirt. Hannah's blood.

She uttered a soft moan. Her lips continued to move after all sound had died.

All sound except Angelica's shrill chant: "Simon! Simon! Simon!"

Hannah died in Simon's arms, her head lying heavily against his shoulder, her soft blond hair brushing his cheek, falling over his shoulder.

Hannah dead. Julia dead.

Angelica shrieked, her eyes shut tight, pulling frantically at her long black hair.

Robert held his brothers, turning them away from the hideous scene before them.

Mrs. MacKenzie sobbed against the wall, burying her face in her apron.

"I—I thought it was Lucy Goode," Simon sputtered.

"Lucy Goode resigned this afternoon," Mrs. MacKenzie

replied through her sobs. "She could not bear Miss Hannah's accusations. She packed her bag and departed."

With a quiet shudder Simon held his lifeless daughter. As he struggled to keep her on her feet, they appeared to be dancing, a strange, sad, awkward last dance.

Hannah is gone, he realized. *Julia is gone. The wonderful part of my life is over.*

"Simon! Simon! Simon!" Angelica chanted.

"I tried to hide from it, Angelica," Simon sobbed. "I tried to pretend it no longer existed. But the curse that follows the Fear family has found us all today."

"Simon! Simon! Simon!" Angelica shrieked behind him. "Simon! Simon! Simon!"

Simon Fear knew that her cries would haunt him for the rest of his life.

PART THREE

Shadyside Village

1900

CHAPTER 22

On a gloomy fall day a young man stepped off the westbound train onto the narrow concrete platform of the Shadyside train station. He was a good-looking boy of eighteen, with slicked-down brown hair, lively brown eyes, and a friendly, open face.

He quickly glanced down the main street of the small town. Shadyside appeared to be prosperous and pleasant with low brick buildings behind shady trees. Then he hailed a carriage with a cheerful cry. "Cabbie! Cabbie!"

The driver, a shriveled old man with white whiskers and long white sideburns beneath a worn blue cap, stopped the horses and hopped down to help the young man with his suitcase.

"I can handle it, driver," the young man said, offering

his friendly smile. "I have but one bag, as you can see."

"And where do you come from?" the cabbie asked, eyeing the boy suspiciously.

"Boston" was the reply. "My name is Daniel. Daniel Fear. And I have come to visit my grandparents."

The old driver's eyes narrowed in surprise. "Daniel Fear, did you say? And you have come to visit Simon Fear and his wife?"

"They are my grandparents. I have never met them," Daniel admitted. He hoisted his bag onto the luggage compartment at the back of the carriage. One of the two horses whinnied. The carriage rocked back and forth.

"My name is McGuire," the cabbie said, touching his cap. "I have been driving this rig in Shadyside Village for a lot longer than you have been alive, son. And you are the first visitor I have ever taken to the Fear mansion."

"Strange," Daniel replied uncertainly.

"Strange indeed," McGuire said, shaking his head. "That house has been dark and closed up ever since the two daughters died. That was some thirty-five years ago, I believe."

"Simon's daughters?" Daniel asked, surprised. "You mean that I had aunts?"

The cabbie nodded. "Who might your father be, son?"

"Joseph Fear," Daniel told him.

"Ah, yes, Joseph," McGuire said, removing his cap to scratch his head. "I remember him well. Good-looking boy. I remember they sent him away to school. A couple of years after the . . . uh . . . after the tragedy with the two girls. Joseph never returned home."

"Yes. We live in Boston now," Daniel said. "None of us has ever been back to Shadyside. My father is a very quiet man, a private man. He never told us much about our family. I did not even know I *had* grandparents here until word came about my grandfather's seventy-fifth birthday."

"So Simon Fear is to be seventy-five," McGuire muttered, rubbing his chin.

"Yes," Daniel replied. "My grandfather wrote a letter and asked to see me. So . . . here I am."

The old cabbie muttered something that Daniel couldn't hear. Then he turned and, with a loud groan, hoisted himself up to the driver's seat. Daniel watched McGuire take the reins, then climbed inside the small carriage, pulling the door closed beside him.

Staring out the dusty window, Daniel watched the small town roll by. The town center with its offices and shops gave way to rows of small cottages, then farm fields, then tangled woods. The overcast sky made everything appear dark and unwelcoming.

Suddenly Daniel heard McGuire shout for the horses to *whoa,* and the carriage bounced to an abrupt stop. Daniel peered out at a tall brass gate. The gate was tarnished.

"Here we are, son," McGuire called down. "The Fear mansion."

Daniel opened the carriage door and leaned out. "Can you not take me up the driveway?"

His question was greeted by a long silence. Finally the old man called down gruffly, "This is as far as I go. Few people would wish to come as near as this to Simon Fear's mansion."

Daniel climbed down and removed his bag. He handed up two coins to the driver, who stared straight ahead, refusing to look at the mansion. Then with a curt "Good luck, son," McGuire whipped the horses, and the carriage sped away.

Daniel pushed open the heavy gate and stepped onto the long dirt driveway that led up to the house. "Oh!" The sight of the enormous mansion looming against the charcoal gray sky made Daniel stop and cry out.

Tall weeds choked the lawn. Shrubs and hedges had grown wild. A fallen tree limb lay across a barren, neglected flowerbed.

The house, a ramshackle, dark fortress, stretched behind a thick veil of bent trees. All of the windows were shuttered. No welcoming light greeted Daniel as he trudged up the driveway. No light escaped from the house at all.

So *this* is where Father grew up! he thought in amazement. What a dreary, frightening old place. No *wonder* Father never talks about his childhood.

Dead, brown leaves rustled at Daniel's feet as he

stepped up to the double front door and lifted the heavy brass knocker. He could hear the bang of the knocker echoing inside the house.

He waited, listening. He knocked again.

Finally the heavy door creaked open.

A stooped, white-haired old woman poked her head out and stared up at him suspiciously. She wore a stained white apron over a black dress. One of her eyes had glazed over. It was solid gray. The other eye squinted hard at him.

Frowning, she muttered something that Daniel couldn't hear.

"I beg your pardon?" he asked, leaning closer.

"Stay *away*!" the old woman rasped. *"Stay away from here!"*

CHAPTER 23

Startled, Daniel stared back at the old woman. "I am Daniel Fear," he said finally. "I believe my grandfather is expecting me."

The old woman sighed but didn't reply. She squinted up at him for a long time with her one good eye. Then she beckoned him inside, gesturing with a bony, gnarled finger.

"I am Mrs. MacKenzie, the housekeeper," she told him, leaning on a white cane as she led him through a long, dark hallway. "I am housekeeper, maid, valet, and butler," she added with some bitterness. "The only servant who stayed."

Daniel followed her in silence, carrying his bag. As they made their way through narrow, dark hallways, he tried to peer into the rooms they passed. They all seemed to be dark and shuttered, the furniture covered with sheets.

"My father did not tell me the house was so large," Daniel said, his voice echoing in the empty hall.

"Your father got away . . ." Mrs. MacKenzie answered mysteriously.

They continued through the dark, gloomy house in silence. The only sounds Daniel heard were the scraping of his boots on the threadbare carpet and the *tap-tap-tap* of the old housekeeper's white cane as she walked.

At the end of a twisting hallway Daniel saw a flicker of orange light from a corner room. "Your grandparents are in there," Mrs. MacKenzie said softly, pointing. She turned, leaving him in the hall, and disappeared around a corner, her cane tapping its insistent rhythm.

Is the old woman completely mad? Daniel wondered. Or just unfriendly?

He took a deep breath and reluctantly approached the doorway. He saw a low fire crackling in a wide stone fireplace. Setting down his suitcase, Daniel stepped into the room.

His grandmother caught his eye first. Angelica was stretched out on a purple velvet chaise longue beside the fire. She wore an elegant black dress with a white lace collar.

She smiled at Daniel as he approached, but made no

attempt to stand up. As she smiled, Daniel saw that her skin was delicate and translucent and tight against the bone, making her face resemble that of a grinning skull. Her hair fell loosely down her back. It was as white as snow.

"Grandmother Angelica," Daniel said with a slight bow. He reached for her hand, but she didn't offer it.

"Put another log on the fire, boy," Angelica ordered.

"I beg your pardon?" Daniel had expected a warmer greeting from his grandmother.

"Do not dawdle. Do as I say," Angelica insisted coldly, waving a slender white hand toward the fire. "Another log on the fire, boy."

Daniel hesitated, then hurried to the fireplace to do her bidding. He could find no logs in the wood basket, so he piled on several sticks of kindling.

Then, wiping his hands, he turned back to his grandmother. "I am so pleased to meet you," he said, smiling sincerely.

"You may go now," Angelica replied curtly. Before the startled Daniel could reply, she started to scream: *"Did you not hear me? Go! Go! Go!"*

Daniel gaped at her, trying to decide what to say or do.

"Pay no attention to her," a high-pitched voice wheezed from behind him.

Daniel wheeled around and saw a nearly bald old man hunched over in a wooden wheelchair. He had a thin brown blanket tucked over his legs. His face was yellow and sickly in the flickering firelight. He stared at Daniel through square-shaped spectacles with his dark eyes, eyes like tiny black buttons.

"Grandfather!" Daniel declared.

Simon Fear wheeled himself closer, both hands pushing at the large wooden wheelchair wheels. "Pay no attention to Angelica. She is mad! Mad as a loon!" He cackled as if he had made a joke.

Daniel glanced back at Angelica, who lay staring at the fire.

"Grandfather Simon, I am pleased to meet you," Daniel said, turning back to the frail old man.

Simon extended a slender, spotted hand to his grandson. Daniel reached down to shake hands. He almost cried out. Simon's hand was unearthly cold!

"Joseph's boy," Simon muttered, refusing to let go of Daniel's hand. Behind the eyeglasses the tiny black sparrow eyes had locked on Daniel's face as if trying to memorize every detail. "Yes, yes. I see Joseph in you," he said and then coughed for several seconds, allowing Daniel the opportunity to remove his hand from the icy grip.

"My father sends his love," Daniel said stiffly.

"Love? What is love?" Angelica chimed in from behind him. "What is love? I would really like to know."

"Joseph has no love for us," Simon said darkly, wiping

saliva from his colorless lips with the back of his hand.

"I beg your pardon?" Daniel exclaimed.

"My son Joseph abandoned us. I tried to make him understand that we Fears have no choice but to stick together, to band together, to hide together against our enemies. But Joseph chose to disobey me."

The light seemed to fade from Simon's eyes. He lowered his head. For a moment Daniel thought that his grandfather had fallen asleep.

"Put another log on the fire!" Angelica ordered impatiently. "Another log, if you please! Why must it always be so cold in here?"

"There do not seem to be any more logs," Daniel told his grandmother.

An icy hand grabbed his wrist. Simon held him with surprising strength. "I told you to ignore her!" he snapped.

Daniel tried to pull free. The cold from Simon's hand seemed to sweep right through Daniel's entire body. "Grandfather—"

"You cannot hide from your blood!" Simon declared loudly, staring up at Daniel, tightening his cold grip on his grandson's wrist. "I told Joseph that when he was just a boy. You cannot hide from your blood and your fate."

"Yes, Grandfather," Daniel stammered, trying to be polite.

"His brothers Robert and Brandon stayed," Simon said. "But now they're gone too."

"I never met my uncles," Daniel replied softly.

"Now you are here, Daniel," Simon said, smiling up at him, a frightening smile that sent shivers up Daniel's spine. "Now you are here to carry on my work."

Daniel swallowed hard. "Your work? I—I came to celebrate your birthday, Grandfather. I—"

Simon ignored him. He had both hands up behind his collar, struggling to remove something from around his neck. Finally he succeeded. With another frightening smile he tucked an object into Daniel's hand.

Daniel took a step back toward the fireplace and examined his grandfather's gift. To his surprise it was a piece of silver jewelry. Disk shaped, it was held by three silver claws, like birds' feet. On the disk were four blue jewels that sparkled brightly in the firelight.

What a strange gift, Daniel thought. He turned the pendant over. On the back he found Latin words inscribed: DOMINATIO PER MALUM.

"What do these words mean, Grandfather?" Daniel asked, studying the strange silver pendant.

"Power through evil!" Simon bellowed. His loud cry caused him to cough and wheeze.

Daniel studied the strange pendant, turning it over in his hands.

"Put it on," Simon instructed him. "Wear it always. It has been in the Fear family since our days in the Old Country."

Daniel obediently slipped the silver chain around his neck.

He tucked the pendant under his dress shirt.

And as the warm disk settled against his chest, he felt a surge of heat—and the entire room burst into flame!

CHAPTER 24

Daniel saw flames before him—the bright image of flames leaping tall into a black sky. A momentary image, a vision, lasting a second or two.

In the flames he saw a girl, a young girl, pretty and blond, twisting in the fire, twisting in agony.

The image disappeared. The girl and the flames vanished instantly.

The pendant still felt warm against his chest.

Simon smiled knowingly up at his grandson.

The strange three-clawed pendant has powers, Daniel realized, feeling fear and curiosity at once.

Daniel heard a tapping sound behind him. He turned to see Mrs. MacKenzie enter the room, bent over her cane, an unpleasant frown on her withered face.

"I have come to take the young gentleman to his room," she announced coldly, glaring at Simon with her one good eye.

Simon didn't reply. He nodded. His eyes closed.

"Put another log on the fire, boy," Angelica ordered. "I'm cold—so cold!"

Mrs. MacKenzie grunted her disapproval of her mistress. Feeling awkward and confused, Daniel picked up his bag and followed the old housekeeper out of the room.

Tapping her cane against the thin carpets, she led him through a twisting maze of dark halls. Then up creaking stairs to a large bedroom on the second floor.

Daniel followed her in. The room was cold. The small fire in the fireplace offered little heat. Mrs. MacKenzie made her way to the window and pulled the shutters open to allow some light in. But the windows were caked with soot.

She offered Daniel a helpless shrug, then hurried from the room, her cane tapping in front of her.

Daniel slumped onto the bed, shivering. "Why have I come here?" he asked himself out loud.

Shaking his head unhappily, he removed his pocket watch and studied it. Hours to go before dinner. And Simon's birthday party is several weeks away.

What will I do here? How will I spend the time?

Staring into the small, useless fire, Daniel wished he had never come.

* * *

Dinner was solitary and silent. Simon and Angelica were nowhere to be seen. Mrs. MacKenzie served Daniel his dinner at one end of the long dining room table. He had little appetite but forced himself to eat.

The next day he made his way into town and strolled around Shadyside Village, delighted to be out of the stale air and gloomy surroundings of the Fear mansion.

He found the town square pretty and pleasant. People smiled at him as he passed. Daniel was so good-looking and friendly, he often drew smiles from strangers.

A crowd of villagers had gathered at the edge of the square to admire a shiny new motorcar, one of the few "horseless carriages" that Daniel had seen in Boston. Eagerly he strolled over to see it. A strange-looking four-wheeled contraption of glass and painted metal.

A red-faced man in his shirtsleeves was straining hard, turning a metal crank at the front of the machine, trying to start it up. But in spite of the enthusiastic support of the crowd, the engine refused to sputter to life.

Chuckling to himself, Daniel stepped away and realized he was quite thirsty, probably from the dust that floated up from Shadyside's unpaved streets.

A small white-fronted general store on the corner caught his eye, and he made his way toward it, thinking of a cold drink.

As he pulled open the door, the aroma of fresh-brewed coffee greeted his nostrils. He closed the door behind him.

Then, stepping past a large wooden pickle barrel and several burlap bags of flour and sugar, he stopped at the long wooden counter at the back of the store.

A young woman dressed in a silky yellow high-collared blouse and long maroon skirt had her back to him. She was reaching up to arrange canisters on a shelf on the wall.

Daniel cleared his throat impatiently.

She turned and smiled, surprised to see a stranger in the store.

And Daniel fell in love.

She is the most beautiful girl I have ever seen, Daniel thought, feeling dazed.

She appeared to be about his age with long dark hair that fell to her shoulders, creamy pale skin, and green eyes that gleamed in the light from the store window.

Her smile, the most beautiful smile Daniel had ever seen, faded. "Are you staring at me?" she demanded. Her voice was lower, throatier than he had expected.

"Yes," he replied. He couldn't think of any other reply.

Speechless. I'm speechless, he thought. Maybe coming to Shadyside was not such a bad idea after all.

He suddenly realized she was gazing at him with concern, her broad forehead wrinkling above the beautiful green eyes.

He blinked. Felt himself blushing.

"Are you feeling well?" she asked, hanging back from the counter.

"I—I apologize," Daniel managed to stammer. "I—I am thirsty. So—"

"Would you like coffee? Or perhaps some apple cider?" she suggested, her smile returning. "It is very fresh."

Daniel adjusted the starched collar of his shirt. It suddenly felt very tight. "Yes. Thank you. Cider would be wonderful."

"Well, it *is* good. I do not know if it is wonderful," she replied dryly. With a sweep of her long skirt she made her way around the counter, carrying a tin cup toward the cider barrel across the aisle.

She walks so gracefully, Daniel thought, following her with his eyes. Like a poem. He suddenly wished he knew poetry.

She handed him the cup filled with cider. He took a sip. "Very good." He licked his lips. He raised his eyes to hers and realized that *she* was now staring at *him.*

She glanced away shyly. "Are you new in town?"

Daniel told her he was. "Can you tell me of some interesting places I should see?"

She laughed. "Interesting? In *Shadyside*?"

He laughed with her. He liked her sense of humor. And he liked the way her chin trembled when she laughed. And he liked her low, velvety voice.

"Surely there must be something worth seeing," he protested.

She narrowed her green eyes as she thought. "I am sorry. There really is not much of interest here—except perhaps the Fear mansion."

Her reply startled Daniel. He decided to play innocent. "The Fear mansion? What is so interesting about that?"

Her expression turned serious. She lowered her voice to a whisper. "It is a very frightening place. Horrible stories are told about it. I really do not know if they are true or not. It is said that the Fears live under a terrible curse, that the mansion is cursed, too. It is said that everyone who enters—"

"Every town has a house like that!" Daniel scoffed, shaking his head.

My grandfather's house certainly *looks* like a cursed place, Daniel thought. I wonder why the villagers tell such stories about it.

"I would not venture near it, even for sightseeing," the girl remarked with a frown.

"I will take your advice," Daniel told her. "Would you care to show me around the rest of your town?"

She blushed. A coy smile played over her full lips. "Why, sir, I do not even know your name."

"It is Daniel," he told her eagerly. He started to reveal his full name, but stopped. He realized he didn't want her to know yet that he was a Fear.

"Daniel? I like that name," she replied, her eyes lighting up. "I was once going to name my dog Daniel."

They both laughed.

"And may I ask *your* name?" Daniel asked.

"Nora," she said, pale circles of pink forming on her cheeks. "Nora Goode."

CHAPTER 25

"Quick—someone's coming!" Nora whispered. She grabbed Daniel's arm and pulled him off the road into the trees.

Daniel laughed. "It's just a rabbit. Look." He pointed to the large brown rabbit that scampered over the carpet of dry leaves at the edge of the woods.

Nora laughed and pressed her forehead against the sleeve of Daniel's jacket.

I love her laugh, he decided.

I love everything about her.

As they walked hand in hand toward the river, Daniel found it hard to believe they had met just five days earlier. He had never felt this way about anyone.

Each afternoon he had waited around the corner from

her father's store for her to finish work. Then, trying to make it appear that they weren't walking together, they would make their way up the broad Park Drive to the Conononka River, which flowed through the woods north of the village.

There they would sit side by side and hold hands under a shady tree. As the sun lowered itself behind the cliffs across the river, they talked quietly, getting to know each other, discussing whatever popped into their heads.

Daniel had explained to Nora that he was visiting his grandparents. But he still hadn't worked up the courage to tell her that his grandparents were Simon and Angelica Fear.

"Do your grandparents not wonder where you go every afternoon?" Nora asked. Her dark hair shimmered in the patches of sunlight that filtered down through the tree leaves.

"My grandparents show little desire for my company," Daniel told her. "Most days they do not come out of their rooms. When I do see them, they ask me little. In fact, they hardly speak to me at all."

"How strange," Nora murmured thoughtfully.

"My grandmother lives in a world of her own," Daniel said sadly. "I am not sure she even knows I am her grandson. And my grandfather . . . he spends his days in his wheelchair by the fire, muttering dreamily to himself."

"You must be lonely," Nora remarked, squeezing his hand.

"Not when I see you," Daniel replied boldly.

She smiled at him, her green eyes catching the light of the lowering sun. He realized that Nora must be lonely, too.

Her mother had died in childbirth. Nora was an only child. She spent her days working in her father's general store. She spent her evenings cooking and caring for her father. They lived in rooms above the store.

"My dream is to move away some day," she had revealed to Daniel. "To a town with wide, paved streets and buildings as tall as the trees, a town filled with people I don't know."

As the red sun flattened against the dark cliffs above them, Daniel worked up his nerve, leaned forward, and kissed Nora.

He expected her to resist. But when she returned the kiss with enthusiasm, he realized that perhaps she was as in love with him as he was with her.

I have to reveal to her that I am a Fear, he thought, wrapping his arms around her and kissing her again. But will she react with horror? Does she believe the frightening stories about my family? When she learns I am a Fear, will it drive her away?

The thought made him shudder. Daniel knew he couldn't bear to lose Nora.

As they walked holding hands back to her father's store, Daniel decided he had to learn the truth. Before he revealed his identity to Nora, he had to find out if there really was a curse on his family, if the terrifying tales the villagers told about the Fears were true.

Once I know they are *not* true, once I know they are all silly fairy tales, then I will be able to tell Nora that I am a Fear with a clear heart, he decided.

He said good night at the edge of town, reluctant to let go of her soft, warm hand. Her eyes glowed happily as she whispered good night. Then she turned and ran to the store, her silky dark hair trailing gently behind her.

Her heart fluttering, the taste of Daniel's lips still on hers, Nora brushed through the dark store, humming to herself. Thinking happily about Daniel, she started up the narrow stairs that led to the rooms she shared with her father.

Nora gasped, startled to find her father waiting for her at the top of the stairs, an angry expression on his face.

James Goode, Nora's father, was a short, wiry man with shiny slicked-down black hair and a black pencil mustache beneath his long, pointed nose. He was normally quiet and good-tempered. But when his anger got the better of him, he would explode with rage and lose control so that he frightened Nora.

Now she hesitated halfway up the stairs, staring up at his angry frown, his blazing eyes.

"Where have you been?" he demanded, struggling to keep his voice low and steady.

"Just out for a walk," Nora told him blankly.

He glared at her, his face set in an angry scowl. He motioned for her to come the rest of the way up the stairs. Then he followed her into the small sitting room.

"Just out for a walk with *whom*?" he demanded, crossing his thin arms over the chest of his undershirt.

"With a friend," Nora replied uncomfortably.

"He is no friend," James Goode said through clenched teeth. "The boy you have been sneaking out with is no friend at all—he is a *Fear*!"

Nora gasped. She dropped down onto the straight-backed wooden chair by the fireplace. "He never told me, Father."

"Of course he didn't!" Mr. Goode snapped. "He knew that no decent girl would be seen walking with a Fear in this town!"

"But, Papa—" Nora's mind whirled in confusion. Why hadn't Daniel been honest with her? Was he afraid?

"Papa, Daniel is wonderful," she said finally. "He is kind and gentle. He is intelligent and considerate and—"

"He is a Fear," her father interrupted with a scowl. He stood over Nora, his hands tensed awkwardly at his sides. "I will not have you seeing a Fear. You know the history of that cursed family. Everyone in Shadyside knows."

"I don't *care* about that!" Nora cried. "They are just wild stories."

"Wild stories?" James Goode exclaimed. "Wild stories?

Why, Simon Fear's own daughters were *murdered* when they were about your age. Murdered!"

"Papa, that was so long ago!" Nora cried. "No one knows what really happened—"

"The two girls were found in the woods with their bones removed!" James cried. "They found only their skins. Their bones were gone! Gone!"

"You know that's just an old story!" Nora screamed. "No one but silly children believes that, Father!"

"Maybe not, but Simon's wife, Angelica, she *is* mad, Nora. She practices evil magic. People have disappeared in the woods behind the Fear mansion. They were Angelica's human sacrifices. They—"

"Papa, stop! These are all wild tales! Gossip and rumors! You *cannot* believe such insane stories!"

James groaned in exasperation, running both hands back through his slicked-down hair, scowling at his daughter. "I *do* believe them," he said, his voice trembling. "I believe them all. This is why I cannot allow you to see that Fear boy again, Nora."

"No!" Nora shrieked, jumping to her feet, her eyes wild. "I *love* Daniel, Father! I *love* him! You *cannot* forbid me to see him!"

"Nora, listen to me," James insisted, his pencil mustache twitching in anger, his slender face reddening. "Listen to me! For your own good, you cannot see him again! I forbid it!"

"No!" Nora shrieked, her anger matching her father's. "No! No! No!"

James Goode's eyes narrowed angrily. His words came out slowly, deliberately, through clenched teeth: "Then, Nora, you have given me no choice. . . ."

CHAPTER 26

That night Daniel waited until the house was silent and dark. Then, carrying a candle, he crept downstairs to Simon's library, determined to learn the truth about his family's history.

Holding the candle high, Daniel could see that all four walls were covered from floor to ceiling with books. The air smelled musty, almost thick with dust from the old volumes.

The floorboards creaked under Daniel's shoes as he crossed the room to get a closer look at the books. To Daniel's surprise, the first shelf he examined held books about magic, the dark arts, strange scientific journals, and volumes about astrology and foretelling the future.

How strange that Simon should possess books of this

nature, Daniel thought, moving the candle along the shelves. Did he and Angelica have a *scientific* interest in such matters?

Daniel searched the library shelves for another twenty minutes but found nothing of interest, nothing that would reveal his family's history to him.

Suddenly hungry and thirsty, he made his way to the kitchen with his candle. The old house creaked and groaned as he walked through the darkness. As if warning me away, he thought, feeling a chill.

A glass of water satisfied his thirst. Then, moving the candle in front of him, Daniel made his way to the pantry behind the kitchen. "Where are those ginger cookies we had at dinner?" he whispered to himself.

He heard the soft scrabble of padded feet. The kitchen cat, no doubt, chasing after a mouse.

He moved the candle over the shelves of tins and jars. No cookies.

Something beyond the pantry shelves caught his attention. A crack in the wall formed a shadow in the flickering candlelight.

Curious, Daniel pressed on the crack, and the wall slid back. *A hidden doorway!* Daniel realized.

His heart beating excitedly, he pushed the door open farther and slipped inside. He found himself in a low-ceilinged narrow room. Holding the candle high, he saw two pillows on the floor, stained by dark mildew, a bundled-up blanket, a girl's doll.

How strange, Daniel thought, bending to pick up the doll. Its dress was covered with dust. Its round blue eyes stared up at him in the candlelight.

Whose doll was this? Daniel wondered, setting it down on one of the pillows. Who used this hidden room? Judging from the dust and mildew, it hasn't been occupied in many years.

He kicked at the blanket, raising a cloud of dust. His shoe hit something solid underneath. "How strange. How strange," he muttered to himself.

He pulled the blanket away and lowered the candle. The light fell over a large dark-covered book. Bending to examine it, Daniel saw that it was an old Bible.

The spine was cracked. The tattered pages smelled of mildew and decay.

This Bible looks as if it has been in the family for many generations, Daniel thought. Why has it been hidden under a blanket in this secret room?

Kneeling on the dusty floor, he began searching through the pages with his free hand. In the back of the Bible he found what he was searching for—a family history.

Tattered, brown-stained pages held the scrawled handwriting of his ancestors. Daniel's eyes eagerly rolled over names and dates, births and deaths.

He saw the date 1692 and read the names Matthew and Benjamin Fier. Wickham, Massachusetts Colony.

Our name was spelled differently then, Daniel realized. I wonder when the change was made—and why.

His eyes eagerly searched the page, reading about other Fiers. So many early deaths, Daniel realized, narrowing his eyes and lowering the candle as he struggled to make out the dates. So many deaths, sometimes two or three at a time.

Bent over the old volume, he turned the page excitedly, his eyes running down the names and dates. Suddenly the candle flickered.

Strange, Daniel thought. There is no breeze in this tiny room.

The candle flickered again.

Had someone else entered the room?

Daniel started to turn as a cold hand was tightly clamped over his mouth.

CHAPTER 27

Daniel tried to cry out, but the hand gripped tighter.

"Sshhhhh. Do not make a sound," a voice whispered.

The cold hand slipped away. Daniel turned to see Mrs. MacKenzie staring down at him, her glazed-over eye catching the light from his trembling candle. She gave him a strange smile.

"Is it the family history you are looking for?" she whispered, lowering her good eye to the Bible on the floor. "You have no need of books, young master. I will tell you all."

"Wh-what is this room? Why is the family Bible hidden here?" Daniel stammered, climbing unsteadily to his feet.

"I thought it would be safe here," the old housekeeper replied. "This is a secret room. Your aunts, Simon's poor daughters, Hannah and Julia—may they rest in peace—would hide in here to whisper and giggle together. They thought I did not know about this room, but I did."

"How—how did they die?" Daniel demanded.

The old woman raised a finger to her lips. "The curse of the Fears caught up with them."

"Then my family *is* cursed?" Daniel cried. His trembling voice revealed his horror.

"Follow me," Mrs. MacKenzie whispered. "I shall reveal all to you tonight."

He followed her through the dark, twisting halls to her quarters. There, in her tiny, nearly bare room, she motioned with her cane. "Sit you down," the old woman whispered, shoving him toward the high-backed armchair. "I will tell you about the Fears. More than you wish to know."

"The family is really cursed?" Daniel asked again, obediently lowering himself to the chair, staring intently at the old lady in the flickering candlelight. "Are the stories true?"

Mrs. MacKenzie nodded, leaning on her cane. "The curse came about because of your first relatives in the New World. Their names were Matthew and Benjamin Fier."

"I saw those names in the Bible," Daniel told her.

"They were treacherous men. Ambitious. They did

not care who they betrayed," the old woman rasped, scowling.

"And the curse? It came about because of them?"

"They burned a young woman at the stake, the Fiers did," Mrs. MacKenzie told him, tapping her cane on the carpet in rhythm with her words. "They burned an *innocent* young woman. Her heartbroken father put a curse on your family.

"From that day on," the old woman continued, "the two families have sought vengeance on each other. Decade after decade, generation after generation, the two families have used all of the evil at their command. They have terrified and betrayed and murdered each other."

She proceeded to tell him the stories of vengeance and betrayal. Daniel listened in chilled silence. Her croaking voice etched the scenes of terror deep into his mind.

"And my grandfather—?" Daniel asked finally, astounded by the old woman's stories.

"Simon Fear thought he could escape the curse by changing the family name. But it followed him. It found him. His young daughters died a horrible death because of it."

The candle trembled in Daniel's hand. He set it down on the arm of the chair.

"Joseph, your father, watched his sister Hannah die. He knew from that moment on that he had to get away from this house, from this village. His brother, Robert, did not get away. He died of a strange fever, many said brought on by a spell from his evil daughter-in-law, Sarah Fear. The other brother, Brandon, and his son Ben—they just wandered into the woods and disappeared. The curse . . .

"The curse of the two families continues to this day," the old woman said, shaking her head.

"The other family," Daniel whispered. "What is their name?"

Mrs. MacKenzie hesitated. She coughed, leaning on her cane.

"Mrs. MacKenzie, please tell me," Daniel urged. "What is the name of the other family, the family that has cursed mine?"

"Their name is Goode," the old woman revealed.

Daniel gasped. "Goode? But that cannot be!" he sputtered. "Mrs. MacKenzie, I—I am in love with a Goode! Nora Goode! She cannot possibly be related to the evil family who—"

"She is a Goode," the housekeeper replied solemnly, staring hard at Daniel, leaning into the candlelight.

"No!" Daniel cried, leaping to his feet. "No! I cannot accept this! Nora is kind and gentle. She is innocent of any evil. I am certain she knows nothing of this curse!"

"Perhaps she does not know," Mrs. MacKenzie replied, leaning on the cane. "Perhaps you and she will be the ones to break the curse."

"Break the curse?" Daniel asked eagerly. He grabbed the old woman, "Break the curse? How?"

"If a Fear and a Goode were to marry . . ." Mrs. MacKenzie said thoughtfully.

"Yes!" Daniel cried, his voice cutting through the heavy, musty air. "Yes! Thank you, Mrs. MacKenzie! That is what I shall do! And the curse will end forever!"

The next morning passed so slowly, Daniel felt as if time were standing still. Pacing his room, he repeatedly checked his pocket watch, waiting for the time when Nora finished work.

Downstairs, preparations for Simon's birthday party were under way. The party was scheduled for that evening. Simon and Angelica had not emerged from their rooms. But a line of carts and carriages pulled up to the back entrance, carrying food and drink and flowers for the celebration.

At a little after three Daniel set off, walking toward town. It was a lengthy walk along a dirt path that led through woods, fields, then finally small houses before reaching the town square. But Daniel enjoyed the walk. It gave him a chance to think of Nora and to rehearse what he planned to say to her.

It was a warm day for autumn, almost summerlike. Daniel unbuttoned his heavy overcoat as he walked. After several minutes more he removed it and slung it over a shoulder.

When the low brick buildings of the town square came into view, Daniel's heart began to pound. He had rehearsed his marriage proposal again and again, repeating the words in his mind.

But what, he wondered, would Nora's reaction be?

Daniel knew that Nora liked him and cared about him. But what would happen when he revealed to her that he was a Fear? What would happen when he told her the long tragic history of their families? When he told her that their marriage would end a centuries-old curse on their families?

Would she be horrified—or overjoyed?

Taking a deep breath, he shifted the coat to his other shoulder and crossed the unpaved street, taking long strides.

The white clapboard general store came into view. Daniel felt as if his heart would burst!

He stepped onto the sidewalk—and stopped short.

The store window was boarded over with pine boards.

The door, normally open, was shut. Behind the small window in the door, the store was dark as night. And empty.

Nora is gone, Daniel realized.

CHAPTER 28

Daniel staggered back, nearly toppling over. "Where is she?" he cried, staring in horror at the boarded-up store. "Where has she gone?"

He stood, trying to make sense of his frantic, rambling thoughts, trying to decide what to do next.

How could she disappear overnight? Vanish into thin air?

As he stood in shock and dismay, a voice floated toward him, calling him, "Daniel! Daniel!" *Nora's voice!*

He uttered a low cry of surprise, then held his breath, listening hard.

Again he heard her voice. Again he heard her calling his name from far away, so far away. So faint and far away that it could be the wind. Or his imagination.

"Daniel! Daniel!"

"Nora, I hear you!" he cried frantically. "Where are you? Where?"

He listened again. It *is* my imagination, he decided miserably.

His shoulders slumped forward. The sky darkened. He felt like collapsing into the dirt.

"Daniel! Daniel!"

The faint, faraway cries were going to drive him mad.

"Daniel! Daniel!"

Desperately Nora called to him, pounding on the frame of her bedroom window above the store until her fists throbbed with pain.

"Look up! Why won't you look up?" she pleaded, watching Daniel, his face darkened by shock and grief.

"Daniel! Daniel! Up here!" she screamed.

Finally he glanced up. Finally he saw her. "Nora!" She could hear his happy cry through the glass.

Wiping away her tears, she pointed frantically to the narrow balcony outside her second-floor window. It took him only a few seconds to realize she wanted him to climb the drainpipe to the balcony.

She watched as he tossed his heavy coat to the ground, grabbed the pipe with both hands, and began to pull himself up.

Behind him, she saw, the village square stood empty,

except for a large yellow hound dog sleeping in the middle of the street. "Hurry! Please hurry!" Nora begged, her hands pressed against the thick windowpane.

A short while later he was standing outside her window, breathing hard. He stared in at her tearstained face. "Nora, what has happened?" he demanded. "Open the window!"

"I cannot!" she called out to him. "My father has locked it! I am locked in my room!"

She watched him grip the frame and struggle to pry the window up. It wouldn't budge.

With a loud groan he pressed his shoulder against the glass and leaned with all his weight. The pane remained in place.

Nora leaped back as Daniel heaved his shoulder into the pane again. She cried out as the glass fell into her room. It landed flat at her feet without shattering.

With a happy cry Daniel burst through the opening and swept Nora into his arms.

"Daniel! Daniel, I thought I would never see you again!" Nora cried, pressing her damp cheek against his.

He hugged her tight. "Nora, what has happened? Why has your father locked you in here?"

She held on to him for a moment, as if proving to herself that he was solid, that he was real. "Father locked me in to make sure I would never see you again. He has gone to the next town to make arrangements. He is taking us far away, Daniel. Far away."

Daniel uttered a cry of surprise. "But why, Nora?"

"He found out that you are a Fear," Nora replied, her body trembling, tears rolling down her flushed cheeks.

"So you know!" Daniel said, feeling his pulse throb at his temples. "You know I am a member of that cursed family!"

"I know, and I do not care!" Nora declared. "I love you, Daniel! I do not care anything about your family or its past!"

"I love you, too, Nora!" Daniel cried, and they embraced again. "But you must know the story of our families. You must know all about the curse."

"No! Take me away from here!" Nora pleaded, her voice trembling. "For Father will never allow us to be together. He will be back in an hour or two. And then—"

"That is time enough for me to tell the story," Daniel insisted. "And then we will be married!"

"Yes!" Nora agreed, squeezing his hand. "Oh, yes, Daniel!" They kissed.

Holding her hands tightly, Daniel revealed to Nora the tragic history of the Fears and the Goodes. She listened in horrified silence, leaning her head against his shoulder.

"So many deaths, so much murder and betrayal," she murmured when Daniel had finished.

"Does this mean that you will not marry me?" he asked, his eyes burning into hers.

"We must be married at once," she replied breathlessly. "We must end the curse forever."

Daniel cried out in happiness. "I passed by the house of the town justice on my way here. I know he will marry us now!"

Nora's smile faded. She gazed at him uncertainly. "But, Daniel, we have no ring to bind the ceremony."

Daniel let go of her hand. His expression turned thoughtful. "No ring . . ." he muttered, frowning. "Oh. Wait!" He reached behind his neck and pulled off the silver three-clawed pendant. "This will serve as a ring, Nora!" he proclaimed excitedly.

"What a strange object!" Nora cried, staring at it. "Where did you get it?"

"It is of no concern," Daniel replied excitedly. "It will serve as a ring." He raised the silver disk to slip the chain around her neck.

As she arranged the pendant, Nora felt a sudden surge of heat at her chest and thought she saw flames rising up around the room. The strange image lasted only a few seconds. When it cleared, Daniel was pulling her by the hand toward the window to make their escape.

"Tonight is my grandfather Simon's seventy-fifth birthday party," Daniel told her, helping her onto the tiny balcony outside the window. "We will announce our marriage at the party!"

"Oh, Daniel!" Nora cried, lingering at the window. "What will your grandfather say? What if our announcement angers him or makes him unhappy?"

"He can only be joyful that a centuries-old curse has ended," Daniel replied, smiling, his dark eyes flashing excitedly. "Come, Nora. Hurry! Tonight will be a night we will long remember!"

CHAPTER 29

That night Daniel walked with his new bride through the gloomy halls of his grandfather's mansion.

"Daniel, this house . . . it frightens me," Nora whispered.

"We shall not stay long, dear wife," Daniel told her, squeezing her hand. "We will leave after the birthday party. I promise. We will not even stay the night."

Nora stayed close by his side as he led her through the dark corridors of Simon Fear's house. "The house is so dark, so cold," she whispered.

"Try not to think gloomy thoughts," he urged as the pantry came into view. "After all, we are married. And after a few hours we never need return to this dreary place again."

Mrs. MacKenzie and more than a dozen helpers, hired

from another town for the evening, were bustling about the kitchen, preparing the food and drink for the birthday party. But the old housekeeper stopped to stare as Daniel led Nora into the room.

"Mrs. MacKenzie, this is my wife, Nora," Daniel announced, unable to keep a wide, excited grin from his face.

"Nora Goode," the old woman muttered, studying Nora intently with her one good eye. Then she smiled, too. "I wish you both joy," she said.

"Please take care of Nora while I attend to my grandparents," Daniel asked, still holding his bride's hand. "When the time is right, I plan to announce our marriage."

He turned before the housekeeper could react and hurried to greet Simon and Angelica in the ballroom.

Daniel stopped in surprise at one entrance to the ballroom.

Where are the guests? he asked himself.

The enormous room was empty. Hundreds of glimmering candles sent a wash of pale light over the walls, festooned with white and yellow flowers.

Daniel's footsteps echoed loudly in the vast emptiness as he crossed the room to greet his grandparents.

The party was scheduled to have begun more than an hour ago, he remembered. Was it possible that no one had come?

As far as Daniel had been able to tell during the

weeks of his visit, his grandparents had no friends. The Fear mansion had been closed to all visitors for thirty-five years.

Did Simon and Angelica expect people to come? Had they invited anyone? Anyone besides Daniel?

Daniel felt a chill of horror.

Am I really the only guest at this eerie party?

"Hello!" he called, trying to sound cheerful. But his voice echoed mournfully in the enormous empty space.

His grandparents hovered near the door.

Angelica wore a solemn-looking black dress more suited to a funeral than a birthday party. Her long white hair was tied behind her head with a black ribbon.

Daniel hesitated and gaped at his grandmother.

Angelica was going through the motions of welcoming guests. "So good to see you," she repeated with a smile, nodding her head at empty air. "So nice of you to come."

Daniel swallowed hard. She has entirely lost her senses! he told himself, watching her smiling and carrying on a conversation with no one at all.

Simon, his dark eyes glowing excitedly behind his spectacles, his face flushed in the candlelight, stared eagerly at the open doorway. He leaned forward in his wheelchair, an expectant smile frozen on his face, as if eager to see who would arrive next.

Daniel took a deep breath. I guess I had better go along with the charade, he told himself with a shudder.

"Happy birthday, Grandfather," he called warmly, rushing up to the wheelchair and shaking Simon's hand.

Simon's hand was as cold as ice. "Thank you, my boy," he replied. "I am happy that at least *one* member of my family saw fit to attend this occasion," he added with some bitterness.

Daniel moved over to greet Angelica. "Did you come with the Bridgers?" she asked. She stared at him as if she had never seen him before.

"You . . . uh . . . look lovely tonight, Grandmother," Daniel managed to say.

"Don't just stand there. Why don't you mingle with our guests?" Angelica demanded. She turned away from him and stuck out her gloved hand. "So good of you to come," she gushed to no one at all. "And how are your lovely daughters?"

Simon continued to stare at the doorway, the expectant smile frozen on his face.

Daniel stepped quickly to the wall, his shoes pounding like thunder in the empty ballroom.

What should I do? he wondered. They are mad, completely mad—both of them!

Should I bring Nora out and introduce her now? Shall I tell them that Nora and I have married?

Or should I take Nora and flee this frightening place?

No. I cannot run. I must stay and tell them.

Watching Simon from across the room, Daniel

wondered how the old man would react. A Fear had married a Goode. Today, on Simon's birthday, the ancient feud between the two families had ended. Hundreds of years of bitterness, of treachery, of evil, had come to an end. The Fears and the Goodes would be one family now.

Will my grandfather share my joy? Daniel wondered.

Daniel heard a rumbling from the far end of the ballroom. He glanced up to see a birthday cake being wheeled in on a cart.

It was an enormous round cake, three tall tiers, frosted in white and yellow. On top were seventy-five candles, creating a blaze of yellow light that shimmered over the cake.

This is absurd! Daniel thought. Such a magnificent cake for such an empty celebration.

Who would bring such a cake into a tomb! A *tomb!*

I've got to get Nora now, he decided. I will tell my grandparents my news. And then Nora and I will flee into the night, never to return!

As the hired servants slowly wheeled the cake toward Simon and Angelica, Daniel hurried to the pantry to retrieve Nora. Holding her hand tightly, he pulled her into the ballroom.

In the gloomy, eerie silence, Simon was preparing to blow out the candles, his face red in the glow from seventy-five candles.

Nora resisted, but Daniel pulled her across the empty ballroom. Squeezing her hand, he gave her a reassuring smile. She looks so beautiful, Daniel thought.

Nora wore a simple pale blue dress with a lacy white collar. The silver three-toed pendant glowed at her throat.

"Grandfather, Grandmother, I have an announcement to make," Daniel declared, his voice booming in the empty room. Nora lingered just behind him.

Daniel saw Simon's eyes narrow. Simon was staring at the pendant at Nora's throat. "Wh—what is this?" he stammered.

Holding tightly to Nora's hand, Daniel took a deep breath. "Grandfather, on this happy occasion I—I would like to introduce my wife to you. I have married Nora Goode!"

CHAPTER 30

"Noooooooo!"

A hideous wail, a cry of anguish and of horror rose over the ballroom, causing a thousand candles to flicker and bend low.

It took Nora a long while to realize that the howl had come from Simon Fear.

Frightened, she took a few steps back as Simon rose from his wheelchair. The old man's eyes were wide with horror. He pointed a trembling finger at the three-clawed disk around Nora's throat.

"Noooooo!" Another animal howl escaped Simon's lips.

Still pointing, he staggered toward her.

But his legs would not support him. He stumbled.

Trying to steady himself, he leaned against the cart and pushed over the cake.

Angelica began to shriek as the enormous cake splattered to the floor.

"Daniel, what shall we do?" Nora cried. But her words were drowned out by yet another howl from Simon and by Angelica's shrill cries.

"Daniel, what is happening?"

A small carpet caught fire first. Then the entire room was ablaze—as if all the candles in the ballroom had suddenly fallen and flared into tall flames.

"Daniel, please! Daniel!"

She couldn't see him. He was hidden behind a bright wall of fire only feet from her.

Flames leaped from the floor and danced off the four walls.

How could the room be burning so quickly? Nora wondered, choking on the thick smoke, choking on her fear. "Daniel? Daniel?"

It was so bright, so blindingly bright.

As she stared into the flames, surrounded by screams and terrified cries, Nora saw a struggling figure emerge from the yellow-orange brightness.

"Daniel? Where *are* you?"

The figure grew closer, clearer.

Nora raised her hand to her mouth as she realized she was staring at a girl about her age, a girl struggling against a dark wooden stake, surrounded by flames, a girl burning, burning, burning, screaming as she burned. Susannah Goode, burning at the stake beside her mother.

And as Nora gaped in openmouthed horror, other tortured figures invaded the room, rising up through the crackling, blistering flames.

Nora saw Rebecca Fier, her neck broken, hanging by a rope from a dark rafter. Old Benjamin Fier rose into the room, impaled like a scarecrow, a wooden shaft pushed up through the back of his skull.

Nora screamed and tried to shut her eyes. But she had to watch, she had to bear witness as the other victims of the past emerged in the burning ballroom.

As she stared in silent horror, she saw Matthew and Constance Fier, skeletons behind their walled-up prison. William Goode, his head exploded, his skull showing through rotted flesh, hovered into view.

The ghost of little Abigail Goode floated overhead. Abigail's mother, Jane, staggered stiffly after her, her face bloated from drowning. Kate Fier rose in front of them, a knitting needle through her heart. Hannah Fear came next, a sword through her chest.

Then Nora saw Julia Fear, scratching the air, scratching at nothing, her fingernails cut and bleeding. Poor Julia, buried alive, but back now to join the other victims of the centuries.

The victims, the phantoms of the past, Fears and

Goodes, roared around the room, their cries louder than the thunder of the flames. They swept round and round, faster, faster, until they became a raging whirlwind of pain, of brutal death.

"Daniel, where are you? Daniel?"

Nora stared into the swirling flame. "Daniel, oh, Daniel!"

Unable to find him, unable to endure the howls of the dead, their cries of agony as they swept around the room, Nora covered her eyes and fled.

Moments later she was in the cool darkness of the night, watching the blaze from the front lawn, trembling from the sudden cold, gripping the silver medallion with both hands as villagers made their way from town and gathered, muttering about the evil of the Fears, about the centuries of evil that had led to this night, to this final fire.

"Daniel! Please come out, Daniel!"

Nora called his name again and again.

But as the flames raged, swallowing the Fear mansion in their eerie light, and the terrifying howls rose up in the night like a symphony of pain and horror, Nora knew she would never see Daniel again.

Epilogue

Nora dipped her pen, but the inkwell had run dry. Yawning, she set down the pen and stared at the stack of pages she had written.

Our marriage ended the feud between the Fears and the Goodes, she thought miserably. But not as we had intended.

No one came out of the fire. Not Daniel. No one.

The house burned for days until the fire finally smoldered out, leaving nothing but a black, charred shell in its place. Leaving the charred ruins of the Fear mansion and a legacy of evil—evil that will hover over the entire village.

This is why I have written my story, Nora thought, flexing her aching fingers. This is why I have spent the night writing down everything I know about the Goodes and the Fears.

Maybe someone reading this will be able to stop the evil before it rises again.

They think I am insane, Nora realized. They think the fire and all I saw drove me mad.

That is why they brought me to this insane asylum. That is why they locked me in this room.

But I am not mad. My story had to be told. It had to be written. I had to stop the hideous evil. I *had* to.

Glancing at the sunlight pouring through the window, Nora heard footsteps. Voices in the hall.

The door to her room opened. Two uniformed nurses entered. Their faces were solemn, their eyes cold. "The doctors will see you now, Nora," one of them said softly.

"Yes. Very well," Nora said, rising from the hard chair she had spent the night in. She lifted the heavy sheaf of papers from the small desk. "Here. They must read this," she told the nurse. "They must read the whole story. They must know about the evil. The evil will destroy us all, you see. They must know—"

Narrowing her eyes, studying Nora's face, the nurse took Nora's pages and tossed them into the fire.

"No!" Nora shrieked. She tried to dive after them, but the nurses held her back firmly.

"It is for your own good, Nora," one of them said softly. "If the doctors saw what you have spent the night scribbling, they would lock you up and throw away the key."

Nora stared at her pages as they caught flame and started to burn, sending thick white smoke up the chimney.

"You do not understand!" she protested, tears forming in her tired eyes. "The evil is still alive. The evil is still there! The word must get out. People must know—"

"Come with us, Nora." The nurse's voice was soft, but her grip was hard and tight on Nora's arm. "Come with us now. Try to forget your wild tale."

"Did you not hear the news?" the other nurse asked brightly. "This will surely cheer you, Nora. The Fear mansion is gone, but the village is to build a road on the property."

"What? A road?" Nora asked, feeling dazed. "But the horror—"

"No more horror, Nora. No more. The road will be lovely. It means that lovely houses will be built there," the nurse told her, edging her toward the door. "And do you know what they're going to call the new road?"

"What?" Nora asked weakly.

"They're going to call it Fear Street."

UNLOCK THE MYSTERY, SUSPENSE, AND ROMANCE.

Kissed by an Angel

New York Times bestselling author
Elizabeth Chandler

From Simon Pulse
TEEN.SimonandSchuster.com

THE WAR BETWEEN
HEAVEN AND HELL RAGES ON. . . .

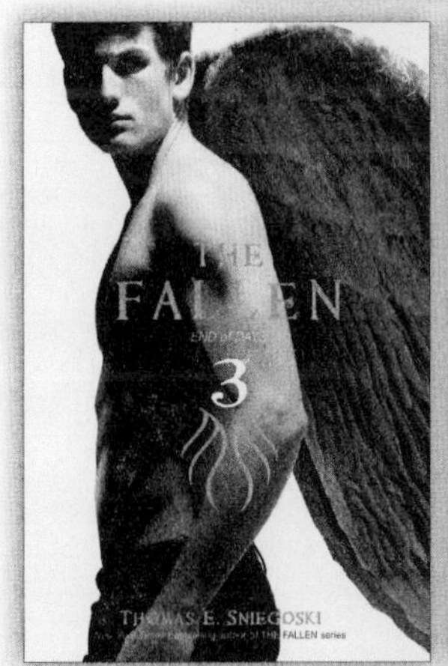

DON'T MISS A MOMENT
OF AARON'S QUEST.

EBOOK EDITIONS ALSO AVAILABLE
FROM SIMON PULSE • TEEN.SIMONANDSCHUSTER.COM